THE
PRODIGAL
SON

Colleen McCullough, a native of Australia, established the department of neurophysiology at the Royal North Shore Hospital in Sydney before working as a researcher at Yale Medical School for ten years. She is the internationally bestselling author of numerous novels, including *The Thorn Birds*, and lives with her husband on Norfolk Island in the South Pacific.

ALSO BY COLLEEN McCULLOUGH

Tim
The Thorn Birds
An Indecent Obsession
A Creed for the Third Millennium
The Ladies of Missalonghi

THE MASTERS OF ROME SERIES
The First Man in Rome
The Grass Crown
Fortune's Favourites
Caesar's Women
Caesar: Let the Dice Fly
The October Horse
Antony and Cleopatra

The Song of Troy
Roden Cutler, V.C.
Morgan's Run
The Touch
Angel
On, Off

The Independence of Miss Mary Bennet
Too Many Murders
Naked Cruelty

THE
PRODIGAL
SON

Colleen McCullough

HARPER

Harper
An imprint of HarperCollins*Publishers*
77–85 Fulham Palace Road,
Hammersmith, London W6 8JB

www.harpercollins.co.uk

This paperback edition 2012
1

First published in America by
Simon and Schuster 2012

A catalogue record for this book is
available from the British Library

ISBN: 978 0 00 739585 9

Printed and bound in Great Britain by
Clays Ltd, St Ives plc

MIX
Paper from
responsible sources
FSC **FSC™ C007454**
www.fsc.org

FSC™ is a non-profit international organisation established to promote
the responsible management of the world's forests. Products carrying the
FSC label are independently certified to assure consumers that they come
from forests that are managed to meet the social, economic and
ecological needs of present and future generations,
and other controlled sources.

Find out more about HarperCollins and the environment at
www.harpercollins.co.uk/green

For CAROLYN REIDY
the best editor I've ever had
a loyal and unflagging publisher
and my very dear friend
with love and thanks

THE
PRODIGAL
SON

Prologue

Friday, January 3, 1969
from
7:30 P.M. until 11:30 P.M.

B reath surrounding him in puffed clouds, John Hall put one not-quite-steady finger on the door buzzer and pushed. The opening chords of Beethoven's fifth symphony answered, an unexpected shock; the last thing he had associated in his mind's eye with this unknown father and family was kitsch. Then the door was opening, a tiny little maid was divesting him of coat and gloves, and dancing at her heels came a young and beautiful woman, pushing the maid aside to attack him with outflung arms, lush lips puckered in a kiss.

"Dearest, darlingest John!" she cried, the lips squashed against his cheek because he had turned his head. "I am your stepmother, Davina." She seized his right arm. "Come and meet us, please. Is Connecticut cold after Oregon?" she cooed.

He didn't answer, too overwhelmed by the greeting, the young woman's almost feverish chatter (his *stepmother?* But she was years younger than he was!)—and the noticeably foreign accent she owned. Davina . . . Yes, of course his father had spoken of her on the phone during their several conversations, but he hadn't anticipated a bimbo, and that was how she presented. A brunette bimbo, clad in the height of fashion: a tie-dyed chiffon pantsuit in all shades of red, very dark hair loose down her back, a flawless ivory skin, full and pouting red lips, vividly blue eyes.

"It was my idea to introduce you to the family at Max's birthday party," she was saying, in no hurry to commence the introductions. A very few people were scattered around an ugly, hideously modern room. "Sixty!" she went gushing on in well structured English, "Isn't that wonderful? The father of a newborn son, and the father of a long lost son! I couldn't bear for you and Max to meet in a less significant way than tonight, everybody looking their best."

"So this black tie is your idea?" he asked, just a trifle ungraciously.

His displeasure didn't impinge; she laughed, her rather ropelike hair swinging as she tossed her head complacently. "Of course, John dearest. I adore men in black tie, and it gives us women an excuse to dress up."

At least her prattle—there was more of it—had enabled him to assimilate those present, even come to some conclusions. Three tall, robustly built men stood together, and were very obviously related; John could say with certainty that they were his father, his uncle and his first cousin: Max, Val and Ivan Tunbull. Their broad Slavic faces were set in lines speaking of undoubted success, their well opened yellowish eyes held confidence and competence, and their thick, waving thatches of brassy hair said that baldness did not run in the family. The Tunbull family . . . *His* family, whom he wouldn't have known before tonight had they chanced to encounter each other at a different black tie dinner party . . .

A briskly professional looking man of about forty was standing with them, his very pregnant wife of around his own age beaming up at him fatuously: *not* a bimbo!

Where were Jim and Millie Hunter? They'd said they would be here! Surely no one could be later than he? It had taken almost an hour for him to get up the courage to ring that bell, striding up and down, smoking cigarettes, shrinking back into the shadows when the professional guy and his pregnant wife came across the street, engaged in what sounded like married couple banter. No, maybe not an hour, but a half hour, sure.

Came another dose of Beethoven in tinny bells; the tiny servant moved to the front door, and in they came, Millie and Jim Hunter. Oh, thank all the gods! Now he could meet his father with a confidence bolstered by knowing that Jim Hunter had his back. How much he had yearned for this reunion!

Max Tunbull was advancing toward him, hands outstretched. "John!" said Max in a gravelly voice, taking John's right hand in both his, smiling on a wall of huge white teeth, then leaning in to embrace him, kiss his cheeks. "John!" The yellow eyes filled with tears. "Oh, Jesus, you're so like Martita!"

When the fuss died down, when all the introductions were safely in the past, when John felt that he could make some choices of his own without his stepmother foiling him, he sought out Jim and Millie, havens in a stormy, unknown sea.

"I was about to head for the hills when you came in," he confessed, more to Jim than to Millie. "Isn't this weird?"

"Three women, six men, and black tie. You're right, it is weird," Jim said, but not sounding puzzled. "Typical for Davina, though. She loves to be surrounded by men."

"Why am I not surprised?" John put his martini glass down with a grimace.

"You no like?" asked a voice at his elbow.

He turned to look, found the midget maid. "I'd much rather have a Budweiser," he said.

"I get."

"One for me as well!" called Jim to her back. "Have you managed to talk to your dad yet?"

"Nope. Maybe at the dinner table. It's as if his bimbo wife doesn't want to give me any opportunity."

"Well, she can't keep that up forever, especially now you're in Holloman," Millie comforted. "Vina has to be the center of attention, from the little I've seen of her. Jim knows her far better."

"Thanks for being home last night when I blew in from Portland," John said. "I couldn't wait to see you."

"I can't believe Max let you stay in a hotel," Jim said.

"No, that's my fault. I figured I'd better have some place of my own to retreat to if I needed, and right about now I'm glad. California or Oregon this ain't."

"Hey, California was a long time ago," Jim said gruffly.

"It lives in my heart like yesterday."

"This is more important, John," Millie said. "Family is all-important."

"With an ugly stepmother in control? All that's missing are the ugly stepsisters. Or should that be stepbrothers?"

Millie giggled. "I see the analogy as far as Davina goes, John, but you'd make a lousy Cinderella. Anyway, it's a role reversal. You're not an impoverished kitchen slave, you're a millionaire forestry tycoon."

When Davina drove them to the dinner table, a wide one as well as long, John found that he and Max were seated together at the head of the table; Davina occupied the foot alone. Down the left side she put, from Max to her, Ivan Tunbull, Millie Hunter and Dr. Al Markoff. On the right side she seated, from John to her, Val Tunbull, Muse Markoff the pregnant wife, and Jim Hunter.

And at last John had a chance to talk to Max Tunbull, who turned a little side on and asked, "Do you remember your mother at all, John?"

"Sometimes I think I do, sir, at other times I'm convinced that what I think I remember is an illusion," John said, his eyes suddenly more grey than blue. "I see a thin, sad woman who used to spend her time typing. According to Wendover Hall, who adopted me, she was very poor, made a living from typing manuscript for a dollar a page, no errors. That's how he met her. Someone recommended her to type a book he'd written on forestry. It wasn't long before he put her and me in a beautiful house at Gold Beach in Oregon. She died six months later. That I *do* remember! I must have been with her when she died, and I wouldn't leave the body. Kinda like a dog, I guess. She'd been dead for two days when Wendover found us."

Max blinked his own tears away. "My poor boy!"

"My turn to ask a question," John said, voice hard, curt. "What was my mother like?"

Closing his eyes, Max leaned back in his chair slightly, as if speaking of his first wife didn't come easily—as if, indeed, he endeavored never to think of her. "Martita was what these days we'd call a depressive, son. Back in the 1930s, the doctors said she was neurasthenic. Quiet and withdrawn, but as lovely on the inside as she was on the outside. My family didn't like her, especially Emily—Val's wife, in case you're not keeping the names straight yet. I never realized how badly Em got under Martita's skin until after she left, taking you with her. That was June of 1937, and you were barely a year old. Of course it all came out afterward, while I was scouring the country looking for you and your mom. Em worked on your mom's insecurities every chance she had to be alone with her—relentless, unbelievably cruel! Convinced her she wasn't loved or wanted." The reddish-tan lips thinned. "Emily was punished, but too late for Martita."

"She's not here tonight—was she expelled from the family?" John asked uncomfortably.

Max gave a short, harsh laugh. "No! That's not how most families work, John. Em just got the cold shoulder from the rest of us, including Val. Even Ivan wasn't encouraged to take her side in anything—and he didn't, either."

"So that's why Emily's not here tonight?"

"Not really," said Max nonchalantly. "Em's grown in her own direction, which suits the rest of us just fine."

"She won't like my advent. It must look to her as if I'm going to reduce her son's share of the family business."

Max looked into this long lost son's face with what seemed genuine love. "On that head, John, I can't thank you enough. It came hard to Ivan to lose half his inheritance to my son Alexis, so to know you're making no claim on me is wonderful."

"I have so much money I'll never be able to spend it," John said, searching his father's face. "Ivan can rest easy. I hope you've told him that?"

"No chance yet, but I will."

Someone was banging a spoon against an empty crystal wine glass: Davina.

"Family and friends," Davina began, each word carefully articulated, "we are gathered here tonight to kill the fatted calf for my darling husband's prodigal son, lost to him for over thirty years. However, we also kill the fatted calf to honor my beloved Max, who turned sixty three days ago."

She paused, eyes roaming the attentive faces. "We know why Emily isn't here, but, dearest John, the absence of Ivan's wife is equally habitual—Lily says she's just too shy to face a room that might contain a stranger. Silly girl!"

Startled, John's gaze flew to Ivan, who was glaring at his stepaunt in furious dislike, and John for one couldn't blame him. What an awful thing to say! Max must really be under the thumb of this—no, not bimbo. Davina was a harpy, she ate people tooth and claw, slavering.

"On October thirteenth of last year," the high voice went on, "I gave birth to Alexis. A son for Max at last, an heir to replace his beloved John." She smiled at Max brilliantly. "And then, a month ago, John phoned from Oregon. He had found out who his family were, and he wanted to return to the fold."

She emitted a histrionic sigh. "Naturally Max doubted John's identity, but as the calls went on and the documents were produced in various lawyers' offices, Max began to hope. And after the ring arrived, who could continue to doubt? Not my beloved Max! John the prodigal son had returned from the dead. So now we gather to celebrate the reunion of Max and John Tunbull. Lift your glasses and be upstanding!"

My name is John Hall, Davina, thought John to himself at the end of this disingenuous, mischievous speech. Not John Tunbull! Now I have to sit here while these people toast us. Prodigal son, for God's sake! She never quite gets the story right, this eastern European harpy.

Embarrassed to look at any of those faces, his eyes went to the diminutive woman who appeared to be some kind of superior servant, moving among the hired help in smooth command. Clad in a shapeless grey dress with a shapeless body underneath, it was hard to arrive at her status in this menagerie. Her face was flat and suggested a cretin, as did the flat-backed skull, but the black, currantlike eyes were intelligent and the tiny, short-fingered hands deft as she wiped a dribbled speck of food from one plate and rejected another as unfit to be served. He had heard various people call her Uda; from what little he had seen thus far, John decided that she was Davina's personal servant owning no allegiance to the Tunbulls. Just who *was* Davina Tunbull?

The meal was fantastic. Iranian caviar and trimmings was followed by the closest Davina could get to a fatted calf, she explained: roast milk-fed veal, lean, pink and juicy, with perfectly cooked vegetables, and an amazing cake for dessert. John ate well—he couldn't resist such delicious fare.

As they rose from the table Davina sprang another surprise with another crystalline tattoo on a glass.

"Gentlemen, to Max's study for coffee, after-dinner drinks and cigars!" she cried. "Ladies, to the drawing room!"

And finally, in a kind of foyer that ran between the dining room and Max's study, John managed to waylay Jim Hunter.

"Do you believe this?" he asked, moving to one side of the traffic flow, six men fleeing from that awful woman.

Jim rolled his eyes, an almost scary expanse of stark white in such a black face. "It's typical Davina," he said. "I know the Tunbulls well after this past year and more putting *A Helical God* to press. But we'll have plenty of time for me to tell you about that now that you're in Holloman."

"It was terrific to reminisce last night when I found you at home," John said. His eyes, returned to blue, rested fondly on Jim's face. "You look great, Jim. No one would ever recognize you for the old Gorilla Hunter."

"For which I have you to thank. I can pay you back for my operation at last, old friend."

"Don't even try!" John frowned. "Millie's still too thin."

"That's her nature, she's an ectomorph." The big, luminous green eyes, so strange in Jim Hunter's darkness, swam with tears. "God, it is good to see you! Over six years!"

John hugged him hard, a strong yet manly embrace that Jim returned, then, emerging, saw Dr. Al Markoff glancing at his watch.

"Another hour, and I'll be able to grab my wife and split. Davina's hard to take tonight," Markoff said, leading the way. "Long lost sons crawling out of the woodwork aren't in her line, no offense, John, but the forestry background makes it an ideal metaphor." He glanced at his watch again. "Not bad, not bad. It's just ten-thirty. Muse and I will be sawing *wood* in less than an hour, ha ha ha. Punsters can't help themselves, John."

A little to John's surprise (though his ego wasn't bruised), Max put Jim Hunter in what was clearly the place of honor in his den: a big, padded, crimson leather wing chair. The whole room was crimson leather, gilt-adorned books, walnut furniture and leaded windows. Artificial. Davina, he would have been prepared to bet.

He drew up a straight chair in front of but to one side of Jim's wing chair, hardly curious about Jim's significance: it would all come out in time, and he had loads of time. Max had gone into a huddle with Val and Ivan, each flourishing a large cigar and a snifter of X-O cognac; the Tunbulls don't skimp on life's little niceties, he thought, and they love to huddle. Dr. Al drew up another straight chair on Jim's other side, and the den settled into two separate conversations.

"Are you the Tunbull family physician, Al?" John asked.

"Lord, no! I'm a pathologist specializing in hematology," Markoff said affably, "which won't mean any more to you than Douglas fir does to me. Now Jim's RNA I find fascinating."

"Is this yours and Muse's first child?" he pressed.

Markoff guffawed. "I wish! This, my bachelor friend, is the forties accident. We have two boys in their teens, but Muse is too scatty to throw geniuses, so they're horribly ordinary."

"I think you'd be a pretty cool father," John said, enjoying the man's easygoing humor as he expanded on the theme of the accidental forties pregnancy; while he talked, John almost forgot what he suspected was going on between Max, Val and Ivan: the non-depletion of Ivan's share of the family business and estate.

He felt suddenly very tired. The meal had been long and his wine glass refilled too often, something he disliked. To gird up his loins for this meeting had taken courage, for there was much of his mother in John Hall, who shrank from confrontations. After Jim and Dr. Al moved on to nucleic acids, John managed a surreptitious peek at his watch: 11 p.m. They had been in the den for a half hour, which meant, according to Dr. Al, another half hour to go before he stood any chance of escaping. Max was gazing across at him with real love and concern, but how could he get to first base with a father shackled to a harpy like Davina? She would be rooting for baby Alexis, and why not?

Sweat was stinging his eyes; funny, he hadn't noticed until now how hot the room was. Rather clumsily he groped in his trousers side pocket for his handkerchief, found it, yet couldn't seem to pull it out.

"Hot," he mumbled, running a finger around the inside of his collar. The handkerchief finally came free; he held it to his brow and mopped. "Anyone else hot?" he asked.

"Some," said Jim, taking John's brandy snifter from him. "It's the end of the evening, why not take off your tie? No one will mind, I'm sure."

"Of course take it off, John," said Max, moving to the dial of the thermostat; the response of cooler air was immediate.

His lips felt numb; he licked at them. "Numb," he said.

Jim had taken the tie off, loosened the collar. "Better?"

"Not—really," he managed.

He couldn't seem to draw air into his lungs properly, and gasped.

11

Sweet cool air flooded in; he gasped again, but this time it was harder to suck in a breath. He swayed on the chair.

"Get him on the floor, guys," he heard Dr. Al say, then felt himself laid supine, a loosely rolled coat behind his head. Markoff was ripping open the buttons on his shirt and barking at someone: "Call an ambulance—resuscitation emergency. Max, tell Muse to give you my bag."

Nauseated, he retched, tried to vomit, but nothing came up, and now he just felt sick, didn't have the strength to retch. His teeth chattered, he was appalled to find his whole body invaded by a fine tremor. Then came an almighty, convulsive jerk, as if it were happening to someone else—why was he so aware of everything that was going on? Not in a disembodied way—that he could have borne, to hover looking down on himself. But still to be inside himself going through it was *awful!*

All that became as nothing compared to his struggle to breathe, an ever-increasing impossibility that flung him into a terror he had no way to show beyond the look in his eyes. I am dying, but I can't tell them! They don't know, they'll let me die! I need air, I need air! Air! Air!

"Heartbeat's weak rather than suspiciously irregular, it isn't a primary cardiac catastrophe," Dr. Al was saying, "but his airway is still patent. Shouldn't have this gear with me, except that I borrowed it for a refresher course in emergency medicine . . . Gotta keep up with the times . . . I'll intubate and bag breathe."

And while he talked he worked, one of those odd people who like to do both simultaneously. With the first puff of oxygen into his lungs, John knew through his mania that he could not have had a better man treating him if it had gone down in the ER itself. For perhaps six or seven blissful breaths he thought he'd beaten whatever it was, but then the gas bag and the strong pressure on it couldn't force his air passages to inflate, even passively.

Inside his head he was screaming, screaming, screaming a blind, utter panic. No thoughts of the life he had lived or any life to come intruded for as long as the width of a photon; no heaven, no hell, just the horrifying presence of imminent death, and he so alive, awake, forced to endure to the last, bitterest . . . In his eyes an electrified terror, in his mind a scream.

John Hall died eleven minutes after he started feeling hot. Dr. Al Markoff knelt to one side of him fighting to keep him alive, Dr. Jim Hunter knelt to his other side holding his hand for comfort. But life was gone, and of comfort there was none.

PART ONE

From
THURSDAY, JANUARY 2, 1969
until
WEDNESDAY, JANUARY 8, 1969

THURSDAY, JANUARY 2, 1969

"**D**addy, what's the procedure when I'm missing a toxin?"

Patrick O'Donnell's startled blue eyes flew to his daughter's face, expecting to see it laughing at having successfully pulled Daddy's leg. But it was frowning, troubled. He gave her a mug of coffee. "It depends, honey," he said calmly. "What toxin?"

"A really nasty one—tetrodotoxin."

Holloman County's Medical Examiner looked blank. "You'll have to be more specific, Millie. I've never heard of it."

"It's a neurotoxin that blocks nerve transmission by acting on the pores of the voltage-gated, fast sodium channels of the cell membrane—or, in simpler words, it shuts the nervous system down. *Very* nasty! That's what makes it so interesting experimentally, though I'm not interested in it per se. I use it as a tool." Her blue eyes, so like his, gazed at him imploringly.

"Where did you get it from, Millie?"

"I isolated it myself from its source—the blowfish. Such a cute little critter! Looks like a puppy you'd just love to hug to death. But don't eat it, especially its liver." She was perking up, sipping the coffee with enjoyment now. "How do you manage to make a good brew in this godawful building? Carmine's coffee sucks."

"I pay for it myself and severely limit those invited to drink it. Okay, you've jogged my memory cells. I have heard of tetrodotoxin, but only in papers, and in passing. So you actually isolated it yourself?"

"Yes." She stopped again.

"I'll do a Carmine: expatiate."

"Well, I had a tank of blowfish, and it seemed a shame to waste all those livers and other rich bits, so I kept on going and wound up with about a gram of it. If taken by mouth, enough to kill ten heavy-weight boxers. When I finished my experimental run I sealed the six hundred milligrams I had left over in glass ampoules, one hundred milligrams to each, slapped a poison sticker on the beaker holding the six ampoules, and put it in the back of my refrigerator with the three-molar KC1 and stuff," said Millie.

"Don't you lock the refrigerator?"

"Why? It's mine, and my little lab. My grant doesn't run to a technician—I'm not Jim, surrounded by acolytes." She held out her mug for more coffee. "I lock my *lab* door when I'm not in it. I'm as paranoid as any other researcher, I don't advertise my work. *And* I'm post-doctoral, so there's no thesis adviser looking over my shoulder. I would have thought that no one even knew I had any tetrodo-toxin." Her face cleared, grew soft. "Except for Jim, that is. I men-tioned it in passing to him, but he's not into neurotoxins. His idea of soup is *E. coli.*"

"Any idea when it disappeared, sweetheart?"

"During the last week. I did a stocktake of my refrigerator on Christmas Eve, and the beaker was there. When I did another stock-take this morning, no beaker anywhere—and believe me, Dad, I looked high and low. The thing is, I don't know what to do about losing it. It didn't seem like something Dean Werther is equipped to deal with. I thought of you."

"Reporting to me is fine, Millie. I'll notify Carmine, but only as a courtesy. It can't be equated with someone's stealing a jar of po-tassium cyanide—that would galvanize everybody." Patrick gave a rueful grin. "However, my girl, it's time to shut the stable door. Put a lock on your refrigerator and make sure you have the only key."

He leaned to take her hand, long and graceful, but marred by bit-ten nails and general lack of care. "Honey, where you did go wrong was in keeping what you didn't use up. You should have disposed of it as a toxic substance."

She flushed. "No, I don't agree," she said, looking mulish. "The extraction process is difficult, painstaking and extremely slow—a lesser biochemist would have botched it. I'm no Jim, but in my lab techniques I'm way above your run-of-the-mill researcher. At some time in the future I might need the leftover tetrodotoxin, and if I don't, I can legitimately sell it to get my investment in the blowfish back. My grant committee would love that. I've stored it under vacuum in sealed glass ampoules, then slowed its molecules down by refrigerating it. I want it potent and ready to use at any time."

She got to her feet, revealing that she was tall, slender, and attractive enough to turn most men's heads. "Is that all?" she asked.

"Yes. I'll talk to Carmine, but if I were you I wouldn't go to Dean Werther. That would start the gossip ball rolling. Are you sure of the amount in each ampoule? A hundred milligrams in— liquid? Powder?"

"Powder. Snap the neck of the ampoule and add one milligram of pure, distilled water for use. It goes into solution very easily. Ingested, onc heavyweight boxer. Injection is a very different matter. *Half* of *one milligram* is fatal, even for a heavyweight boxcr. If injected into a vein, death would be rapid enough to call nearly instantaneous. If injected into muscle, death in about ten to fifteen minutes from the onset of symptoms." Such was her relief at sharing her burden that she sounded quite blithe.

"Shit! Do you know the symptoms, Millie?"

"As with any substance shutting down the nervous system, Dad. If injected, respiratory failure due to paralysis of the chest wall and the diaphragm. If swallowed, nausea, vomiting, purging and then respiratory failure. The duration of the symptoms would depend on dosage and how fast respiratory failure set in. Oh, I forgot. If swallowed, there would be terrible convulsions too." She had reached the door, dying to be gone. "Will I see you on Saturday night?"

"Mom and I wouldn't miss it, kiddo. How's Jim holding up?"

Her voice floated back. "Okay! And thanks, Dad!"

Snow and ice meant that Holloman was fairly quiet; Patrick made his way through the warren of the County Services building sure he would find Carmine in his office—no weather to be out in, even black activists knew that.

Six daughters, he reflected as he plodded, did not mean fewer headaches than boys, though Patrick Junior was doing his solo best to prove boys *were* worse. Nothing in the world could force him to take a shower; two years from now he'd be a prune from showers, but that shimmered on a faraway horizon.

Millie had always been his biggest feminine headache, he had thought because she was also his most intelligent daughter. Like all of them, she had been sent to St. Mary's Girls' School, which for masculine company tapped the resources of St. Bernard's Boys. Including, over eighteen years ago—September 1950, so long ago!—a special case boarder from South Carolina, a boy whose intelligence was in the genius range. On the advice of their priest, an old St. Bernard's boy, his parents had sent him to Holloman for his high schooling. With good reason. They were African Americans in a southern state who wanted a northern education for their precious only child. Their Catholicism was rare, and Father Gaspari prized them. So Jim Hunter, almost fifteen, arrived to live with the Brothers at St. Bernard's: James Keith Hunter, a genius.

He and Millie met at a school dance that happened to coincide with her fifteenth birthday; Jim was a few days older. The first Patrick and Nessie knew of him came from Millie, who asked if she could invite the boarder at St. Bernard's for a home cooked meal. His blackness stunned them, but they were enormously proud of their daughter's liberalism, taking her interest in the boy as evidence that Millie was going to grow up to make a difference in how America regarded race and creed.

It had been an extraordinary dinner, with the guest talking almost exclusively to Patrick about his work—not the gruesome side, but the underlying science, and with more knowledge of that science than most who worked in the field. Patrick was still groping his way into forensic pathology at that time, and freely admitted that conversing with Jim Hunter had administered a definite onward push.

A shocking dinner too. Both Patrick and Nessie saw it at once: the look in Millie's eyes when they rested on Jim, which was almost all the time. Not burgeoning love. Blind adoration. No, no, no, *no!* That couldn't be let happen! Not because of a nonexistent racial prejudice, but because of sheer terror at what such a relationship would do to this beloved child, the brightest of the bunch. It couldn't be let happen, it *mustn't* happen! While every look Millie gave Jim said it had already happened.

Within a week Jim and Millie were the talk of East Holloman; Patrick and Nessie were inundated with protests and advice from countless relatives. Millie and Jim were an item! A *hot* item! But how could that be, when each child went to a different school, and their teachers disapproved as much as everyone else? *Not* from racial prejudice! From fear at potentially ruined young lives. For their own good, they had to be broken up.

The fees were a burden, but had to be found; Millie was taken out of St. Mary's and sent to the Dormer Day School, where most of the students were the offspring of Chubb professors or wealthy Holloman residents. Not the kind of place parents with five children and a sixth on the way even dreamed of. But for Millie's sake, the sacrifices had to be made.

An instinct in Patrick said it would not answer, and the instinct was right. No matter how many obstacles were thrown in their way, Millie O'Donnell and Jim Hunter continued to be an item.

Even looking back on it now as he tramped through County Services was enough to bring back the indescribable pain of those terrible years. The misery! The guilt! The knowledge of a conscious social crime committed! How could any father and mother sleep, knowing their ethics and principles were colliding head on with their love for a child? For what Patrick and Nessie foresaw was the suffering inflicted on Millie for her choice in boyfriends. Worse because she was prom queen material, the most gorgeous girl in her class. The Dormer Day School seethed with just as much resentment as St. Bernard's and St. Mary's—Millie O'Donnell was living proof that a black man's penile size and sexual prowess could seduce even the cream of the crop. Girls hated her. Boys hated her. Teachers hated her. She had a black boyfriend with a sixteen-inch dick, who could possibly compete?

The trouble was that their teachers couldn't protest that the friendship caused a drop in grades or a lack of interest in sport; Jim and Millie were straight A-plus students; Jim was a champion boxer and wrestler, and Millie a track star. They graduated at the head of their respective classes, with a virtual carte blanche in choice of a college. Harvard, Chubb, or any of the many great universities.

They went to Columbia together, enrolled in Science with a biochemistry major. Perhaps they hoped that New York City's teeming, hugely diverse student population would grant them some peace from their perpetual torments. If so, their hopes were dashed at once. They endured four more years of persecution, but showed the world they couldn't be crushed by graduating *summa cum laude*. Patrick and Nessie had tried to keep in contact, go down to see them when they wouldn't come home, but were always rebuffed. It was as if, Patrick had thought at that time, they were growing a carapace thick enough and hard enough to render them invulnerable, and that included shutting out parents. He and Nessie had gone to their graduation, but Jim's parents had not. Apparently they had given up the fight, just as strenuous on their side to sever their son from his white girlfriend—and who could blame them either? It takes maturity to know the pain . . .

The day after they graduated, Jim and Millie married in a registry office with no one there to wish them well. It was near Penn Station; they walked, carrying their suitcases, to board a crowded, smelly train to Chicago, traveling on student passes. In Chicago they changed to another crowded, smelly train that ambled on a poorly maintained railbed all the way to L.A. For most of the two and a half days they sat on the floor, but at least at Caltech they'd be warm in winter.

At the end of the two-year Master's program Jim was starting to be known, his color beginning to be an advantage north of the Mason-Dixon Line—until people learned he had a beautiful white biochemist wife. However, the University of Chicago was willing to take Mr. and Mrs. Hunter as doctoral fellows—back to cold winters and cheerless summers.

When they received their Ph.D.s they seemed to meet a solid wall of opposition. No matter how much a school wanted Dr. Jim Hunter, it wasn't prepared to offer employment to his wife, Dr. Millicent Hunter. He was one of the biggest whales in the vast protean ocean, whereas she was a sprat. As post-doctoral fellows *or* as faculty, the financial outlay for two Hunters was considered excessive. If this was complicated by the inter-racial nature of their union, no one was prepared to say.

After six years in Chicago they were poorer than ever, never having actually held a job. Their grants contained a subsistence-style living allowance, and on that they subsisted, dressing from K mart and eating supermarket bargains. A Chinese meal to go was a luxury they indulged in once a month.

Then their luck turned.

In 1966 the President of Chubb University, Mawson MacIntosh, was actively looking for racial misfits—and also for potential Nobel Prize winners. Jim Hunter looked good on both counts; M.M. was determined that Chubb would stay in the forefront of academic integration at all levels. Without any idea that Dr. Millicent Hunter was the Holloman Medical Examiner's daughter, M.M. sent a quiet directive to Dean Hugo Werther of Chemistry that the Doctors Hunter be given two faculty positions. They were not in the same lab, and her post involved some teaching, but they were both in the Burke Biology Tower and would be seen together. Dr. Millie pleased M.M.; biochemistry was a discipline that visibly changed while you looked at it, so teachers were rare. Whereas Dr. Jim Hunter was a

23

breaker of new ground, his mind that of a true genius. Only his having a beautiful white highly educated wife told against him, and that could not be seen to matter. The couple had been married for years, so probably had nothing left to learn about racial discrimination.

Thus it had been that over two years ago Millie had phoned out of the blue and asked if she and Jim could beg a bed for a couple of nights. Admittedly four of the O'Donnell daughters were gone, but of spare bedrooms there were none; Carmine had come to their rescue by giving them use of his apartment in the Nutmeg Insurance building before he sold it upon his marriage.

Overjoyed though they were at the return of Millie and Jim, Patrick and Nessie discovered very quickly that whatever they could offer was too little, too late. The Doctors Hunter were armored against the world so strongly that even parents couldn't find a weakness in the rivets. And what could they have done differently? Fear for a child leads to all sorts of hideously wrong decisions, Patrick reflected as he tramped up a set of cold stone stairs. If only Jim had looked like Harry Belafonte or at least been an ordinary brown! But he didn't, and he wasn't.

If the relationship between the Doctor's Hunter and her parents was a rather distant one, it was also genuinely friendly. What Patrick and Nessie continued to fear was simple: how could a fifteen-year-old possibly own the wisdom to choose the right life's partner? One day either Millie or Jim was going to wake up and discover that the childhood bond was gone, that a cruel world had finally managed to separate them. So far it had not happened, but it would. It would! They had no children, but that was probably deliberate. Until now, they plain couldn't afford a family. The steel in them! It amazed Patrick, who had to wonder if his own comfortable marriage to Nessie could have taken one-tenth of the blows Millie and Jim took every day.

Over two years last September since they came to Holloman!

Carmine was in. As he came through the door, Patrick had to smile. His first cousin was napping in the extremely efficient way he had perfected over hundreds of hours waiting to be called as a trial witness. What had happened last night?

"Did you and Desdemona toast the New Year too lavishly, cuz?" he asked.

Carmine didn't jump or twitch; he opened one clear eye. "Nope. Alex is teething and Julian is like his daddy—a very light sleeper."

"You would have them so close together."

"Don't look at me. It was Desdemona's idea." Carmine swung his feet off the kitchen table he used as a desk and opened both eyes. "Why are you slumming, Patsy?"

"Have you heard of tetrodotoxin?"

"Vaguely. It's been suggested in a sensational Australian case some years ago—the symptoms fit, but they couldn't isolate a poison of any kind. The Japanese flirt with it, I found out during my years in the occupation forces as a Tokyo M.P. Blowfish, blue-ringed octopus and some other marine nasties. According to my sources, it's fully metabolized and out of the system before autopsy can detect it," Carmine said.

Patrick blinked. "You perpetually amaze me, cuz. I presume it has to be logged in a poisons register if it's anywhere near the general public, but what happens if it's nowhere around the general public, yet goes missing?"

"That depends on whether you're ethical, or the type who covers his ass. Ethical, and you report its loss to *someone*. If inclined to cover your own ass, you write 'accidentally destroyed' or 'out of date and discarded as per regulations' in a register. But I presume this victim is ethical, right?"

"Right. My problem daughter, Millie. She's been working with the stuff, had enough left over to kill ten heavyweight boxers, divided into six glass ampoules of a hundred milligrams each—yes, yes, I'll slow down! She put the six ampoules into a beaker, stuck the skull-and-crossbones on it, then shoved it in the back of her lab refrigerator." Patrick frowned. "She didn't tell anyone it was gone until she came to see me. I advised her to remain silent, to tell no one further."

"Who else knew it was there?"

"Only Jim. She told him, in passing. Not his field."

"Was it labeled, apart from the poison sticker?"

"She didn't say. But while she may be too honest to forge an entry in her register, she is highly organized, Carmine. It would have been coded rather than named. Anyone poking through her refrigerator wouldn't have known what he was looking at," Patrick said. "My girl's worst fault is that she's too trusting. An untidy worker she's not. The trust baffles me, I confess. How can you trust a world that shits on you the way Millie's world shits on her?"

"It's her nature," Carmine said gently. "Millie is an honest-to-goodness saint." He caught sight of the railroad clock on his wall. "Lunch at Malvolio's?"

"Sounds good to me."

As soon as Merele cleared the dishes away Carmine returned to his cousin's problem.

"You'd better look up tetrodotoxin's clinical symptoms," he said. "If anyone took it with nefarious intentions, a gurney holding a victim is going to roll through your morgue doors, and the faster you can screen for tetrodotoxin, the better your chances of finding it. In fact, why don't you tell Paul you're running a little unofficial test to keep your technicians on their toes? Tell him they're to look for abstruse neurotoxins like tetrodotoxin. It won't fool Paul, but your technicians are used to your—er—unofficial exams. Let Paul in on it, he's no gossip, Patsy."

"Well, I have to keep my technicians on their toes now my lab is the major one in the state. I'll look, Carmine—and look hard." His face puckered; he fought for control and found it. "This isn't fair! Millie doesn't need extra grief."

"She did exactly the right thing in reporting her loss," Carmine said, voice level. "Had she concealed the theft, you might easily have missed a tetrodotoxin death at P.M. If the thief's motive was nefarious, he was looking for a rare and undetectable poison. And that means he's knowledgeable. A biochemist or biologist, or maybe a doctor." Carmine frowned, toyed with his spoon. "Given Jim's relationship to Millie, he's out of the picture, and that means someone else knew about the tetrodotoxin."

Patrick shivered. "Carmine, don't! You're talking as if the thief really does have murder in mind. I mean, this is all pure hypothesis! A bottle washer does her glassware once a week, there are electricians and plumbers—Millie doesn't work in a vacuum."

"Calm down, cuz, of course it's hypothesis. We'll cross the bridges as we come to them, but it never hurts to be fully prepared. I can already note that Dr. Millicent Hunter informed the Medical Examiner and the police that she found six hundred milligrams of tetrodotoxin missing from her laboratory refrigerator—what else could she have done? The substance wasn't named, though it bore a generic poisons sticker—that really is suspicious, Patsy. She's sure nothing else went missing—hang on." Carmine slid out of the booth. "I'll be back in a minute—and lunch is on me."

Patrick watched his cousin say something to Luigi, who pushed a phone across the counter. Carmine made a couple of calls, the second one the longer of the two, then returned.

"Nothing else is missing, even sterile water. The substance in question was coded—no indication of its real identity."

"So she can't be blamed? Ought it to have been locked up?"

"Given that she locked her lab door even if she was only going to the bathroom, Judge Thwaites would probably rule that the circumstances of Millie's research routine made locking it up unnecessary, given its anonymity. A white powder in a glass ampoule—it could be anything from cocaine to flour. Honest, Patsy, Millie's okay."

Carmine gave his cousin a look that held as much love as exasperation; one's children caused torments and apprehensions just not possible in any lesser beings. Patrick was caught in the web of his fear for this most worrisome daughter.

"You know, I don't label my stuff poison," Patrick said.

"You don't have to. Your lab is off limits to those who don't have

27

clearance, especially now there's a viewing room two floors up for identification," Carmine said comfortably. "All it took was the installation of an elevator shaft between your floor and ours."

"I keep all the known poisons in a safe, of course," Patrick went on, grappling the problem like a dog an old and meatless bone. "Trouble is, there are so many toxic ways to die, from Drano to household bleach. It used to be much easier when people just used rat or wasp poison—Carmine, don't let life hurt my Millie yet again!"

"I'll give it my best shot, I promise. How long have they been together now?"

"Eighteen years last September. They're thirty-two."

"What drew them together, Patsy?"

"I asked Millie that a long time ago, before they went to Columbia. All she said was that their eyes met."

"Doesn't happen that way for many."

"Never did for me." Patrick sounded desolate.

"Nor me, though I did love the color of Desdemona's eyes. Like pack ice, that eerie blue."

"I deemed them cold. That was why I disliked her."

"We do go on the eyes, Patsy, no argument there."

Patrick put his hand over Carmine's on the table. "But not for a long time now, cuz. She's a great woman, your wife."

Carmine changed the subject. "M.M. whispered to me that the Chubb University Press expects Jim Hunter's new book to be a popular bestseller. It's about the hand of God in our design for life—I didn't really get it, but M.M. says that anyone who reads the book will. He read it in manuscript and he's wild about it. Lucky for Jim that Don Carter lasted as Head Scholar of C.U.P. through to the end of the publication process. Tom Tinkerman, the new Head Scholar, is not a Jim Hunter fan—too Christian in the orthodox sense, brands Jim an atheist."

A look of horror flashed into Patrick's eyes. "Carmine, no! Tell me things are going to continue to go well for Jim! He and Millie need to start a family soon, and they're counting on extra income from book royalties—Don Carter gave him a generous contract, from what Jim said to me."

"And Tinkerman can't tinker with that, Patsy. I think M.M. is more concerned with making sure C.U.P. throws its weight behind Jim's book," Carmine said, wondering if there was anything that wouldn't alarm Patsy when it came to Millie.

"Tinkerman is a sanctimonious pedant!" Patrick snapped. "Why the hell did the Chubb Board of Governors give him the Head Scholar's job? He's not equipped for it, Jim says."

"From what M.M. told me, blame the Parsons. Man, that crew! I well remember them from the Hug case."

"And I," Patrick said, sounding grim.

"They have this collection of European art, reputedly the biggest and best in America," said Carmine. "The head of the family bequeathed the collection to Chubb along with many millions in endowments, but he didn't put a delivery date on the art collection. The surviving Parsons decided to keep the art. M.M. didn't push, hoping that when they did deliver, they'd donate a gallery to hold the collection. Until the banker guy with the wrong last name had one drink too many at the last Parson meeting with M.M., and told him they figured they could hang on to the paintings for another fifty years." The broad, handsome face broke into smiles; Carmine's amber eyes glowed. "M.M. got his dander up—a very dangerous state of affairs."

"Jesus!" Patrick's breath escaped in a hiss. "Did the banker guy fancy suicide, or something?"

"Must have. M.M. announced that he'd sue very publicly unless the entire collection down to the last Leonardo cartoon was delivered to Chubb's Curator of Art within a month. The Parsons were fucked, and knew it. Their revenge on M.M.? A new Head Scholar named Thomas Tarleton Tinkerman."

"And here was I thinking federal politics were dirty!" said Patrick, grinning. "Still, not a victory for the Chubb University Press. Or Jim."

"Care to bet how long Tinkerman lasts as Head Scholar? Not many moons beyond the receipt of the last Parson painting."

"But too long for Jim," Patrick said gloomily, "unless he can hold off on publishing."

"I don't pretend to be an expert on C.U.P., cuz, but I do not think that's possible," Carmine said, voice gentle. "Once a book's in print, it takes up a lot of space. They ship it out."

"I don't think I'll go on Saturday night."

"Patsy, you have to go! Desdemona and I can't wave all the flags for Jim," Carmine said sternly. "What would Millie say if you and her mom weren't there?"

"Pah!" The fresh, fair face screwed up in disgust. "Millie and Jim are the only reason I will be there, that's for sure. It seems wrong to give a banquet in honor of someone whom not a soul wanted in the position—even, now you tell me, M.M. Though I guess the Parsons will be there to cheer for Tinkerman."

"Bound to be."

"At least it's the relative comfort of black tie," Patrick said, looking evil. "You won't have to wear your dress uniform, just your academic robes."

"You'll be in the same boat, Patsy—academic robes."

FRIDAY, JANUARY 3, 1969

"Think of this as good practice," Millie soothed. "By the time the banquet rolls around tomorrow night, you'll be a true veteran." She made an adjustment to Jim's tie and stepped back. "Perfect! So handsome! There won't be anyone in your league."

Sentiments that were, he knew after listening to them for eighteen years, utterly mistaken. His looks had improved out of sight, but he'd never be Harry Belafonte. The only reason he turned heads was the ravishing white woman on his arm.

Old enough now to be settling into his ultimate physique, Jim Hunter was several inches over six feet in height, had a neck so thick and strong that it tended to dwarf his head, massive shoulders and upper arms, and a barrel of a chest. When he walked he waddled thanks to bulging thighs, but the right knee injury that had put paid to any hopes of a football scholarship made him favor the right leg in a noticeable limp.

The face, to those seeking it atop so much raw power, used to be no disappointment, for it had been brutish. Jim Hunter's skin was nigh impossibly black, as black as the blackest native African's; when he was photographed, even in color, his face was so dark it lost whole layers of definition. To see what he really looked like necessitated seeing the living man. His bones were unobtrusive, the cheekbones flat, and his nose in the old days had splayed outward with hugely gaping nostrils. At St. Bernard's he had instantly been nicknamed Gorilla, a huge insult compounded by his uprooted bewilderment, this all-

31

white environment so far from home: the days of black immigration from the South were still to come, so he was a true novelty in Italian-American East Holloman. Adolescents are cruel; to find the Gorilla could ace them all in a classroom without even extending himself didn't go down well. Nor, when almost immediately he took up with the St. Mary's belle Millie O'Donnell, did that go down well. Add Jim Hunter's temper plus his tendency to harbor grudges, and the pattern was set. He fought. Dozens of fights against ever-increasing numbers of opponents had eventually destroyed his superficial, even some of his deepest, sinuses as well as afflicted him with agonizing pain in his facial nerves. While the gorilla look grew worse.

Only John Hall's loan of ten thousand dollars for surgical repair had saved Jim's life, and in more ways than one. After the surgery the gorilla look had vanished; his nose was straight and quite narrow, its nostrils small and unobtrusive, he had bones in his cheeks and a good jawline. Finally his one great natural endowment, a pair of large, astonishingly green eyes, could come into their own and dominate his face beneath a high, broad brow.

But the psychic scars persisted down to this moment when his beautiful white wife tied his black tie and told him he looked so handsome. These were the great years of the Black Revolution, of last-ditch stands by fanatical whites against the inevitable opening up of all horizons to the black man, and Jim Hunter knew it, acknowledged it, even understood it. What he couldn't shake off was his deep conviction that much of his own ordeal was due to his marrying a white prom queen. She had been with him since his fifteenth birthday, so much a part of him that she was a cause. A cause? No! *The* cause.

A sensible streak had whispered to Jim that, appearing so very African, he must not go the Afro route; his hair was close-cropped and he wore the apparel of a post-doctoral fellow—chinos, white cotton shirt, loafers, a beat-up tweed jacket.

Except when, as now, he was being squeezed into the biggest tuxedo the formal-wear shop hired out.

"Don't flex your muscles," Millie was warning.

He hardly heard her, thinking how he'd gotten there. The years at Chubb had been a landslide of discoveries and seminal papers, or maybe a roller-coaster was a better analogy. Most of those who talked excitedly about Professor Jim Hunter had no idea he was a black ex-gorilla married to a dishy white chick. His reputation was made; now all he had to do was hang in there over this coming twelve months, during which he would enjoy fame of a different kind: a celebrity author. Though when Don Carter had started to describe some of the things he would be called upon to do, he shrank away in horror. Most of all, he was not ready to face the whole of a vast nation as the blackest of black men with a beauty queen white wife.

Millie was standing there, gazing at him with the eyes of love. Her sister Kate, a clothes horse, had lent her a dress, kind of wispy over a plain lining of lavender blue, the wisps the same shade, but varied in intensity. She looked out of this world. Her legs were on display because miniskirts were in for evening parties, Kate said. And Kate had good taste, down to the loose cord of sparkling rhinestones around Millie's hips.

She didn't look happy, despite the love. Poor little girl! The guy who pinched her tetrodotoxin ought to be shot for the major crime of worrying her. And then there was John Hall . . .

He took her face between his huge hands, holding it like a single rose. "You are so beautiful," he said in the back of his throat. "How did I ever get this lucky?"

"No, how did I?" she whispered back, stroking his hands. "One look, and I was done for. I will love you until I die, James Keith Hunter."

His laugh was almost too quiet to hear. "Oh, c'mon, honey! Death is just a transition. D'you think that our molecules won't shift heaven and earth to be together as long as time endures? We may die, but our molecules won't."

Her laugh was silent. "Just taking the mickey, my love, my joy—my dear, dear love."

"This time next year we'll be comfortable, I promise."

"A promise I'll hold you to." She twisted a scarf around her neck and shrugged into a sweater before he helped her into her down coat, old and weeping, but Chicago-warm. "Oh, winter! I can't wait for spring this year—1969 is going to be ours, Jim."

His own Chicago down coat was a better fit than the tux, creaking at its seams. "At least it's not snowing."

"I dislike these people," she said as she watched him lock the front door. "Fancy John turning up their relative."

"You know what they say—you can choose your friends, but not your relatives. Though the Tunbulls aren't too bad once you get to know them."

"Poor John! I wonder how he'll feel when he meets his stepmother. From what he said last night, most of his contact with his father concerned proving that he was the long lost son," said Millie.

"That's logical," Jim answered. "Don't worry, Millie, it will all come out in the wash sooner or later." He looked suddenly hopeful. "Just think! I'll soon be able to pay John back for that sinus operation if my book does what they say it will. Ten thousand dollars! Yet one more debt. A hundred big ones in student loans . . ."

"Stop it, Jim!" she snapped, looking fierce. "We're Chubb faculty now, you're about to be famous, and our income will pay back every last debt."

"If Tinkerman doesn't suppress *A Helical God*. Oh, Millie, it's been such a long, hard road! I don't think I could bear another disappointment." Jim removed the stick from the old Chevy's gas pedal. "The car's good and warm. Get in."

Davina and Max Tunbull lived in a big white clapboard house on Hampton Street, just off Route 133 in the Valley, and not more than half a mile from the invisible boundary beyond which the Valley became a less salubrious neighborhood. There were actually three

Tunbull houses on this longish, rambling street of mostly vacant lots, but Max and Davina lived in the dominant one on the knoll, by far the most imposing. A house on the far side of the street had some pretensions to affluence, but there could be no doubt whose residence kinged it over all others.

When Millie and Jim arrived they found themselves the last, dismaying—had it really taken so long to squeeze Jim into his hired tux? What an idiocy! *Black tie!*

It wasn't the first time she had met Davina, but the woman still jarred and disturbed her. Millie's life to date had been spent in traditionally unfeminine pursuits and with mostly male peers, a pattern set very early on thanks to her liaison with Jim. So the Davinas of this world were more foreign even than this Davina really was; they chattered of things Millie knew nothing about, nor hungered to know about.

John Hall was almost pathetically glad to see them, which made it all worthwhile; despite Jim's importance to Max, they probably would have declined this invitation had John not visited last night and implored them. The poor guy was terrified, but that was typical John, a loner, shy, unsure of himself until he settled into the kind of friendship he had enjoyed with the Hunters back in California.

But of course Davina wouldn't leave them alone. Not surprising to Millie, who knew of Davina's reputation: see an attractive man and go for him, then, when he became too ardent or amorous, run screeching to husband Max for protection. John, with genuine good looks skating on the verge of female, was a logical Davina target. The weird servant, Uda, had obviously assessed John to the same conclusion, and plied the poor man with martinis he had the sense not to drink. What was Uda's stake in it? wondered Millie, eyes busy.

It was the only way to make the time go, especially in this almost all male assembly. Under ordinary circumstances Millie would simply have barged into the middle of the men and demanded to be included in conversation whereof she knew she could hold her end up. But with Davina present, no luck! Not to mention the pregnant

Mrs. Markoff, the only other woman, and not, from the look on her face, a Davina admirer.

Mentally Millie ran through what she knew about Davina from Jim, the source of all her information on the big team who were responsible for putting his book into print, from the Head Scholar of the Chubb University Press to Tunbull Printing and Imaginexa Design. Oh, pray that *A Helical God* did what everyone said it was bound to!

A Yugoslavian refugee who had been in the country for ten years and was now twenty-six: that was the first item. She had been lucky enough to be "discovered" by a big agency and became a top model, especially famous for taking a bubble bath on TV—an ad, she was quick to point out, that still paid her good royalties. But her heart was in visual design, and she was, so the Chubb University Press people insisted, a superb exponent of the art of making a book irresistibly attractive to browsers. Her chief market lay with trade publishers, but because Max was sole printer to the Chubb University Press, she had deigned to take over their output as well.

Millie didn't think, somehow, that dear old Don Carter, who had been Jim's mentor through the writing and editing of the book, would have had the steel to deny Davina entry to a rather peculiar world, that of the minor academic publishing house. So whether C.U.P. wanted it or not, Davina took over their "book look" as she put it.

Could she honestly be just twenty-six years old? No, Millie decided, she's thirty at least, has to be. Tall, stick-thin yet graceful, and lucky enough, thought Millie, eyeing her clinically, to have a narrow skeleton; a big, wide pelvis would have put a huge gap between those arm-sized thighs. Good, B-cup breasts, not much of a waist—that fit with the skeleton—and a long torso above shortish legs. She dressed extremely well, and her brown-black hair was thick enough to take the loose-down-the-back fashion, though it tended to clump in ropes. *Beautiful* clear white skin, carefully plucked and arched brows, long lashes, and startlingly vivid blue eyes. Yet, Millie's thoughts rambled on, her lips were *too* large and her nose, though straight, was broad. Good cheekbones saved her face, together with those weird eyes. An enlightenment burst on Millie: Davina looked as Medusa the Gorgon must have looked before the gods stripped her of her beauty!

"I haven't got my waistline back enough for miniskirts," Davina was saying to Millie, the foreign accent lending her high, fluting voice some much needed character.

"I didn't think dresses with miniskirts emphasized waists," Millie said. "How old is Alexis?"

"Three months." She gave an airy laugh. "I thought I was giving Max a much needed heir, and now—John turns up! So now I kill the fatted calf for the return of the prodigal son."

"But John isn't a prodigal son," said Millie. "That son was banished for loose living or some such thing, I thought, whereas John is just a victim of circumstances beyond his control."

The derisive eyes clouded, became uncertain; Davina gave a shrug and flounced off.

The room was very modern, but Millie quite liked it and found a comfortable chair to people watch in peace while she could. Except that there were too few people. Her gaze rested upon Jim, talking to John, and her thoughts slipped backward in time; his advent out of the blue last night had shocked her, though Jim—no, not expected it, seemed to have sensed it was coming.

They had met in California when all three enrolled in the biochemistry Master's program at Caltech; that they had clicked was probably due to John's solitary habits, which fitted well into their own isolation. For reasons he never elaborated upon to them, John Hall too was armored against a cruel and inquisitive world. He wasn't short of money, but learned not to intrude his wealth into their friendship. With John as third wheel, those two years in California had held many pleasant moments; they did a lot of sitting on public beaches, counting their nickels and dimes for a boardwalk lunch somewhere, listening to Elvis Presley, the Everly Brothers and the

Coasters, all very new and exciting at the time. Women found John immensely attractive and threw lures, but he ignored every overture. Whatever chewed at his core was shattering, subtle, sorrowful. That it had all to do with John's dead mother they had gathered, but he never told them his whole story, and—at least while Millie was present—they never asked. Jim, she suspected, knew more.

The glowingly bright corner John Hall occupied in Millie's mind went back to his astonishing and totally unsought generosity. When Jim's facial sinuses literally threatened his life, John Hall went out and commissioned the finest sinus surgeon in L.A., and, without telling them, threw in a plastic surgeon for good measure. Ten thousand dollars of surgery later, Jim Hunter emerged a changed man. Not only could he breathe easily, not only was all threat of brain infection removed, but he had also lost all resemblance to a gorilla. He was pleasantly negroid, no longer even remotely apelike. And Jim had actually stomached the gift! Jim, who would accept charity from no one! Millie knew exactly why: easy breathing and safety from cerebral abscess were wonderful, but not even in the same league as losing the gorilla look.

When they went to the University of Chicago, John returned to Oregon. But he kept in touch, and when Jim sent him the postcard saying they were now faculty in the Chubb Department of Biochemistry, he sent a huge card he'd made himself, delighted that good fortune had smiled on them at last.

Then, out of the blue, he'd called them from the airport to say he was on his way to Holloman, and would they be up for a cup of coffee if he came around? Only last night! With all this torment on his mind, he'd talked of the old times, nothing but the old times, and feeling his eyes rest on her, Millie had given a shudder of fear. Not that too!

Millie jumped, so deep in her reverie that Davina's voice came as a shock.

"To the table, everyone!"

With so few women, no surprise to find she occupied the middle slot on one side of the table with the pregnant doctor's wife opposite her. Ivan was on Max's side of her, Dr. Al Markoff on Davina's side; Jim sat opposite her down one next to Davina, and Val sat on Muse Markoff's other side. Not a remote table of several conversations; everyone was within good hearing distance. Millie winked at Jim, whom Davina was already monopolizing.

They had to go through that awful speech about the fatted calf, the pointed references to the absentee Tunbull wives—she was a monster! Some of the tendrils of her hair, thought a fascinated Millie, were stirring to form snakes—wasn't that a head and a forked tongue in there? This woman speaks with a forked tongue!

The first course was Iranian caviar.

"Of course Russian would have been better," said Davina, demonstrating how to eat it, "but this is still Caspian sturgeon of malossol variety. What silly rules a cold war causes! No Russian caviar. No Cuban cigars. Silly!"

Iranian caviar is good enough for me, thought Millie as she piled a toast finger high and tamped everything down with sour cream; minced egg and minced onion had an annoying habit of tumbling off, and she wasn't about to waste one of those tiny, heavenly black blobs.

"I've died of sheer bliss," she said to Muse Markoff.

"Isn't she amazing?" Muse asked as the plates were whisked away. "Even to having Uda, the perfect housekeeper. Things sure have changed in the Tunbull zoo since Max married Davina."

"Muse! How did you get that name?" Millie asked.

"A father steeped in the Classics. He was an associate professor at Chubb, poor baby. Sideways promotion. Once an associate, never a full."

"And how have things changed for the Tunbulls, Muse?"

"This passion for Max's Russian roots. I always thought they were Polish roots, but Davina says they're Russian."

"Just as well the McCarthy era is over."

Muse winced, patted her huge tummy. "That was rich for a first course. I hope I last—my liver doesn't like rich food. D'you think the roast veal will be terribly fatty? The way Davina spoke, I see it kind of swimming in fat."

"No, no fat," said Millie, smiling. " 'Fatted calf' is a stock phrase, like—um—'lean pickings.' Roast veal isn't at all fatty, I promise."

Nor was it. The veal was plain but perfectly cooked, very thin slices of pinkish meat with a gravy rather than a sauce, mashed potatoes, steamed broccoli, thin and stringless green beans. Muse, Millie noted, ate with enjoyment, and made no complaints about her sensitive liver.

When Millie overheard Max and John talking about Martita, more of the puzzle fell into place. From her own little speech, Davina must have worked feverishly to disprove John's story—what was the ring reference all about? So even through their phone conversations, Max must have kept to legal matters, Davina probably literally breathing down his neck. Those two poor men are not going to have an easy time of it . . .

A glance at Davina revealed a head of living snakes. If she caught their eyes, she'd turn them to stone.

What was with this Emily, the persecutor of John's mother? Absent because she'd grown off in her own direction rather than because she had offended. Though so many years would soften anything, and she was Val's wife, Ivan's mother. Ivan . . . How did he feel, seeing his share of the family business steadily depleting? Though John had said last night that he had no wish or intention to be a part of the Tunbull business. Maybe the Tunbulls had no idea as yet how rich John was, how little he need depend on anyone after Wendover Hall dowered him. It seemed one of Davina's ways of amusing herself was to snipe at Ivan—look at her crack about his wife.

Oh, John, John, I feel so sorry for you! Millie cried to herself as the cake came in.

"Uda made this with her own hands!" Davina fluted, the snakes writhing. "Each layer of cake is no more than five millimetres thick, and the butter cream is also five millimetres thick, flavored by Grand Marnier. The top is sugar-and-water boiled to crisp, transparent amber glass. And the entire cake is for the many years John has been away, while the glassy top, which must be broken before the past can be eaten, is tonight. Eat up, my friends, eat up!"

"A minute, Vina, give me a minute first!" Max shouted, surging to his feet. "First of all, I want you to lift your glasses to Dr. Jim Hunter, whose book on nucleic acids and their possible philosophical meaning is shortly to be published by the Chubb University Press, whose printers we have been for over twenty years. Head Scholar Carter assures me that it's going to be a popular best seller. To Dr. Jim Hunter and his amazing, thought-provoking book, *A Helical God!*"

Good old Max, thought Millie, letting the most divine cake she had ever tasted dissolve gradually on her tongue. He could not resist showing Jim off for John's benefit, always assuming that he had no idea we knew each other in the old days. And why would he know that? John's advent is a shock.

Then the worst fate of all struck Millie; she was herded to the drawing room with Muse Markoff and expected to have coffee apart from the men, all gone to Max's den. Not fair! What can I talk about, for God's sake? They wouldn't know a benzene ring from a curtain ring or an hydroxyl ion from a steam iron!

Luckily Davina and Muse, living across the street from each other, had plenty to talk about; Millie sat back and sipped much better coffee than she was used to, stomach pleasantly full and most of her spare blood supply more concerned with digestion than deep thoughts. Her eyelids drooped; no one noticed.

The door flew open upon a white-faced Max.

"Muse, Al needs his medical bag urgently," he said.

Good wife, she was gone in under a second for the front door, the tiny maid Uda running at her elbow to steady her.

"What is it?" Davina faltered, all resemblance to Medusa vanished. "Let me see!"

"No!" he barked.

To Millie's astonishment, Davina sank back into her chair at once. "What is it?" she repeated.

"John's having some kind of attack. Ambulance!" And he rushed to the phone, gabbled into it that Dr. Al Markoff needed a resuscitation ambulance *immediately*—uh, yeah, address . . .

By this time Muse had returned, Uda carrying a seemingly heavy black leather doctor's bag. Max snatched it.

"Stay here, all of you," he said.

The minutes ticked by, marked out on a gigantic, fanciful clock sculpted into a wall; the women sat frozen, mute.

An ambulance came very quickly; the vigilant Uda let in two equipment encumbered physician's assistants and ran them to the den, then returned to take up her station beside Davina, who looked wilted and terrified.

Jim appeared, went straight to Millie.

"John is dead," he said abruptly, "and Dr. Markoff says it's suspicious." The green eyes were stern, level. "I thought of the missing tetrodotoxin."

Her skin lost all its color. "Jesus, no! How could it have gotten *here,* for God's sake?"

"I don't know, but if you can help, Millie, then help. Call your father and tell him what's happened. The symptoms sound as if it was injected. If the pathologist acts quickly enough, there may be a chance he can find tetrodotoxin in the form of its last metabolites. There's blood drawn, so get a motorcycle cop here to siren it into town. Then your dad's got a fighting chance. Call Patrick, please."

She obeyed, pushing Max away from the phone.

"By the time the road cop picks the sample up, Dad, I'll have drawn a schematic of tetrodotoxin's molecular structure," Millie said to Patrick a moment later. "I think Jim's crazy to suspect it, but what if he's right? What if whoever stole the stuff is selling it as the undetectable poison? That's why you have to assay the victim's blood a.s.a.p.—more chance of a last metabolite or two. Gas chromatography first, then the mass spectrometer. Humor Jim, Dad, please! I mean, it can't possibly be tetrodotoxin, these people have no connection to me."

"I'll send Gus Fennell. I have to recuse myself, Millie," said her father's voice, "and I'm guessing Carmine will too. It will probably be Abe Goldberg. Oh, shit!"

"Tell me about it." She hung up.

Max Tunbull and Al Markoff were arguing.

"You've got it all wrong, Al! John's mom died at about the same age, and John's her spitting image—it runs in that family!" Max said.

"Crap!" said the doughty doctor. "Bitch all you like, Max, I'm not convinced John died from natural causes. The time span between onset of symptoms and death was nearly lightning. Pity I was too busy to time it."

"I timed it," Jim Hunter said. "From his saying the word 'hot' to his death, eleven minutes. You're absolutely right, Al, it's suspicious. John was a healthy guy."

Whereupon Davina, eyes distended, uttered a shriek, went rigid, and fell to the floor. Uda knelt beside her.

"I put Miss Vina bed," she said. "Mr. Max, you phone her doctor now. She get needle."

"No way," said Muse Markoff. "The cops will want to see her, Uda—unsedated."

"Thiss not Iron Curtain!" Uda snarled on yellow teeth. "Big function tomorrow night for Miss Davina, she be ready!"

And, thought Millie, remembering tomorrow night, Davina would go through hell to be ready for it. No matter what the cops might want, Davina's doctor was going to knock her out until late tomorrow afternoon. "Or," said Millie to Jim, "I'm a monkey's uncle."

He grinned, brushed her cheek with one finger. "That, my love, you are not." His eyes followed the servant, supporting her mistress to the stairs. "To get to Davina, first get past Uda. If I've learned nothing else, I've learned that."

Lieutenant Abe Goldberg appeared a few minutes after the motorcycle cop picked up the test tubes of blood for the M.E.; with him came Dr. Gus Fennell, Deputy Medical Examiner, and his own pair of detectives, Sergeants Liam Connor and Tony Cerutti.

"What do you really think, Millie?" Abe asked, his fair and freckled countenance looking unusually grim. Millie Hunter's marital history was well known, and she was loved.

"John's symptoms sound very supicious, but the rapidity of his death suggests injection rather than ingestion. If he'd eaten it, especially given the good meal he consumed, I would have expected considerable vomiting and fecal purging. And it wouldn't have come on so fast. Tell whoever does the autopsy to look for a puncture mark, and tell Paul the dose might have been as small as a half of one milligram. John was about six feet, but he wouldn't have weighed more than one-sixty." Millie kept her voice low, glad Davina Tunbull wasn't watching. Hysterics, my eye!

"Now's not the time or place, Dr. Hunter, but I gather you were aware your wife had tetrodotoxin at her laboratory?" Abe asked Jim, his voice courteous.

"Yes, she mentioned it."

"Were you aware how dangerous it is?"

"In all honesty, no. I'm not a neurochemist, and I would not have recognized it as a toxin if I'd encountered it, at least before I determined its molecular structure. That always gives a lot of things away. But it's only tonight, after watching John Tunbull die, that I understand how lethal it is, particularly for such a tiny dose. I mean, it's lethal at the kind of dose you might give yourself by sheer accident!"

"Who suspected the death, Dr. Jim?"

"Dr. Markoff. Said flatly it was a coroner's case and the police had to be called in. He's impressive."

"Did you think the death suspicious?"

Jim considered that carefully, then shook his head. "No, I guess I just thought it was a heart attack, or maybe a pulmonary embolus—I'm not totally medically ignorant, but I'm not a physician either. Except for his age, John's death looked pretty routine to me. Millie wasn't so sure because someone stole her tetrodotoxin—it's absolutely lethal stuff, Lieutenant."

"Did you know about the theft, Doctor?"

"Sure I did—Millie and I tell each other everything. But I never thought of connecting it to John—I have no idea what the symptoms are, except I guess I thought they'd be the usual symptoms of poisoning—vomiting, purging, convulsions. None of which he displayed. The only poisons I know behave the way John behaved are all gases, and since no one else felt a sign of what John went through, it can't have been a gas. Tetrodotoxin isn't a gas either. It's a liquid that can be reduced to a powder, or vice versa." Jim gave a half-hearted grin. "By which, Lieutenant, you know that Millie and I do discuss things."

Abe's large grey eyes had narrowed; so this was the black half of a famous alliance! Wherever he might have met Jim Hunter, under what circumstances, his eyes betrayed enormous intelligence, innate gentleness, a huge capacity to ponder. Carmine liked him: now Abe saw why.

"May my wife and I find a quiet, out of the way corner, Lieutenant?" Jim asked.

"Sure, Doctors. Just don't leave the house."

Abe kept his questions to the dinner guests brief and to the point: just events at the dinner, in the den, trips to the toilets, John's sudden illness. The only one he suspected of real duplicity was Mrs. Davina Tunbull, who had retreated into hysterics Millie whispered were fake. They were always bad news, those women, even though mostly they had nothing to do with the commission of the crime. They muddied the waters simply to be noticed, treated specially, fussed over. And there was no way he was going to get to see her or the servant, Uda, tonight.

With their details written down in his notebook and John Tunbull's body gone to the morgue an hour since, Abe wound up his investigation shortly after midnight and let people go home.

"Though that's really only us," said Millie, wrapped against the cold as she and Abe stood on the crunchy doorstep. "The rest are close enough to walk home. Oh, dear, there's Muse vomiting in the garden. I daresay she does have a sensitive liver after all. Her husband's very kind to her, I see."

"Where do you live, Millie?"

"On State Street. Caterby is the next intersection."

Jim drove up in their old Chevy clunker; Abe opened the passenger door to let Millie slide in, then watched them drive away, the white fog issuing from their tail pipe telling him that the temperature had dropped below 28°F. This was a cold winter.

Those two unfortunate people, Abe thought, mind on the Doctors Hunter. Still dirt-poor, to be living out there on State. Paying back the last of their student loans, no doubt. Just as well Dr. Jim is the size of a small mountain. If he were a ninety-pound weakling, that neighborhood would be hell for a mixed-race couple, full of poor whites and an occasional neo-Nazi.

SATURDAY, JANUARY 4, 1969

Desdemona took the tuxedo by its shoulders and shook it out.

"There, Millie! It will not only hold throughout tonight's boring festivities, it will actually feel reasonably comfy."

Beaming in pleasure, Millie hugged as much of Desdemona as she could reach. "Thank you, thank you!" she cried. "Aunt Emilia said you could do anything with a needle, but I hated invading your privacy, the busy mother. However, unless Jim's book is a big seller, we can't possibly afford a tailor-made dinner suit for him."

"Looks to me as if he's going to need one in the years to come. When you can afford it, ask Abe Goldberg where to go. His family has more tailors than detectives. Carmine can't buy his suits off the rack either—clothing manufacturers don't cater for men who are massive in the shoulders and chest, but narrow in the waist." Desdemona turned her sewing machine upside down and watched it disappear into its cradle. "There! Come and have a cuppa with me—tea or coffee, your choice." A hand reached down to scoop Alex out of his daytime crib. "Yes, sweet bugger-lugs, you've been very patient," she said, balancing him on her left hip.

"You manage so effortlessly," Millie said, watching Desdemona make a pot of tea and shake chocolate chip cookies on to a plate, all holding Alex.

"Oh, Alex is easy. It's the first one causes the headaches," Desdemona said, settling into the breakfast booth—a new addition to the kitchen—with Alex on her knee. She dunked the edge of a cookie in her rather milky tea and gave it to Alex to suck. "I would have been horrified at the thought of giving a sugary cookie to a nine-month-old baby when I had Julian, but now? Anything that shuts them up or keeps them happy is my motto."

Such a beautiful child! Millie was thinking as she watched enviously. I want to be her—I'm sick of laboratory experiments! I want a delicious little baby Hunter, some shade of brown, with weirdly colored eyes and a brain as big as his or her Daddy's . . .

"Where are you?" Desdemona asked, snapping her fingers.

"Putting myself in your place. Wanting to be a mother."

"It's not always beer and skittles, Millie," Desdemona said wryly. "I'm still recovering from a post-partum depression."

"But you're okay, right?"

"Yes, thanks to an understanding husband."

In came Julian, toting a huge orange cat that was giving him all its considerable weight. Desdemona handed a cookie down.

"Ta, Mommy."

"Julian, you're developing your muscles splendidly, but how is Winston going to get any exercise when you carry him everywhere? Put him down and make him walk."

Down went the cat, which began to wash itself.

"See? That's why I carry him, Mommy. Every time I put him down, he washes himself."

"To get rid of your smell, Julian. If he is to sniff out rats and mice, he can't have Julian all over him."

"Okay, I see that." Julian wriggled up beside his mother and looked at Millie with topaz eyes. "Hi," he said.

"Hi. I'm Millie."

Out of the corner of her eye Millie saw an ugly pit bull dog join the cat; they ambled together toward the back foyer.

"You can be nice to Julian," Desdemona said gravely. "He's through his most annoying phase, at least for the time being."

"What was your most annoying phase, Julian?" Millie asked.

"Daddy said, I was a defense attorney." Julian reached for his mother's tea cup and drank its entire contents thirstily.

"You let him drink *tea*?" Millie asked, appalled.

"Well, drinking gallons of it from infancy didn't stop us Brits from ruling most of the world," said Desdemona, laughing. "I put extra milk in it if Julian drinks it, but tea's good value." She gazed at Millie sternly. "Come! Talk to me about you and Jim."

"That does it!" said Julian loudly, sliding down from the seat with a flick at Alex's cheek that Millie supposed was love. "I have to supervise Private Frankie and Corporal Winston. See ya!" And off he went.

"His speech is dreadful," his mother said. "Try though I do to limit them, he's full of Americanisms."

"He *lives* in America, Desdemona."

She sighed. "The quintessential gun culture. But let's not talk about my sons. Who interviewed you last night?"

"Abe. Thank God for a friendly face."

"Don't say that too loudly. Carmine doesn't want an outside agency invited in to investigate because of propinquity." She chuckled. "Such a peculiar word to use!"

"Not much chance of that," said Millie. "I called Abe Lieutenant Goldberg and was as stiff as a poker. It was dreadful, Desdemona! Jim was right next to John when he took ill."

"Someone had to be next to him," Desdemona comforted, and poured more tea around the encumbrance of Alex, still sucking at his cookie. "I gather that further questioning is to wait until tomorrow maybe Monday for you and Jim."

"I must say that Abe took Davina's absence calmly. Even after her doctor told him she'd have to wait until Sunday for questions, he just looked long-suffering."

Desdemona grinned. "They encounter women like her all the time, Millie. All she's doing is postponing what will be a nastier interview because she did postpone it. And enough of all that! Have you a nice frock for tonight?"

Millie's face clouded. "Unfortunately, no. Kate let me pick through her enormous wardrobe, but tonight is a long dress that has to hold up academic robes, so I'm back to my graduation black dress. Men have their ties to hook robes and hoods around, but women don't. You and Carmine are coming tonight, I hope?"

"We'll be there, Millie," said Desdemona, smiling.

"You said tonight was an annoying inconvenience, Mommy," said Julian, stomping in like a soldier back from the wars.

"He's turned into a parrot," his mother said. "I absolutely despair of sensible conversation with him."

"Why do you absolutely despair of sensible conversation with me, Mommy? I know lots of big words."

"You know them like a parrot."

"Pooh, nonsense!" said Julian.

"Oh, lord, I said that weeks ago, and he won't forget it!"

Alex opened his mouth and grinned, revealing teeth.

Ivy Hall was one of the oldest buildings at Chubb University, it-self nearly three hundred years old, and Ivy Hall had been preserved with loving care. Built of red brick in 1725, it had been the original classroom, though for the last hundred years it had been used only for important banquets. Until Mawson MacIntosh, fondly known as M.M., had taken over as President of Chubb, its accommodation had been on the spartan side—scarred wooden benches and refec-tory tables. With his unparalleled genius for fund raising, M.M. had persuaded the Wicken family to donate a large sum to refurnish Ivy Hall; it now had proper dining tables of the finest mahogany, with upholstered mahogany chairs.

Its walls were hung with priceless Flemish tapestries between floor-to-ceiling Georgian windows, with space for long paintings of landscapes here and there. The oak floor had been treated, and the dais designed to take a high table given a much needed spit and polish.

The official reason for giving this particular banquet was to mark the retirement of the present Head Scholar of the Chubb University Press, and the assumption of the title Head Scholar by his successor. How the man responsible for the administration of C.U.P. had come to be known as its Head Scholar was lost in the mists of time for most: in actual fact it went back to the founding of C.U.P. in 1819, and was supposed to reflect Chubb University's charter principles. This night, however, also marked another fact about C.U.P.: it was 150 years old, and celebrating its sesquicentenary. For that reason, the heavy place mats bore a beautifully chased design based on the number 150, dreamed up by C.U.P.'s associated design firm, Imaginexa; it was therefore the brain child of Davina Tunbull, who had gone further and put a few festive gold-and-silver touches on the hall that not the most conservative of academics could have damned as in bad taste.

Four tables had been laid, decorated with gold-and-silver 150s cunningly wrought out of metal to form something like epergnes. One, the high table, sat upon the raised dais at the end of the hall, and because of its orientation, the three tables down on the floor of the hall were also laid from side to side of the room, which gave the whole assemblage a discriminatory feel, as it went high table for the major dignitaries, then the Chubb University table, followed by the Chubb University Press table, and, farthest from the high table and closest to the food ingress and egress, the table of Town dignitaries.

Each of the four tables held nine couples, which meant that a total of seventy-two people would sit down to what would be a function most didn't want to attend but couldn't not; the speeches and the involuntary exposure of many to people they tried to avoid summed up the negative side of being there, while the quality of the food, the fairly comfortable chairs and the chance to catch up with old friends represented the positive side. Tradition demanded that academic robes be worn by all the men but only by those women holding Chubb faculty positions, which added to the torments; police captains like Carmine Delmonico and Fernando Vasquez voted it an utterly wasted evening.

"Whoever planned this setup made a boo-boo," Commissioner John Silvestri said as he ensconced his still beautiful wife in her chair and sat down next to her. "They put Nate Winthrop on the high table and Doug Thwaites down on the floor—man, they will rue that!"

Carmine, to whom this remark was made, gave his boss a grin. "They need Delia," he said.

"We could rent her out, a thousand bucks an hour."

"No, we won't. M.M. might grab her."

"M.M. won't be pleased when he sees he's gotten Nate but no Doug," said the District Attorney, Horace Pinnerton. "Yes, Marcia, I'll see if I can get you an extra cushion. They never cater for shorties," he said to Fernando Vasquez.

"Or long drinks of water," Fernando said, nodding at the two metres-plus of Manfred Mayhew, Holloman's Town Clerk, once a famous basketballer. His wife, of course, was barely five feet tall. Another cushion coming up!

"And for this, Ginny and I have to miss our free night," said the Fire Chief, Bede Murphy, who didn't wear a robe.

His wife was giving Liza Mayhew the look of a martyr. "Bede doesn't fit his tux anymore," she said, low-voiced, "and my long dresses went out with Norma Shearer. Sometimes I hate Chubb! Academic gowns, tuxes, long dresses—pah!"

"The place mats and decorations are superb," said Desdemona pacifically. "Millie told me that Davina Tunbull designed them. Is that her on the next table up?"

About to sit down, Carmine turned to tally the C.U.P. table. "Your instincts are amazing," he said. "From Abe's description of a woman who'd gone to bed in hysterics and wasn't even on display, that's her in silver and gold."

"Well, she's so beautifully dressed, and matches the decor," said Desdemona, and gazed down at the table with a sigh. "My back will be giving me gyp at the end of this. Why are dining tables so low, or chairs so high?"

Carmine seated himself, pleased that he was on the correct side of the table to look up the hall. Davina Tunbull was a looker, but what took his eye was the dramatic difference in age between her and her husband. Max looked his sixty years—why hadn't they begged to be excused tonight? Everybody would have understood. No, she had wanted to come, no matter how Max felt. Dressed in slinky gold and silver panels that left her knobby back bare, she was queening it over the rest of the women at her table—or in the hall, for that matter. Why did women starve themselves to look good in clothes? They resembled greyhounds.

All the Tunbulls had come—Max and Davina, Val and Emily, Ivan and Lily. After Abe's perceptive reportage, Carmine had the men in his memory now. They represented the printing side of C.U.P., so presumably the others at the table belonged to C.U.P. itself. Interesting! Several of the executives were women; no mistaking who was the professional boss in a relationship, and these women were towing escorts or tame husbands. No equal partnerships here. Three women executives, three men executives.

His eye went to the high table, farthest away, but also the easiest to see, up in the air six feet. Jim and Millie Hunter were seated on it; so were the two senior Parsons, Roger Junior and Henry Junior. Hmm . . . That was right, then, the Parsons had bludgeoned Chubb into appointing Thomas Tarleton Tinkerman the new C.U.P. Head Scholar. Easy to pick him: his facial expression was reminiscent of Martin Luther having a bad day with his hemorrhoids. Jesus, were they the Parson wives? They could have been sisters to their husbands—the same austere, bony faces—and the same watery blue eyes, he'd be willing to bet if he got close enough to check.

"You're enjoying this, you ruthless blighter," Desdemona was whispering. "Grist to your copper's mill."

"Yep," he said amiably, lifted her hand and kissed it, eyes glowing. "None of them can hold a candle to you."

She blushed. "Flattery will get you permission to massage my back later tonight, otherwise I'll be a cot case tomorrow."

"Deal," he said, and grinned at Patrick and Nessie, down between

Horrie Pinnerton and Dave Zuckerman, the head of Social Services. Derek Daiman and his wife, Annabelle, had just come in too; he had gone from Principal of Travis High to Director of Education. It felt good to have a black couple on the Town table—more than Chubb could boast.

"Generous width of seating," Derek said, sitting opposite Carmine. "If the meat's tough, I can fly my elbows."

"Don't hesitate to put them on the table when they're not flying," Carmine said. "This is your first banquet, you and Fernando, but it's my skeedy-eighth."

"*Will* the meat be tough?" Fernando asked anxiously.

"Put it this way, guys: If the meat is tough, then the next banquet will serve roast caterer for the main course. M.M. is a stickler for good food at these functions." He raised his glass of amontillado. "Cheers! Here's to many more Chubb banquets."

"Speaking as a cop, may they all be boring," Fernando said, and sipped. "Hey, this is good sherry!"

"Chubb is well endowed, gentlemen."

"Who's at the first table below the high one?" Derek asked.

"Chubb U. dignitaries. The rest of the Governors—Dean Bob Highman as senior dean—three specimens of Parson in Roger III, Henry III, and he of the loose mouth, Richard Spaight. But don't feel sorry for Doug Thwaites, he'll make mincemeat of them all."

Thomas Tarleton Tinkerman, now Head Scholar of the Chubb University Press, was holding forth to the Parson Brothers while the entire high table listened, some politely, some happily, some incredulously.

"C.U.P. will return to the spirit of its charter," he was saying, "and leave scientific publishing to those academic institutions with the interest and resources to do it properly. C.U.P.'s niche under my care of the imprimatur will be in those neglected fields whose students may be few, but whose ideas are so vital to Western philosophy that they have shaped it. In our present climate of worship for the technocrat and the machine, no one publishes them anymore. But I will, gentle-men, I will!"

"I'm not sure how the technocrat and the machine fit in, but I take it you dismiss twentieth century philosophy?" Hank Howard asked, wondering if he could be baited.

The haughty face sneered. "Pah! One may as well call Darwin and Copernicus philosophers! The kind medical students read!"

"I think it's great that medical students read anything not con-nected to medicine," Jim Hunter said mildly.

Tinkerman's face said "You would!" but his mouth said "Not so, Dr. Hunter. Better they should confine themselves to medicine than read metaphysics for monkeys!"

A small, startled silence fell: Tinkerman had sounded too per-sonal, and several of his auditors resolved to deflect him.

"I've known medical students who read Augustine, Machiavelli and Federico Garcia Lorca," said M.M., smiling easily.

"Perhaps they're a little off the track of this discussion, Tom, but if novelists like Norman Mailer and Philip Roth were offered to you, surely you'd publish them?" Bursar Townsend asked.

"No, I would not! *Never!*" Tinkerman snapped. "Disgusting, filthy, pornographic trash! The only philosophy they can offer is in the gutter!" His chest heaved, his eyes flashed.

"Ah!" M.M. exclaimed. "Food! Tom, your blood sugar seems a trifle low. We are shamefully neglecting Roger and Henry, not to mention the ladies. My apologies."

"The man's a Dominican in modern academic robes," said the outgoing Head Scholar to Secretary Hank Howard, not bothering to keep his voice down.

Academic robes were also absorbing Solidad Vasquez, Annabelle Daiman and Desdemona. The two first-timers were overawed at the fantastic array.

"Is there anyone not in academic robes?" Solidad asked.

"By tradition, the only ladies have Chubb posts, like Dr. Millie

Hunter. The Town men wear theirs not to be entirely outclassed," said Desdemona, looking at her generous plate of smoked salmon with brown bread-and-butter enthusiastically. "Carmine has a Master's from Chubb, and I see Fernando is in Master's robes from— where?"

"University of Florida." Solidad giggled. "It isn't fair, but I notice that it's a Holloman joke that any Florida school is a place that awards degrees in ballroom dancing and underwater basket weaving. Well, Fernando's degree is in sociology, and it's a respected one."

Annabelle looked insufferably smug. "Derek's doctorate is from Chubb," she said.

"The hall does look as if it's populated by peacocks," said Desdemona. "The gold detail on some of the robes is truly astonishing. And ermine! Head Scholar Tinkerman's purple-and-gold is the Chubb School of Divinity."

"So that's what's wrong with him!" Nessie O'Donnell called.

"It's so pretty," said Annabelle, gazing around. "What's the scarlet and ermine?"

But that, no one knew, though all agreed that its wearer stood out brilliantly.

Fernando was quizzing Carmine. "Is that really black guy on the high table Dr. Jim Hunter?"

"Yes. His wife's the only woman wearing academic robes."

"I noticed them coming in, each wearing the same gown. A handsome couple. Man, he's *huge!*"

"Champion boxer and wrestler ten years ago. Came in handy."

"I bet."

Fernando's remark about the Hunters as a handsome couple had intrigued Carmine; people usually didn't see them that way, and he applauded Fernando's perception.

But inevitably his attention went back to Dr. Thomas Tarleton Tinkerman, looking magnificent in his doctor of Divinity robes. Well, Carmine amended, he was the kind of man who would manage to make sackcloth and ashes look great. Tall and ramrod straight, he gave an impression of considerable physical strength—no nerdy weakling, he. More like a West Point graduate full bird colonel who divided his mental energies between stretching for the next promotion and coping with a new attack of hemorrhoids. Tonight was definitely a hemorrhoid night: maybe not Martin Luther, but Napoleon Bonaparte?

Handsome in a Mel Ferrer way, chiseled features that said he had the asceticism of a monk. Grey hair went well with light eyes. The corners of his mouth turned down as if he despaired of human frailty in the full knowledge that he himself had none. *Conceited!* That was the word for Tinkerman.

The whole of C.U.P. knew that he didn't want to publish *A Helical God*. It was written for ignoramuses by an ape, not a scholar, and it cast doubt not so much on the Christian God as it did on His ministers, their reluctance to accept science as a part of God's grand design. How Tinkerman must be writhing at the thought that he dared not use his most powerful tool—racial prejudice. No, he wouldn't run the risk of being accused of that. His tactics would be oblique and subtle.

How expressive was a feminine back? Surprisingly so, Carmine concluded, going down the row of the high table's ladies' backs, all he could see. Angela M.M. bobbed up and down like a sleek yet busy bird, the two Parson wives sat haughtily straight thanks to old-fashioned corsets, and poor little Mrs. Thomas Tarleton Tinkerman looked like a plucked fowl, her shoulder blades vestigial wings, her backbone knobby beads. It was more difficult to catalogue Millie, in a University of Chicago Ph.D. gown, but certainly she wasn't hunched over in defeat; just, it was plain, ignored by all the other women save wafty Angela. How she must be missing Dr. Jim, almost the distance of the table away from her—and who had placed her between the Parson wives?

Neither Millie nor Jim had gone to the expense of buying doctoral robes; theirs were hired, which meant a generic robe mixed-and-matched. It showed as what it was—shabby, much used by many, and not the right size.

Heart feeling twinges for the Hunters, Carmine's attention returned to his own table to join in a merry discussion with Derek Daimon and Manny Mayhew about the merits of teaching Shakespeare to hoods.

Once Mrs. Maude Parson ascertained that the rather common girl next to her had a doctorate in biochemistry, she dried up defensively, while Mrs. Eunice Parson on Millie's other side didn't seem to speak to anybody. Only Angela M.M. knew that the billionaire ladies were abysmally educated, and utterly intimidated at being in this kind of company. Had Millie only known, she would have made an effort to talk to them, but what happened in reality was a Mexican stand-off: one potential conversationalist was terrified by so much money, the other two by so many brains. Poor M.M. was carrying the major burden of conversation, Angela helping valiantly, but it was not, the President of Chubb said to himself, one of the better banquets. That was what happened when you let someone like Hester Grey of C.U.P. do the seating arrangements. And Nate Winthrop instead of Doug Thwaites—was the woman mad, to demote Doug to the floor? If anyone he hated wound up in his court within the next six months, he'd throw the book at them—and his chief target would be M.M., innocent.

Millie did have a memorable exchange of words with the new Head Scholar, seated almost opposite her. It commenced when he looked her up and down as if he felt she would be more appropriately situated peddling ass on a street corner.

"I believe your father is the Holloman County Medical Examiner, Dr. Hunter?" Tinkerman asked, inspecting his chicken breast to see what the filling was—ugh!—garlic, apricot chunks, *nuts* for pity's sake! Whatever happened to good old sage and onion stuffing and giblet gravy?

"Yes," said Millie, demolishing her broiled scrod with unfeigned relish; expensive foods were rare on the Hunter table. "Dad has turned an old-fashioned coroner's morgue into a forensics department without parallel in the state. It can perform the most difficult assays and analyses, and the autopsy techniques have changed almost out of recognition."

"Oh, science!" said Tinkerman, screwing up his mouth. "It is the cause of all our human woes."

Millie couldn't help herself. "What an asinine thing to say!" she snapped, having no idea she was thrilling the Parson wives, who would have given their billions to say that to a man in doctor's robes. "I would have said God was the cause of human woes—look at the wars fought in God's name," she said.

If she had thrown him into a vat of cement, he could not have grown any stiffer. "You blaspheme!" he accused.

She lifted her lip. "That answer is like trotting out a block of wood as a remedy for plague! This is 1969, not 1328. It's permissible to question defects in the nature of God."

"Nothing permits anyone to question anything about God!"

"That's like saying our Constitution would be improved if it forbade freedom of speech. Science too comes from God! What we discover are more revelations about the complexity of God's design. You should come down out of your heavenly clouds and stare through a microscope occasionally, Doctor. You might be amazed, even awestruck," said Millie, very angry.

"I am amazed at your blindness," he said, floundering.

"Not I, Doctor, not I! Look in a mirror."

"Speaking of which, Tom," said M.M. affably, "are you all set for your speech? The main course is here."

In answer Tinkerman got to his feet and rushed off on a bathroom run; when he finally came back he seemed to have gotten over his flash of frustrated temper, for he sat down, smiling. Millie too had had time to let her anger cool; feeling someone edge behind her, she looked beyond Mrs. Eunice Parson to see Mrs. Tinkerman settling. Their eyes met—was that sympathy?

"Do you have a degree, Mrs. Tinkerman?" she asked, sure of affirmation; Doctors of Divinity must have highly educated wives!

"Dear me, no," said Mrs. Tinkerman. Her brown eyes blazed a moment, then went out. "I was a secretary."

"Do you have children?"

"Yes, two girls. They went to the Kirk Secretarial College and have very good jobs. I believe that there are so many Ph.D.s in sociology that they have to work as cashiers in supermarkets, whereas good secretaries are as scarce as hen's teeth."

"They are indeed," said Millie warmly. "Lucky for your husband too—no university fees to pay."

"Yes, that was a consideration," Mrs. Tinkerman said, her voice devoid of expression.

The peach pie arrived—yum! Poor woman, Millie thought as she smoothed her melting ice cream all over the still hot pie. She doesn't even hate her husband, she just dislikes him. It must be hell to have to lie in the same bed. Or perhaps she doesn't. If I were her, I would have taught myself to snore very, very loudly.

Time for the speeches, thought Carmine, shifting restlessly.

"M.M. ought to dispense with that fool high table," said Fire Chief Bede Murphy.

"I agree," Carmine said, "but why, Bede?"

"Fire hazard, for starters. Too narrow for a table seating people down both sides. I've been noticing it all evening. On a bathroom run they have to squeeze past, and some of the guys put their palms on the shoulders of those sitting down. Must be annoying. I mean, would you want to palm M.M.'s acres of gold detail? Or that snooty bastard who's the incoming Head Scholar? And tell me why Chubb thinks the Town would be offended if it weren't invited to these bean feasts? The whole Town and Gown rigmarole gives Ginny and me the shits. Our Saturday nights are *ours!* We went to a lot of trouble to make sure no babysitting the grandkids on a Saturday, and then what? We're here! The food's good, but Ginny can broil scrod too."

"A brilliant summation," said Fernando, grinning.

"I mean, the bathroom run palming is unnecessary," Bede went on. "There's plenty of room down here on the floor to put a fourth and even a fifth table. Then they could put marble busts of Tom Paine and Elmer Fudd up on the dais, surrounded by orchids and lilies."

"The one who really dislikes being palmed on a bathroom run is our new Head Scholar," said Carmine, winking at Desdemona, whose eyelids were beginning to droop. Come on, M.M., turn down the thermostats!

"According to Jim and Millie, Tinkerman despises the whole world," said Patrick. He sipped, grimaced. "Oh, why do they always fall down on the coffee?"

"C.U.P. doesn't like its new Head Scholar," said Manfred Mayhew, contributing his mite. "It's all over County Services that he's a Joe McCarthy kind of fella— witch hunts, though not for commies. Non-believers."

"I fail to see how the head of an academic publishing house can conduct witch hunts," said Commissioner Silvestri.

"That's as may be, John, but they're still saying it."

"Then why haven't I heard the slightest whisper?" the Commissioner demanded.

"Because, John," said Manfred, taking the plunge, "you are an eagle in an eyrie right up in a literal tower, and if it's built of brick instead of ivory, that's only an architectural reality. To those of us who live below you, John, it is a genuine ivory tower. If Carmine and Fernando don't tell you, you don't know—and don't say Jean Tasco! She's got a titanium zipper on her mouth."

Gloria Silvestri's coffee had gone down the wrong way: Carmine and Fernando were too busy fussing around her to make any comments—or let their eyes meet. Masterly, Manfred!

Mawson MacIntosh had slipped the cord holding his reading half glasses around his neck and had gathered his notes together; he was a wonderful speaker and as extemporaneous as he wished to be— tonight, judging from his notes, only partially. Not before time, thought Carmine, feeling the cool air on the back of his neck. M.M.

had turned the thermostats down, which meant no naps in a warm hall. Desdemona would wake up in a hurry, as would all the women, more scantily clad than the enrobed men.

"Ladies and gentlemen," M.M. said, on his feet and using the most democratic form of address, "we meet tonight to celebrate in honor of two men and one institution . . ."

What else M.M. said Carmine never remembered afterward; his attention was riveted on Dr. Thomas Tarleton Tinkerman, still seated, and looking very distressed. His crisp white handkerchief was out, fluttering at his face, beaded in sweat, and he was gasping a little. The cloth billowed down to the table as he put his hands up to his neck, wrenching at his tie, more constricting than usual because it held his hood on and kept his gown in perfect position.

"Patsy!" Carmine rapped. "Up there, up there!" Over his shoulder he said to Desdemona as he followed his cousin, "Call an ambulance, stat! Resuscitation gear on board. Do it, *do it!*"

Desdemona was up and running toward the banquet supervisor as Carmine and Patrick mounted the dais, scattering its occupants before them. M.M. had had the good sense to be gone already, his chair thrust at a startled waiter.

"Down, everybody, off the dais!" M.M. was shouting, "and get your chairs out of the way! Women too, please. Now!"

"Nessie will have sent someone young and fast for my bag, but we're parked over on North Green," said Patrick, kneeling. The new Head Scholar's gown, hood and coat were removed and the coat rolled into a pillow; Patrick ripped open Tinkerman's dress shirt to reveal a well muscled, laboring chest; he was fighting desperately to breathe. Came a very few weak retches, some generalized small jerks and tremors, then Tinkerman lay staring up at Patrick and Carmine wide-eyed, in complete knowledge that he was dying. Unable to speak, unable to summon up any kind of muscular responses. Eyes horrified.

Millie hovered in the background: Patrick turned his head. "Is there any antidote? Anything we can at least try?"

"No. Absolutely nothing." She sounded desolate.

The ambulance arrived three minutes from Desdemona's call, bearing resuscitation equipment and a physician's associate.

"His airway's still patent," Patrick said, slipping a bent, hard plastic tube into Tinkerman's mouth. "Everything's paralyzed, but I was lucky. I'm in the trachea. I can bag breathe him and keep oxygen flowing into his lungs, but he can't expand them himself, not one millimetre. The chest wall and the diaphragm are totally nerveless." Again Patrick turned to Millie. "Is he conscious? He seems to be."

"Higher cerebral fuction isn't affected, so—yes, he's conscious. He'll remain conscious. Watch what you say." She pushed in beside him and took one hand. "Dr. Tinkerman, don't be afraid. We're getting lots of air to your lungs, and we're taking you to the hospital by ambulance right now. You just hang on and pray—we'll get you through." She got up. "Like that, Dad. He's terrified."

By the time the ambulance screamed into the Holloman Hospital E.R., Head Scholar Thomas Tarleton Tinkerman was dead. The tiny muscles that fed vital substances to his internal organs and pumped the waste products out had succumbed to the poison. Fully conscious and in complete awareness of his imminent death, not able to speak or even move his eyelids, Tinkerman was pronounced dead when awareness left his gaze: to Carmine, who had seen many men die, it always looked like literal lights out. One moment something was there in the eyes; the next moment, it was gone.

The body was expedited to the morgue at the express command of the Medical Examiner, but the syringe containing a blood sample beat the corpse by an hour and a half. Paul Bachman had sent a technician on a motor cycle to Ivy Hall to collect it. On analysis it revealed the dwindling metabolites of tetrodotoxin. No one knew its half life, so the dosage was at best a guess.

"It would seem to me," said Patrick, "that Dr. Tinkerman received more of the toxin than John Hall. There's a fresh puncture wound on the back of his neck to the left side of the spinal column, so I'm assuming it was injected. Not enough gastric symptoms for inges-tion, and death was too swift. About ten minutes from the onset of noticeable symptoms. Had the blood been examined for toxins at the usual pace, it would have metabolized to nothing before any screen for neurotoxins was suggested. The cause of death, while highly sus-pect, would have been a mystery. The same can be said for John Hall, though we were slower, the traces fewer."

Carmine sighed. "So Abe gets John Hall and I get Dr. Tinker-man. Thomas Tarleton Tinkerman—a poseur, hence the fancy mid-dle name, Tarleton. Tinkerman wouldn't have suited the ideas our Head Scholar had about himself. He was a conceited man." He had removed his bow tie and opened the collar of his shirt, and looked more comfortable.

They were sitting in Patrick's office with a pot of his excellent cof-fee; Delia, Nick, Buzz, Donny and four uniforms were at Ivy Hall taking down names, addresses, phone numbers and brief statements, and Delia had already confiscated the table plans. There was no point in asking Judge Thwaites for a warrant to search any persons pres-ent; he was as cross as only he could be when things did not go to plan—and especially when he'd been kicked off the head table to make room for that kiss-ass mediocrity, Mayor Nathan Winthrop. It would be many weeks before the Judge forgave anyone present at the banquet, even if for no greater crime than witnessing his humili-ation. If John Silvestri refused to beard him, no one could.

"So someone is going to waltz out of Ivy Hall with a home-made injection apparatus in his pocket," mourned Patrick.

"Not necessarily," Carmine said. "How many people know Doug Thwaites as well as we do, huh? Depending who the guilty party is, the gear might be in a trash can. Delia's got it under full control, the trash cans are sequestered under guard along with the rest of Ivy Hall. For this kind of case, we're limited in manpower, so the foren-sic search of Ivy Hall may be postponed a little."

"Delia is going to wind up Commissioner," Patrick said.

Carmine flashed him a grin, but refrained from taking the bait.

"I'm hoping the injection apparatus has been abandoned," he said. "There won't be any more injection murders, I'd be willing to bet on that. Or any more murders at all. So why keep the device? It's not a hypodermic and syringe in the formal sense, is it? Couldn't have been done in either case—too public, and you can't make giving an injection look like anything else. I see something no bigger than one of Desdemona's thimbles, though what can replace a piston-plunger is beyond me. A very short, fine gauge hypodermic he had to have, but attached to something other than a syringe. A man would hardly feel the prick, especially if it were accompanied by a comradely slap. Look at snakes and spiders. They have a reservoir for the venom and a channel down the back of a tooth or a tube through the middle of a fang."

"You really do believe he expected to get away with it!" Patrick said, astonished.

"What poisoner doesn't? This is one cocksure bastard, Patsy. I had a funny feeling tonight, so I watched Tinkerman closely, but I can't remember anyone's acting suspiciously. Bede and his bathroom runs! He had the right of it."

Suddenly Patrick looked his full fifty-eight years. "Oh, cuz, I give up!" he cried. "I'm going home to Nessie and a sleeping pill. Otherwise I won't be worth a hill of beans in the morning. I am to recuse myself completely?"

"Yes, Patsy," Carmine said gently.

"Keep me in the loop?"

"I can't. Think what ammunition we'd be handing to a defense attorney. You have to stay right out and right away."

Desdemona had despaired of a back massage and gone to bed, from which Carmine hauled her out and subjected her to fifteen minutes of pain from sheer guilt.

"Feel any better?" he asked at the end of it.

"Not at the moment, you sadist," she said grumpily, then relented. "But I will tomorrow, dear love, and that's the most important thing.

If caterers have extra cushions for the shorties, why don't they have a couple of chairs with the legs sawn off for the giants like me and Manny Mayhew?"

"Because people are allowed to be five-foot-nothing, but not way over six feet," said Carmine, smiling. He pushed a stray wisp of hair behind her ear, then leaned forward and kissed her. "Come on, my divine giantess, I'll get you into bed with the pillows packed how you like them."

"Is it Millie's poison?" she asked, settling with a sigh of bliss; only Carmine knew how to get the pillows right.

"I'm afraid so."

"It isn't fair, Carmine. After all the years of struggle, she and Jim have to go through this?"

"Looks that way, but it's early days. Close your eyes."

He wasn't long out of bed himself, thankful that Patrick had folded and his sergeants had gone home at Delia's command—how exactly had she assumed command?

SUNDAY, JANUARY 5, 1969

T hey met in Carmine's office at ten in the morning; no need yet to annoy wives with early Sunday starts, and the singles liked a sleep-in quite as much as the marrieds.

Abe, Carmine reflected as he gazed at his oldest and loyalest colleague, was settling into his lieutenant's authority as quietly as he did everything, but there was a new smoothness and placidity in his face, caused by an extraordinary piece of good fortune. The German chemicals giant Fahlendorf Farben had awarded his two sons full scholarships to the colleges of their choice when they reached college age, to be ongoing as far as doctoral programs. For the father of two very bright boys, a huge relief; saving college fees kept parents poor. The grant had arisen out of Abe's own police work; forbidden to accept a posted reward, Abe had declined it. So Fahlendorf Farben had given scholarships to his boys, signed, sealed, the money already invested.

Abe always worked with Liam Connor and Tony Cerutti, his personal team.

Liam was in his middle thirties and had been Larry Pisano's man, but much preferred working for Abe now Larry was gone. Married and the father of one girl, he kept his private life well apart from his police career, which indicated, Carmine thought, a proud man in a moderate domestic situation, neither heaven nor hell. He was barely regulation height but kept himself fit, and had a pleasant face: grey-blue eyes, a lot of sandy hair, good bones. His reputation in the Holloman PD was of a man who did nothing to excess—probably why he and Abe clicked. Rational men.

Tony Cerutti was of that East Holloman Italian American family that bred many cops, his degree of blood relationship sufficiently removed from the Commissioner and Carmine, both half Cerutti. Thirty years old and a bachelor, he was dark, handsome and charming in a slightly street-rat way; Abe always sent him after women suspects of a certain class. He was still learning to damp down the wilder side of his enthusiasm, but he was a good man, and absolutely attached to Abe, who awed him.

Carmine spoke first, outlining the disappearance of Dr. Millie Hunter's tetrodotoxin.

"Because Paul acted so fast, both victims still had traces in their systems," he said. "Each had a puncture wound in the left side of the back of the neck, into muscle and fat, not near bone. The injection would have been absorbed at an intramuscular rate. The dose was almost microscopic—about one half of one milligram. That makes it a hundred times more potent than cyanide. There's no antidote and no treatment. Worst is that the victim is fully conscious until death."

"Holy shit!" Donny exclaimed, face white. "That's awful!"

"Very cold-blooded," Carmine said. "Though it's out of sequence, I'd like to continue for a moment about the poison. There must be at least five hundred milligrams left—a lot of death, though this doesn't feel like a killer at the start of a spree, so the leftovers are more likely to go into storage. It seems that neither victim felt any pain on injection, yet we also know the killer didn't use an ordinary hypodermic and syringe. So what's the method of delivery, and how long before the first symptoms appeared?"

"I've seen Gus Fennell and Paul Bachman again this morning," Abe said, "and they've been doing a lot of reading as well as done a better time line of the physical course of John Hall's symptoms. An intramuscular injection had to have been administered inside Max Tunbull's den, it couldn't have been given before they went in. No one left the room, even on a bathroom call. Gus and Paul both insist no more than twenty minutes passed between the injection and death, and all six men were in Max's den for *thirty* minutes. That means you're right about the method of delivery, Carmine. No hypodermic and syringe."

"The real stumbling block in our murderer's plans was Millie Hunter," said the pear-shaped voice of Delia Carstairs. "If she hadn't reported the theft of her tetrodotoxin to her father, both these deaths would have been impossible to prove as murder."

Carmine's eyes rested on Delia with a smile in them. It was way below freezing outside and the wind was up, contributing a chill factor; Delia had dressed for it in outer wear of fake fur striped like a red-and-black tiger. The outfit underneath was also striped tiger fashion, but in pink-and-black, and it bore touches of bright blue because her heart craved color, color, and more color. She was way below regulation height and built like a barrel on grand piano legs, had no neck, and a huge head adorned with frizzy, brassy hair; there was so much mascara around her twinkling brown eyes that they always looked marooned in tar. Her bright red lipstick had a tendency to daub her slightly buck teeth as well as sneak into the pucker-wrinkles around her mouth, but no one's smile was more genuine than Delia's. Her nature was perfect for police work, since she was meticulous to the point of obsessiveness and she never gave up; no one could see more in a sheet of numbers or a floor plan, which made white-collar crime her most relished pleasure.

The blood niece of Commissioner John Silvestri on the Silvestri side, she was English, the child of a prestigious Oxford don, and despite her sartorial eccentricities she enjoyed a relatively high social position within the city of Holloman's hierarchy (her posh accent assured it). Those who didn't know her well tended to dismiss her as something of a fool. Wrong! thought Carmine. Having Sergeant Delia Carstairs was like being a closet dictator owning a secret ICBM.

"Expound," said Carmine.

"I think I've already hit the nail on the head, chief. Our awareness of his murder method has ruined everything for him," Delia said.

"Not one, but *two* murders, both at banquets, yet of utterly opposite kinds. Nine suspects for the death of John Hall, seventy-two for Dr. Tinkerman. If one presumes that the only viable suspects attended both banquets, we have Max and Davina Tunbull, Val Tunbull, Ivan Tunbull, and Jim and Millie Hunter."

"Not Millie!" said Tony Cerutti instantly.

"Why not?"

Carmine stepped into the breach with a glance at Tony. "I guess Millie's a part of the clan," he said calmly, "and I for one would be confounded were she to turn out the guilty one. We—we *know* her. But you're right of course, Deels. She has to go on the list of suspects."

"As far as I'm concerned, she and Jim head the list of suspects," said Abe. "Who else could have brought that particular poison to the Tunbull dinner? The thief? How would any Tunbull have known about tetrodotoxin?" Abe looked grim. "My instincts say it isn't Millie. That leaves Jim."

"Who has good reason to want to kill Tinkerman, but why John Hall?" Liam asked.

"How do you know that?" Carmine asked.

"Easy. Everyone does. Dr. O'Donnell hasn't been silent about Tinkerman's attitude to Jim Hunter's book," said Nick Jefferson. "Gossip around County Services says Tinkerman hates Jim Hunter." His handsome black face grew stern. "I believe someone stole the poison—*and* used it!—to implicate Dr. Jim."

"Too many speculations on too little evidence," said Carmine with a sigh. "We know murder was done on two different occasions using an instrument the killer thought undetectable. It's surely logical to assume that the same hand is responsible for both the deaths. But motive? We have no idea. Is the thief of the toxin also the killer? We have no idea."

"It's dig time," said Donny Costello.

He was the last of the sergeants, moved up from the pool a few months earlier, and he was eager, thorough, a trifle sideways in his thinking. A husky, chunky man just turned thirty-one, he had recently married, and existed in that happy haze of the newly wed husband: home cooked breakfasts, plenty of sex, a wife who never let him see her hair in curlers or her temper in tatters.

"Right on, Donny!" Abe cried. "Dig, dig, and dig again."

"Who stands to benefit or profit?" Carmine asked. "What kind of link can there possibly be between a West Coast timber tycoon and an East Coast divinity scholar? Did they die because they knew each other, or because they couldn't be let to know each other?" He frowned. "Candidly, Jim and Millie Hunter look suspicious in more ways than the rest put together."

"It's *not* Millie!" said Tony pugnaciously.

"Jim Hunter's book is involved," Carmine went on as if no one had interrupted.

Abe interrupted. "Max Tunbull told me that he and Val, his brother, made an executive decision just before Christmas and ran a twenty thousand first printing, though C.U.P. hadn't authorized it. And Davina Tunbull printed twenty thousand dust jackets."

"Delia, you interview Davina," Carmine said.

"And what are you going to do, chief?" Delia asked.

Alone among them she called him "chief" or "boss"; recently Carmine had come to think this was part of her assumption of extra, entirely unofficial, power. If he didn't adore her—but he did, with all his heart. His ICBM.

"I'm seeing M.M.," he said. "Abe will decide who interviews whom apart from Davina. And don't forget for one moment that Donny's the new broom—you'll have to dig hard to go deeper."

M.M. was impenitent about one aspect of the Tinkerman murder. "It got the Parsons off my back," he said, pushing the plate of fresh apple Danish at Carmine.

"Did they really blackmail you into Tinkerman, sir?"

"My fault. I should have kept the iron fist sheathed in velvet a little longer. But oh, Carmine," said the President of Chubb, blue eyes fiery, "I was fed up with waiting for those holier-than-thou bastards to hand over Chubb's collection of paintings! I don't care about the Rembrandt or the Leonardo—well, I do, but you know what I mean—I wanted the Velasquez, the wartime Goyas, the Vermeer, the Giotto and the el Grecos! Who ever sees them? The Parsons! I want them hung where all of Chubb and however many visitors can see them!"

"I understand," said Carmine, biting into a pastry.

"When that idiot Richard Spaight said they were going to hang on to Chubb's paintings for another fifty years at least, I—I *snapped!* Hand 'em over within a month, or I sue! And I meant it," said M.M.

"And they knew they couldn't buy the court," Carmine said.

"I am not without influence," M.M. said smugly. "That's their trouble, of course. They have billions, but they don't cultivate the right people, whereas we MacIntoshes do—and we're not short of a dollar either."

"A pity the Hug folded. The Parsons were happy funding such important research, but it was fatal to hand administration over to a psychiatrist."

"Why is that, Carmine?" M.M. asked, his famous apricot hair now faded to a pallid peach.

"Desdemona says psychiatrists with business heads are in private practice. The ones in research tend to be enthusiastic about loony projects or stuff so far out in left field you can't see it. So the Hug folded. It's better as it is, a simple part of the medical school rather than full of weirdos."

"The Parsons hold me responsible, as far as I can gather just because I'm President of Chubb. The paintings? Sheer spite."

"No, I disagree," said Carmine, remembering a lunch with the Parsons in a blizzard-bound New York City. "They really do enjoy looking at the paintings, Mr. President. Especially the el Greco at the end of the hall. Greed tempted them to keep the lot—greed of the eyes. As for spite—it's a part of the Parson persona."

"Hence Tom Tinkerman. Nothing of interest would have been published during his tenure at C.U.P.," said M.M. flatly. "I am really, really glad that he's dead."

Carmine grinned. "Did you kill him, M.M.?"

The determined mouth opened, shut with a snap. "I refuse to rise to that bait, Captain. You know I didn't kill him, but—" A beautiful smile lit up M.M.'s face. "What a relief! The Board of Governors can't be blackmailed a second time because there's no Tinkerman left among the candidates. So soon after Tinkerman's appointment, we'll just slip in the one we wanted all along. I don't think you know him—Geoffrey Chaucer Millstone."

"Auspicious name," said Carmine gravely. "Who is he?"

"An associate professor in the Department of English—a dead end academically, but he's not professorial material. Too brisk and pragmatic. Hard on the undergrads and harder still on fellows of all kinds. Ideal for C.U.P.—no leisurely publication of abstruse treatises on the gerundive in modern English usage."

"Darn! I've been hanging out for that. Is he good for things like science and Dr. Jim's book?"

"Perfect," said M.M. with satisfaction. "There's no denying either that C.U.P. can do with the funds a huge best seller would bring in. The Head Scholar will have money to publish books he couldn't have otherwise. C.U.P. is well endowed, but the dollar is not what it used to be, and these days alumni with millions to give think of medicine or science. The days when the liberal arts received mega-buck endowments are over."

"Yes, that's inevitable. A pity too," said Carmine; he was a liberal arts man. "Last name Millstone? As in the Yankee Millstones, or the ordinary old Jewish immigrant Millstones?"

"The ordinary old Jewish immigrants, thank God. Chauce, as he's known, is worth a whole clan of Parsons."

Carmine rose. "I'll have to see people I'm bound to offend, sir. Be prepared."

"Do what has to be done." The good-looking face was at its blandest. "Just get Dr. Jim out from under, please. It has not escaped me that he's bound to be the main suspect."

Her tiger bonnet on her head to keep her ears warm, her short arms encumbered by folds of fake fur, Delia drove her cop unmarked out to Route 133 and found Hampton Street. An odd neighborhood for relatively affluent people, but her preliminary research had revealed that Max and Val Tunbull had each built on Hampton Street in 1934, just as America was recovering from the Great Depression, on land that had cost them virtually nothing, and using building contractors grateful for the work. Probably they had believed that Hampton Street would become fairly ritzy, but it had not. People wishing to be ritzy had preferred the coast or the five-acre zone, farther out.

Max Tunbull's house was imposing. Delia parked her Ford in the driveway so that other cars could get around it, and rang the doorbell: it chimed the first notes of Beethoven's fifth symphony, a choice she abominated.

In spring, summer and autumn there would be a pleasant garden around the knoll upon which the house stood, though whoever selected the plants seemed indifferent to what ice did to Mediterranean things. Someone homesick for the Dalmatian coast, perhaps? wondered Delia as she waited.

One of the tiniest women she had ever seen opened the door. Four feet six, no more, and shapeless, clad in a shapeless grey uniform dress. She looked what Delia's father would have called "wrong"— the skull structure of a cretin, yellow, speckled skin too. But the very dark little eyes were full of intelligence as they surveyed Delia, no giant herself.

"What you want?" she demanded, her accent thick and Balkan.

Delia flashed her gold detective's badge. "I am Delia Carstairs, a sergeant in the Holloman police, and I have an appointment to see Mrs. Davina Tunbull."

"She sick, no see."

"Then she has ten minutes in which to get well, and she *will* see me," said Delia, stepping adroitly around the gnome. "I'll wait in the living room. Kindly show me the way."

Rage and fear fought for domination; the fear won, so the gnome conducted Delia to a large room furnished in an unconventional way: mismatched chairs and coffee tables, shelves of mementos and art pieces, a wall of leather-bound, gilded books, a large thick rug that bore a pattern reminiscent of a Paul Klee painting. The colors went together well, the chairs were comfortable but the fabric very modern—the decorator loved Paul Klee. There were several paintings on the walls that Delia fancied were genuine Klees. An interesting choice, to feature a post-impressionist master not well known outside art circles. This Davina Tunbull might have as many layers as flaky pastry.

"What is your name?" she asked the gnome.

"Uda."

"You're the housekeeper?"

"No. I belong Miss Vina."

"Belong?"

"Yes."

"Then please go and inform your mistress, Uda, that she cannot avoid this interview. If she is ill, I will accompany her to the Holloman Hospital and question her there. Or, if she thinks not to grant me an interview at all, I will arrest her for obstruction of justice and see her at the Holloman Police Department in a proper interrogation cell."

Extraordinary, the effect the word "interrogation" had on eastern Europeans! Uda vanished as if conjured out of existence while Delia divested herself of her outer garb; the room was well heated. Someone was a smoker, but no odor of cigarettes lingered in the air, so the ventilation must be excellent. Odd cigarettes that Delia knew well, having smoked them herself in days gone by. Sobranie Cocktails, made of Virginia tobacco with gold paper tips and several pastel colors of paper—pink, blue, green, yellow and lilac. At night the Cocktails smoker apparently switched to black Sobranies—gold paper tips, black paper encapsulating pure Turkish tobacco. There were no butts in any of the immaculate modern glass ashtrays, but there were six boxes of Sobranie Cocktails and three boxes of black Sobranies scattered around the coffee tables.

Davina Tunbull tottered in, supported by her servant. She was wearing a purple satin nightgown and had a billowing lilac chiffon negligé over it. Long black hair, white skin, blue eyes, a bonily beautiful face of the kind Delia fancied Mata Hari might have owned. She looked like a mistress, not a wife. One long, graceful hand was pressing red fingertips to her brow, the other clutched at Uda, who must be remarkably strong. Mrs. Vina Tunbull wasn't feigning giving her a lot of weight to support.

"Sit down, Mrs. Tunbull, and cut out this utterly ridiculous nonsense," Delia said crisply. "Hysterics are wasted on me, and histrionics make me want to laugh. So none of either, please. Sit up straight and behave like a very intelligent woman who owns and runs a highly successful business."

The lush mouth had fallen open; evidently Mrs. Tunbull wasn't used to such plain speaking. "Pink!" she rapped at Uda, who opened a Sobranie Cocktails box, removed a pink cigarette, lit it, and handed it to her mistress. "What do you want?" she asked Delia rudely, the smoke trickling from her nostrils like a lazy dragon not prepared to stoke its furnace.

"First of all, what prompted you to have a formal dinner party in your home last Friday?" Delia asked.

The pink cigarette waved around as Davina shrugged. "It was overdue," she said, her accent more an asset than a liability; without it, her voice wasn't attractive. "My husband, Max, had his sixtieth birthday at New Year, that was one reason. For another, I wished to celebrate the birth of our son, Alexis—I have been very slow recovering. Finally, John had come back from the dead." Her lids went down to veil her eyes; she handed the partially smoked cigarette to Uda, who stubbed it out. "It really was the prodigal son returned, my dear Sergeant Delia Carstairs."

Well, well, so Uda told her my name and rank and everything, thought Sergeant Delia Carstairs.

"Max and his brother, Val, certainly regarded John as long dead," Vina went on. "There had been a huge police search for John and his mother in 1937, and it was not abandoned for some years. It is traditional to kill the fatted calf when the long lost prodigal son returns, and I did—I had roast veal for the main course—wasn't that clever of me?"

"Very clever," said Delia dryly. "Was Mr. Tunbull sure that John was his son?"

"In the end he was quite convinced," Vina said. "John had his mother's engagement ring. Oh, there were many documents and papers, but it was the ring slew Max, who believed his eyes. Martita—John's mother—had admired the stone in a geology shop, and Max had it made into an expensive ring for her. It is an opal, but the opal is in bands striped through a solid black stone, like a zebra. I will show you," she said, literally snapping her fingers at Uda, who went to a box on a shelf, opened it, and brought a huge ring to Delia.

Amazing indeed! Delia had never seen anything like it, even when thumbing through the books of gemstones police sometimes had to consult. The stripes, black as well as white, were about two millimetres thick, the black dull and opaque, the opal white flashing from red to green fire as the stone was moved. The stone—about twenty carats—was mounted in yellow gold.

"As a gem it's probably not all that valuable," said Delia, handing it back to Uda, "except for its rarity, which would raise its worth considerably."

Uda had put the ring away and returned to stand by Davina; waiting for the next snap of the fingers?

"There were physical similarities too," Vina said. "John was different in coloring and features, but his facial expressions were pure Max. Ivan saw it immediately. Ivan is the nephew."

"Why did you invite the Doctors Hunter to your dinner?"

"To please John. He knew them in California, and I thought it would be nice for him to have some friends of his own there." Another shrug; she used them for all sorts of reasons. "After all, Sergeant Carstairs, Max, Val, Ivan and I all know Dr. Jim very well through C.U.P. It was his wife we didn't know."

"I understand you have high hopes for his book?"

"Naturally!" Davina said impatiently. "If *A Helical God* is a big best seller, then Tunbull Printing and my own Imaginexa stand to make a lot of money. We do well out of printing any C.U.P. book, but Dr. Jim's is unique. Max has already printed twenty thousand copies."

"But isn't the title still a matter of debate?" Delia asked blankly. "Wasn't it rash to go to press?"

"It was my idea," Davina said triumphantly. "Dr. Jim is in love with his title. So if the book and its cover are already in print bearing his title, we win!"

"You could as easily wind up in a court battle with C.U.P. that could go on for years," said Delia, hardly able to credit her ears. She reasoned like a small child! And Max and Val and Ivan had actually risked their business on her instincts? When in the right environment, Davina Tunbull must be able to sell the Brooklyn Bridge ten times a day!

"You have the cow by the feet instead of the ears," Vina said, sounding blithe. "We only stood in danger if Tinkerman was the Head Scholar, and I knew he would not be. I asked Uda to look in the bowl of water at the future—she is never wrong! She said Tinkerman was going to choke to death at the banquet, and that is exactly what happened. Dr. Jim will keep his title. We stand in no danger now that Tinkerman is dead."

Yes gods, the woman *is* a child! thought Delia, alarmed. "Mrs. Tunbull, I think it's time I reminded you that you are entitled to have a lawyer present while you're being questioned," she said urgently. "I've endeavored to keep our conversation neutral, but you are incriminating yourself out of your own mouth. Juries are not impressed by soothsayers. Do you wish to continue to speak to me, or would you rather have a lawyer present?"

"I need no lawyers," said the lady loftily. "I did not kill the man. I went nowhere near him. As for my dinner—why should I kill poor John? He told Max and me that he didn't want Alexis's inheritance. His adopted father is very rich and has already settled millions on John. If I were you, I would look at Ivan. He thought he would be the big loser."

"Thank you for this most illuminating interview," Delia said hollowly. "Is there anything else I ought to know?"

"Only that John—" Vina's voice dropped to a whisper "—was enamored of me. I could not tell Max, and I did not tell Max! But it was a good thing John died in that respect, Sergeant. He was so ardent that I had to fight him off with my teeth and my nails. Then Uda came in, and I was saved. Is that not so, Uda?"

"Yes."

"When did this happen, Mrs. Tunbull?"

"Last Friday. At the dinner. He got me alone."

"Bad man!" said Uda, glowering.

"At the dinner, Mrs. Tunbull, did you go into the den at any time after the men repaired there?"

"No," said Davina.

"No," said Uda.

"I do advise you to ask your husband to seek legal counsel, Mrs. Tunbull. You have a tendency to be indiscreet," said Delia, rising to depart.

"Indiscreet! What a good word! I will remember it. Now I will be indiscreet on a different subject, Sergeant. Your clothes are very bad. Very, very bad."

Her best poker face didn't betray her; Delia looked curious. "Are you qualified to judge?" she asked.

"Oh, yes. I was model in New York City. TV commercials. My face was on some billboards. My legs too. Davina Savovich, but as model I was just Davina. About you, Sergeant. You need to lose at least thirty pounds," the high, remorseless voice went on, "and seek the right exercises to get a waistline at least. Wear slacks to hide your legs, they are beyond all hope. When you lose the weight, come back to me, and I will dress you."

By this, the tiger bonnet was on and its ribbons tied beneath Delia's chin; Uda was holding the door open, her black currant eyes lit with derision. Delia stepped out onto the mat and turned with a brilliant smile.

"It is a miracle to me, Mrs. Tunbull, that nobody has ever murdered *you*," she said, and stomped off to her car.

"Impudent bitch!" she yelled to the freezing air as she wrenched open the Ford's door. In the driver's seat, she turned the rear vision mirror down to regard her face in its framing bonnet; her fury died. "What rubbish!" she said as the car moved. "My dress sense is impeccable. Aunt Gloria Silvestri says so, and look at her! The best dressed woman in Connecticut, according to the Hartford *Courant*. That skinny bitch is a fashion ignoramus."

However, she was still tending to stomp when, on the off chance, she called in to the morgue on her way to her office. Luck at last! There at a desk, carefully writing up notes, was Dr. Gustavus Fennell, Deputy Coroner. He was as anonymous as many in the business of handling the dead tended to be: neither tall nor short, fat nor thin, fair nor dark. Mr. Average and Totally Forgettable.

"Gus, did you post John Hall?" she asked.

Down went the pen; he considered the question. "Yes."

"Did the body bear any bruises, bites or scratches? The sort of marks a man might have if he tried an unsuccessful rape?"

"No, definitely not."

"Could bruises develop post mortem? Is he still here?"

"In the big room. We can look," said Dr. Fennell, getting up. "It would be unusual for post mortem bruises to develop on a clear, unblemished skin at autopsy," he said, ambling to the wall that held the cold room door.

"Business is brisk," said Delia, gazing at several occupied gurneys.

"Two additionals from unexpected murders make a difference. Were it not for Mr. Hall and Dr. Tinkerman, it would have been an average weekend intake. There was a shoot-out on Argyle Avenue, but the rest are just routine investigations requested by puzzled G.P.s." He peeled away John Hall's sheet.

Gloved, they examined the body together, front and back, from head to toes and in between.

"Not a sausage," said Delia, stripping the rubber off her hands. "I had a funny feeling that would prove to be the case. His stepmother is accusing him of trying to rape her last Friday."

"Shades of Phaedra and Hippolytus," Gus said with a chuckle.

"You know your Greek mythology, sir."

"Yes, but it's an extremely rare woman willing to back up her accusation by killing herself, which is what Phaedra did. Perhaps your Phaedra killed this Hippolytus?"

"I wouldn't put anything past her. Thank you, Gus dear."

"So," she said, reporting to Abe in his office, "I can assure you that if Mrs. Davina Tunbull tells you John Hall tried to rape her, she's lying. I've had Gus Fennell add a *post scriptum* to the autopsy report stating specifically that the body bears no marks of teeth, nails, fists or feet. What an extraordinary case this is! People lying so blatantly you wonder about their mental competence. It's been like that from the start, Abe. Were I Millie, I think I would have shrugged and not bothered to report the loss of the poison."

A frown had gathered; Abe stared at Delia oddly. "That is very perceptive, Sergeant Carstairs. If she were anyone other than our Millie, my tortuous mind might have sniffed a plot, with her husband's collusion."

"That's our downfall, Abe. Our minds are *too* tortuous. As Carmine says, the first impression is usually the most significant one. What was yours, since I wasn't at the Tunbulls?"

"That Dr. Jim did it. Gut instinct, nothing else."

"It doesn't add up, though, unless you want to make *his* mind tortuous enough to use the poison on John Hall as practice for the real event—poisoning Tinkerman."

"You can look at it that way, Deels," Abe said. "Or you can interpret the whole thing as an attempt to frame Dr. Jim."

"Oh, I loathe frame crimes!" Delia cried. "It's that extra layer of Saran Wrap makes it impossible to get the pie out unbroken."

"Good metaphor. Thanks, Delia—and for getting Gus to look at the body again too. I accept your opinion of Davina's lies as well. It takes someone super smart to act super dumb." Abe put a hand to the back of his pate, where the hair was thinning. "Anyone in the den could have administered the poison, though it would be a great help if we knew the instrument of delivery."

"Are you considering Dr. Markoff a suspect?"

"Until I prove he had no motive, yes."

"Who stands to benefit the most from John's death?"

"Ivan, Val's son. Baby Alexis cut him out, I guess, but a baby isn't the same threat as a grown man. John, they all say, kept emphasizing that he wasn't interested in Max's business or money because his adoptive father is very wealthy and had already endowed him. My research to date does indicate that this Wendover Hall owns half of Oregon."

"Dig deeper into John himself," Delia said.

"I will. I mean, our line of work teaches that people never seem to have enough money. John Hall could be heir to the Vanderbilts and still covet Max's little bit."

"Davina's the one needs research in that house, opinionated skinny bitch that she is!"

Abe didn't make the mistake of probing into Delia's sudden detestation of Davina Tunbull; if his exquisitely sensitive nose whispered that it had to do with Delia's apparel, that was even more reason to shut up. So he confined himself to generalities.

"The Yugoslav background?" he asked.

"No, the New York City modeling career. I smell a very dead rat, Abe—there was some sort of funny business involved. She's also potty," Delia said sternly. "She kept telling me things no one in their right mind would say without an attorney present, yet when I cautioned her a la Miranda, she ignored me. Whatever else you do or don't do, make sure you have two witnesses present when you question her. Otherwise she'll probably accuse you of raping her, and Uda will back her up."

"Is she genuinely dumb?"

"If she's dumb, so is Oppenheimer. That's why I prefer to call her potty. She thinks the way she thinks we think women think."

From Abe's office Delia went to her own. It had belonged to Lieutenant Corey Marshall, now Senior Lieutenant of Uniforms with Captain Fernando Vasquez, and had lain vacant for less than half a day before Delia swooped, announcing that she needed space for spreading out huge sheets of paper. Carmine had pointed out that she had masterminded his own removal to Mickey McCosker's suite of offices to have ample spreading room, but he may as well have saved his breath. Yes, but that space was actually Carmine's, she spread out her sheets on sufferance, she needed her *own* space . . .

Silvestri gave in, whereupon his niece badgered him for better furniture that, she wheedled, "betrayed the domain and the hand of a woman." In like manner she had usurped the quite unofficial position of second-in-command of Carmine's team; if Carmine were absent, Nick, Buzz and Donny all looked to her to issue the orders. How it had happened was a mystery, except that Carmine for one knew how much of the Commissioner lay in her nature. Hesitate, and Delia would take over.

This case was interesting, she thought as she hung up the tiger outerwear and went to a long, narrow table already bearing four large sheets of paper: her C.U.P. banquet seating plans.

The Chubb table, first of those down on the floor, was the most intriguing, she decided, whizzing on her wheeled chair until she hovered over it. Four Chubb Governors and their wives, three of the Parsons and their wives, His Honor Judge Douglas Wilbur Thwaites and his wife, Dotty, and Dean Robert Highman and his wife, Nancy. The four governors occupied one end of the table, the three Parsons the other, with Dean Highman next to the Parsons and Judge Thwaites next to the governors. As Bobby Highman's college, Paracelsus, was a Parson endowment, it made sense to seat him in proximity, but no wonder Doubting Doug was in such a royal snit—Governor William Holder, next to him, had once made mincemeat of D.A. Thwaites by getting a guilty-as-sin defendant acquitted. Which might have been all right, save that Holder continued to rub the defeat in every time he saw the now Judge, who rightly blamed the jury, not Holder's defense.

Two of the Gentleman Walkers of Carew were seated at the C.U.P. table, Delia noted: Dapper Dave Feinman, escorting the editor in chief, Fulvia Friedkin, and suave Gregory Pendelton, squiring the director of design, Hester Grey. Publishing, Delia reflected, attracted females, and actually offered them some top management positions—rare in business. The Doctors Hunter were at the high table, but the three Tunbulls and wives were all seated with C.U.P. That meant they must do all C.U.P.'s printing—how interesting!

Very well: coffee with Dotty Thwaites, a chat with Nancy Highman, a long and charming interview with Hester Grey, and— would Abe mind if she tackled Emily Tunbull? The two cases were so entwined, and it would take a crafty woman to prise the lid off Emily's pot of malice, sheer hearsay though it was. Then, of course, she had to see how the search through the banquet's detritus was progressing . . .

Carmine walked through the door.

"Oh, goodie!" said Delia. "Chief, may I please have the C.U.P. table? It's stuffed with women, and you have your work cut out dealing with the men."

He had lost a little weight and was looking, thought his most devoted fan, extremely well. With winter upon them, she had expected a return of last winter's rather rheumatic gait, but thus far he was moving like a supple youth. Such a very attractive man! Knowing herself a platonic admirer insofar as that were possible, Delia appreciated Carmine for what he was: a man of forty-eight, built like a bull but trim, with the face of a Roman emperor—autocratically good looking, with a pair of jewel-colored eyes that saw clear through to the soul.

Thinking he'd be teaching school, he'd majored in English and Math at Chubb, but after going to his great love, police work, he had pursued a leisurely Master's degree that discussed the rising tides of urban violence in terms of the huge changes in literary metaphor as evidenced by the Raymond Chandler school. It had been a good but not important thesis that wouldn't have procured him a doctorate, but ambition wasn't why he had done a Master's. That belonged to the boredom of the bachelor years.

"You look well," she said before he could answer her first question. "No arthur-itis."

"Desdemona filled some horse-sized capsules with turmeric—you know, the powder turns a curry yellow? She read somewhere that it's good for rheumatics, as she calls them. And she's right— or something is. No aches and pains this winter." He came to look at the C.U.P. table plan. "Yes, Deels, this one is definitely yours. Abe tells me that Mrs. Davina Tunbull is heavily into incriminating herself." He perched the edge of his rump on the table.

"I reminded her of the Miranda decision, boss, but she ignored me. I think you should see her yourself, Carmine. Something's going on—all this rubbish about the deceased trying to rape her! Only don't see her without witnesses. Her cretinous servant will back up any lie Davina tells."

"If there is cretinism there, Delia, then Uda can't possibly be intelligent. Mental retardation is a part of the syndrome," Carmine objected. "You can't be half a cretin."

"I disagree!" Delia said vigorously. "I have seen it before in other cretinous looking individuals, and I stand by the evidence of my eyes. Cretins can sometimes preserve their brains, and Uda is one such. Perhaps the syndrome is only partially established, I don't know, but Uda has as good a brain as Davina."

Carmine stood upright. "Go home, Delia. It's still Sunday, and

Ivy Hall won't be ready for your attentions until tomorrow. Davina Tunbull can wait, so can the rest."

"Gus Fennell likened Davina and John Hall to Phaedra."

"The young wife of Theseus's old age, who fell in love with his son by the Amazon queen," Carmine said, smiling.

Home for Delia was a beachfront apartment in Millstone, on the easternmost edge of Holloman County; Millstone Bay was a scallop in the coastline beyond the Busquash peninsula, and was one of the more expensive places to live. That Delia had recently been able to buy her condo was thanks to a tidy bequest from her father's sister; it had made all the difference to her financially.

Not everyone's idea of beauty, perhaps, but it was Delia to the enth degree, from its theme of rust, yellow and bright sky blue, to its dozens of daisy-embroidered doilies, knickknacks and very comfortable furniture; she even had an easy chair and a table chair designed for Desdemona.

Divested of her outerwear, she took her glass of sherry to the plate glass window that formed most of the front wall of her living room, and stood looking with pleasure at a winter world. The stony beach was littered with eerily beautiful chunks of ice washed up from some shattered berg drifting down in the arctic current—the water was below air freezing, still liquid because of its salt content—and the trees showed forth in the splendor of their lacy grey skeletons. Not much snow, considerable ice; it could happen that way, and Holloman had had a true ice storm two days before Christmas that left pendulous icicles on eaves and branches still. Long Island was visible, but only just; more bad weather coming, given that black snow sky. Glorious! Delia loved her beachfront view in all its seasonal moods, and prayed, along with everyone else in Millstone, that this year they'd have the big storm that put the sand back on the beach. It had been snatched away eleven years ago as part of some cycle; the local Yankees swore it was due to reappear soon.

She had made a big pot of pea-and-ham soup, one of the happier aspects of being a spinster, she reflected as she pigged out on it and buttery fingers of toast. She could fart all night and offend no nose save her own.

That awful Davina Tunbull popped into her mind as she put her plate, cup and bowl into the dishwasher. Lose thirty pounds, indeed! Live on lettuce leaves and black coffee instead of pea soup and buttery toast? I could run her down inside a hundred yards, the smug bitch! They may not look good on a Times Square billboard, but my legs are made for *using*, not looking at.

Carmine was staring at the same wintry, watery landscape, but his was a busier view, encompassing the harbor and its shipping. The ice was crusted around the East Holloman shore, but it wasn't going to be the sort of winter saw the ice breakers working to clear a channel to the hydrocarbons farm. The black sky said lots of snow, but the absence of mackerel said it wouldn't blow a gale to pile up snowdrifts.

He had ignored his front door, halfway down the sloping two-acre property he called home, in need of some salt in the air and a sense of a wider world than the one at present occupying him in its worst manifestation: close blood relatives were implicated in the crimes he and his detectives had sworn an oath to pursue to a successful conclusion. What he had to do was banish the specters of Jim and Millie Hunter, assemble them with the rest of the suspects, and admit that, as things stood at the moment, they were the most likely suspects.

The worst of it was that as yet he hadn't encountered many of the participants—nor would, unless he usurped Abe Goldberg's position as chief investigator of the Tunbull dinner party. And that he would not do. Under ordinary circumstances it would not matter, but these two cases were inextricably linked through the mechanism of the two deaths—Dr. Millie Hunter's esoteric neurotoxin. Luckily he could see anyone involved in the Tunbull death from the aspect of Thomas Tarleton Tinkerman's death, save for Uda, whom he was dying to meet. Whatever Davina was, Uda had a hand in it. If Davina was a poisoner, then Uda had a hand in that too.

Dr. Jim had to be his next subject. Word had already gone to him that he was expected in Carmine's office at the Holloman PD at nine tomorrow morning. The East Holloman kids had used to call Jim "Gorilla"—the flat nose and gaping nostrils, of course, plus the black, black skin. How cruel children were! To an East Holloman kid in 1950, before the great waves of black immigration from the South, Jim Hunter may as well have been an alien from Mars. Holloman had "gone black" in the Fifties, when factory owners like the Parsons and Cornucopia had realized this work force was both capable and grateful for regular employment, even if the wage scale was lower than for whites. The Hollow had always been black, but not as populous, and Argyle Avenue was a fairly recent overflow. Georgia and the Carolinas would always be home, but they weren't where the work was; the South was not industrialized, even in 1969.

A digression, Carmine. Back to Dr. James Keith Hunter, an African American of enormous promise, one black child who had to be saved, hence his importation to Holloman in 1950. And his impact on Patsy's family, on East Holloman in general. So ironic, that the vagaries of life should have led him back to Holloman, where he was still living the life of a poor black, albeit as much of an enigma to his own people as to others. Unless his book lifted him out of debt, put money in the bank that meant a nice home, Dormer Day School fees for his children, and freedom for Millie. At going on thirty-three, they were finally at a point where the comforts of success were a definite probability. Not, however, under Tinkerman!

Now Tinkerman was dead, and the Head Scholar replacing him was very much a Jim Hunter fan.

The biggest puzzle was whereabouts John Hall fitted into all of this, if the two murders were committed with the same end in view. And how could they not be? What had John Hall known—or, failing that, what threat had he represented?

Damn weekends! The real enquiries couldn't start until tomorrow, which gave the murderer time to cover his tracks.

Something banged hard into Carmine's leg; startled, he looked down upon an ugly doggy face trying desperately to smile. Frankie had grown tired of waiting for the beloved steps to come through the front door, and gone to find out why they hadn't.

"Hi, guy," Carmine said, hunkering down to run a silky ear through his fingers. "It's cold out here, you crazy mutt."

Frankie groaned.

"Okay, I give in! Come on, hound."

They walked up the path together, the dog a respectful half pace behind to guard Carmine's flank.

Desdemona was in the kitchen. Carmine slid into the booth and sat watching her as the dog took up its usual post at her heels, adept at getting out of her way.

"Smells great. What is it?" he asked.

"Filet of beef with a chateaubriand sauce, potatoes simmered in beef stock, and green beans," she said, grinning. "This case meant no Sunday midday dinner, and scrod doesn't fill your tummy for more than two hours, so depending on lunch at Malvolio's, I thought you might need a treat." She dropped a block of unsalted butter into her sauce and emptied a saucer of freshly minced tarragon on top of it. "There, we can relax while it melts, after which I have to stir."

"The kids in bed?"

"As per usual. Alex is asleep, Julian is watching cartoons."

"I'll be back."

Alex was sound asleep, impervious to the racket emanating from the nursery TV set, another Prunella suggestion while she had been in residence with them helping Desdemona get over her depression. It was blatantly reward-and-punishment, but it worked, and Julian had abandoned his defense attorney persona in favor of a more like-able confidence trickster. As neither impressed his father, he looked away from Bugs Bunny and held out his arms.

"Hi, Daddy."

"Hi," said Carmine, kissing him. "Is Fort Delmonico safe?"

"As houses," said Julian, full of his mother's sayings.

"Sorry we didn't get our walk today—work intruded."

"I know *that!*" Julian's eyes were drifting back to the television set. "Did you catch them yet, Daddy?"

"No. It's a difficult case."

"Night-night," said Julian absently.

Carmine kissed both his sons and left.

His drink was waiting by his chair; he sank into it with a sigh as Desdemona came to join him.

"I'll start the meat soon, but I thought you needed a couple of drinks first tonight."

"Perceptive as ever, lovely lady. How do you know?"

"Emilia. She and Maria are cot cases over Millie. I get hourly updates from one or the other."

Carmine drank gratefully, and had just put his glass down when his lap suddenly filled with orange fur. "Oh, Jesus, Winston, leave me alone!"

"It's your hands, Carmine. They stroke so beautifully. Blame them for Winston's passion. He's a lap cat."

"At his size, he's a menace."

Desdemona drank her gin and tonic, grinning. "I can hear him purring—what a motor!" She got up and went to the kitchen, returning quickly. "Meat's on, we'll eat soon, and you're going to enjoy it as it should be enjoyed—no bolting it down."

"I take it the back massage worked?"

"Like a dream. I told you, Carmine, it's your hands. A pair of miracle workers. Isn't that true, Winston?"

MONDAY, JANUARY 6, 1969

This was a general conference, held in Commissioner Silvestri's office, some compensation for the 7 a.m. callout. The coffee was as good as Luigi's and the Danish and raisin bagels fresh.

"Patrick's had to recuse himself completely," Silvestri said, clad in his usual high-necked black sweater and black trousers, "but I talked to Doug Thwaites and we agreed that you shouldn't recuse yourself, Carmine. Millie's not your daughter, and she is a cousin to at least half of the Holloman PD. Gus Fennell will be acting on the pathology front, and Paul Bachman will do the forensics. Patrick will be busy handling the rest of the Medical Examiner's intake. I would prefer that he not be kept in the loop at all, is that clear? Paul and Gus already know, I told them personally."

"Patsy would never run off at the mouth, sir," Carmine said.

"I know, but we don't want some publicity-hungry defense attorney down the track implying that he did." The sleekly handsome face didn't change its expression. "Never forget that the quality of defense attorneys is on the rise. Our police work will be squeaky-clean, and the cop who disrupts the evidence chain is looking at a six-month suspension without pay. Signed, sealed and delivered in triplicate, just like Captain Vasquez prescribes. Is that understood?"

Heads nodded solemnly all over the room; Donny Costello, to whom these high stratum conferences were new, looked quite pale and fearful. Getting into Detectives was a triumph, but it sure had its down side.

91

Silvestri finished scanning the faces, satisfied. "Carmine, how are you going to proceed?" he asked.

"First off, sir, we have to monitor activity in both ghettoes, the Hollow and Argyle Avenue. Nick's been undercover there for four months now, and I don't want to stop that."

Nick looked a little torn, but was more elated than he was disappointed; Carmine's sole African-American detective, he was doomed to remain so for at least several more years, for it took time to produce detectives. Fernando was enlisting black cops and their quality was high, but always with detectives it boiled down to time.

So Nick Jefferson held the African-American fort alone. He was thirty-four years old and the father of two children, and last year the family had suffered a terrible setback when his wife had a serious brain bleed from which she was still recovering. They were modestly well off and lived in the Valley not far from Hampton Street and the Tunbulls; his kids went to the Dormer Day School on part scholarships and a general Jefferson family will to keep them there. His present work held an element of danger, as he performed it in two skins: one was as the hip black detective, the other as a middle-aged malcontent tied to Mohammed el Nesr and the Black Brigade. If it were possible to put the two skins next to each other, even a close observer would not have guessed that they were both Nick Jefferson.

"It's going to be a violent spring in racial terms," said Carmine, "and I can manage without Nick, if he's willing to stay with his project."

"I'd prefer that, Carmine," said Nick firmly.

"Thanks for that, it's appreciated. Abe, Liam and Tony will concentrate on the Tunbull murder without weakening their manpower by chasing after the poison. That job goes to Buzz, who isn't very well known to any of the participants, including the Doctors Hunter." He paused, looked suddenly autocratic. "Attention, all men on this case! Don't be alone with Davina Tunbull, who cries rape and is backed up by her servant, Uda."

More solemn nods.

"Delia, you're on the Ivy Hall seating and whatever subtle signs that gives you. There are some odd placements—why, for instance, was Nate Winthrop at the high table and Judge Thwaites marooned next to a mortal enemy? You can question any woman suspect at any time because you see women differently."

Today Delia was wearing a bright mauve angora sweater with a knobby tweed jacket and skirt in dull reds and yellows, and she had slung the most amazing necklace of what looked like dyed and painted sewing spools around her shoulders. Everyone snuck peeks—somehow the word had gotten around that she and Davina had had a spat about clothes, so no one had the courage to stare, and of course no one in his right mind would comment on her clothes beyond telling her they were gorgeous. But not, they divined, today.

"Certainly, Carmine," she said heartily.

"Donny," Carmine said, looking almost as catlike as the Commissioner, "you receive your baptism of fire by interviewing the Parsons— all five of them, plus five wives—who are at the Cleveland Hotel and not pleased at being told they can't leave town. You have an appointment at two this afternoon, which gives you this morning and lunchtime to read up on them. My notes on the Ghost case will be a help—I've put them on your desk and marked the relevant pages. After you're satisfied there's nothing more to be gotten out of them, let them go back to New York City. Then I want you to see the two Gentleman Walkers at the banquet—Dave Feinman and Greg Pendleton."

He looked at John Silvestri. "And that's it for the moment, sir. Anything I've forgotten?"

"If there is, I can't see it." The Commissioner rubbed his hands together. "Now we can have some breakfast."

It felt odd to be promoted to the Captain's sidekick, Buzz thought as he followed Carmine into the most cheerful of the interview rooms—which wasn't saying much. It still stank of sweat and fear, it still had that hard cop look and feel to it.

Dr. Jim Hunter was already seated in the suspect's chair, his head in a massive book whose pages he riffled as a teller did assorted bank notes. If he were genuinely reading, then he got through a page at a glance. As the two men came in he stood.

"Dr. Hunter," Carmine said, extending his hand. "This is Sergeant Buzz Genovese."

"A pleasure," said Hunter, sitting and closing the book.

"As I would like to record our conversation, would you like to have a lawyer of your choice present?" Carmine asked.

The brows lifted above tranquil eyes. "Am I under arrest?"

"No."

"Then why reschedule to stuff a fourth person in an already crowded room? A recorded conversation surely protects me as much as it assists your case," Jim Hunter said. "Let's get on with it."

Carmine switched the tape on. "Monday, January six, nineteen sixty-nine, time oh-nine-hundred-and-two. Present are Dr. James Keith Hunter, Captain Carmine Delmonico, and Sergeant Marcello 'Buzz' Genovese." He leaned forward, linking his hands together loosely and resting them on the table.

"Dr. Hunter, please tell me what you know about Dr. Millicent Hunter's tetrodotoxin. I want every word of every exchange that went on between you about this substance, no matter how unimportant it might seem. This is a fact finding exercise, Doctor, and your own profession indicates that you understand the significance of all the facts. If we are to get to the bottom of this affair, we need everything. Please proceed with that in mind."

The eyes, Buzz was thinking, are amazing in a face that doesn't bear much—if any—resemblance to a gorilla. I wonder why they called him that when he was a kid? He doesn't have huge nostrils or a flat nose, and a gorilla's eyes are black and fill the whole of its visible orbit—unhuman. This man's eyes are as human as eyes can get—the color! In this too-bright room, a brilliant darkish green. Cognizant as few men's eyes are; as if he already knows everything that the interview will unearth. He too folded his hands on the table, their pink palms a striking contrast to the rest of his skin.

"First, you must understand that my wife and I work in very different fields," he began, his voice low-pitched and calm. "After so many years together, we don't share every detail the way we did in earlier times, but we always know what each other is doing. Millie— I will call my wife that—is interested in the biochemistry of neural breakdowns. By that, I mean localized breakdowns that affect only one part of the body or one organ, as well as generalized breakdowns that end in shutting the whole nervous system down. It isn't largely known, and she may not have told you, but her grant ultimately originated with a government agency that is interested in nerve gases like those disseminated on the battlefields of the First World War, and toxins that might be put into, for example, a town water supply. If you want further information, I can't help you—it will depend on your security clearances."

He drew a breath; the hands had not tightened at all. "The tetrodotoxin was a catalyst rather than an end in Millie's experiments—a tool, you might say. It's too difficult to isolate in large quantities ever to be considered a weapon. The first I heard of it was when Millie asked me to come and see her fish. She had a large tank of blowfish, and I quite understand why she wanted me to see them. They're delightful, look a little like marine puppies. I had no idea they were poisonous until she told me about tetrodotoxin, which she intended to isolate herself because the substance is hard to get and very expensive. Millie is a superb technician, I knew obtaining it was well within her level of skill. But it didn't really impinge, if you know what I mean. That day I was on the verge of making another discovery of my own, so what she was prattling on about was as far from whereabouts my mind was as Mercury is from Pluto. I went back to my own work and forgot all about Millie's tetrodotoxin."

"Even though you knew all about this government agency?" Carmine asked incredulously. "Scientists are in the forefront of opposition to exactly the kind of thing this government agency is encouraging, and now I find you actively praising your wife's source of funding?"

The eyes flashed magnificently. "You squeezed a great deal out of very little, Captain, if you inferred *that*. What you also appear to forget is that this was Millie. I would never do anything that made her work harder, and the agency involved is, after all, interested in enemy action against us. I know Vietnam is a cancer and I don't believe a word Nixon says about getting our boys out of there, but Millie's research has nothing to do with Vietnam or who is in the White House, no matter how shifty—*I* voted for Hubert Humphrey!" He sat back, folded his arms across his mighty chest, and looked as if he was quite willing to take on half of the Holloman PD.

Carmine let him calm down during five minutes of silence, then: "When did her tetrodotoxin next impinge?" he asked.

"When she came home and told me someone had stolen six hundred milligrams of it. Last Thursday. She was upset enough about it to have gone to her father for advice, so I knew she regarded the theft very seriously. She asked me then if I'd mentioned the stuff to anyone, and I said no because I hadn't."

"Did you know where it was? How she'd stored it?" from Buzz.

"Frankly, no. If you'd asked me, I wouldn't have been able to tell you if it was water-soluble, or actually in solution. In fact, I assumed it was in solution, but I was wrong—she said she'd put it into vacuumed ampoules and refrigerated it. You don't usually bother doing that with powders, but it added another step to preparing it for use, and once I realized how absolutely lethal it was, I admired her thoroughness."

"Did she tell you at the time how it affected a victim?" from Carmine.

"No. I was too concerned with cheering her up. And I freely confess that my mind was elsewhere—I was busy with the problem Dr. Tinkerman was going to be. I was terribly worried."

"Not any more," said Buzz.

Hunter shot him a reproachful glance. "Oh, come on, guys, what else would I be than worried?" he asked. "All that work writing the book, then the chance of some extra income going down the gurgler because of one man's power and prejudice? Worried? Sure I was worried! So would any of you be!"

"You have some powerful allies at Chubb, Doctor," Carmine said. "Instead of churning with worry, why weren't you trying to have Tinkerman's stand reversed?"

Jim Hunter writhed, apparently in frustration. "For reasons you wouldn't understand!" he snapped. "Tinkerman could not halt publication of *A Helical God*—he couldn't even bludgeon me into a less intriguing title—but what he could do was refuse to put C.U.P.'s weight behind the book once it was in the stores—take too long shipping orders, refuse to authorize more print runs—that's how he would have gone about it. Tunbull Printing stands to make big profits—so does C.U.P. itself, for that matter!—but Max already did a bad thing in printing without authorization, and it wouldn't have been let happen again. So before you decide I'm the one with motive for Tom Tinkerman's death, you'd better look at the Tunbulls. Or," he said, leaning forward, excited, "look at any of the other authors who are publishing with C.U.P. but whom Tinkerman detests. He's the kind of scholar who'd damn a fellow scholar for quibbling about a minor detail in the life of Jesus Christ. There are suspects up the wazoo!"

"Okay," said Carmine cheerfully, "let's go through it again, Doctor."

That surprised Dr. Jim; clearly he had expected to tell his story and then be dismissed. Now he stared.

"Must we?"

"Oh, I think so. You haven't mentioned John Hall, and I need to know all about your previous contacts with him."

"*John?*" Dr. Jim seemed astonished at this new line of questioning. "He was a friend. A true friend. We met when we enrolled in the Master's program in biochemistry at Caltech, and I guess—no, I'm sure—he made the running. Introduced himself to Millie and me.

97

Normally Millie and I don't pal up with others, but somehow John got under our guard. Millie thought it was because he didn't have any feelings about mixed marriages—black with white. He genuinely seemed to see why I loved Millie, and why Millie loved me. He was a loner, a real loner. It was a while before we realized that he had more money than he could spend—he never pushed it at us, or insulted our pride by offering to pay. I mean, we used to sit on the public beach and count our nickels and dimes to see if we had enough for a cheap boardwalk lunch, and he'd produce the same number of coins we did. He was in forestry, but his adoptive father, Wendover Hall, wanted him to know all about wood biochemistry, and since it's not a curriculum item, he did the same work we did—just advanced biochemistry. Millie, who's a great teacher, used to translate it for him in ways he could use." Hunter shrugged. "And that's it, Captain. We were just—friends."

"Equally? You and Millie, I mean, with John?" Buzz asked.

A question Dr. Jim considered carefully; he was now fully aware of the police purposes, and probably, thought Carmine, twenty paces ahead of them. He was very clever.

"No, I guess I was more committed to John than Millie was, but there was one big reason for that." He drew an audible breath. "I wasn't well. Over the eight years I spent in Holloman and New York City, I must have had dozens and dozens of fights. If the fight was one against one I stood in no danger—I could even hold my own two against—but my opponents weren't honorable. I'd get jumped by up to six guys and get the shit kicked out of me. Then I'd get myself home and have to deal with Millie—crying, in despair, wanting to give up and give in—it was very hard, Captain. By the time we went to California I was moving into an age group that exacted punishment in other ways than force, so the fights ceased. Mind you, even grossly outnumbered I left a few marks on them."

"Where was the worst damage?" Carmine asked.

"God knows what bled inside my chest and belly, but they seemed to heal, and I don't have symptoms that suggest anyone did permanent damage. Worst was my face—the sinuses. I couldn't breathe through my nose anymore, and I used to get attacks of face pain that dropped me like a poleaxed steer—I was a mess. At the beginning of our first summer break—June of 1959—John tricked me into seeing some wizard sinus surgeon who begged to repair my sinuses for nothing—he said it was the most fantastic challenge, one he couldn't let go. But I had a job fixed up, and I knew Millie and I wouldn't manage unless I worked it."

He stopped; Carmine and Buzz sat in silence, unwilling to prompt or push. When he had the next chapter assembled and sorted in his head, he'd go on.

"That was when John confessed about having literal millions from Wendover Hall. And he begged me even harder than the surgeon to have the operation. If I wouldn't take the money as a gift, he said, take it as a loan. One day, when I was a full chair professor, I could pay him back. I crumbled when Millie joined him in the begging, and I confess that the attacks of nerve pain were horrific. The surgeon said once he levered all the broken bones off the nerve channels, the pain would disappear. Also the threat of cerebral abscess. All up, between the operation, a week in the hospital and a summer spent recovering, I borrowed ten thousand dollars from John Hall. It weighs on me, so you have no idea how glad I was to think that at last I could pay him back. And then he died. That was not fair! Just not fair!"

Emily Tunbull walked down the short section of road between her house and Davina's, quietly boiling. How was it that a twenty-four-year-old floozie from God knew where had danced off with Max's house, business and fortune right under her nose? But who could have guessed it when the skinny bitch had appeared at Tunbull Printing with a portfolio of her work, fluttering her false lashes at Max as she explained that she had just opened this art design studio on the Boston Post Road, and would he be interested in putting a little work her way? And Max, stupid old goat, had whinnied, pawed the ground and deluded himself that he was not an old goat: he was a stallion in his prime.

He had been cunning. No one in the family had suspected what was going on for six solid months—six months during which Max had taken the bitch out to dinner, given her expensive gifts, handed her the contract for the dismally plain dust jackets C.U.P. wrapped around its works. Val had noticed the signs, but not divined the cause. The dust jackets had brightened up, but in an inoffensive way—their coloring, the lettering, a subtly more modern feel—and Max had been open about the source: Imaginexa, the new design firm on the Boston Post Road not a half mile away. That Max himself had smartened up his appearance and was having the outside of his house painted seemed natural, logical; after all, he was fifty-eight years old, due for a sprucing up.

Emily hadn't worried about Ivan's inheritance in many years. Once Martita vanished together with her son, Emily had known it would all come eventually to Ivan, as it should. Who else was left, who deserved to inherit more than Ivan? He had worked very hard to impress Uncle Max, done as he was told, moulded himself in Max's image. And *pleased* Max, who may have mourned his lack of a son, but knew Tunbull Printing was in safe hands under Ivan.

Until Davina Savovich, the model from New York City who filled Max with grandiose ideas about his importance to C.U.P. What other printer in Connecticut could cope with the demands of a university press, with its strange publications and limited print runs?

At the end of their secret six months, Max and Davina had married; no one was present to raise objections. Instead, the marriage had broken over Emily, Val and Ivan like a half-frozen Niagara Falls! Silly old goat Max had married a woman nearly one-third his age, and when her belly began to swell, Emily for one knew her life's purpose was shattered. Yes, naturally the bitch had littered a son! Alexis, yet! Davina was nutty about the Russian czars, insisted on calling her offspring by a Russian name. And old goat Max had consented, as he consented to everything Davina suggested, even insanities like huge, unauthorized print runs. Now it became obvious why Max had painted the exterior of his house: it was waiting for its new mistress to put her touch on its interior—bizarre shapes and colors and patterns, homage to an obscure master named Paul Klee.

Ivan was such a good boy. Never a trouble, never a worry. In high school he had expressed a wish to become a pilot, but when Val explained his position as Max's heir, he had given up every youthful aspiration, gone to U Conn for a degree in precision engineering, and joined the printery. His choice of bride was perhaps more down-market than Emily for one would have liked, but Lily turned out to be a dear little thing. If her origins showed in her grammar, that was bearable compared to Max's choice of a wife, thought Emily, still boiling as she trod up the path to the front door. Choice in *wives*, for that matter. Martita had been too stuck up to fraternize with any of the family, now here was Davina trying to tell the family with whom to fraternize! A loathesome bitch, so sure of herself, so sure of Max. Time to unsettle her . . .

Emily rang the stupid doorbell with its stupid tune, and was thrown completely off balance when Davina answered the door herself—where was horrible Uda? And dressed, yet! No satin nighties and negligés? Emily was even gladder that she had "dressed" to visit her sister-in-law, who was staring at her.

It was a long time since Waterbury, and Emily Tunbull had learned, as you had to when your men mixed with really important people in the course of their business. The Pollack social climber had learned so well that she hardly ever remembered her maiden name had been Malcuzinski. So she was slim and attractive in a late-forties way, attended the beauty parlor once a week for hair styling and manicure, and shopped for dresses during sales in superior stores. Today she was wearing a well tailored, darkish blue dress, and the shoes she slipped on her feet once divested of her boots were dark blue Italian kid. A sapphire-and-diamond brooch sat on one lower shoulder. As a young woman she had been ravishingly pretty, but that never lasts; her features had set into a handsome, rather masculine mould, and she wore her crisp dark hair short, expertly cut. Her eyes were dark and very busy: Emily Tunbull missed nothing. As she was about to let Davina know in the sweetest possible way.

"Where's Uda?" she asked, perching in a chair.

"Doing something for me in the kitchen."

"How is Alexis?"

"In perfect health."

"That's not really what one means when one enquires after a baby," said Emily, watching Davina light a Sobranie Cocktail cigarette; it was wrapped in green paper.

The thin black brows rose. "La-de-da! What else could you mean, Emily?"

"Davina, he's a baby! They're so lovely, and growing all the time—he must be full of tricks and cute stories."

Now the brows frowned. "At four months he tells stories?"

"No," said Emily, striving to stay cool. This stupid gold-digger *pretended* to understand the nuances of English! "I mean that when I ask about him, you should tell me lots of cute stories about him."

Davina yawned. "Uda could, I suppose, if her English were better. And I have a girl sees to him as well—washes his diapers, bathes him, keeps his linen fresh." She lifted an impatient shoulder. "But why ask me this today, Emily?"

"I guess I haven't gotten around to it before. You haven't been much in evidence since his birth, have you?"

"I hemorrhaged, and it exhausted me. The fools of doctors left it too late for a Caesarean. I am only just recovered."

"If you ate more sensibly, you wouldn't have suffered."

"Pah! Thin is in! Alexis was a small baby."

"You dieted the strength out of yourself. Bones were made to be covered, not seen."

The developing argument ceased when Uda came in; Davina turned to her gratefully. "Coffee," she said curtly.

"You treat that poor woman like dirt, Davina."

"She is my servant, bonded to me. This you know."

"In Yugoslavia, I guess anything's possible, but not here in America. Uda is free, not bonded."

"The country makes no difference to a bond. Her family has provided mine with servants for five hundred years."

"Lucky you," said Emily dryly.

They sat then in an uneasy silence until Uda returned pushing a cart loaded with coffee, savory nibbles and pastries.

"There's no need to go to so much trouble," Emily said, her coffee cup in one hand and some kind of curryish bun in the other. She bit into it, nodded. "Very good! But unnecessary."

"What are you here for, Emily?" Davina herself took black, unsweetened coffee and ignored the edibles.

"To clear up a few things I've noticed over the past year."

Down went Davina's cup. "What things?"

Emily took another tiny curry bun. "Oh, come now, Vina! Must I spell them out? You know very well what I'm getting at."

Her answer was a sneer; then Davina shrugged. "When you start getting mysterious, Em, I become the Thomas who doubts."

"You, doubt? Never!" said Emily with her own sneer. "It's surprising what there is to see and hear, and how it all adds up."

The white skin had lost its luster; Davina's rather flat chest heaved on a breath. "You are just making mischief!"

"Max home, is he? I thought I didn't see him drive out."

"We expect the police."

"You'll suffer more if I open my mouth and tell Max."

"Tell Max what? Your usual lies? You're like the scum that rises to the top of anything left standing, you trouble-maker!"

"I want Ivan to inherit half of the business," said Emily.

Recovered from her alarm, Davina inspected her long, red-lacquered nails. "Pah! You know nothing because there is nothing to know. This is how you drove Martita away, not so? The slurs, the innuendos . . . Always convincing her that you said the truth. Well, I am no Martita. I am not a fragile depressive. I am not vulnerable either. You are a proven liar."

"Perhaps I can prove I'm not a liar—this time." Emily took a third bun. "You know what I'm driving at, Vina. These are delicious! May I have the recipe?"

"I will tell Uda to write out the recipe in ounces and pounds, yes?" Davina smiled. "Uda is a cook to die for."

"Do we have a deal?" Emily asked. "Half to Ivan."

"If you like," Davina said, sounding indifferent. Then she raised her voice in a shout. "Max, dear! Coffee and company!"

The elegant Ivy Hall furniture had been moved to a pile at the back of the hall, the spot where it now rested having been thoroughly checked by Paul Bachman's team. That left the vast remainder of the room to examine, including its trash. Donny and Delia represented Detectives; the bulk of the work fell to the Medical Examiner's people.

Two forensics technicians had already done the worst job—going through the four cans used to receive food scraps. It was the only aspect of the work that wouldn't wait until this Monday.

So on Monday Delia and Donny, Paul and two others, clad in coveralls, bootees, gloves and caps, did the ordinary trash. This had been deposited in ordinary small metal containers of the most ubiquitous kind, receptacles scattered in corners, against walls, down the corridors to entrance and toilets, the toilets themselves, and the kitchen.

They worked on a huge sheet of blue plastic, onto which each searcher emptied a container before inspecting the empty interior, complete with a flashlight, for anything that might have adhered or stuck in a seam. The trash itself was gone through meticulously, then thrown into a big drum.

"When the menu is smoked salmon, your choice of chicken breast or broiled scrod, and peach pie a la mode, why the hell would you bring these?" Donny asked, sitting back on his heels and holding up an empty Cheez Whiz packet.

"Not everyone likes food food," Delia answered, head down and tail up. "I've found Twinkie wrappers by the score, as well as part of what looks like a theory of the universe written on a tatty piece of paper. It must have been wrong—the genius threw it out, anyway."

"Who had a baby at this junket?" Paul asked, holding up a soiled disposable diaper.

"No one was supposed to. It must have been in a basket of rushes. Oh, the mysteries inherent in a nation's trash!" Delia exclaimed, holding up a can of mosquito repellent. "At *this* time of year? Really!"

"I've found a Rubic cube, a book of crossword puzzles and five jigsaw pieces," said one of Paul's technicians, sniggering. "I guess some people come prepared for the boring speeches."

They had nearly finished; it would be, they hoped, the least palatable job concerned with this case.

Donny yelped. "Hey! Found something, Deels!"

She scurried over on hands and knees and looked into the palm of his glove, the others crowding around too. It held a metal saucer about a half inch in diameter and a quarter inch deep at its center. Underneath, soldered to the saucer's center, was the business end of a fine bore hypodermic needle perhaps five-eighths of an inch long. It was plugged with a tiny cube of cork. On the top rim of the saucer a rubber cover had been stuck using a glue that partially dissolved the rubber, thus fusing it extremely efficiently to the steel saucer.

"Bingo!" Paul breathed. "I can't believe he threw this out in the trash."

"Carmine was right," Delia said. "The killer didn't know we stood no chance of getting warrants to search people before they left. So he ditched it at first opportunity."

"He respects the poison, making sure that none could accidentally enter his own flesh as he carried it—a pocket of his jacket would have been ideal, but fiddling around to get it out—yeah, he might have pricked himself," Donny said. "It was still risky, though. I wonder when he removed the cork? And why, having used the thing, didn't he just drop it and kick it under the table? Except I don't see how it was done."

"Carmine has to see this right now," Delia said, scrambled to her feet and made for a wall phone.

Ten minutes later he was there, leaving Buzz to continue grilling Dr. Jim Hunter. With him he brought a half gallon of distilled water, a ten cc syringe armed with a short twenty-gauge needle, some test tubes and a kidney dish.

"Okay, Paul, you get to do the rinsing," Carmine said. "If there's tetrodotoxin in this contraption, it's potentially lethal until, Gus says, it's been rinsed to death, which we do by pushing water into the saucer through the rubber diaphragm and collecting it in test tubes or, if worst comes to the worst, in the kidney dish."

It was a painfully slow business, as the fine bore needle soldered onto the saucer's base dripped the water at a dreary rate, but finally Paul pronounced himself satisfied, and rinsed the device's exterior into the kidney dish.

"Do you know what?" Carmine asked, taking the device. When no one answered, he spoke again. "I reckon all our work has been for nothing. I don't believe this thing has ever held a drop of tetrodotoxin."

A gasp went up; everyone stared at Carmine, shocked.

Donny recovered first. "How does it work?" he asked.

"Like this, I think." Carmine took the device and tucked the hypodermic end between the first and the middle fingers of his right hand so that the needle tip just protruded adjacent to his palm. This saw the saucer rest against the backs of the same two fingers. "The saucer is filled with tetrodotoxin and he holds the thing like so. Then he puts his hand, palm side down, on the side of his victim's neck. The needle goes in as far as his fingers let it. Then he put the thumb of his other hand on top of the rubber diaphragm and pushes at it the way he'd push at an eyeball. That drives the poison out of the saucer, through the hypodermic and into the victim's flesh. It's done in literal seconds, and that left hand covering the right one completely obscures what he's actually doing. As soon as it's done, the hands come down. He must have a way of being positive he can get the needle tip plugged with his cork before it floats free in his pocket. I'd say he practiced the whole operation until he could do it in his sleep. There would have needed to be an incident that diverted people's attention—made everyone look to the wrong side, maybe. More important at the Tunbull dinner."

Carmine shook his head, a dissatisfied look on his face. "At the banquet he would have been behind every man in the row of diners, there was no one to notice what he did with his hands apart from the women opposite, who saw hands on shoulders every time a man got up to go to the bathroom. Ingenious and effective."

"Yet you don't think it was used?" Delia asked.

The cork went into a tiny baggie, the device was put into a lidded jar, where it rolled around like a fallen top.

"How did he fill it?" Donny asked.

"The same way we rinsed it—injected the substance into the saucer with a hypodermic," Carmine said.

"Then filling it was a bitch."

"Speaking of filling things, Donny, aren't you supposed to be doing homework on the Parsons? You see them at two."

"I haven't forgotten, Captain," said the culprit hastily, before Delia could go to bat, "I read your Ghost case notes and sweet-talked a newspaper morgue librarian into searching all the Parson articles out. Looked to me as if all hands were needed at Ivy Hall, begging your pardon."

Carmine grinned. "Forgiven, but get your ass moving now."

"He's a good man," said Delia after he had gone.

"You are not wrong," Carmine said.

She returned to the device. "I didn't know you could solder stainless steel," she said.

"Soldering is like most things, Deels. Be scrupulous in cleaning your surfaces—wipe them down with ether, say—and solder will hold for long enough."

Paul and his technicians were packing up to leave; only Carmine and Delia stood at apparent leisure.

"Where did he get the saucer thing?" Delia asked.

"I have no idea, but it must be part of a piece of lab equipment," Carmine said.

"Ah, the Hunters again," said Delia.

"Or workshop people like printers," said Carmine.

Only something vital would have dragged Carmine away from the interrogation of Dr. Jim Hunter, but when the Captain sent him a second wheel in the shape of a uniform cruising the pool of potential detectives, Buzz Genovese understood that he was to continue. Because Dr. Jim had already coughed up most of his guts on the sinus surgery, Buzz decided to settle the new face into Dr. Jim's world by pressing for more details.

"There's more to it than just a simple operation, Doctor," he said as the uniform endeavored to disappear into the woodwork.

"*Simple* operation?" Hunter stared. "It was anything but, Sergeant. I was in the O.R. for eleven hours and unbeknownst to me, Zimmerman the surgeon had brought in a facial plastic surgeon named—uh—Feinberg or Nussbaum or something. So when I came out of the O.R., I needed a new picture on my driver's license—the pair of them had changed my face. Oh, I didn't turn into Sidney Poitier, but I sure didn't resemble a gorilla anymore. Still ugly, but they gave me my *own* face. It didn't remind anyone of anything."

"Were you pleased?" Buzz asked.

"That's putting it mildly! I was—I was very grateful. For that gift alone I could never lay a hand on John Hall. The surgeons insisted it wasn't cosmetic surgery, just a full reconstruction of the sinuses that altered the exterior of my face, as apparently it does. If there was any genuine plastic surgery involved, it was to my nose. They gave it some shape and grafted me new nostrils."

"How did your wife feel about all that?"

"She was delighted, especially when I lost most of the nerve pain. I went from several attacks a day pre-operatively to one every six months post-operatively. And my face felt—oh, kinda *light*. I could breathe properly, even in deepest sleep."

"Remind me, when was the operation?"

"June of 1959. It was real pioneer surgery, so I got written up in a couple journals."

Hunter had been in the room now for two hours, suffering the oft-repeated questions as most highly intelligent people did, in some bewilderment that his interrogators could be so dense, a sentiment that inevitably led to irritation. It is a rare genius who can continue to put up with the questions of fools unruffled, a fact Carmine and Buzz were relying on. Though Jim Hunter had endured the slings and arrows of racial prejudice, he was also a campus idol. In his work place he was the source of all knowledge, the boss of a whole team of "acolytes" as Dr. Millie called them, and universally adored. He was tolerant, humorous, forgiving and permanently afire with enthusiasm, which made him a wonderful research team leader; no one who worked for him would say or do anything that might incriminate Big Jim, as they called him. It was a sobriquet of total love.

Therefore let the questioning be repetitive, remorseless and, to a Jim Hunter, well-nigh senseless. His ego and his work had conditioned him to expect that his answers would be accepted the first time he gave them; now here he was, being jerked around by utter idiots.

An hour after Carmine had vanished saw Dr. Jim remove his tie; he was sweating, even though the room was chilly.

Every minute of the interminable interview since Carmine left had been devoted to his relationship with John Hall, with Dr. Jim sticking to his guns: he and Millie had known John in California, hung out with him, enjoyed marvelous conversations on subjects that ranged from the Big Bang to the mysteries of genetics and the hunger of the human race to ruin its habitats.

"C'mon, Doctor," Buzz said with a sneer, "there had to be a down side because there always is a down side. Friendships aren't static or idyllic! They go up and down like marriages and snotty brothers and pushy sisters. I mean, it sounds to me as if your wife was very much the third wheel in this ideal give-and-take friendship between two men."

Then it happened, so suddenly that to Buzz it seemed to come out of the blue. Hours of calm, of understandable but well controlled irritation, and now—wham! Hunter exploded!

"You fool!" Hunter snarled, muscles audibly creaking. "Oh, Jesus, you cops are stupid! I'm like, down on kindergarten level, crawling! Millie wasn't the third wheel—she was the fulcrum! John was nuts about her, and she liked him too much—I almost lost her to a man I liked, respected, and was in debt to—how do you think that made me feel?"

He stopped, but whether from horror at having broken, said too much, or rather to give himself precious seconds to think of his next tack, Buzz just couldn't tell. After fifteen years as a cop and innumerable interrogations, Buzz Genovese knew himself as a raw beginner. Oh, why wasn't Carmine here to witness this? With any other person he would have taken events at face value, yet some instinct in the cop part of his mind whispered that Dr. Jim was as much in possession of his wits now as he had been until now. How could that be?

"John was a rich guy," Jim Hunter said, voice level. "If I was working all night and didn't need Millie, he'd take her out to dinner in places I couldn't even afford to drink the water in the finger bowls. A couple times he gave her little presents—a necklace of really good-looking fake pearls, a rhinestone pin. I let him because it let me work without needing to worry about Millie. Usually she worked as my technician, but there were times when she would have been in the way. Literally, I mean. Space is not something universities are generous with." He stopped again.

"When was all this?" Buzz asked.

"Right at the end, thank God. We left for Chicago the day after it all came out in the open. Millie dealt with John—I never saw him at all."

"How did it come into the open, Doctor?"

"I came home early and caught them kissing. Millie swore it was the first time, and that John kissed her against her will, but it sure looked reciprocated to me. He'd just given her the pearl necklace, and I grabbed at it—it broke, pearls went everywhere on the floor. Millie got down on her hands and knees to pick them up, howling, nose running—she said the pearls were real, and the rhinestones were actually diamonds. I remember I took her face between my hands—I could have crushed her skull to pulp if I'd wanted." He drew in a great, sobbing breath. "But I couldn't. Not Millie! I just knew I was going to lose her."

"And did you lose her, Doctor?"

"No. She put the pearls and the diamond pin in a parcel and took it to him in person."

"Wasn't he still present?"

"No. He shot out the door while Millie was gathering pearls."

"So she took him the gifts. What happened between them?"

"I don't know. She didn't tell me, and I didn't ask."

"How did this affect your marriage?" Buzz asked.

The full upper lip lifted. "That's none of your business. I will only say that Millie and I are joined at the hip—no one and nothing can break us apart."

"So meeting John Hall again can't have been all pleasure."

"I hadn't seen him since the end of July of 1960. That's now eight years ago. Certainly I didn't see his advent as any kind of threat to my marriage, Sergeant. I'm even in a position to pay him back for the surgery, and his death can't change that, it's a debt of honor. I'll pay his estate," Jim Hunter said.

"So your wife's state of mind wasn't a concern?"

"Absolutely not."

"Let's get back to the poison, Doctor. Did you take it?"

"Absolutely not."

"But you must have been tempted."

"Why? John Hall was no threat to me."

"His emotional involvement with your wife is motive."

111

"California was over eight years ago. Passé, Sergeant."

"Have other men than John Hall pursued your wife, Doctor?"

"Not that I've noticed, and she's never said so."

Buzz looked at the clock. Over three hours. He was itching to continue, but the man had waived the presence of an attorney, and Buzz was aware that he was skating dangerously close to what an attorney could later term harassment. The wrong time for lunch, but it would have to happen.

"Lunch break," he said briskly. "I'll send to Malvolio's for a tray— brisket, rice pudding and decent coffee sound okay?"

"Indeed it does. May I stretch my legs?"

"Of course, but inside the County Services courtyard."

Carmine was back, looking satisfied; after Buzz reported, his mood soured a little.

"I just can't be sure of the guy," Buzz said as they ate at Malvolio's. "Even when he broke about Millie, I wondered. The cop in me shouts that he's playing with us, that everything he says, how he says it, what he looks like when he says it, *everything* is calculated. Yet it all makes sense."

"Then, if it is calculated, why did he need to insert Millie and infidelity into the equation?" Carmine asked. "It attributes motive to him that we didn't know about before, so *why?*"

"Maybe when he realized we were serious enough to detain him for way over the usual time span of a questioning, he thought we'd do the same to Millie. He's no dummy, he knows the pair of them are our main suspects. Jim Hunter doesn't break, but Millie just might. So he paved the way," Buzz said.

"Very, very good!" Carmine said, smiling broadly. "That is exactly what he did. Paved the way for Millie to crumble."

"Do I get Millie in?"

"Definitely, as soon as possible. Give her lunch too. I'm going upstairs to the Commissioner."

"I have a feeling there's more to come," he said to Silvestri after filling him in.

"So do I. For instance, is Dr. Jim himself free from sin? He's an idol on the science campus," the Commissioner said.

"If it's half as good as M.M. says, his book will make him an idol on every science campus in the country. Not to mention a lot of homes and institutions. With the death of Dr. Tinkerman and the eclipse of the Parsons, nothing is going to stop *A Helical God* hitting the bestseller lists and staying there for many months."

"Did he write it consciously to sell, Carmine?"

"Sure, he must have, though someone else gave him the idea. Family legend has him pictured as completely absorbed in his work, a man who never reads an ordinary book or watches the news on television. His isolation from popular scientific publishing is a good point, John, that we have to explore. I gather Dr. Jim wrote *A Helical God* very quickly, effortlessly—and recently. So where did he get the idea?"

"Millie?" asked Silvestri.

"Yes, she's the most likely one." Carmine shrugged. "The trouble with that pair is that it's hard to get beyond them. Yet Millie is no more *au fait* with the world of commercial book publishing than Jim is. However, we'll pursue it."

"It's early days yet, I know, but you think it's the Hunters behind both murders," Silvestri said, tone dispassionate.

"Unless we dig up something really unexpected, it does look that way. But which one? Or was it both? Today we have to get a better idea about what makes the Hunters tick, as Desdemona would put it." He looked thoughtful. "There's huge family opposition to so much as the idea that Millie might have been involved, and I tend to side with that myself, having known her since she was born. Despite her history, she's no black sheep."

"Unfortunate metaphor," Silvestri said dryly, "but I get your drift. Keep on digging, Carmine, and don't worry about Patsy. I'm keeping him close to me, so he and Nessie don't feel utterly alone in their troubles. Gloria's a tower of strength."

*   *   *

Millie arrived bewildered, but very glad to see Jim, whom she was allowed to see in passing only—no chance for a talk.

She was in jeans and a sweatshirt; her down-stuffed outer clothes were hanging outside the room to which she was taken. No make-up, no hair styling; her looks did not preoccupy her, never had as far as the family knew. Her thin body was not the product of strict diets, it was due to a combination of trying to eat the right (and more expensive) foods, giving the lion's share to Jim, and often plain forgetting to eat because the work called. But she moved with grace and dignity, held her head proudly atop a swanlike neck, and had plenty of shape in her physique—small but lovely breasts, a tiny waist, swelling hips. Set her side by side with Davina Tunbull and you would see the real thing next to a caricature. In K-mart clothes, Millie turned heads; in Fifth Avenue clothes, she'd be offered movie contracts.

"Why am I here?" she asked Carmine.

"A few things have come up about John Hall, Millie. You never told us that he hit on you in California, gave you expensive jewelry— that he kissed you, if nothing more."

She went so white that Carmine almost left his chair to go to her, but she recovered quickly, lifted her chin. "It was my business, no one else's, Captain."

"In a murder enquiry? When the person who hit on you is the victim? That doesn't wash, Dr. Hunter, and you know it. Did you have an affair with John Hall?"

"No, I did not," she said, steady now. "He kissed me once—and not at my invitation. He'd just told me that the pearls were real, and the rhinestone pin was diamond. I'd automatically assumed they were fake, but when he kissed me and told me he was in love with me, he told me their real value. I told him that I couldn't return his love, and gave them back." She shivered. "It was one of the most awful days of my life."

"I understand that you and Mr. Hall were surprised in the act of kissing by your husband, who tore a string of pearls from around your neck. He accused you of infidelity," Carmine said.

"No, I refuse to believe that in his heart of hearts Jim thought me capable of betrayal," Millie said huskily. "He was jealous, and that made him angry. But Jim's not a hot man, his temper cools quickly. So when it did, his ability to think things through returned, and he saw immediately that I was innocent."

An explanation couched in feminine drama, using words like betrayal and innocence, thought Carmine. In an odd way, they defused what had been an explosive situation, one of the worst days of her life. Had she hated John Hall for exposing her, the perfect wife, to Jim's ire and disappointment?

"When did this happen in relation to your time in L.A.?" Carmine asked. "I should tell you that we know about your husband's sinus operation and the loan from John Hall to finance it, and that it took place in June of 1959."

"We left California in August of 1960," Millie said slowly, "and John hit on me about six months before that—around the end of February of 1960, it would have been."

Ah! thought Carmine, astounded. He says it happened the day before they left for Chicago, she says it was six months earlier. It's Hunter lying, not his wife—but why?

"So your last six months in L.A. weren't spent in company with John Hall?"

Now she looked astounded. "Things went on the same after as before," she said. "Why wouldn't they? It was just a temporary aberration, Captain. John apologized to Jim, and that was the end of it." Her brow creased. "Infatuation, that's all it was."

"And how did you fit after the incident?"

"Me? I was just relieved it all blew over. I wasn't nearly as vital to John as his bond with Jim was." Her hands moved, as if they could convey what words couldn't. "You see, John was one of those people who worship at the feet of genius, and every time John saw Jim, the genius hit him between the eyes. There was nothing homosexual in their relationship, but it was tight—very tight. My own theory was that John could compete with Jim in one way only—his attraction for women—and he set out to see if he could steal *something* from a genius, if only a wife."

"You make it sound as if a wife is unimportant to a genius."

"No, no! I don't mean I'm unimportant to Jim! But the wife is separate from the genius—at least, that was what John Hall thought. He assumed that the space I occupied in Jim's life was all to do with making sure he wore more clothes than a fig leaf, ate regular meals, put my feminine body next to him in a bed. California saw the worst period of Jim's ill health, so my importance to Jim as a colleague in his work wasn't on its usual full display. He lost sight of the fact that I'm a biochemist too, and that that allows me to serve a genius in ways wives can't. Until we came to Chubb, I was Jim's chief technician, even though I was never on his books. These days he has so many acolytes he doesn't need me the way he used to." She smiled. "However, I sometimes appear after eleven of a night, when he's all alone, and work as his best technician. No one is my equal."

She stopped, her eyes suddenly full of tears. "John never picked up on that, and once Jim cooled down, he understood what had actually happened—the stealing from a genius."

"But Jim forgave him."

"Yes, of course."

"Did he forgive you, Millie?"

"He had nothing to forgive."

"Your husband said this incident with John Hall occurred the day before you left for Chicago."

She laughed merrily. "He would! In fact, he may even think it was. Jim's not good on time spans and dates. Science is his all, he's neither perceptive nor poetic, I'm afraid."

"Yet I'm told that *A Helical God* is both perceptive and poetic. How come?"

"Work, Captain, that's his work! A different compartment entirely from ordinary living. Where his work's concerned, the genius comes roaring up out of the depths of his brain and you wouldn't know him for the same person. Jim is split."

"Have there been infidelities on his side?"

Millie looked stunned. "Jim? Unfaithful?" Her eyes danced. "If it had ever occurred to him, maybe he might have been, but women have the wrong skeleton. It's not a helix. Physically he is the strongest man I've ever encountered, but he doesn't waste his strength on things that aren't helical."

"Whose idea was it to write *A Helical God*?" Carmine asked.

For a long moment Millie looked absolutely taken aback, then she drew a breath as if she had forgotten that to breathe was a necessity. "What a fascinating question, Carmine! Do you know, I just can't answer it? He didn't say anything to me, he just sat down at our old IBM typewriter one night and started hammering the keys. I wasn't even aware he knew such a thing as a best seller existed until he explained what he was doing when we went to bed about four in the morning. Oh, his mind! It came out already parsed, analyzed and edited, Dr. Carter said. Every chapter in sequence, the jargon dumbed down to exactly the right extent. His prose was amazing! So poetic! I was awed, Carmine, awed."

"When did he start to write it, Millie?"

"Um —" She paused to consider. "As far as I remember, it was September of 1967, because he was through it and had a good manuscript by the end of 1967—a year ago. The only one who'd seen it was me, and I was determined he should take it to a commercial publishing house that would know exactly what to do to market it." She clenched her fists in frustration. "But Jim wouldn't consider a commercial publisher. He wanted it to be a best seller, yes, but he wanted the kudos of the Chubb University Press imprimatur on it, same as his two textbooks. I couldn't budge him, and look at the trouble it's led to! All the idiocies of Head Scholars and the overall good of the house outweighing the income from a big best seller—when we heard that Tinkerman had replaced Dr. Carter as Head Scholar, I think Jim would have done almost anything to get out of his C.U.P. contract. But he couldn't. His own craving to maintain his academic laurels had tied him to C.U.P. no matter what."

Carmine smiled. "Did you say, 'I told you so!'?"

She giggled. "No, I did not. Otherwise murder would have been done, with me the victim. A cut-and-dried case."

Lunch a memory, Buzz battled on with Dr. James Hunter, to no effect; he wasn't about to lose his cool again.

Then Carmine sent in a note.

"Who gave you the idea for *A Helical God*?" Buzz asked.

Hunter blinked. "Idea?"

"Yes, idea. Whose idea was it to write that book?"

"Mine," Jim Hunter said.

"And there are pigs flying everywhere . . ." Buzz taunted. "Dr. Hunter, bona fide scientists don't get sudden inspirations to write popular books. People with a commercial axe to grind suggest them, maybe help push the project along. Who helped you?"

"Me, I, and self."

"No one so much as whispered the idea to you? You didn't dream it in your sleep?"

"Absolutely no one contributed, even my sleep-brain."

"Would you go on oath to say that?"

"What a ridiculous question!" Hunter said, but not angrily. "My book is not under suspicion of murder, Sergeant, so I fail to see why you bring it up."

Carmine entered. "Dr. Hunter, a pleasure," he said.

"I wish I could say the same."

Reaching into his pocket, Carmine produced a small glass jar. "Would you participate in an experiment, Doctor?"

"With what object?"

"Possibly clearing you of suspicion of murder—or, if the contrary, making it highly likely that you did commit murder."

"Captain Delmonico, I will gladly participate in any kind of experiment that might prove my innocence. Bring it on."

"It's not intimidating," said Carmine, smiling as he took the lid off the jar. "Give me your right hand, please, palm facing downward, fingers extended but together."

Hunter did as he was told; Carmine looked at the size of the hand with a lifting heart. The injection apparatus came out. "I need you to separate your fingers very slightly, Doctor, while keeping your hand extended and steady."

Carmine positioned the steel saucer over the gap between the index and middle fingers, then, gently, making sure he didn't catch the skin, he thrust the hypodermic between the fingers until the saucer rested on their backs.

"Tighten your fingers together to grip the tube I've just put between them," Carmine instructed, and turned the hand over, palm side up. There was no sign of the tip of the hypodermic.

"Keep your fingers tightly together while I fiddle," he said, probing into the fissure between the two fingers. There! The tip of the hypodermic was a good three millimetres short of protruding out the palm side of Hunter's hand.

"Okay," he said, "now we'll try the other fingers, then the other hand as well."

Finally the tip of the hypodermic did barely show, between the right hand's third and pinky fingers. Not enough control to do the job, Carmine decided.

"Thank you, Doctor. You may go home. Millie is here too, and we've finished with her as well. Go home together."

Millie and Jim looked at each other, but didn't speak until they were safely in their own car, driving out of the County Services parking lot.

"What a terrible day," she said, not knowing where to start.

"How long were you there?"

"From noon."

He grinned, trying to make light of it. "Beat you by three hours, kid."

"We're the main suspects, Jim."

"Well, that was inevitable once they found out we knew John in California. We're the missing link."

"Since I know it wasn't us, who was it?" she asked.

"I wish I knew. Whoever it is, the cops haven't found him yet," said Jim in a flat voice. His eyes slid sideways toward her, flicked back to the road. "What did you say about John's hitting on you in California?"

"I tried to make them see how unimportant it was, but it's so hard trying to tell people who weren't there what it really was like." She squeezed his thigh. "You got the time wrong, was the worst. I could see their ears prick."

"Oh, Jesus, did I? By much?"

"Not at all!" she said airily. "A mere six months. I tried to explain that was normal for you, but they found that hard to credit. Honestly, Jim! The day before we left for Chicago?"

"Wasn't it? I thought it was, but a lot's happened since."

"How can we persuade them that it wasn't the end of the world for us?" she asked.

"Don't let it chew at you, honey. Everything sorts itself out sooner or later, so they're going to find their suspicions fade away. There's a big difference between suspicion and proof we were involved, because we weren't involved."

"It's Davina Tunbull!" Millie cried.

"Has to be," Jim agreed. "John Hall was a threat to her precious Alexis, and Tom Tinkerman to her prosperity. I mean, even if John told her and Max he didn't want any part of Tunbull money, he may have lied. Davina's got a shady past."

"How do you know that?" Millie asked curiously.

"She drank a little too much champagne back when the book was in manuscript, and said a few things she shouldn't have."

WEDNESDAY, JANUARY 8, 1969

It was barely dawn when Liam Connor double-parked on a street in Queens not far from JFK airport; he walked up five steps to a pale blue front door, found the sticker that said Q. V. Preston, and rang its bell. Clearly things had gone to plan; the door clicked and opened, though Liam didn't need to enter. His quarry was coming out, bundled up for a winter ride to Connecticut.

"Freeze the balls off of a brass monkey," said Mr. Q. V. Preston as he settled into the passenger seat and actually groped for a seat belt. That told Liam that he didn't ride around in many cars; the seat belt advocates were having a hard time of it convincing the populace to buckle up, and cops were the worst offenders—too much like restraints.

"Car's warm, Mr. Preston."

"Are we allowed to stop for breakfast in this great little diner in Co-op City?"

"Sure," said Liam, under orders to be nice.

The three-hour journey (with breakfast included) passed very pleasantly; Mr. Q. V. Preston was full of interesting stories, and the diner in Co-op City was superb. Liam earmarked it for future sallies to the Big Apple.

Most importantly, Mr. Q. V. Preston thoroughly enjoyed his outing, plucked from his everyday routines as he had been, he explained to Carmine, who welcomed him and put him into Delia's office for his interview, as its chairs were more comfortable and it did indeed bear a woman's touch, like vases of dried flowers. He would conduct the questioning, but all of his or Abe's teams who could be here were, scattered casually around the room as for a nice chat.

They had had an extraordinary stroke of luck when Liam began enquiring from Immigration and Naturalization about a pair of Yugoslav refugees named Davina Savovich and Uda X: the man who had handled their case was still in the department, still working in New York City, and professed to remember them well.

His full name, he told the tape recorder, was Quinn Victor Preston, and eleven years ago he had been working with the Port of New York.

"The two girls had stowed away on an Italian freighter out of Trieste, and by the time they got to me, they were in a bad way. Davina spoke a little broken English—enough that I didn't use an interpreter. They always screw meanings up, in my experience. Vina and Uda were Slovenes, which translates as the most western-oriented of the Balkan principalities that Marshal Tito combined under one government as Yugoslavia. There isn't a lot of love lost between the various principalities, especially the ones where Muslims and Christians are pretty evenly distributed. Not a problem in Slovenia, which loosely comprises the Yugoslavian alps—few Muslims, if any.

"Davina struck me as highly intelligent," said Preston, warming to his story. "Her English actually improved with every sentence we exchanged—I could see her mind filing away its grammar, always the hardest aspect of English for an eastern European. She was as thin as someone out of a Nazi concentration camp—skin stretched over bones, maybe eighty pounds. Uda was just as bad. They had no papers, and literally threw themselves on my mercy—I was the head honcho there at the time. Now I'm on airlines, a different world."

He sat back and sipped his cop coffee without complaint—I & N coffee must be equally bad, Carmine thought, unwilling to hurry him. A man nearing retirement age, apparently living alone, and not the kind of man widows hunted—too much fat around the midline, too little hair, too uninspiring in the face, too shabbily dressed. He probably had plenty saved up, just didn't spend it on trying to be a ladies' man when the TV set could offer him sports and his refrigerator beer. Yet the adolescent Davina Savovich had made an impression.

He put his mug down. "They'd walked across the mountains— real alps!—to Trieste, hiding by day, moving by night. Stealing food when they could. They discovered that the *Cavour* was sailing for New York, and somehow got aboard. The first thing I checked out was whether Davina had prostituted herself to achieve it, but she hadn't. As time went on, I understood better that sex was not how she preferred to attain her ends. I suspect she'd been gang raped somewhere, and it had turned her off sex, even as a tool."

"It usually does," said Carmine, topping up his mug.

"They asked for asylum in the United States of America," Preston went on. "My rejoinder was to ask her how she intended to make a living if she was granted asylum. By working, she said, at whatever work she could find. Whatever she did, Uda would also do. Her plan was to go to one of the big hotels—as usual, The Plaza was the one she knew—and offer their services as cleaners. I knew the manager of a less famous hotel—the Grand Lion—and called him to see if his establishment could offer them employment. He—uh—jumped at them, thought they might be easier to discipline than Puerto Ricans."

"Does that mean you ran a kind of racket, sir?" Tony Cerutti asked to freezing glares from many eyes—dumb, Tony, dumb!

It didn't faze Mr. Q. V. Preston in the slightest. "I could only run a racket, sir, if I accepted kickbacks, and I did not," he said calmly. "It is not, strictly speaking, the function of an I & N official to run an employment agency, but sometimes these things do happen through sheer accident. I had a friend. My friend had a hotel. I needed to reassure myself that any individuals to whom I granted visas would be honorably employed, and my hotelier friend had job vacancies. Hey, Preston!" He chuckled at his own little pun.

"But the girls were under age," Tony objected. Tony, Tony!

"I knew *that!* However, they had no papers of any kind, and Davina swore she and Uda were twenty-one years old." He shrugged.

"I had two choices. Deny them asylum, which meant sending them back to turbulence and penury that could well result in their death. I do that every day, gentlemen, but it is never something I relish. My other choice was to send Davina and Uda to my friend with the hotel as bona fide workers." His face screwed up. "I had such a strong feeling about Davina! That she'd manage, and one day be an asset to this country. Something I can't say about many of the refugees who appear at my desk."

"So they got their papers and went to work at the hotel?" Tony asked, blithely unaware that this wasn't an inquisition.

"Yes. I had a stern talk with Davina, warning her that I could remove her immigrant status any time I felt she wasn't holding up her end of the bargain. So no prostitution and no theft. Davina promised they'd do it the hard way, and they did."

"How can you be sure, Mr. Preston?" Abe asked courteously.

"I made the pair of them report back to me at the end of every six months. And of course I kept in touch with my pal at the Grand Lion." A reminiscent smile crossed Mr. Q. V. Preston's face. "The change when I saw them at the end of the first six months was incredible. They'd both put on weight and Davina had found time to visit a beauty parlor—she was just gorgeous! And Uda? Well, Uda stayed Uda, just fatter. They'd been put to work in the hotel kitchen and shamed the Puerto Rican kitchen hands so much that they'd been threatened. Davina wasn't a tad intimidated. She laughed at them and said if they tried anything, she'd castrate them—everyone has to sleep, she whispered. Any other woman would have been found with her throat cut, but Davina was *believed*. They thought her a witch."

"I can imagine that," said Carmine, smiling.

"When I approved of them, my friend put Davina in the restaurant as hostess—her English had improved in leaps and bounds. Uda went with her as her personal assistant." Preston sighed happily. "Davina had been the hostess for almost six months when the proprietor of a model agency dined there and offered to put her on his books. I told her to go for it."

"As easy as that," said Carmine.

"Yes, it really was, but only after much suffering, never forget that, Captain." His face saddened. "I only saw them once more, when Davina was on billboards and kicking her heels in TV bubble baths. There were more beautiful models, but Vina had an extraordinary gift—looking at pictures of her made you firmly believe that the product she was advertising simply *felt* better than its rivals. I closed my files on them with a note that they should be awarded citizenship at the earliest possible time, and that was the end of it. Or—almost." He stopped.

"What, Mr. Preston?" Carmine asked.

"I heard that after she and Uda became citizens, she got herself mixed up with a shady guy named Chez Derzinsky—it had to do with fraud, I believe. There's a police lieutenant in Brooklyn used to be in one of the Manhattan midtown precincts can tell you a lot more—Milton O'Flannery."

Liam was already writing it down.

"But you never saw her again in person, sir?" Carmine asked.

"No. I never expected a nostalgic visit—she never looks back, that girl. But I would love to hear her Connecticut story."

"I'll take you to lunch at Malvolio's before we drive you home, and you shall hear it. But first, what more can you tell us about Uda?" Carmine asked.

Q. V. Preston looked surprised. "I always thought that was one of Vina's finest characteristics," he said. "She never at any stage abandoned her damaged sister."

"*Sister?*"

"What, isn't that known? How amazing! They're twins. The family is a very old one, and apparently much intermarried. Davina told me that in an effort to counteract the intermarriage her great-grandparents and grandparents and their siblings had contracted some peculiar unions—Chinese, Negro, you name it."

"None of this is known in Connecticut, even, I suspect, to her husband and his family," Abe said.

"With Davina, who knows?" Preston said. "She was the senior twin, and perfect. Uda was born looking strange, though it's purely her looks. Her mind is as good as Vina's, I reckon."

Tony Cerutti had been deputed to return the immigration official to his home, but instead of lunch at Malvolio's, he had to chew on a vicious lecture from Carmine.

"Dumb, Tony, downright, outright, unbelievably dumb! The man's a very senior member of a much bigger organization than the Holloman PD, and he gave up his day to come give us desperately needed information about two suspects in murder. And what do you do? Make him feel like a suspect with tactless questions! I swear I'm tempted to throw you back into uniform, Tony, if over a year in Detectives hasn't honed your sensibilities better than this. You still get to drive him home, but God help you if you say one word out of line! I want him back in front of his TV feeling like he had a good day out. Now go away and bury yourself somewhere I can't see you!"

After which, naturally, he had to hear the same lecture from Abe Goldberg, a sharper cut because from a kinder instrument.

Carmine raised a brow at Liam and Abe. "What sort of sister obeys a snap of the fingers?" he asked.

Liam grinned. "No kind my family ever heard of. If Sheila snapped her fingers at Pauline, you'd hear the fight in Stamford, Hartford and New London."

"My sisters too. I suppose looking brain-damaged would affect how a sisterly relationship functioned, but Davina, I gather, really does treat Uda with contempt. Or maybe," Carmine went on in a musing voice, "it's all an act for our benefit."

"And the benefit of the Tunbulls, who really do believe Uda's some kind of slave," said Abe, equally thoughtful. "We have to look at that pair as a pair more closely, Carmine."

"Who do we put on it?"

"Delia," said Liam instantly.

"Delia," said Abe, turning it into a chorus.

"My feeling entirely. Delia, tomorrow morning. Pity she wasn't here to meet Mr. Preston."

Later that afternoon Carmine called a meeting in his office; the only one not present (apart from Nick) was the disgraced Tony, driving Q. V. Preston back to Queens. The news of his fall from grace had already spread out of the PD and into City Planning, Welfare, and a dozen other inhabitants of the County Services warren. No one ever knew how it happened; it just—did.

"We've hit the doldrums," Carmine said, "in a case that's going to be built on circumstantial evidence. Lucky for us that the other crimes needing our attention have been simple, with straight, hard evidence and witnesses. But this one is a swamp, not any place with a current. The pool of suspects is small and the motives are obvious. John Hall was killed because he knew something about someone concerned in the Chubb University Press publication of books, possibly the book known as *A Helical God*. Dr. Tinkerman was killed to remove him from his position as Head Scholar of C.U.P. Again, the book *A Helical God* springs to mind. However, we ought not to focus on this work as a given. It may be a blind, a red herring. The motive for both murders may lie in personal relationships having nothing to do with books as books." He took a turn about his office, scowling slightly.

"The Tunbulls are the key. Whoever was present at Davina's dinner is suspect for John's murder, which evidence suggests can't have been committed by an outside agency of any kind. And all those suspects were present at the banquet where Tinkerman died."

He wrote on his blackboard: *"James and Millicent Hunter. Max and Davina Tunbull. Val Tunbull. Ivan Tunbull.* And, let us not forget—*Uda Savovich.* Who wasn't at the banquet."

Down went the chalk. "That's it. One of those people did double murder. On first glance I am inclined to dismiss Dr. James Hunter because the apparatus we found was too small for the size of his hand and fingers. However, a second glance reveals that the device could have been a deliberate plant by Hunter, who has another that fits his hand comfortably."

He returned to the board after a quick stroll. "Paul's report is in. The device Donny found has never held a drop of tetrodotoxin. Which leaves us in a cleft stick—was this the way the killer delivered his poison, or did he use something else? We may never know. Abe, what do you have?"

Abe stood up, face placid. "The influence of Davina on the Tunbull family is pronounced," he said. "Decisions have been made that would never have been made had Davina not pushed. In the main, the twenty-thousand print run of *A Helical God* that C.U.P. didn't authorize. Davina's reason? That it would cement Dr. Jim's chosen title, to which Tinkerman was opposed. He was all for *Nucleic Acids*—not a title to attract a bookstore browser. If the gossip is true, Tinkerman considered Dr. Jim's book an affront to God, and was determined that the title should omit all reference to the Creator. His policy—and, stemming out of that, C.U.P.'s policy—was to decry the book scholastically and ensure that it failed as a popular success. So I guess I'm harping on the book as a reason for murder."

Delia huffed. "According to Davina, the print run was no risk at all. Uda had prognosticated Tinkerman's future, which was to die at the banquet. Davina believed Uda's vision implicitly—Tinkerman was going to die. Which is not the same thing as saying Davina—or Uda—killed him. Though I confess, boss, that the phenomenon of the unauthorized print run baffles me."

"Me too," said Buzz. "I mean, Max has been associated with C.U.P. for over twenty years. He's sophisticated as well as a shrewd businessman. So why *did* he do that?"

"I suspect there are answers, but that we haven't located the right oracle yet," Carmine said, smiling. "The man who can give us the answers is the old Head Scholar, Don Carter, who's on my list of interviewees. In the meantime, I suggest you all just take the print run as more logical than it seems."

"Okay," said Buzz, and grinned wickedly. "Here's another question, Carmine: Tinkerman's pals the Parsons were influential enough to push M.M. into doing as he was told: why not put M.M.'s name on your board as a suspect?"

"I agree he *should* be a suspect, Buzz," Carmine said with heavy irony, "but I for one do not have the intestinal fortitude to write *Mawson MacIntosh* on this blackboard. M.M. is quite capable of murder in defense of his beloved university, but his speciality is assassination—of your character first, and if that doesn't work, of your very soul. Luckily he's on the side of the angels, and his victims are always straight from hell."

Buzz winced, lifted his hands in surrender.

Abe spoke. I may be off the subject, folks, but has anyone seen Max and Davina's baby? The famous Alexis?"

A question greeted by blank silence until Delia answered. "I haven't, and I imagine that means none of you has. What do you suspect, Abe? I'm intrigued."

"I guess I started out by wondering if there were something wrong with the baby. Then I progressed to wondering if there was a baby at all. I've had a couple chats with Emily Tunbull—a nasty piece of work, that one!—and she alerted me when she said *she* had never really seen Alexis, just a bundle so wrapped up it could have contained a doll," said Abe. "Her theory is that Alexis is a figment of Davina's imagination and does not really exist. Emily believes Davina's tricked the family with Max's connivance. Emily's passion is her own son, Ivan, whom the arrival of Alexis dispossessed."

"Aren't families interesting?" Delia asked. "What any outsider sees is only what the family intends shall be seen."

"I'm glad you feel that way, Delia," Carmine said, "because you are going to examine the existing parameters of the Tunbull family, armed with what we now know about Davina and Uda. Talk to Emily. And demand to see the unswaddled baby." He threw his head back and laughed. "I'd love to go to His Honor the Judge and ask for a warrant to produce an unswaddled baby!"

"He's just persnickety enough to give you one," said Abe.

Prunella, still in residence with her parents, had taken Julian and Alex for the day and night to give Desdemona a rare chance to be alone all evening with her husband. Carmine's experience of weekdays had led him to pick Wednesday as his treat, on the theory that if it went as Wednesdays usually did, he would be home early. And he was right; the tetrodotoxin murders had indeed foundered, and he was through the door by five.

"How lovely," said Desdemona, smiling as her eyes rested on him in his chair, free of a child, yes, but hampered by Winston, a big, fat, orange cat. "I admit that the pets are worse for you, as they crave to sit in your lap, but Frankie makes such a wonderful foot rest." She rolled her bare heels and ankles across Frankie's side, an activity that produced the dog's awesome groans.

"Family life is always different from the life of lovers." He sipped his drink, knowing he had the leisure to make it last and still have another couple of weakies before dinner. So he asked: "What's for dinner?"

"One of your favorites. Saltimbocca alla Romana, with ziti in a plain tomato sauce on the side, and a green salad with walnut oil vinaigrette. After that, a deliciously smelly, runny cheese that cost a bomb."

"I have died and gone to heaven."

"Tell me about the case."

He did so through that drink and the next; she listened intently, frowning occasionally. At the end she got him a third drink, then sighed. "Poor Millie," she said obscurely.

"Why single her out, lovely lady?"

"She was so terribly young when she made her decision, and she's far too stiff-necked ever to renege on it. Fifteen! The last of the gilt would have worn off the gingerbread by her mid-twenties, by which time all her friends from high school would have been married at least once, had a couple of children, and spent much of their time moaning over furniture Millie would have deemed palatial. What did Millie have, in her mid-twenties? A selfishly genius husband whose color had given her endless pain, a series of vile apartments full of Good Will furniture, a shared old car, hardly a dime in her purse, and not the faintest echo of children's laughter—or tears."

"Put like that, given her background, you paint a terrible picture, Desdemona."

"Think of her in California! She wouldn't have been human if she hadn't hankered for a better life, and California was the time she saw the pattern of her life unfolded beyond a shadow of a doubt. John Hall could not have appeared at a moment better suited for his purposes than sheer accident dictated—a very sad and disillusioned Millie, ripe for his attentions. Did she know the pearls were real, the rhinestones diamonds? It hardly matters. The important thing was that this personable, charming man noticed *her*, gave his gifts to *her*. Millie is terribly clever, but the biochemistry was a way to hew to Jim, a guarantee that they'd always have table and pillow talk when prosperity arrived. She had thought it would well before he earned his doctorate. In California she finally understood that it never would arrive at all."

Carmine stopped stroking Winston's head. "I'm getting out of my depth," he said, brow wrinkling.

"Jim puts their money into his work," Desdemona said, on her way to the kitchen.

Carmine tipped an outraged Winston onto the floor and followed her with a detour to the sink to wash his hands before he slid into the booth. "He can't do that," he said.

"Whether he can or not, he does. Jim sees some new piece of apparatus he can't afford, and fiddles the books to buy it with his living money, or for her lab with her living money. It never occurs to Jim that in stripping both their grants bare, he denies Millie the dignity of her position." Desdemona busied herself at the stove. "When finally they became salaried faculty here at Chubb, Millie was thirty. Now here she is, pushing thirty-three, living out on State Street. *Chubb faculty living out on State Street?* Come, Carmine! Everyone knows the really great universities pay in prestige, but they're not on subsistence money. I mean, how can a man who possesses a whole floor of the Burke Biology Tower be living on a pittance? M.M. knows he's a potential Nobel laureate, so I'd be willing to bet that Jim's pretty well paid. Paying off student loans? They should have done that some time ago—including the sinus reconstruction money from John Hall, which I gather John never honestly expected to see paid back. No, Jim ploughs it all into his work with blind compulsion. I'd feel more sympathy toward that sort of drive were it not for the fact that Jim plunders his wife's salary and grant money as if they were his own." Desdemona struck her hands together. "Grr!"

"How come you see all this when no one else seems to?"

The meal was in the pan, the ziti sauce was stirred, the pasta boiling: she blinked. "I ran a very large research unit, Carmine. I know all about researchers."

"You make me want to despise Jim Hunter, and that's a brand new feeling."

The salad was picked over, the jar that held Desdemona's homemade vinaigrette shaken vigorously. "You mustn't despise Jim, honestly. The answer doesn't lie with him—it never did, and it never will. Millie has to put a stop to it, that simple. She just has to say, 'No, Jim, my money is mine, my equipment is mine, and I want a comfortable life. That means you give me some of your money for a change so I can make a nest and have my babies.' She's never said it because she thinks he'll leave her—what a load of old codswallop! Jim Hunter could no more leave Millie than the Moon could abandon the Earth."

Head spinning, Carmine laid out knives, forks, the French sauce spoons Desdemona insisted upon for scooping up the last liquid on a plate. "A shiraz?" he asked.

"That nice light Chilean one." She was getting ready to serve.

"Don't dump on Jim, he's a special case," she said. "As a man, he has no idea what women are, or what they need. He's only ever known one woman—Millie. Who turned herself into a doormat for him—*at fifteen!* How can he possibly know that she isn't really a doormat? She's given him no clues."

The bowls of ziti and sauce had appeared, the salad bowl and two empty china bowls in which to place helpings; then came the plates beautifully arranged with the saltimbocca. Carmine picked up his knife and fork. "Well, all I can say, my most glorious Desdemona, is that there's something radically wrong with a man who doesn't let his wife make a nest—and learn to cook like a Cordon Bleu graduate. Even that fool cat is a part of the home you've made for me and our sons. And don't think I haven't tumbled to the fact that you think it does my blood pressure good to stroke twenty-two pounds of Winston."

"Well, it does so too do you good," she countered, sitting down and sniffing. "Oh, it *does* smell good! Tuck in, Carmine."

He obeyed orders and tucked in, but after they had made a gooey mess of the runny, smelly cheese and retired to the living room with a pot of tea, his mind returned to what Desdemona had said about Millie Hunter. Frustrated as well as unhappy, and beginning perhaps to think that even if there were a best seller, all Jim's royalties would be invested in his research, leaving nothing for Millie or the children Desdemona said she longed to have.

PART TWO

From
THURSDAY, JANUARY 9, 1969
until
FRIDAY, JANUARY 17, 1969

THURSDAY, JANUARY 9, 1969

When Delia beat on Emily Tunbull's door with the brass knocker she preferred to Beethoven's fifth, no one answered. How odd! Emily was the reclusive among the Tunbull women, she had been led to believe, and her smart new Cadillac Seville was parked in the garage, its door up as if she had intended driving off, but had been diverted. After five more fruitless minutes, Delia walked around the back; some crazy women, she was aware, hung their washing out on lines to freeze rather than use a dryer. But no Emily Tunbull was pinning out wet clothes to freeze.

The house was a nice one, and a peek through a window revealed a nice interior, safely beige, with classy pieces of furniture. Tunbull Printing obviously did well enough to support all its owners in considerable style. The backyard was a tidy one, partitioned off with a chain link fence, though one side and behind were vacant lots; Ivan and Lily's equally nice house lay on the other boundary, where the fence contained a gate. Sure enough, the backyard did contain a clothesline—and two sheds besides, but their doors were padlocked; the far shed looked substantial, perhaps even lined.

Delia gave up and walked down Hampton Street to the house on the knoll, where Uda opened the door.

"Is Mrs. Tunbull home?" Delia asked, face serious.

"Wait. I see."

Cooling her heels on the stoop didn't last long; Uda came back and held the door wide. "In," she said.

"I imagine," said Delia to the walls, "you understand all the nuances of the English language, Uda. You just don't show it."

Davina was in the living room, fully clad in a violet pantsuit and matching Italian flatties—the matriarch at home?

"Sergeant Carstairs," she said. "Coffee?"

"Thank you, no." Delia found a chair that was low enough to permit her to rest her feet on the carpet; Davina was quite tall and Max a tall man, so it was a Delmonico kind of house in that respect. "Mrs. Tunbull, why do you treat your twin sister like the vilest of servants?"

The blue eyes swung to her face, arrested, then their lids fell— her usual evasive trick. "I see. You have been talking to Mr. Quinn Preston."

"Yes. In actual fact he gave the pair of you a glowing report, so you've no need to worry on the immigration front."

"I certainly do not! Uda and I are American citizens!"

"Pursuant to Uda, why do you treat her so abominably?"

"That is insulting!"

"Not as insulting to you as your treatment of her is insulting to Uda."

A snap of the fingers saw Uda turn to go.

"Kindly stay, Miss Savovich!" Delia said, voice commanding.

"This is *my* house!" Davina snapped.

"This is *my* murder investigation, ma'am. If its consequences are inconvenient to you, I am sorry for it, but that cannot alter your obligation to answer my questions. Why do you treat your twin sister like the vilest of servants?"

"That is how families work in my country," Davina said with a pout. "Uda was born defective. I have cared for her as she cannot care for herself. She has a comfortable bed in a most luxurious apartment of her own, and all the good food she can eat. I am the family breadwinner. Uda takes her bread from me. My price is her labor and her obedience."

"How do you feel about this one-sided contract, Uda?"

"I am happy. I like work. I care for this house, I care for Vina," said Uda, accent still thick, but grammar somewhat improved. "I am necessary, Sergeant Carstairs. Without me, my Vina could not manage."

"Ah!" Delia exclaimed. "Then you appreciate power."

"Doesn't everyone?" Davina asked.

"Of course. However, using it wisely is another matter. Would you say, Mrs. Tunbull, that you took a terrific risk in persuading Mr. Max Tunbull to print twenty thousand copies of *A Helical God* before that was authorized by C.U.P.?"

"Pah!" spat Davina, as if people's denseness amazed her. "I have already said that I knew Thomas Tinkerman would die at the C.U.P. banquet—where was the risk?"

"You incriminate yourself out of your own mouth."

"Nonsense!" Davina said. "I believe in Uda's gifts from long acquaintance with them. When she gazes into the water bowl she is never wrong. And you cannot prove I killed Tinkerman because I did not. I went nowhere near him that night."

Time to change the subject, thought Delia. "I have another request, Mrs. Tunbull. I want to see your baby."

That transfixed both of them. Davina, tracing the patterns on the arm of her chair, dug into it so suddenly that Delia heard the nails break. Uda, hands on the back of Davina's chair, lost color and clenched the fabric fiercely.

"I am sorry, that is impossible," Davina said, staring at her ruined nails in exasperation.

"Why?"

"Because I do not choose to show him to you."

"Then, ma'am, I will be back with a warrant—after I've posted police guards to make sure you don't remove the child."

"You cannot! This is America!"

"I can—and I will." Delia slid off the chair and stood in all the glory of her purple pantsuit, its orange blouse, the long, bright pink scarf dangling on either side of her head. "Come, Mrs. Tunbull, show me this baby everyone hears so much about, yet no one ever sees. This morning we are private. If I return with a warrant I will be accompanied by two male police witnesses. It will be a circus. Show Alexis to me now, and it remains among the three of us."

The Savovich sisters said nothing for a moment; then Davina sighed. "Very well, Sergeant. I will bring Alexis."

The news was too urgent and vital to trust to the police radio, and Delia didn't feel like finding an unvandalized phone booth to call Carmine in advance; she simply radioed that she was on her way back to County Services, and needed to see the Captain.

Delia bursting with news, Carmine thought as she skittled in like a crab discovering the joys of forward locomotion, was one of the greater pleasures his police work afforded.

"You look like Pandora bearing her box," he said.

"I feel more like Mauna Loa on the verge of an eruption," she said with a squeak in her voice.

"Then hit me with your lava, Deels."

"There is a baby, and he's absolutely gorgeous," Delia said. "One of the loveliest children I've ever seen. I would have to say, though, that the greatest factor contributing to his beauty is the color of his skin. He's black."

A pin dropping would have sounded like a minor explosion. Jaw sagging, Carmine gaped at her for what seemed a very long time before he shut his mouth and looked himself.

"Black," he said then. "How black, Deels?"

"Medium. Not black black, but darker than café au lait." She stopped, took a breath, and dropped the real bombshell. "His eyes are green, the exact color of You-know-whose."

Carmine felt the hairs stand up on his neck. "Jesus!"

"I had to ask her, of course."

"What did she say? What could she say?"

"Denied it absolutely. Confessed that there was black blood in her own family—a pair of great-grandparents and a grand-parent, father of her father. Her grandfather wasn't a full blood, she said, but he was

African to look at. Except for his red hair and his green eyes." Delia flopped onto a chair.

"And what does Max Tunbull say? Did you get onto that, or did the Savovich ladies dry up?"

"Dry up? Anything but! Once I had Alexis on my knee, they seemed relieved someone else was in on the secret. Apparently Max is so besotted he'd believe anything Davina told him, including the negro family history. That Jim Hunter could be the father has never even crosssed Max's mind, Davina swears. I confess I am inclined to believe her. She bewitches men, that woman."

"Did she mention Jim Hunter?"

"No. Just blamed the world for its dirty mind when her baby came out that color. Of course the eyes are only just a known fact— it takes time for babies to color their irises. So for Davina the green eyes are a very recent worry. Instinct prompted her to hide the baby for as long as she could. Emily snipes at her, but Davina holds firm." Delia propped her chin on her hands. "It is a damnable situation for a woman, I see that. Whether Jim Hunter is the father or the unprovable negroid family history is true, for a white woman to produce a black baby is—oh, dreadful! Davina has enemies, even among the Tunbulls. She knows the day of revelation must come, but she hoped to postpone it until after Jim Hunter's book is a big seller, and the Hunters have moved away from her a little."

"Does Jim Hunter know there's a black baby?"

"No. Nor does Millie. The only ones who know are Max and the Savovich twins—and me now, of course. I told her that I'd try to keep her secret," Delia said. "I actually felt sorry for her, Carmine! What if the family history's true?"

"It shifts the epicenter of this business," Carmine said, pacing up and down. "However, for the moment I think you and I will keep Davina's secret. True or not, everyone will infer Jim. Millie would be devastated, although she'd insist the black family history was fact. That attitude wouldn't save her from malice and speculation from workplace to the O'Donnells. Besides, how does the negro look skip generations? I thought the gene was dominant, that it overwhelmed the caucasian gene."

"As time goes on, that gets less cut and dried," Delia said. "In Mendel's time the laws of inheritance were ironclad, now they're not. Ask Jim Hunter—biochemistry's his field."

"But people are not educated in modern ideas on it."

"Precisely."

"Oh, Deels, this is terrible! Let's say the father *is* Jim Hunter—when could it have happened?"

"Alexis was born at full term on October fourteen, which would put his conception around the New Year of 1968," Delia said. "From August of 1967 until that Christmas, Jim wrote *A Helical God* as well as bore his full research load, coming to its fruition right about then into the bargain. He wouldn't have had a second to devote to a love affair, especially with Davina. Whereas she would have been among the very first to see the finished manuscript, given Max's submission to her. A very small window indeed, Carmine, around a year ago."

"Of course he'd known Davina from earlier books."

"Yes, why is that?" Delia asked. "Working in Chicago, yet published by Chubb."

"Max Tunbull should be able to answer that," Carmine said.

"Or the old Head Scholar. What a pickle!" cried Delia.

I need a walk, said Carmine to himself, shrugging into his down jacket and making sure his gloves were in a pocket. Then it was down to the cobbled yard between the vast twenty-year-old County Services building and the old annex containing the cells.

Sheltered from the worst of the wind, Carmine yanked the hood over his head and began the familiar trek every tormenting case seemed to provoke. Up and down, around the perimeter, then two diagonals before starting again. Whom would he meet today? He always met some other tormented soul.

Today, Fernando Vasquez, having a hard time adjusting to a Connecticut winter after years of Florida.

"You look like Scott of the Antarctic," Fernando said.

"Thanks a million for comparing me to the guy who didn't make it," Carmine said stiffly.

"Yeah, but he did it the hard way. Amundsen had dog sleds and more dog sleds and all that Scandinavian know-how. Scott was an Englishman, doing it on a shoestring, walking to the Pole. I mean, it almost feels like Amundsen was *cheating*."

"You're not a Spanish grandee! You're a British bootstrapper. Who's been indoctrinating you? Are you and Desdemona *cheating* on me? In a dog sled? 'Mush, Fernando, mush!'"

Their steps went well together; they strode in silence then for several complete rounds, smiling.

"How's the uniformed division going?"

"Slow but steady. They're getting used to the forms and the reports, especially after I brought in that hotshot lawyer Anthony Dora to give them a seminar on police roles in evidence as well as demystifying courtroom procedures. He's impressive. They tended to believe him whereas they had ceased to believe me—new broom's bristles worn to stubble and all that shit."

"We got you just in time, Fernando. How are the loots?"

Vasquez threw his handsome head back and laughed. "Great! Especially Corey. He has a feel for the work."

"More than he ever did for my kind of looting. But he's not your favorite, is he?"

"With Maureen for a wife? Shades of Torquemada! No, the one I lean on is Virgil Simms."

"Makes sense. Speaking of him and certain events, have you heard how Helen MacIntosh is going?" Carmine asked.

"Gun happy as ever. She's leaving her Manhattan precinct for the greener pastures of Nashville."

"Whom did she kill?"

"Four hoods in three separate incidents. Came out squeaky clean from the internal enquiries, but her colleagues were beginning to step ten paces around her and even then worry if it were far enough to avoid stray bullets."

"Good luck, Nashville." Carmine smiled reminiscently. "She won't last long any place. Gun happy."

Delia returned to Hampton Street, determined to see Emily Tunbull. Another tattoo on the knocker produced no result, but the garage door was still up and the Seville sitting waiting. She had to be at home, and she wasn't over at Lily Tunbull's because their cars were both absent and the house silent. Had she perhaps gone out with Lily and the kids? Not, Delia was convinced, without first closing the garage door. It worked on a remote, no effort involved. No, something was *wrong*.

Back to the yard, still deserted. Nothing had changed; no one had visited it and left evidence of that visit. Delia peered in every downstairs window—no Emily, even sleeping in a chair or on a couch. That established, she threw pebbles at the upstairs windows, to no effect. Back to the yard.

Two sheds. One was probably to hold wood, the other perhaps for some hobby of Val's; it was difficult to think of Emily as having a hobby requiring a shed. Neither padlock was a serious challenge for a police detective; Delia picked the one closest to the house first, to find wood of the kind used in fires for visual pleasure rather than actual heating. The second padlock snapped open with equal ease; Delia unhooked it and opened the door.

The poor woman had suffered terribly. Her clothes had been ripped off by her own fevered hands, probably in an effort to sop up some of the frightful mess she was making, couldn't stem or control. The confined place reeked of vomitus and feces, strewn around as Emily flailed, then convulsed. Her naked body was twisted into a huddle that presented the viewer with her buttocks and perineum, her legs apart continuing the view as far as the mons, all covered in mess. Her upper torso was splashed and smeared with vomitus where the left side had lifted away from the concrete, yet her face looked as if a gigantic hand had squashed it into the ground. The agony written on it was horrifying; Delia leaned against the shed wall and wept in a combination of shock and outraged pity. No one deserved to be seen in death like this! It was appalling, it was inhuman, it was—Delia sobbed.

As soon as she could move she closed the door and put the padlock back in place, then went to the back door—a credit card did the job. Inside, she sat on a chair and pulled a phone on the countertop toward her.

"Carmine? It's Delia. I've found Emily Tunbull . . . I want personnel who really respect bodies—" She sobbed again. "—no, I insist on it! The poor woman is desecrated, I've never seen anything like it. I don't want her family or any fool setting eyes on her until she's been tended to, is that clear?" And she hung up without another word, without waiting for Carmine to answer her or give her directives.

He came himself, siren shrieking, Paul Bachman and Gus Fennell not far behind.

"Delia, what on earth's the matter?" he asked, coming into the kitchen. "Is she inside? Paul and Gus need to know."

"She's in the far shed. Pick the padlock, it's easy. Then look." Delia tried to repair run mascara, broke down again. "Oh, Carmine, it is *awful!* Tell Paul and Gus that the photographs are to be sequestered."

Carmine disappeared, came back shortly after, white-faced. "I can see why you're so upset. It's unconscionable! Don't worry, Paul and Gus are there, everything will be okay, that's a promise." He went into the living room, returned with an unopened bottle. "Here, drink this," he said, giving her a cognac from the bottle. "Go on, drink it, Deels, please."

She obeyed; a little color returned to her face after she retched, fought, kept her gorge down. "I will never forget it," she said then. "Carmine, I beg you, light a candle for me that I don't die that way! Every shred of dignity gone—awful, awful! I'll never forget it! What happened to her?"

"Tetrodotoxin by mouth is my guess," he said, chafing her hands. "Much worse than strychnine, even."

"Light a candle!" she insisted.

"I'll light a hundred. So will Uncle John. But we have a secret weapon—Mrs. Tesoriero. We'll get her on the job as well, Delia. It won't happen to you, I guarantee."

She started to cry again. Carmine let her, then ordered that she be driven home. She would be all right, he knew, but with her make-up smeared all over her face, she was not fit for public exhibition.

Abe was there when he got back to the shed.

It turned out that Emily had pursued a hobby after all. The shed belonged to her, and contained the paraphernalia of a sculptor. Her medium was ceramic clay, and examples of her work stood on shelves: portrait busts, horse's heads, cats in various poses. The walls were lined; light came from the roof, of transparent plastic, and air from a ventilator at the top of two opposite walls. No one could see in, which led Abe to wonder how many people knew of her hobby.

"No one's mentioned it to me," Abe said, "including her."

"She's aiming to sell the pieces to gift shops once she's glazed and fired them," Carmine said, "and she was disliked in the family. I think she was waiting to shock them, take some of the wind out of Davina's sails."

The portrait busts were probably not for eventual sale, and per-haps would never be fired, but they showed a talent the other pieces didn't. Emily could suggest character in her potraits, as in the bust of Max—a tired old man trying to be young. And, had Millie Hunter only set eyes on it, she would have agreed with Emily's interpretation of Davina: Medusa, down to the last snake on her head.

The body had been removed, but the mess that hadn't stuck to Emily was still there, and a faint suggestion of putrefaction.

"Did Gus say how long she'd been dead?" Carmine asked.

"The best part of twenty-four hours," Abe answered. "He thought yesterday afternoon, some time after four."

"No food in here?"

146

"None. Just a carafe of water and a glass. Paul took both of them," said Abe. "I hear Delia was upset?"

"Very. The obscenity of the act really got to her."

Abe looked slightly displeased. "I wish Gus hadn't moved the body before I got here," he said.

"At my orders, Abe. I saw it, and it couldn't have told you a thing beyond obscenity. The poor creature had torn off all her clothes during her agony, and died twisted into a pretzel. Delia asked that no one should see, and I obliged her. You'll get the photos, but keep them to yourself. Liam and Tony don't need to see them. It's a female thing, and I respect it."

"Fine by me." Abe had turned to go when his eye lit upon a small box sitting on a shelf between a curled up cat and a cat with its paws tucked under. He picked his way across the soiled floor and took the box down. "Funny place for it," he said, opening it, then holding up its contents: a home-made glass ampoule containing about as much white powder as would thinly cover a dime. Even gloved, his grasp was delicate; then he put it back in the box and put the box back on the shelf. "I have to wait for Paul," he said.

"Padlock the shed and put a uniform on guard, Abe. We need to go through the kitchen before the husband gets home."

Val Tunbull arrived escorted by a squad car; he had not been told of Emily's fate, just that his presence was required at home.

Abe met him at the front door and escorted him into his own living room; the kitchen was a hive of activity, and they dared not offer coffee or tea. An unopened bottle of bourbon stood on the bar cart; that would have to do when the time came.

A man in his middle fifties, Val Tunbull had a pleasant, open and good looking face crowned by a mass of brassy yellow hair Abe and Carmine had come to associate with the Tunbull men.

"What's up?" he asked, puzzled, but without aggression; he was the second-string man in a family business, and it wasn't his place to bluster or bully.

The news of his wife's death visibly shook him, but he refused the liquor. "Tea, I'd like some tea," he said, tears rolling down his face.

Abe made up his mind. "I'm very sorry, Mr. Tunbull," he said, "but we've had to confiscate every kind of food and drink in your house. Your wife was poisoned, and we don't know where she got the poison. Is your son home?"

"Yes. When the cops came for me, he followed."

"Then how about you and I walk to your son's house? You can have your tea there, and company as well."

Val Tunbull rose at once. "Yes, please. I have to tell Ivan—it will break his heart."

Abe guided him out the front door. "Did your wife have any enemies, sir?" he asked, putting a hand beneath Val's elbow.

Val's footsteps faltered; he leaned on Abe a moment. "I guess so. She—she hated Max's first wife, Martita, and that led to big trouble." He stopped, wiped his eyes, blew his nose. "Max found it hard to forgive her, but it's such an old business now that I can't see how it figures. Emily disliked Davina too, but Davina put her in her place. Martita could never have done that. That's why I didn't worry about Emily's campaign against Davina. She's a tough cookie." He was talking fluently, as if much of this had been bottled up for want of a willing ear to listen. "And Emily had discovered sculpting in clay— she loved it, just loved it! I thought some of her work was great, and I encouraged her. She'd be out in her shed day and night—I had it lined, made real comfortable—having a ball—she was so happy at last." He cried desolately.

Abe compelled him to stop walking until he had composed himself; they continued slowly.

"Did your wife ever say anything about the poisoner?"

"She told me she knew who it was, but honest, Lieutenant, I didn't believe her. Telling those kind of whoppers was Emily's besetting sin—she loved to stir people, you know? But I'm sure she was making it all up. Truth is, Emily would have loved to be like Davina—pushy, glamorous, smart as new paint."

"Did she say anything specific? Mention a name?"

"You're missing my point, Lieutenant. She never did say anything convincing. This time she said she knew where the poison stash was—stash? No, I think that's my word for it. Emily said hoard, I think. Anyway, you know what I mean."

"I do."

"But I couldn't get anything more out of him," Abe said to Carmine a few minutes later. "We *know* she had one ampoule of it, but that's not a stash. The poisoner has at least three ampoules left, maybe more, if he saved what he didn't use when he took his injection doses."

"Whatever," Carmine said, "we're not going to find any tetrodotoxin in Emily's kitchen, are we?"

"No, we're not. My guess? It was in the water carafe."

A conclusion also reached by Gus Fennell.

"There was nothing left in her stomach at all," he said to Carmine and Abe. "Her vomiting was so intense that the samples of vomitus we scraped up contained intestinal matter as well. Tetrodotoxin was present, but the nature of the food was impossible to determine beyond the fact that it was soft, quickly digested and non-fatty in nature. The one item we could reconstruct was some bread wrapped around a kind of curry filling, but that held no poison at all. I'm guessing her water from the carafe."

"Does it have a taste?" Abe asked, curious.

"Who knows? Want to try it?" Gus asked.

"No, thanks!"

"Did you manage to make her presentable, Gus?" Carmine asked.

The nondescript face fell. "No. Once rigor passed off I was able to straighten her out and arrange her body decently, but the face is marred. Her husband will have to identify her, but it's a closed casket funeral, can't be otherwise."

"Time of death?"

"Between four and six p.m. yesterday."

"Val Tunbull did say she worked day and night in her shed, but he didn't mention that she wasn't home at all last night."

"I think Emily's hobby has enabled her to get out of domestic or connubial duties she no longer feels much enthusiasm for," Carmine said. "There was a very comfortable couch in her shed, and a good heater. My guess is that Val didn't mention her absence because it's a regular occurrence. Any bets he eats a lot of meals at his son and daughter-in-law's next door?"

Paul came into Gus's office. "Want the news about the ampoule?" he asked, dark face inscrutable.

"Why not?" Carmine asked.

"Flea powder. No tetrodotoxin whatsoever."

"Shit!" from Carmine.

"Any prints?" from Abe.

"Only Emily's. I think we've been handed a genuine red herring," Paul said.

"More to the point, so was Emily handed a red herring," Carmine said on a Bronx cheer. "It takes a lot of gall to play with a potential victim before doing the deed. Abe, what next?"

"Depends. Did you break the ampoule, Paul?"

"No. I drilled a hole in its bottom and emptied it that way. The actual gizmo is otherwise intact." Paul pulled a face. "All I will add is that whoever made it is a total amateur."

"I'm taking it to Millie Hunter," Abe said. "She ought to have a few illuminating things to say."

Abe found her in her laboratory, though it was surely time, he thought, for a married woman to be heading home to fix dinner. But not in the Hunter household, he divined; that was a domicile run on TV dinners that they burned because they forgot what hour they'd put them in the oven.

She worked in an inside room ten feet by eight feet—a cross between a lab and a cupboard, given the wealth of shelving on its walls. The floor was cluttered with nineteen-inch racks holding electronic equipment, cables had been taped down to prevent being tripped over, and a tiny sink with a swan-neck faucet seemed to be her only source of water apart from carboys marked "Distilled" or "Deion-ized." She did her procedures on a stainless steel cart meticulously covered in linen savers, had a small but adequate autoclave on a shelf, and, in a gap, a refrigerator/freezer that bore a steel flap and a padlock.

The room was very well lit by banks of fluorescent tubes under diffusers in the ceiling; Bach was playing from another shelf, where a cheap tape recorder cum radio sat. Everything was as neat as a pin, Abe thought as his eyes roamed around; his tidy soul applauded the kind of person who could fit so much into so little. This room's owner was one highly organized and obsessive person. It took one to know one.

"I wish I could say it's great to see you, Abe," Millie said, perch-ing on the room's only chair, a high stool with a padded seat that revolved.

Abe stood in a vacant space, elbows tucked in. "I know, Millie, and I echo that. Can't they find you a bigger lab? This is more over-crowded than a Sing Sing cell."

"Not an important enough fish," she said cheerfully. "I'll never win the Nobel Prize, but I will contribute some tiny scrap of knowl-edge about the functioning of the central nervous system, kind of like a missing piece of blue sky in a jigsaw of blue sky. It's Jim's work is ground-breaking, which is why he has a whole floor of the Burke to himself these days."

"Well, I think you're wonderful to cope with this."

"And I think you're wonderful to say that." Her lovely face so-bered. "What can I do you for, Abe?"

He produced a box and unearthed the ampoule. "Did you make this, Millie? No, it's not dangerous. It held flea powder."

She took the ampoule curiously, shaking her head even as she did so. "No, this isn't my work. Too crappy, and I'd go farther by saying it wasn't made by anyone who can heat glass well under lab conditions. I mean, we're always heating and bending glass. Whoever made this sawed two standard test tubes in half, put his—flea powder?—oh, I like that!—in the bottom one, held it upright in a clamp, heated the top rim, heated the rim of the other one, and just fused them together while they were gloppy. There's no way he aspirated the air to get a vacuum inside. I made mine from two different sizes of thin-walled glass tubing, and by the time I finished with them, I had something that looked pretty professional," said Millie.

"If he heated the top rim with the powder in the tube's bottom, wouldn't the powder be affected?"

"No. Glass is a very poor conductor of heat."

"Any idea who made this one?"

"No idea at all, except it wasn't a lab technician. I'd fire anyone who couldn't do better than this a month into the job training."

"Any idea why he picked flea powder?"

"I'd say it means he's seen tetrodotoxin. The color and the consistency are closer than, say, talcum or icing sugar."

"Thanks, Millie." Abe took the ampoule from her, put it back in its box and slipped the box in his pocket. "What time do you go home, honey?"

"I'm closing down here right now, as a matter of fact, but then I'll go up to Jim's floor and see if he needs help."

Abe walked back to his car through the cold dark evening, aware of a lump in his throat. Were Jim and Millie ever going to make a *home?* Or perhaps, he thought, fair man that he was, they already have all the home they want or need—a laboratory. But that's poor comfort in old age.

An unhappy day for Delia, who, upon arriving home, ran a bath and stayed in it until she was as wrinkled as any prune. No scrap of make-up or mascara was left on her face, her wet hair was slicked against her skull, and she lay understanding the bliss of being rocked in a cradle of amniotic fluid. One of those lucky creatures with positive buoyancy who couldn't sink, toward the end of her immersion she dozed, and the sleep did its healing thing. When she awoke she was able to get out of her bath, wrap herself in an old checkered dressing gown and fluffy slippers, and actually think of food. The sight of

Emily Tunbull had been buried in her cerebral sludge, to reappear only in death that came in the same guise—and in nightmares.

She unearthed four proper British bangers from her freezer and put them in her warming oven to thaw: no hurry. If there were (few) things about England she missed, a British banger was top of her list. For reasons that entirely escaped her, the Americans had no idea how to make a decent sausage; all they produced were those tough, horrible little things they ate for breakfast smothered in *syrup!* But Delia knew a butcher up the other side of Utica who made proper British bangers, and every six months, armed with a polystyrene laboratory chest and a sack of dry ice, she made a banger run to stock up her freezer.

Tonight she would have bangers and mash with mushy peas,—but not until she'd had several sherries. She lit her imitation fire, found the excellent thriller she was halfway through, and moved with a glass, the sherry bottle and her book to the window. The most comforting buffer in the back of her mind was that Uncle John, Carmine and Mrs. Tesoriero were all lighting candles. She was definitely *safe*.

FRIDAY, JANUARY 10, 1969

The cure had worked so well that Delia came into County Services in one of her best outfits, a wool dress in great swirls of dark red, bright red, orange and yellow, like a rainbow that ran out of steam just as it was contemplating going green.

"I think we should look at bathroom runs again," she said before anyone else could get a spin on the ball.

There was a universal groan.

"No more hands on shoulders!" Donny cried.

"Tch, of course not! I mean in the dark corners on the way to the toilets, inside the toilets themselves," Delia said.

"We've spent loads of time on that," Buzz said.

"Well, I'm not convinced we've spent sufficient. Are we absolutely positive that no one met someone else going to or from? Not necessarily off the high table—the C.U.P. table people, for instance. How do we know we've eliminated every and all possibilities?"

"You're right, Delia," Carmine said. "We can't know, and we never will know. If by this time people haven't come forward to tell us that they met X or Y on a bathroom run, then they never will. The C.U.P. banquet is a leaky sieve, and the Tunbull dinner an exact opposite. No one left Max's den, even on the shortest bathroom run, after the men went in and Max shut the door. All the men swear it, and I believe them."

"I'm seeing Max Tunbull this morning," Abe said.

"What about the ampoule?" Carmine asked.

"Not Millie's. She regarded it with contempt, said any lab technician could do better after a mere month on the job. However, she did say that the joker's use of flea powder indicates he knows what tetrodotoxin powder looks like."

"Captain, do we have a main suspect?" Donny asked.

"You're as much a member of this team as anyone, Donny, so what do you think?" Carmine asked.

"Dr. Jim Hunter," he said, hardly hesitating. "Tinkerman's death got him out of a big hole."

"What about John Hall's death?"

"There has to be something there, boss. Is the old guy from Oregon coming—Wendover Hall?"

"He's supposed to arrive this weekend, staying with Max. If he doesn't fill in the blanks, we're up that creek." Carmine looked at Liam. "What do you think?"

"I vote for Davina and her spooky sister. That huge print run gives all the Tunbulls motive, Captain."

"Buzz?"

"I vote for Dr. Jim Hunter."

"Tony?"

"Dr. Jim Hunter."

"Delia?"

"Dr. Jim Hunter." Her voice was loaded with significance: she knew about the baby.

But Carmine didn't ask Abe, a courtesy. "I see Dr. Jim's a hot favorite," he said, "and I don't mind anyone's having a favorite provided no mind skews the evidence. But none of you will do that, you're too professional. Liam is just as right when he says all the Tunbulls have a stake in this. John's death affected how Max's empire might be divided. We have to find out more about him—he's a shadow."

And so the meeting broke up. Delia remained behind.

"It's hard being privy to information we're not sharing," Carmine said to her, "but in spite of that, we continue to keep Davina's baby our secret for the time being. I'm going to see the old Head

Scholar, Dr. Donald Carter. Delia, follow whatever scent your nose thinks best."

The outgoing Head Scholar of the Chubb University Press had held his post for a full ten years and had seen many triumphs, including, five years ago, a popular best seller on earthquakes and volcanoes that had astonished every seismologist in the nation—save, naturally, its author, vindicated.

"I don't know why people in the field were so surprised," Dr. Carter said to Carmine over good coffee and blueberry muffins. "It's my experience that ordinary folk are fascinated by how Mother Earth works, or how God sews our molecular design together, or how the Universe got going. It's my opinion that at least one expert in a field should write a book about it for the layman, even if the result is not a best seller—it will sell well enough to make a profit, which is all one can ask. Jim Hunter's book is sheer genius. I admit that I had no idea he could express himself so beautifully. But then, scientists are often like that. Look at Feynman's lectures—what a wonder!"

"Before we get down to Jim's book per se, Dr. Carter, I need to know a great deal more than I do about the relationship between the Chubb University Press and Tunbull Printing allied to Imaginexa Design," Carmine said.

The prawnlike white eyebrows climbed toward a head of splendidly white, waving hair; Dr. Don Carter's dark eyes took on the expression of internal calculation. A formidable man.

"Then I'd best start with C.U.P.," he said. "There are university presses and university presses, Captain. I mean, consider the two giants—Oxford and Cambridge. Were it not for their example, maybe no university would have gone into an esoteric field like publishing, but originally the university publisher filled a gap by providing a print medium for authors who stood no chance of publishing for profit. I guess no one in the beginning ever thought how much money there was to be made out of dictionaries and histories, but every profitable book also meant a scholar who could be published at a loss."

He nibbled a muffin. "C.U.P. was founded to publish the unprofitable scholars, and never developed into a giant—or even a potential giant. Its list is modest and esoteric save for that one accidental best seller, *Fire Down Below*. And Max Tunbull just happened to have the right kind of printery to suit our needs. We hadn't published during the War, but by 1946 we had a couple of manuscripts that needed to be books—seminal stuff, one religious, one on syntax. Max tendered, was awarded the contract, and we were so pleased we've just never looked elsewhere." Dr. Carter picked a blueberry out of its surrounding cake, and ate it with relish.

"Tunbull Printing is in such close proximity to Chubb, for one thing," he went on, still fishing for fruit, "and in all fairly small operations, Captain, there is a tendency to form into a family unit. Which is what happened with Max."

"What about Davina and Imaginexa?" Carmine asked, a part of his mind wondering why people needed to pick the eyes—or fruit out of things. "Is it customary to hand over design of university textbooks to an outside firm?"

"Depends on the designer," said Dr. Carter. "I was never happy with the way C.U.P. books *looked*. Without mentioning any names, our visual designer is so hidebound she'd have the books identical to those published in 1819. And I got tired of waiting for her to retire. Even small university presses have to move with the times, especially now that we're contemplating things like soft cover editions. Davina is brilliant, make no mistake!"

"Thank you, that answers some of my questions," Carmine said, pouring more coffee. "Was the original idea for Jim Hunter's book his, Doctor?"

"I always assumed so," Dr. Carter said mildly.

"I have some reason to query that."

"Well, you are a captain of detectives, so I bow to your far superior experience. *Could* the idea have been implanted?" he asked himself musingly. "Given the pace at which Jim works, you may be right, yes. That gigantic head is stuffed with ideas, but all about his work. To think of explaining what he does to people who wouldn't know RNA from the NRA wouldn't occur to him—or at least that's how I read him. Until he gave me the manuscript, which was definitely typed on their old IBM, no other machine. I was staggered."

"Could Millie have suggested it?"

The seamed face, almost a caricature of the scholar, fell into shadow. "Ah, Millie! Poor, poor little girl . . . She is as much Jim Hunter's slave as Uda is Davina's."

"How did that happen to Millie, Doctor?"

"Her passion, which is immense. She wrapped all of it in one single parcel, Jim Hunter, whom she adores. Jim has colossal charisma. Millie sweeps out the inner sanctum, goes into places in his life where no other human being is allowed to go. It is enough for her until the specter of childlessness rears its cobra head, as it will. Then she will demand that Jim give her children, and he'll obey. But the impetus must come from her. This book is the turning point in their relationship."

"She was too young," Carmine said abruptly.

"At fifteen? No! Think of Romeo and Juliet, of teenage suicides. Don't forget that Jim was only fifteen too. No seasoned seducer, he. I pity him even more than I do her—he is the black half. But what you must remember first of all, Captain, is the massive nature of their *shared* pain."

Carmine flinched. "How long has Jim known the Tunbulls?"

"About four years. C.U.P. has already published two works, one in 1965 and one in 1967. Both were learned tomes, if one can apply that phrase to biochemistry, which is more foreign to me than assembling a do-it-yourself nuclear submarine."

"So he knew the Tunbulls *before* he came to Chubb?"

"Max, certainly. He wrote both while he was at Chicago, but I personally pirated him as an author—there were rumors of a future Nobel Prize even then. The second book came out right at the time Jim moved to Chubb."

"And then he embarked on *A Helical God*. You imply that he hadn't known Davina before it?"

"If he had met her, it would have been socially only, maybe a dinner. But *A Helical God*—Davina was in her element! Instead of having to reproduce diagrams and graphs, she had to find ways to illustrate cellular goings-on for laymen, and to gain the knowledge to do that, she had to huddle with Jim. How they huddled! They got on like a house on fire."

"Affair-type fire, sir?"

Dr. Carter blinked, then giggled. "She should hope! I do know the lady well, Captain, but I know Jim Hunter far better, and I don't think she got to first base. Besides, she's a cock teaser, not a man eater. I'd be willing to take a bet that Max has the only key can open Davina's chastity belt."

"I see. Tell me about the unauthorized print run."

"I thought it was a good ploy, actually, in dealing with Tom Tinkerman. Pah! What a poseur! I've already told you that a small university press concentrates on the more unpublishable scholars, but in 1969 no university press can ignore the sciences. Which is what Tinkerman intended to do. The man was such an unscrupulous liar that he even convinced Roger Parson Junior that C.U.P. never published treatises upon obscure philosophies and medieval Christianity. While I held the imprimatur, it did—often! I can forgive a man confabulations based in hunger to see his own pet projects favored above all others, Captain, but I cannot forgive a man who lies to achieve the suppression of other forms of knowledge. That was Tinkerman. Like Hitler, he was by nature a burner of books and ideas." Dr. Carter's face screwed up. "However, he had the Parson ears—all of them."

"But the print run, sir?" Carmine persisted.

"As said, a good ploy. Tinkerman wouldn't have sued, he was too careful of his public image, and I dropped a little word in his ear about how the public Press could make a bigot look. I said I'd told Max to go ahead and print."

"And had you?"

"No!"

Carmine rose to go. "Thank you, Dr. Carter."

"Oh, one more thing," said Dr. Carter as Carmine donned his coat. "One very important thing."

"Sir?"

"Talk to Edith Tinkerman. A man's widow is more honest than his wife can ever be."

Carmine started the engine of his beloved cop Fairlane, but did not put the car in Drive. His notebook . . . Mrs. Edith Tinkerman, in that limbo of widowhood without a body to bury until the Coroner deigned to release it . . . Yes, there it was. Dover Street in Busquash. Admittedly not the beach front or the real heights of the peninsula, but a very good neighborhood even so.

The house was exactly what one might have expected Thomas Tarleton Tinkerman to inhabit: medium in size and price range, dove-grey aluminum siding that looked like board but kept the heat in during winter and the heat out during summer. It would have three bedrooms, a living room, dining room, kitchen, and a family room that undoubtedly functioned as a large study for the late Dr. Tinkerman.

Edith Tinkerman lived in the kitchen, which some merciful architect had made large enough to hold a dining table and chairs for everyday use; this was Edith's personal property, littered with fabrics, spools, and an electric sewing machine.

"I take in dressmaking," she explained, more comfortable when Carmine elected to sit at her work area rather than in the living room, which looked as if it were never used.

"For interest or income, Mrs. Tinkerman?"

"Income," she answered immediately. "Tom was parsimonious, Captain, unless to spend money could enhance his position."

Jesus! thought Carmine, this case is replete with poor little put-upon women! All neglected for the husband's career! Don't these guys realize that it's like amputating a limb, to put the wife on an outer orbit, deny her a share of the spoils?

"Did he make a will?" he asked, refusing refreshments.

"Yes. It was in his desk, which he kept locked. Once I was sure he was really dead, I busted the lock and found it." She looked smug. "I get three-quarters of everything, though I'm sure Tom thought of it as an interim will only. He was sure he was going to live forever. I thought he would too."

"Do you have children?"

"Two girls, one twenty, one twenty-two. Tom was very disappointed, but his budget didn't allow for more children, so he has no son. On the other hand," she went on dreamily, "having girls was good for his billfold. Education is for men, he said, so the girls went to secretarial college and are working."

"Were you educated, ma'am?"

"Oh, no! I might have given him an argument. I too was a secretary—his. Though twenty-four years of marriage to Tom gave me plenty of big words to use when I feel like it."

"Was your marriage happy?"

"No, but I never thought it would be. Marriage to a Tom is better than being an old maid, Captain, if you're not really educated. I had a husband, he gave me two lovely girls, and I have managed to eke out my housekeeping allowance by sewing. Tom only had enough love for one person—himself." Her plain face assumed a look of ineffable satisfaction. "I willed myself to have girls. There was no way in Creation I would have given him a son to ruin."

"You're very candid," Carmine said, out of his depth.

"Why not? Tom is dead, he can't hurt me now. As soon as his estate is probated, I intend to sell this property, cash in his stocks and shares, and divide the proceeds equally among Anne, Catherine and me."

"What happens to the other quarter of his estate?"

"He left it to the Chubb School of Divinity."

"Can you give me an estimate of the estate's worth?"

"About a million dollars."

"More than I imagined," Carmine said.

"Captain, Tom still had the first nickel he ever earned on a paper route. This house was bought for cash, no mortgage."

"How much contact did you have with him at the banquet?"

Her greying hair, Carmine noted, was home-permed, and not very well; even at nineteen, he decided, she would never have been a pretty woman, but she would have been exactly what the divinity scholar was looking for: a housewife with no appeal for other men.

Finally she answered. "Apart from walking in with him, I only had one contact," she said. "Typical Tom! My dinner got cold. I had to give him his B-12 shot."

Carmine sat up so suddenly that he felt his neck crunch—the turmeric still had a way to go, obviously. "B-12 shot?"

"Yes. Tom had no acid in his stomach, which made him a dreadful eater—none of this, none of that, on and on! Meat and shellfish were difficult for him, oils and fats too. In fact, he was happiest eating jelly sandwiches or toast. And he flagged because he couldn't absorb B-12. It had to be injected into his muscle."

"Achlorhydria," Carmine said slowly. "Yes, I know it."

"A shot of B-12 perked him right up," said the widow. "I have bottles of it, but also some single-dose ampoules so I can put one in my purse with a TB syringe. He was nervous—this was a big occasion for him, I knew that, and B-12 was like a—well, I imagine like a snort of vodka to a drinker. When he gave me the signal for a shot, I wasn't surprised. He got up to go to the bathroom, and I followed. I went into the Ladies, broke the neck on the ampoule, sucked up the B-12, put the cap on the needle and the ampoule back in my purse."

"Did no one see you?" Carmine asked incredulously.

"No one. The Ladies was empty and the main course was being served. As I said, mine got cold. Tom was waiting at the end of the passage in the corner, and was terribly annoyed with me because there was nowhere to put the injection. The more he hounded me, the more upset I got. In the end he snapped at me to put it in the back side of his neck—everywhere else was smothered in robes, coats, shirts, cuff links—I was in tears. He turned side on and bent down and I gave him the shot in the soft part of the back of his neck, just as he had instructed. The minute the needle was out, he went back to the table, while I tidied my face and put the syringe in my purse."

"You threw nothing in a trash can?"

"Tom would have lynched me! I'm all too aware of law suits if a cleaner gets pricked or cuts herself on the glass. Tom was emphatic about it."

"What color was the injection, Mrs. Tinkerman?"

Her brown eyes widened. "B-12 colored, of course."

"And what color is B-12?" he asked patiently.

"A beautiful ruby-red," she answered, bewildered.

"The color was the same as always?"

"Identical, as far as I could see in the light."

And take that, you cop fools! Carmine told himself, driving away with mind whirling. *Edith Tinkerman* as an arch-poisoner? A sat-on academic wife deliberately chosen by an ambitious husband intent on ensuring that his children were his and that the dinner table would hold no conversational stimulation? No, it was not Edith Tinkerman. It couldn't be! She was the poisoner's patsy, nothing more. The administration of an injection of vitamin B-12, beautiful ruby-red cyanocobalamin.

He'd mixed his dose and colored it, then inserted it in the ampoule and melted it shut again. But had he really entrusted his plan to such a chance? How much of a chance was it? He must have known how atrociously Tinkerman bullied his wife, known too of his psychological dependence on a substance he deemed vital to his welfare, his ability to perform a task. Yes, this poisoner would have taken the chance, knowing it was no chance at all. And sure enough, Tinkerman and his wife left the table, returned with him elated and her flustered. The device Donny found in the trash was always a blind.

Abe saw Max Tunbull in his office at Tunbull Printing, a large and typically ugly factory-style building on the Boston Post Road not far from Davina's firm, Imaginexa. A more attractive front had been tacked on to the printery, however, to tell people that it was too successful to take orders for wedding invitations or In Memoriams to commemorate funerals.

The office was fairly spacious and bore Davina's hand in its color scheme of crimson and pale lemon yellow; Abe found the combination disquieting, but apparently Max did not, for he gazed around his premises with obvious pleasure.

In the few days since his sixtieth birthday dinner and its shocking events, Max had visibly aged. A tall man with a good body, he and it had subtly sagged, and the mass of waving, brass-gold hair had suddenly dimmed. Given the short time, Max had gone astonishingly grey. His features were Slav, the face broad and slightly flat, the cheekbones inclining to the oriental; his determined mouth had lost some of its firmness. Only the eyes, Abe sensed, remained as they had been: yellowish in color, they were well opened and fringed with very long lashes. Under ordinary circumstances he would be called an attractive man.

"I would like you to tell me everything you know about your son John," Abe said, having declined coffee. "We're experiencing trouble learning anything about him, and while I know that his adoptive father, Wendover Hall, is on his way to Connecticut, I would still like to hear what *you* know before I see him."

Max looked at where his hands lay in his lap, frowned, and put them on his desk, not linked together, but holding on to the desk's edge as if to a float in an angry sea. "Frankly, Lieutenant, I thought John was long dead. As God is my witness, I searched for him and his mother for years," Max said, voice husky. "As time wore on, I guess I abandoned hope. So when he called me up and said who he was,

I plain did not believe him. Until he produced the papers and the ring—the opal zebra ring, one of a kind. Then I had to accept him."

"What did he tell you about himself?"

"That his mom had been taken in by Wendover Hall, who married her and adopted John. Martita was calling herself and John by an assumed name, Wilby. Wendover sent John to the best schools and encouraged him to make his career forestry, which he did. John said he loved the work. But the name on the many transactions was either John Hall or John Wilby. He knew nothing about the Tunbulls until, on his thirtieth birthday, long after his mother's death, Wendover Hall gave him a box from her that she had stipulated wait until John was thirty. Even knowing, he took over two years to decide to contact me and, as he put it, open up old wounds."

"Given the birth of your second son by your second wife, sir, did John's advent create testamentary problems for you?"

Max laughed, it seemed with genuine amusement. "None at all, Lieutenant! He was obviously well off, it showed in his clothes. Wendover Hall, he told me, had already settled millions on him. He said he wanted no part of my estate, and I believed him. Certainly I've made no new will since he came back into my life." Suddenly Max looked extremely uncomfortable. "I just wish I could say the same for John! Yesterday a lawyer named Harold Zucker called me from Portland, Oregon, to tell me that John made a new will on the last day of 1968. It leaves everything he has to be divided equally between my son Alexis and Val's son, Ivan."

Boy, thought Abe, winded, that sure came out of left field! "A shock, huh?" he asked.

"You can say that again!"

"Have you informed anyone in your family yet?"

"No. I knew you were coming this morning, and I thought it wiser to wait and tell you first. But I didn't know—I swear I didn't know!" Max cried. "How could I?"

"I'll have to talk to Mr. Zucker myself," said Abe, "but may I offer a word of advice? Don't mention this bequest to anyone for the moment. Your family, including you, is suspect in a murder investigation."

"I'll try, but I won't promise," said Max wretchedly. "I lose my son, then I find my son, now I lose him again. It's too cruel! Alexis is too young to care, but Ivan is a grown man, and I owe him, I owe him!"

"Just try. How did your family feel when the proof said John really was your son?"

"Davina was glad for me. That's one wonderful woman! She was delighted to think Alexis had a brother, she really was. It wasn't about inheritances to Vina, it was about having another strong arm to help. Val was glad for me too. He's a true brother—the best brother."

"What does Val do for Tunbull Printing?" Abe asked.

"Looks after the actual printing process. I do all the overseeing and planning—layout, bookbinding—Davina has been a tower of strength to me. A university press is extremely specialized, even has a look. C.U.P. is purple calf with gold print, and some volumes are still exquisitely tooled. Now we do a line of textbooks for undergraduates in subjects as disparate as physics and English, we put them out cheaply, but they still look like purple calf—imitation. We keep the price right down and the look right up." Max shrugged. "Gold-edged pages? We hardly do that anymore, it's a sop for snobs."

"Snobs like Dr. Tinkerman?"

Max sneered. "He was going back to all gilt edges."

"What does Ivan do?" Abe asked.

"Ivan's our traveler. Visits the great university bookstores from coast to coast, as well as other stores catering for the university press market. He monitors competing prices, and also attends all the wholesale shows where we might find new materials, paper, advances in ink and typesetting. Though the wholesale shows are more important, he also mans our booth at the A.B.A. each year."

"A.B.A.?"

"American Booksellers' Association convention. That and the Frankfurt Book Fair in West Germany are the two major trade publication shows each year, but they're important for us too."

"Did you like John as a person, sir?"

"I think I would have, had we had more time together. He was so like Martita! We're comfortable, Lieutenant, the money is no compensation for losing a son twice over."

"How did Mrs. Emily Tunbull regard him?"

"Actually she never met him, but I guess she hadn't been enthusiastic about his reappearance. She was convinced John would cut Ivan out, and that she didn't like." Max frowned. "I heard a weird story from Davina—that Emily told her she knew about some suspicious events that had been going on for a year. When Davina tried to pin her down, she shied away. That's Em!"

"How do you mean, 'That's Em!'?"

"Always full of mysterious accusations. When Martita was my wife, Em was so new to us that we didn't wake up to what kind of mischief-maker she was, so we tended to believe her stories. Well, not anymore, Lieutenant, not anymore!"

"Mrs. Davina Tunbull told Sergeant Carstairs that John Hall had physically attacked her during the dinner party."

"Oh, Vina, Vina!" Max cried, clenching his hands into fists and raising them heavenward. "That," he said grimly, "is typical Davina. She fantasizes that every personable man who meets her tries to make love to her." Suddenly his exasperation vanished, he grinned. "Stick around, Lieutenant, and she'll do it to you."

"I wasn't aware you were aware of her failings, sir."

"By the time Davina and I married in May of 1967, I had her summed up. Don't get me wrong, I'm nuts about her, but I know all her tricks too. For instance, she had the hots for Jim Hunter, who never so much as noticed her on that level. That only made her try harder, until I told her what a fool she was making of herself. Vina is my wife, and I have very good reason to be sure that she's faithful to me. But at the same time, she has to throw out lures to other men."

"You're remarkably perceptive, Mr. Tunbull."

"That's why our marriage will last. I'm an ideal husband for Davina—authority figure as well as lover and father."

Abe changed the subject. "How do you think C.U.P. will go with Dr. Geoffrey Chaucer Millstone as Head Scholar?"

Max's face lit up. "Fantastic! Better than Don Carter, in many ways. I envision more and more titles in the sciences, though he won't forget the humanities. Moving with the times is the hardest task an academic publisher faces, especially the concept of cheap, soft cover texts for undergraduates. I predict a wonderful and fruitful collaboration," said Max. "I mean, Chauce understood why we did that twenty thousand print run."

"What did he understand about it?" Abe asked, curious for a new slant on an old conundrum.

"Best sellers move like lightning," said Max, "and we're not geared to producing them at Tunbull Printing. To have twenty thousand in reserve ready to go is what gives us a fighting chance to keep supply up to demand."

"That," said Abe, relieved, "makes perfect sense."

"Publication Day will be upon us in no time," Max said.

"And when is Publication Day?"

"Undecided, but I'm guessing around the beginning of April."

By the time everyone met in Carmine's office at four that afternoon, the atmosphere had changed. Somehow, and absolutely undefinably, people knew that things had happened to knock cop theories down like pins in a bowling alley.

"John Hall's will is legal and extant," said Abe, "and it appears that both baby Alexis and Ivan Tunbull are now the richer by several millions each. Which wasn't known at the time he was killed—we *think*. But bear in mind that John might have told someone who isn't owning up, or told the poisoner, who killed him anyway. Mr. Zucker the Portland lawyer has acted for John and Wendover Hall for many years, and could tell me what John's old will said. Namely, it left everything to a halfway house for recovering psychiatric patients in San Francisco because John had spent almost two years in and out of it during his late teens and early twenties."

"So his old will left nothing to the Hunters?" asked Delia.

"Nothing. However, he didn't have much to leave. Wendover Hall's endowment is very recent—last December, more or less synchronously with John's new will, which is prudent."

"But both Hunters maintained he was rich," Buzz objected.

"He was, but an allowance kind of wealth. Whatever he needed or asked for he was given, and not grudgingly, Zucker says. Nor apparently did the old man ever contemplate disinheriting him. Wendover Hall wanted to see what John decided about his real family before making the major endowment. He was very pleased by John's decision to have two families."

"Does he know how John disposed of his gift in the will?" Buzz asked.

"Zucker says no. He does now, of course, but has no wish to fight it. The money was John's to do with as he willed."

"It doesn't take the heat off Ivan," Donny said.

Abe sat silent for a moment, recollecting his interview with Ivan and Lily Tunbull following on his seeing Max.

"Ivan looks great for the murder of John Hall," he said now, "but I don't buy it. He's a man of Hall's own age, very settled and domestically happy. That stuck out like a sore thumb. His mind set is his work, which he really enjoys, and he's not really hurting financially. I suspect his mother's ambitions for him were just that—his mother's. If I had to sum him up, I'd describe him as an intelligent, hardworking, modestly ambitious man who can't get over his luck at finding Lily for a wife. Ivan wallows in his family, and, having met Lily, I quite see why he's crazy about her. She's adorable, and it's not a facade. The kids are great, his job's secure no matter who inherits, and he's too good at it to be replaced, even for spite."

Strong words coming from Abe Goldberg. Carmine took over, feeling irritable and curiously foiled. "What kind of killer goes to the trouble of making a device he—or she—has no intention of using? Because it screams to me that if Edith Tinkerman was tricked into vectoring the poison to her husband, then John Hall was also killed by injection with a proper syringe and hypodermic. The device wasn't used at the Tunbull dinner party either. Somehow, by a feat of legerdemain we don't suspect, John Hall was injected while a room full of men enjoyed their port, cognac and cigars. No one made a bathroom run, Dr. Markoff swears to it, and he's the one outside constant I can't overlook or dismiss. The guy's as nosy as Pinocchio and has a better memory than a quiz show king, and he says no one left the room. The men were in it for about thirty minutes when John's symptoms began to appear. Too long for the shot to have been administered before they went in."

"Then it had to have been the device," Donny said.

But Carmine shook his head. "It's too risky. Too many factors might have prevented the poison from leaving its reservoir. Look at the junction of the hypodermic and the metal saucer, Donny! Solder? A 25-gauge needle? That's so small."

"What's left, no matter how improbable, has to be the answer," Delia said, on Donny's side.

"It presents too many dangers to its operator," Carmine said. "That's how I know he didn't use it."

"What about Emily?" Liam asked, tired of going in circles.

"The water carafe. Paul found a trace of tetrodotoxin in it, so that at least is certain," Carmine said.

"Have we enough on Dr. Jim to make an arrest?" Buzz asked.

"What evidence we have is completely circumstantial, so I'd have to say, no."

"How about we arrest Uda Savovich on suspicion and see what eventuates?" Tony asked. "I just feel that until we can arrest someone, there's a chance another death might happen."

"For what reason?" Carmine asked.

"None, but it's something to *do*, sir."

"Have you a strategy, Deels?" Carmine asked.

"It's been thumping in my head that I ought to have one, yet I don't. Oh, I detest poison cases!" she burst out.

"John Hall's inquest is next Monday," Carmine said. "We wait until after that, then reconsider."

"And Tinkerman's inquest?"

"Wednesday. I'm afraid Mrs. Tinkerman is going to have to testify that she gave her husband a shot of vitamin B-12 at the banquet, but I'll make sure that Paul testifies how well the poison was disguised. When does Wendover Hall arrive?"

"Sunday. He'll be on a red-eye out of Seattle and should be at Max Tunbull's house by noon," said Abe. "He's staying there."

"Be waiting for him, Abe. He's the answer to our problems with John Hall. In the meantime, have a good weekend."

SATURDAY, JANUARY 11, 1969

When Millie came out of the bedroom, still blinking sleep from her eyes, she was astonished to see Jim sitting at the table over coffee, with a box of bagels and a bar of Philadelphia cream cheese sitting by her own place.

She came around the table to stand behind him, her cheek on his hair, inhaling the scent of his skin. "Not in the lab?"

"No," he said, smiling and putting down his hefty sheaf of papers. "It occurred to me that it's Saturday, the rest of the world isn't working, and when I took a walk, the smell of fresh bagels hit me like a truck." He reached up and pulled her onto his knees. "I don't know why, but I realized that it's about two years since we last had toasted bagels and cream cheese for our breakfast. I couldn't afford the lox, but I got you the rest."

She pressed kisses against his lips, which always ravished her: silky-soft, yet muscular. "Jim, how thoughtful!" She began to scramble off his lap. "I'll start the toasting."

But he rose, picked her up and put her on her chair. "No, this is my treat, I do the toasting. You can watch."

Head spinning slightly, she followed his movements—he was so efficient! Within ten minutes she was spreading Philly on a hot, brown bagel and chewing in bliss.

"I should have taken you out for breakfast," he said.

"No, bagels taste better at home, especially made on a lopsided toaster." She sipped her coffee. "Jim! Colombian?"

"It's one of those mornings, Millie. I love you."

"Well, I know that. I love you back."

He wetted his lips, hesitated, then plunged in. "I had a serious talk with Davina yesterday."

At mention of the name she stiffened, lifting clouded eyes to his face. "Since when is she a fount of knowledge?"

"About some things, she's the only fount of knowledge," he countered. "Don't get your dander up, Millie, hear what we talked about first. I know your first time of meeting her properly wasn't happy— John dying and all that, but I've known her for a long time, and in some matters I trust her opinions."

"I looked at her and saw Medusa."

He took her hands, chafed their backs with his thumbs. "I accept your feelings, Millie, but try to get past them this once! *A Helical God* is going to turn our world upside down, and none of the C.U.P. people is in touch with reality the way Davina is. Like us, they're academics. Something Davina knows very well, which is why she decided to stick her oar in. Believe me, Millie, she apologized all the time she gave me her thoughts, and after a few hours thinking about what she said, I think she's right."

His earnestness was unmistakable; knowing her dislike of the woman was as illogical as instinctual, she tried to do as he asked, be detached at least. "Very well, Jim, you talked."

"We have to change our lifestyle, she says. If the book's a big success and the general public discovers that Chubb's brightest biochemistry star lives in a semi-slum on State Street, it will harm both Chubb's image and our own. It would look as if I, a black man, was being exploited, underpaid, and the truth is that I'm not. My fault entirely that I plough the money back into my work, but Davina says the adverse publicity could rebound on the book." The full mouth tightened, the eyes hardened. "We have to be living better well before Publication Day, April second."

"And where do we get the money?" Millie asked, voice harsh.

Jim looked enthusiastic. "Oh, Davina fixed that up! C.U.P. will give us an advance against royalties. Some thousands."

"She's a wonder. Is there anything she hasn't thought of?"

His laughter was spontaneous. "Not a thing! She even says we ought to have a baby on the way to vindicate our years of pain and struggle."

Millie's eyes glazed, as if the brain behind was so swamped with new ideas that it couldn't cope with more shocks. When Jim mentioned the baby her lashes fluttered, moisture dewed them, and she swallowed convulsively. "A baby?" she asked.

"Yes. Is a baby okay with you?"

The dew became rain; Millie wept soundlessly, tears pouring down her face. "A baby is the only answer," she said clearly.

He leaned back to stare at her, brow furrowed. "I never realized . . ." he said, trailing off.

"Why would you until an outsider pointed the way?" She got up and began to clear the table. "You don't see beyond your work, I've always known that. I guess even Davina noticed."

"Where do you think we ought to live?" he asked as he took down his coat, squeezed his huge feet into rope-soled boots.

"East Holloman, near my parents."

"Can I leave it to you to look?"

"How much rent can we afford?"

"Whatever the market says, sweetheart. Davina says we'll get whatever we need from C.U.P. For clothes and things too."

And he was out the door, leaving a dazed Millie to shower, put on some clothes, and head for the bus stop. Oh, typical Jim! Things sorted out to his satisfaction, he hadn't paused to wonder if she was going to the Burke Biology Tower too. A ten-minute wait, and he could have driven her. As it was, the bus. He didn't mean it, and under normal circumstances she would have hung onto his jacket and told him to wait for her. Today had been such a huge shock, she was completely off-balance.

Her growing anger roared to the surface as she was trudging to the bus stop and stopped her in her tracks. The next moment she had turned on her heel and walked in the direction of the tired little park the city had put adjacent to Caterby Street. Shaking with rage, more tears pouring down her face. Not that there was anyone to see. At eight o'clock on a Saturday morning, the district was still recovering from the night before.

She found a bench and her handkerchief—they couldn't afford tissues, so she still washed handkerchiefs—had her cry, then mopped up.

It was, she thought, exactly like awakening from a very long and not unpleasant dream. Before this morning, she was Millie Hunter, adoring companion and wife of eighteen years; now she was Millie Nobody, citizen of a world she didn't know, could not yet begin to assess.

A glamorous, selfish, sophisticated old acquaintance of Jim's had sat him down and told him what was wrong with the life he was living, then given him explicit instructions how to fix it—before April second, if you please! A really nice apartment or house, nice things in it, nice food on the table, and a baby on the way. If they were presented with that background, the media sharks would glide off to other feeding grounds.

And Jim had listened. Listened with respect and obedience. Just who was Davina Tunbull? What slot did she fill in Jim's frantically busy life? Was she just a professional acquaintance, or was she something more? Wonderful Jim, for whom Millie would have died, whose integrity was infinitely above all other men's, had listened, seen the logic, decided to obey. The big question was, if it had been she, Millie, to issue these ultimatums, would Jim have listened, understood, obeyed? In the aftermath of this morning, Millie had to ask herself why she hadn't got in first.

The next spasm of rage was directed at herself, at all those lost chances. This time she didn't cry, she simply endured it, felt it burn out, sat empty, hollow, vacant. The baby she had been planning for the moment prosperity arrived was now implanted in Jim's mind as the concept of Davina Tunbull. Whenever Jim looked at their first-born child, he would thank Davina for its existence. Millie's moment had gone, snatched from her grasp, and she could never get it back. When Jim thought of Millie and motherhood, he would first have to think of all those childless years together, and how she had agreed they couldn't possibly have children. No matter that it would be Millie carried the baby; it was Davina's idea.

She knew too that she wasn't being reasonable, that what really lay at base of her anger was the intrusion of another—and particularly offensive—woman into matters that were no one's business save hers and Jim's. But how dared Davina? How dared she! Just when I'd taken myself off the Pill and was dreaming of telling Jim that there would be a baby at last, Davina—how did he put it?—sticks her oar in. He can't have liked her interference, despite which, he took her advice. Oh, it wasn't fair! While she, Millie, waited for the perfect moment to speak, Davina Tunbull, having no perfect moment, spoke anyway. Not fair, not fair!

Everything was so muddled . . . At fifteen I already knew that Jim's was going to be the important work, and, loving him, I gave every atom of my being to advancing his career, from my money to my right arm. I never grudged it, never! I never thought of myself as Jim's inferior, as his uncomplaining servant, but clearly that is how Davina sees me—as a kind of up-market Uda. I never saw a shred of evidence that Jim thought me his inferior—we were too close, too much a team. That's what Davina hasn't understood. If she esteemed me, she would have spoken to both of us together; as it was, she spoke to Jim alone as the arbiter of my destiny as well as his own. It's not *like* that! How many of our decisions did *I* make? Answer: about half. Jim and I are both biochemists, this has never been about my career versus his, it's always been about our joint career, even if the name on it is Jim's, not mine. I always thought Jim understood that my turn would come, now I'm not so sure, and that's a source of deep hurt. Of anger. When our eyes met at fifteen, it was the exchange of two equals, and all the battling since has seen us equals. Can I honestly be an Uda to my man of eighteen years?

No, I refuse to believe it! Without me, Jim couldn't have gotten there. He knows it as well as I do. That we've never discussed it is immaterial: it's a core fact. Now here he is, the pawn of an ambitious, utterly self-centered woman who flirts with him or any other personable man she meets—is that all it is, flirtation? Yes, yes! Everything she does is to feather her existing nest, not make a new one, and she's not privy to any of Jim's less admirable qualities. I hate her, I hate her! She's a blowfly lays its maggots in the juiciest substrate, and Jim's book means a lot to her and Max. Jim's book, Jim's book . . .

The rage was entirely gone. On this Saturday morning, Jim had entirely lost sight of Millie the equal. What was success going to do to him? And, more importantly, to his marriage? Could she continue to summon up the strength to deal with him? I am the only person who knows his secrets, his insecurities, his nightmares, his ghosts.

She got up and returned to the bus stop. As usual, the bus was late; she caught it by the skin of her teeth at the end of a sprint, and sat, gasping for breath, with a smile for her fellow travelers, all of whom she knew. As she sometimes joked to Jim, she was the only white person on board with an intact brain; the bus was for black people full of intelligence and vigor, and white people who were either physically or mentally handicapped.

By the time she walked through her parents' back door she was smiling, looked happier than in years.

"Dad," she said to Patrick, buried in the *New York Times*, "are there any houses for rent in East Holloman, perhaps with a view to buying later on? Jim and I are joining the fleshpots."

When Val sidled through his office door, Max Tunbull looked up in surprise. Val wasn't the sidling type.

"What's the matter? Why the skulking?"

"Chester Malcuzinski is here."

The pencil fell from Max's hand; he went pale. "Christ!"

"We'll be calling on the Name of the Lord a lot. He wants to know why Emily was murdered," Val said, subsiding into a chair.

"How did he find out?"

"Saw some cable TV news program that's made a big production out of the mystery poison. You know, undetectable, sinister, some poisoner on the loose, cops stymied, the usual bullshit."

"Did Lily stock your kitchen again?"

Val's face softened. "Yes. Good girl, my daughter-in-law. Never even cheated on the bills for the insurance company."

"More than you could have said for your brother-in-law."

"Tell me about it, the bastard!"

"How's he cheating the world these days?" Max asked.

"He's in real estate in Florida—the Gulf side, Orlando. More and more northerners are moving to Florida to retire, and Chez helps them spend their money. He builds luxury apartments, so he has people going and coming." Val shivered. "I bet there are a few corpses in the foundations."

"How old is Emily's little brother now?" Max asked.

"Early forties. He adored Em, I have to give him that, but I had a hard time convincing him that I didn't let him know she was dead because I didn't have any idea where he was. I guess what made him believe me in the end was that no one in his right mind would offend Chez Malcuzinski."

"How long is he staying?"

"Until Em's killer is caught, he says. He's moved into Ivan's old room and taken the spare bedroom next door to it as a kind of office and sitting room." Val waved his hands around. "He arrived at seven this morning, and by nine the cable guys were giving him his own feed to a huge TV set. They hadn't gone when the phone guys turned up to give him his own phone line and telex. He moved a table out of the basement to use as a desk—all by himself, can you imagine? He's fit, Max, very fit."

"There's more to it than this."

"I agree."

Apparently reaching a decision, Max got up and locked his work away, something he didn't normally do: with Chez in town, nothing was safe from prying eyes.

"I'll follow you home, Val. If I don't warn Davina what kind of man Chez is, things might get out of hand."

An admirable resolution, but doomed to failure. When Max let himself in the front door he could hear the coquettish peal of Vina's laughter emanating from the living room, and felt his battered heart sink.

The Chester Malcuzinski he remembered had been a pimply youth and then a pimply man in his twenties, but the fifteen years that had elapsed between the last time he had seen Chez and today had wrought wonders. Today's Chez was tall, lithely athletic, had a skin free from pustules, and considerably more good looks than his sister, whose early prettiness had not fared well. He was the picture of a fashionable man, from his carefully coiffed, shoulder-length hair to his bell-bottomed hipster trousers and the full-sleeved shirt open to show a hairy chest. In coloring he was dark, yet, despite his reputation as a thug, his appearance was neither vulgar nor greasy. In fact, he would be immensely attractive to the wealthy women who formed his clientele—a very smooth operator, Max saw at a glance. And Vina was responding as Vina always did to personable men; she was flirting outrageously, giving him the impression that she would be on a bed with her legs open at the soonest possible moment. Oh, Vina, Vina! Not with this man!

All that aside, Max came into the room smiling, his hand extended. "My dear Chez!" he said, shaking the manicured member given him. Then his face saddened. "I wish it were a happier occasion."

And, Chez being Chez, he turned his back on Davina to give his attention to someone he thought could help him. "What happened, Max? Tell me."

"I wish I knew, but none of us does, and that's the truth. My long lost son, John, was poisoned at a dinner here a week ago yesterday, then the new Head Scholar of the Chubb University Press was poisoned at a banquet in his honor a week ago today. Finally poor little

Em was poisoned in her sculpting studio last Wednesday, though her body wasn't found until Thursday afternoon," said Max in the most conciliating voice he could summon.

Chez stiffened. "You mean Val didn't miss her on Wednesday night? Is he cheating on her?"

"No, no," Max said pacifically, noting out of the corner of his eye that Vina was pouting—she didn't like being ignored. "Emily was right into her sculpting, she often stayed in her studio overnight if the clay was going right—don't ask me, I'm not a sculptor!—and Val was delighted. Absolutely delighted! She'd found a satisfying hobby now Ivan was a family man. As the only one without printing skills, we suspect Em had felt like a square wheel, so when she took to sculpting, we helped her in every way we could."

"That's true, Chester," said Davina.

He spared her an impatient glance, then focused on Max again. "How was she poisoned?" he demanded.

"In a carafe of water. You needn't fear there's poison in any of the food, it's all been replaced. Lily did that."

Chez lunged to his feet, fists clenched. "I want to see."

"You can't, Chez," said Max, alarmed. "The shed's sealed."

"Fuck that!"

Max hurried in his wake, but not before turning to Davina. "You, madam, stay right here until I get back. I want a word with you." He encountered a glare from Uda, and glared in return. "That goes for Uda too. Right here, understand?"

He caught up with Chez halfway to Val's house. "The shed has a police seal across the lock," he said to Chez, panting slightly from so much effort and emotion.

"Fuck that!" was the only answer.

The piece of police tape was ripped away, Max compelled to tender a small key.

The stench hit them both; Max reeled, refused to enter, but after an angry glance at Max, Chez walked in.

"Who cleaned up?" he asked when he emerged, white-faced.

"Her daughter-in-law, Lily. A wonderful girl. I think she felt it was the least she could do."

"I'll do something for her. From the stink, it must have been terrible. You're right, Max, Lily is a wonderful girl."

He produced a wad of tissues and ran them over his face. "Emily was amazing, eh? Them—*those* cats and horse's heads—clever as well as pretty. Tell Val I want them—all of them," said Chez, jaw rippling.

"We'd like to keep the family busts," Max said timidly, "but you can have the rest. None of her pieces is glazed or fired yet, though."

"I'll have that done in Florida." Chez blew his nose quite daintily. "See you later," he said, and went off toward Emily's house.

Max allowed himself to tremble, but by the time he came in his own front door he was calm and composed. Which was more than could be said for Davina, in a temper.

"How dare you, Max!" she began.

He cut her short with a chop of his hand through air that whistled, the gesture was so fast. "For once, Davina, you will shut up and listen!" he snapped. "You're a cock-teaser who can't resist teasing cock, but don't try it on Chez Malcuzinski. He is a gangster—a *real* gangster! He'd as soon put a bullet in the back of your head as look at you. If you tease him into making a move, you'd better be ready to deliver, because he won't like no for an answer after you've led him on. And you'll look in vain for me to rescue you, because I won't lift a finger for you. I love you, but I love living more."

Her lusciously lipsticked mouth had dropped open, her fixed blue eyes had forgotten to blink; she had never seen this side of her husband, and it came as a shock. "I . . ." she said feebly.

"I haven't gotten where I am by being unintelligent and naive, Vina. I may not have a college degree, but I've been associated with C.U.P. for over twenty years, and the culture wears off as well as the learning. So I'll repeat my warning about Chez Malcuzinski—he's a bad man, stay clear of him." He transferred his attention to Uda. "As for you, take care of your mistress. Now I'm going upstairs to play with my son."

While Max played with his baby, Davina went for a walk: a long one. A mile up Route 133 sat Major Minor's Museum of Horrors and Motel, which happened to be Davina's destination.

It had changed out of all recognition since the days (not so very long ago) when it had catered for afternoon trysts between businessmen and their feminine targets. Now it was run in conjunction with a house on the opposite side of the road that contained a chamber of horrors that had rocked Holloman, Connecticut and the entire nation. Major F. Sharp Minor had found his metier at last, renovated his motel into premises some felt better than the Cleveland Hotel downtown, and, besides a haute cuisine restaurant, offered an excellent coffee shop. Here Davina shed her outer wear and walked to a table in a secluded corner.

"I guess you had to come, but I wish you hadn't" was her opening remark, then, with a smile to a hovering waitress, "Coffee with cream, nothing to eat, thank you."

"Was Val's story about not being able to find me true?" Chez asked, eating mixed breakfast grills with pleasure.

"Of course it was!" she said rather crossly, then smiled at the returning waitress, who thought her beautiful in every way—such manners! "I couldn't very well inform him that I knew where you were. As far as the Tunbulls are concerned, you and I don't even know each other. Otherwise it might be a bit difficult to explain how I just happened to appear at Max's printery from my new premises down the road that you just happened to help me buy. As well as pointing my nose at Max."

"What's going on?"

"I wish I knew, but I don't. On one level, this poisoner got us out of a hole, but on another, he's put us in the soup. The cops are breathing down our necks, and they're not stupid. When this stranger called last December and announced he was Max's long lost son, I was stunned. Well, don't sit there, stupid! You must know all about Martita and John because Emily always got the blame for their running away."

"That was never fair! Thirty years ago I was just a kid—no way I could help Em."

"Your beloved sister, Chez, was a bitch," Davina said, chin out. "She tried her tricks on me too, but I'm no Martita."

The dark eyes flashed. "You're asking for trouble, Vina."

"Crap, I am! I go down, you go down, Chester Derzinsky. Save your malice for people you can terrify."

"Yeah, you're safe," he admitted reluctantly. "So you had to kill the long lost son to protect your son, right?"

"That's just it, I didn't!" cried Davina. Her voice fell to a whisper. "The poison is some stuff so rare that only a handful of people can make it. I know the husband of the woman who did make it, but no one seems to suspect her—she's related to half the police force and her dad's the Medical Examiner. It's not foxgloves or nightshade, things I could make. Even if I had some, I wouldn't know how to use it."

His breakfast finished, Chez lit a cigarette and beckoned for the waitress and coffee. "You trying to say we're mixed up in this by accident?" he asked incredulously.

"That's exactly what I'm saying." Her eyes widened. "Chez, I'm afraid! I'm deliberately being incriminated, I know I am!"

"Don't the cops have other suspects?"

"A black man—I mean a *black* man! A genius biochemist who's written a popular book on his work. The long lost son, John, knew him and his wife in California. The wife—she's white—is very beautiful. She could have been a model, except that she's another biochemist, the one who made the poison. They're a striking couple, Chez. When I saw them at the C.U.P. banquet, I was amazed. She looks at her husband as if he's God."

"Anything else to report?"

"No. And I hope you remember that I've paid back my loan."

He laughed. "I don't need your dough, Vina. There's not a high end property in my part of Florida doesn't come through me, and some of my commissions run into six figures. You're safe, and you have to admit that Max Tunbull was just what you were looking for."

"I admit it freely. I had no intention of continuing to model until the work stopped coming in, Chez. But never think you masterminded me through a marriage connection. You didn't. I have a great talent for design that suits book publishing. I am grateful for the loan that enabled me to buy Imaginexa. Grateful too for the hint to approach Max Tunbull. But my debts are all paid back and I owe you no favors, my shady New York friend. That part of *both* our lives is best kept closed."

"Are you still smoking Sobranies?" he asked.

"When I need to make an impression."

Chez leaned across the table, his head close. "Did the same guy poison my Em as well as the other two?"

"The cops think so."

"But no one knows who it is, except it's a man."

"They're not even sure of that." She prepared to leave. "Now I'm going home to my baby."

"How old?"

"Three months."

"Did the worst happen?"

"Yes."

"And the guy who wrote the book is black?"

"Yes."

"Caught on the horns of a dilemma, Vina?"

"No. Max is a very good and a very loyal husband."

Ivan and Lily gave Val lunch; Chez had gone off somewhere in his rental car, a Cadillac, without saying when he would be back, and Lily was the kind of wife who would effortlessly produce a lunch for Uncle Chez when he returned.

His advent was the main topic of conversation.

"He seemed very nice to me," said Lily, who was one of those fortunate people who can find nothing to dislike in others. "I love his hair, it's so trendy." She ran an affectionate hand over Ivan's thatch, which did cover his ears as a homage to the fashion, but longer than that he would not go. "And his clothes! Hip as well as trendy."

Lily was far lower class than Emily had hoped for in Ivan's wife, but it hadn't taken Emily long to understand that there was no social class for saints, and Lily was definitely a saint. So she had never suffered the sharp edge of her mother-in-law's tongue, and didn't appreciate for one moment the significance of Davina's gift for her—a strappy garden plant called mother-in-law's tongue.

The two children came in, panting and laughing. Maria was seven, had the Tunbull hair and yellowish eyes, and promised to be very pretty when she matured; Billy was five, the same in coloring, and a little rotund; he had his mother's sunny nature and a lust for adventure that kept her in a lather of worry.

"Mom, it's starting to snow," said Maria. "Please may we stay outdoors a while?"

"Yes, yes!" Billy trumpeted.

Lily considered it, smiled and nodded. "An hour," she said. "Maria, keep an eye on your watch, you can tell the time. Bring Billy back whether he wants to or not."

Off they trooped; she sat down.

"Chez has changed out of all recognition," said Val, still prone to dissolve into tears. "Em would have been so impressed."

"I hardly remember him," Ivan said, tackling his creamed chipped beef and toast with enthusiasm; he hadn't much liked his mother, especially after he married Lily and discovered how lovely women could be. "Except," he said, swallowing a delicious mouthful, "he looked like a greaser. *And* a hood. Didn't he hang out with Vito Gianotti, Dad?"

"He sure did. He must have been arrested a dozen times for this or that, but the cops always had to let him go. He had a brain. He also had a high opinion of himself. About fifteen years ago he moved to New York City and never bothered to come back, even on a visit. But he sent Em really good jewelry on her birthdays and Christmases. It'll all go to you now, Lily. A New York City cop up here making enquiries told me he was running a racket involving good looking, sexy girls, but not as prostitutes. Used them to blackmail old guys of some pretty big payments. If one was uncooperative, he had a special girl he'd send to see the wife. But he was clever, the cops couldn't pin a thing on him or his stable. Then about five years ago he skipped. Even Em had no idea whereabouts he'd gone," said Val, less fond of creamed chipped beef.

"Did Emily like him?" Lily asked.

"No. She thought he dragged the family down."

"Not anymore," said Ivan, running a finger of toast around his plate. "He doesn't look like a businessman, but he sure doesn't look like a greaser or a hood. In Florida, what he wears is probably what businessmen wear instead of suits."

"When are you away again?" Val asked his son.

"The week after next. I have to be here for the inquests, I can understand that. But it's time to distribute reader's copies of the book."

"Is Jim going to do signings?" Val asked.

"I hope so. The Tattered Cover wants him, so does Hunter's—his namesake bookstore, huh?"

"Somehow I can't see Jim sparing the time."

A car engine sounded; Ivan looked out the window. "It's Uncle Chez." He looked puzzled. "Why *is* he here, Dad? Sure, Mom was his sister, and we know he loved her, but it doesn't make a lot of sense. He's always eased his conscience with diamonds. No, Uncle Chez is here for a different reason."

"That's as may be, Ivan, but whatever you say, don't say that," Val implored. "He may not look crooked, but Chez is."

The door opened, Chez strolled in bearing a package. He came around the table to Lily and pressed the package into her hand. "Thank you, Lily," he said.

"What for?" she asked, bewildered.

"Cleaning up after Emily."

The package contained a magnificent diamond bracelet.

"You just let me know if anyone ever makes you unhappy," said Chez to Lily once the bracelet was on her wrist. "Anyone does, he's a dead man."

Lily laughed. Ivan smiled. Val looked horrified.

MONDAY, JANUARY 13, 1969

The inquest into the death of John Tunbull Hall was a brief business that tendered a verdict of murder by a person or persons unknown.

Carmine's concerns were not for the inquest. John Tunbull Hall's adoptive father, Wendover Hall, had not thus far arrived in Holloman. His booking on Saturday night's red-eye special out of Seattle had not been canceled, and no further booking had been made. Though he lived in Gold Beach, Oregon, he had chosen to shuttle to Seattle rather than to San Francisco. Two brief conversations with Wendover Hall had convinced Carmine he did have information to impart, but disliked conversing with people whose faces he couldn't see. He would save his news for a face-to-face confrontation in Holloman.

At noon on Monday, the inquest over, Carmine called Hall at Gold Beach. No one answered. Not for one moment did foul play cross Carmine's mind; if Hall stood in danger, it would be after he got to Holloman. Even so, he called the local cops to see if they knew anything, like whether Hall was still home.

"The poor old guy died of a heart attack Saturday morning on his way to Seattle," said a cop voice that obviously knew Wendover Hall in person.

"Natural causes?" Carmine asked.

"Without a doubt. Silly old geezer shouldn't have been traveling anywhere, his heart was so bad." Came the rustle of papers. "On autopsy, a massive myocardial infarct."

Delia was looking enquiring; Carmine hung up. "Died of a heart attack, doesn't seem any doubt about that. And we are fated not to know more about our first victim."

"Sometimes it seems to me that this country is *too* big," said Delia, sighing. "West Coast people are quite different from East Coast people, and the people in the middle are very different again. Not to mention northerners and southerners. Poor old man! We should have gone to see him."

"Try telling Accounts that," Carmine said ruefully.

"Where now, Chief?"

"I wish I knew."

"Do you have any ideas—as to the guilty party, I mean?"

"Jim Hunter is still my chief suspect, but unless I can prove he took the poison from his wife's refrigerator, the evidence is pure supposition. Nor does it answer the riddle of why John Hall had to die. Tinkerman is obvious. Had his been the only death, we could have built a circumstantial case. Then there's Emily—what on earth could she have known?"

"If Jim Hunter is guilty, then the first and the third deaths could be red herrings. You know as well as I do that killing one person is enough to institute a mind-set. If more deaths ensue, the killer doesn't seem to experience additional remorse, or emotional travail of *some* kind. If the first and the third victims take the heat off Jim Hunter, they have a purpose."

"True."

Delia coughed delicately. "Um—have you considered Millie Hunter at all?"

Carmine lifted his head as though someone had speared him through the chest. "Yes, Deels, of course I have."

"She could have done all three, Carmine. She knew John was in town because he visited her and Jim out on State Street, and she could have lain in wait for him immediately before the men went into Max's den. She could have laced Emily's water carafe, and tell me who better to substitute the B-12? The tetrodotoxin belonged to her."

"Then, first of all, why did she declare the tetrodotoxin missing? And did she—or Jim, for that matter—know about Tinkerman and his problem absorbing B-12?" Carmine asked.

"Let me see Mrs. Tinkerman," Delia said eagerly.

"Sure, whenever you like." Carmine got to his feet. "I think it's time I saw Dean Wainfleet."

"Who's he?"

"Dean of Divinity. Therefore Tinkerman's old boss."

If I have any complaints about Carmine Delmonico, Delia thought as she drove to Busquash, it is that he fails to see that some women witnesses should be questioned by a woman—*me!* The moment Mrs. Tinkerman told him about the B-12, he was out the door. Whereas I would have stayed for a cup of tea and a chat: those who drop one bombshell sometimes have two tucked in their bomb bays. Mrs. T. strikes me as the two-bomb type.

Though she had never set eyes on Edith Tinkerman before, one look told Delia that a weekend contemplating a future minus her husband and plus a quarter of a million dollars to spend had benefited the lady greatly. The home perm was still there and the clothes still made by her own hand, but the brown eyes sparkled and the face held no care-lines. A week ago, Delia divined, the eyes would have been dull and the care-lines many.

"I hope I don't intrude?" Delia asked in her very poshest Oxford accent. "There are just one or two things to clear up."

Nothing had the power to frighten Mrs. Tinkerman now that Tom was no more: she smiled. "Tea?" she asked, taking a punt on the accent.

"Oh, lovely! Yes, please." Delia gazed around the kitchen. "How nice you've made it look. I always think that of all the rooms a house possesses, the kitchen gives its mistress away best. Oh, a choice! Twining's, too! Thank you, Earl Grey."

The table, she was interested to see, had been cleared of the dressmaking impedimenta Carmine had described; Delia sat down, content to wait until the tea and her hostess arrived.

The Earl Grey was accompanied by sugar cookies—pounds to peanuts, thought Delia, that Mrs. T. hadn't been allowed to make sugar cookies. She'd gone on a baking spree at the weekend.

"How long were you married?" Delia asked after expending sufficient effort on putting Edith Tinkerman at her ease.

"Twenty-four years."

"All spent at Chubb?"

"Yes, at the School of Divinity. Tom was an ordained and fully functioning Episcopalian bishop, though his diocese was just Chubb and the Divinity School. He was also a prominent scholar of the Middle Ages. Dean Wainfleet's interests lay elsewhere, so Tom was the school's expert in his field."

"You call him Tom. I would have thought your husband the kind of man who preferred to be addressed as Thomas."

"Oh, he was! But I called him Tom." She cleared her throat. "I'd feel more comfortable if you called me Edie, Sergeant."

"Only," said Delia with a magnificent gesture, "if you call me Delia. What did Tom call you?"

"Edith."

"And was Tom potty about his work?"

Edith Tinkerman blinked. "Er—potty?"

"Nuts. Insane. My papa was an Oxford don before he retired—quite, quite potty, poor old dear! He has an atom bomb shelter in the backyard. My mother's having a frightful time persuading him that he doesn't need to shut himself up in it now that Mr. Nixon is President."

"Your papa sounds interesting, at least. I'm afraid that Tom wasn't interesting. He was very boring."

"How long had he suffered from the B-12 business?"

"A long, long time," said the widow vaguely. "I always thought it was Tom's attempt to be interesting. Certainly he made no secret of it anywhere."

"Did he not, now? That *is* interesting! Wasn't he worried that when people knew he was shooting up, he'd be thought an addict to some nefarious drug?"

"No. B-12 is such a striking color, and he always waved the syringe around, or the ampoule, and it looked legitimate—or he thought it did, anyway. He made such a production out of needing his B-12 shot—had to sit down, fan himself, gasp a lot, complain of feeling faint. My guess is that most of those who saw him were convinced he had some malign disease, and he loved that. Then the minute he was given his shot, he'd jump about as if he'd been cured by Jesus Christ."

"That's impossible," Delia said flatly.

"Tell me about it, Delia. The doctors all said it takes days for the shot to have any effect, but that didn't impress Tom. He was convinced it worked immediately."

"So it was really an attention-seeking mechanism," Delia said. "However, he was fairly furtive at the banquet, yes?"

"That fit too," said Edith. "He was too pedantic to be any kind of speaker except a boring one, but he thought he spoke well because his sentences were properly parsed and analyzed—Tom had a passion for correct English. It had been years since he had had a wider audience than Divinity students, and he was very nervous. M.M. disliked him, and he knew it. And, of course, he knew M.M. had fought against his appointment as Head Scholar strenuously. Roger and Henry Parson got him the post, and they were in his audience too. So he was petrified, Delia."

"I understand, Edie. Go on, dear."

"M.M. reminded him that he was only minutes away from his big moment, and he panicked. The only thing that could calm him down was a shot. Even from where I sat three over from him, I could see it coming—sure enough, he signaled me. So I left the table at once, did my thing with the ampoule and the TB syringe, then left the Ladies. He was waiting in the corner, in a real stew. His agitation made me nervous, and I started to cry." She shivered, remembering. "Anyway, I gave him the shot in his neck and he rushed back to the table. I don't think anyone even noticed I was missing."

"Where did you get that particular ampoule, Edie?"

"That was weird!" she exclaimed. "It was sitting with the syringe right next to my handbag, but I don't remember putting it there. I must have, I guess—Tom was in a bad mood before we started out, and I get—got—flustered when he was in a bad mood. I put the things in my bag."

"Where do you keep the B-12?"

She got up and went to a full length door that opened into a pantry—a closet shelved at intervals on three sides that contained groceries and stores of non-toxic items from toilet paper to washing powder. A wooden box about half the size of a shoe box sat on a shelf; Edith Tinkerman carried it to the table and Delia.

"There, that's where I keep it."

Delia opened it to discover order and method: ten tuberculin syringes in sterile paper packets, a 10cc bottle of ruby-red cyanocobalamin with a rubber diaphragm in its top, six 1cc glass ampoules of the vitamin for single doses, and a box of swabs.

"Who knows it's there?"

"At least half the Divinity school."

"How come?"

"Sometimes Tom would send a student home for the box—he never kept any supplies at school."

"So he gave himself a shot if necessary?" Delia asked.

The brown eyes widened incredulously. "Oh, no! Never! He hated even looking at the needle. There were several people at the school who were willing to give him a shot."

"Was he a bit of a joke at the school?"

"A lot of a joke, I'd say. Tom was so pompous, and I've always thought pompous people make the best joke material. One year it even crept into the student concert—a sketch about Tom and his B-12. I laughed myself sick."

"What did Tom do?"

"Pretended it never happened."

Delia scooped up the box. "I have to confiscate this, dear. For all we know, it might contain more poison."

"Am I going to be arrested?" The widow gave a harsh laugh. "It would be just like the rest of my life to be thrown in jail for Tom's murder."

"No, Edith, you're definitely not going to be arrested," said Delia in her most soothing voice. "You were simply what we call a vector—a method of transmitting the poison to its target. As far as you were concerned, the syringe contained vitamin B-12. Everybody understands that, I do assure you. Let me help wash the dishes."

"You've set my mind at rest, Delia," said Edith over the dish mop. "I was worried."

But, thought Delia, you haven't set my mind at rest, Edith! Somewhere in your bomb bay there's another bomb, and I haven't located it. So she said, "May I come again?"

"Oh, I'd love that!"

"Are you going to stay in Holloman?"

"No. The girls and I talked it over yesterday, and we've decided to go to Arizona. We're going to buy three apartments next door to each other. The girls will work as secretaries and I'll take in dressmaking. Our inheritance money we'll save to go on cruises and long vacations," said the widow, painting a picture that perhaps would not have been everybody's idea of bliss, but clearly twenty-four years of Thomas Tarleton Tinkerman had lowered the expectations of all three Tinkerman women.

"Your daughters might find husbands," Delia said.

A giggle erupted. "And pigs might fly!"

Dean Charles Wainfleet was upset at the manner of Dr. Tinkerman's passing, but immensely pleased to be rid of him.

"The most painful bore ever wished on this school," he said to Carmine frankly.

"Would you have tolerated him were the Parsons not his most ardent patrons?" Carmine asked, smiling. The Dean was a formidable Renaissance scholar who had incorporated philosophy and history into his school, but, as his answer to Carmine's question revealed, he knew which side his bread was buttered on.

"Without Parson patronage, he would have been gone," said Wainfleet cheerfully. "As it was, Tom brought a lot of Parson money our way in the form of endowments for several chairs—including his own, I add. The humanities and religion are not pulling in the number of students they used to, but Chubb Divinity has enjoyed relative prosperity thanks to the Parsons, including the number of students enrolled in the college. They endow in many ways."

"Is there anything I should know about Dr. Tinkerman that is known only within these college walls?" Carmine asked.

"Only that he didn't give up his Chair of Medieval Christian Studies when he assumed his role as Head Scholar. He thought he could combine both, though he had taken a sabbatical for his first year at C.U.P. After that, both would function equally well. I didn't agree, but the Parson Brothers did."

"Either the man was a fool, or a demon for work."

"A little of each, actually. For instance, he had managed to read every book C.U.P. had on its publication list, not only definitely to be published, but also possibly. Including several scientific works that can have meant nothing to him. He said he was reading them for—er—*style*."

"That's the fool," Carmine said.

"Perhaps, but only perhaps, Captain. Tom Tinkerman wasn't a critic of the colloqualism per se, nor even of what Percy Lee would call sloppy prose. His passion was style, and he really believed every author had a unique one. Dr. James Hunter was his obsession—he read *A Helical God*, he read Jim's two other books, and every paper he ever published. *A Helical God* offended his ideals, ethics and principles, but style entered into it too, as it did Jim's other works. He would rant in his stiff, quiet way about God's taking as much offense from style as from content—isn't that extraordinary? I always felt that race lay at the bottom of Tom's fixation on Hunter—at heart he was a bigot. Tom's idea of God was of a white man, and black men with Jim Hunter's degree of intellectual excellence had to be torn down."

"That's a terrible indictment, Dean."

"I know it. Had he not died, anything might have happened."

"Did Dr. Tinkerman and Dr. Hunter ever lock horns in public?"

"Once, that I know of. Just before Christmas, at one of M.M.'s professorial shindigs. Tom attacked Jim Hunter as if he'd personally crucified Jesus Christ. It was embarrassing."

"Do you remember the gist of it?"

"Lord, no! We all moved out of earshot. It seemed wiser."

"Just before Christmas? So the new Head Scholar's identity was known?"

"Yes. Christmas Eve. M.M. was oozing bonhomie and Yule-tide cheer—principally the egg-nog."

"Did M.M. hear it?"

"No. Bobby Highman was telling one of his better stories."

"How did Jim take the attack?"

"Nobly. A trifle pinched around the mouth, but he kept his cool. It was Tom who lost it."

"As only uptight guys can lose it, I imagine. Thank you for that, Dean. It gives me one idea." Carmine grimaced. "I'm not sure I can follow where the idea leads, but I can try."

An extraordinary idea, but one that wouldn't go away. Yet it had nothing to do with style, or with confrontations. It just popped into Carmine's brain along with Dean Wainfleet's verbal description of how things looked at a distance, when nothing could be heard, but much inferred from, when it all boiled down, very little.

Gus Fennell was just out of the autopsy room, and tired. "Oh, what now?" he demanded crossly, then gave himself a visible shake. "Sorry, Carmine. Having Patrick sequestered makes for too much work in my court and not enough in his."

"We'll move to fix that as soon as possible, Gus. Now sit down and I'll get you a coffee."

"I'd rather tea," Gus said, still peevish.

Carmine brought him tea. "Lemon, or milk?"

"Just plain, thanks." He sipped, closed his eyes. "Ah, better! What are you after, Carmine?"

"The answer to a question. Did you do histology on John Hall's neck puncture?"

"Sure."

"What did it show? I must have skimmed over it."

The file was on his desk; Gus opened it. "A definite invasion of tissue, but very shallow. In fact, epithelium only." He reached for his half glasses and read, frowning. "I see why you don't remember. Whoever did the actual histology made a botch of it. I guess the lab was in a panic over this new and undetectable poison, and Paul had his best guy on that as well as himself. They pinch-hit, which is why they're so good—no matter what the forensic task is, one of them can do the analysis or histology or ballistics or—or—it's a long list. We don't have the money or the work for separate technicians. But I remember this because he was a new guy—Brad. Turns out his skills are in ballistics, guns, that kind of thing."

"So we don't *know?*" Carmine asked.

"About the depth of the penetration, no."

"Could you possibly look at the slides, Gus? I'll buy you lunch at Malvolio's any day you like if you do," Carmine wheedled.

"Lucky for you all the tetrodotoxin cases are still in the lab," said Gus, intrigued by now. He found John Hall's box of specimen histology, and the dozen slides on the neck wound.

"Actually they're okay," he said, surprised, looking up from his microscope with raccoon's eyes from pressing too hard. "I'd say the deeper layers of cells weren't penetrated at all. I think your guy received a subcutaneous injection, not an intramuscular one."

"What exactly does that mean in terms of symptoms, Gus?"

"Slower onset. This is very precise, if Brad the technician didn't botch his sections. I must tell Paul to erase any black marks on Brad's record. The needle lifted the skin and slid just under it, which you could do if the substance were concentrated and all you had to inject was a drop or two, rather than a full cc. Also, it couldn't have been done at all with that gizmo you showed me—not nearly precise enough." Gus heaved a sigh of satisfaction. "I must rewrite this."

"How much of a delay would subcutaneous injection cause?"

The pathologist thought about it. "Depends on how rich the subcutaneous tissue was in blood vessels, but the slides say it wasn't fatty—the deceased kept himself fit, I'd say. So taking all that into account, anything from an extra ten to an extra twenty minutes."

"Gus, my man, you are a pearl beyond price, and lunch at Malvolio's just became lunch at the Lobster Pot."

From the M.E.'s domain Carmine went to the Commissioner's.

"Did you know that human fat or adipose tissue is rich in blood vessels?" Carmine demanded as he walked in.

"Well, bless my Aunt Annunziata's arm flaps! To what is this germane, O honored Captain of Detectives?"

Silvestri in skittish mood meant his day was going well; Carmine stifled a sigh. "John Hall's neck is germane, O great and wise Commissioner of Police. It had no fatty tissue worth a dime, therefore no wealth of subcutaneous blood vessels, and no needle punctured his muscle tissue. In other words, he had a lightly built man's scraggy neck. Our poisoner was very crafty indeed, John. He administered a highly concentrated injection of tetrodotoxin just under John Hall's epithelium—no more than a drop or two, Gus thinks."

"So the time window has opened up," Silvestri said softly.

"The deed was done *before* they went into the den."

"How did we miss it, Carmine?"

"Human error, oversight, false premise, take your pick. No one's fault, really, except they put a new technician on taking the histology sections, and, expecting a needle track, blamed the technician when it wasn't there. The kid was right, Gus wrong."

"What made you wonder about it now, Carmine?"

"I don't honestly know, except that something Dean Wainfleet said on an unrelated subject caused a weird shift in my mind, and I suddenly wondered if a subcutaneous injection would slow the reaction time down enough to enable the deed to be done before the men went into the study. Once the symptoms appeared, Hall died quickly—eleven minutes. That says the stuff was concentrated. It was worth a visit to Gus Fennell, I thought."

"Well worth it. Not that it advances proof of guilt."

"Exactly." Carmine sighed. "You know, I could really do with a decent bank robbery or a shoot-out in the Chubb Bowl just for sheer recreation."

"Always the way with poison cases," said Silvestri. "It ought by rights to be a woman, but the pickings are lean."

"Women like a more normal brew. However, there is a woman— Millie. It's her poison, she made it."

"Millie didn't do it," the Commissioner said abruptly.

"I know, she's an open book," said Carmine. "There are two other women with motive, but they don't have the know-how, John. Davina Tunbull and Uda Savovich. We've been digging for a week and come up with nothing that suggests either woman would know tetrodotoxin from tetrachloride—unless Davina is in cahoots with Jim. The only death I can see the Savovich women perpetrating is Emily Tunbull's. She fits their bill, the others don't. I keep coming back to Jim Hunter, but if he did it, he's likely to get away with it because there's nothing in evidence that points to him that doesn't point to Millie as well, and Millie's sacrosanct."

"With good reason," Silvestri said stubbornly.

"And around we go again."

"Did you search Tinkerman's study at his home?"

"Every last sheet of paper. He dealt with his bills himself, paid them. A testament to his stinginess. Tinkerman even listed his wife's allowance as a bill." Carmine put his elbows on the desk and his chin on his hands. "We found nothing."

"Is there some other glaring mistake we've overlooked?"

"With Delia on the job? I doubt it."

"So do I."

This time Davina drove to Major Minor's to meet Chez; she hadn't realized how far it was to walk, and the days of the Yugoslavian Alps were long past. She parked around the back and walked to the coffee shop through an arcade of grisly photographs. Major Minor, thought Davina, is a pervert.

"At the rate the cops are going, you might be here until Christmas and still not see Emily's killer," she said, sitting down and flashing that smile at the waitress.

"Does anyone in the family know why Emily was killed?"

"No, and Uda hasn't heard anything."

"What am I going to do with you, Vina?"

Her eyes narrowed. "In relation to what?"

"Certain New York City activities."

"Ah! *That's* why you're here! Worried that you might be extradited from Florida to New York for something?" Davina asked sweetly. "I knew it wasn't Emily. You'd just send her a diamond wreath."

"Shut up!" he snapped.

"Relax, Chez, I'm not going to upset your apple cart any more than you're going to upset mine. So far the cops haven't noticed you, but they will, and they're smart, Chez. I'm an ostrich with my head in the sand, but I'm well aware what a good target my ass makes." She leaned forward; the waitress would not have liked this smile. "Leave me alone! I am set for life, and I like the life I'm living. You don't scare me! Nothing does! If I need help, I have Uda, never forget that. I am cultured now. I have a child I adore. I am not letting you ruin my life! I—am—not!"

"I want Em's killer caught."

"I don't care what you want. Leave me alone!"

He really does make a room look small, Max Tunbull reflected as he sat, an attentive expression on his face, gazing at Dr. Jim Hunter.

"Publication Day is April second," Max said.

"Three months off," Dr. Jim said, smiling. "I can hardly believe it. I always thought writing the book would be the worst agony, but it was nothing compared to Tinkerman. I wish harm to no one, but with Dr. Millstone as Head Scholar, things will be different. He's everything I could ask for."

"Davina had a talk with him," Max said, then stopped.

Jim looked enquiring. "And?"

"I don't honestly know how to say this, nor do I understand why I was given this duty, but the crux of the matter is that C.U.P. has no publicity department," said Max, laboring. "It never really needed one, even for *Fire Down Below*—the book about earthquakes that was a big best seller five years ago. But everybody from Davina to the Board of Scholars thinks that your book needs a professional publicist. Fulvia and Bettina have found one for you. Her name is Pamela Devane, she's a freelance working out of New York City, and she's the best in the business. Chauce Millstone and Davina have both talked with her—she's on the ball! She's planning a month-long publicity tour for April—New York City, Boston, Chicago, Washington D.C., Atlanta, San Francisco, L.A., Seattle, Denver, St. Louis—about twenty cities in all. Some, like New York and L.A., take several days. TV talk shows, radio shows, newspaper and magazine interviews, a few more esoteric things. Millie has to go with you to participate in some interviews . . ." Max trailed off, disconcerted.

Jim was staring at him in horror. "I can't do that!" he cried, the words erupting as if they didn't belong together. "I can't leave my work for *half* a month, let alone a month! Not at this stage! I figured I'd have to drive down to New York City for one or two interviews, not traipse around the nation—Jeez!"

"Vina said it would come as a shock, but none of us believed her," said Max, flustered. "She insisted we bring in Pamela Devane to support you through it as well as make you see why you have to do it. I thought she was over-reacting, but Chauce was out on a limb—he's too new in the job to understand something as unusual as the potential of *A Helical God*. But sometimes my wife can be uncanny, she just seemed to know how you'd react." Max put out a hand. "Jim, be reasonable! A publicity tour is vital."

"Spend a month saying the same things over and over to a bunch of tiros?" The eyes were incredulous. "Waste my time on something so *stupid?* No!"

Max sighed. "Go home and talk to Millie," he said.

But a visit to the Burke found no Millie—she was at the apartment? In the middle of the afternoon? What was the matter? *What?*

He drove out on State Street to Caterby Street, burst through the door as if pursued.

"Don't tell me you came home to help," she said, kissing him.

There were boxes everywhere; she must have looted every shop's trash to have collected so many. And books. Piles and piles of books, journals, photocopies.

"Dad found us a house on Barker Street in East Holloman, and we're moving. Imagine it, Jim! Moving out of this dump into a great house—and it's a great deal as well! The Tucci Realtors own some houses for rent as well as for sale. Our house is one of them, and if we find a down payment on it within a year, the rent we've paid in the meantime will be contributed toward the purchase price—isn't that wonderful? It has three bedrooms, a room that will make an ideal study for you, a decent kitchen, a huge family room, a laundry, a backyard, a two-car garage—oh, Jim, I'm so happy!"

Millie happy took his breath away; Jim kissed her to limp ecstasy, then, lifting her as if she weighed a feather, carried her to the bedroom to kiss her back to frenzied, tumultuous, exalted response. With each other in the most secret and sacred of ways, they forgot publicity tours, books and boxes.

"You still turn me on," she said, head on his chest, feeling as much as hearing that massive heart beat, beat, beat . . .

"Ditto," he said, a laugh in his voice.

"Can you help me pack?"

"Sure. Walter can deal with the lab." He slid out from under her and headed for the bathroom.

It was over, but it had been a wonderful gift. He was usually so tired, so desperate for sleep, so tormented when he did get to sleep. Who knows? she thought as she left the bed, this hour of afternoon delight might have set me on my way. I've calmed down; even though the canker of Davina will continue to gnaw, a pregnancy is far more mine than Jim's. The baby will belong to *me*.

"Why did you come home?" she asked, back with the books.

Distressed, he told her of his talk with Max. "People are taking over my life, Millie," he said. "How come you never told me about the down side of a best seller?"

"It never occurred to me," she confessed. "I mean, writers of best sellers don't talk about publicity tours, you just see them or hear them or read about them, and the pieces of the puzzle are just that, pieces. Like you, I thought it would be a few interviews done in New York City."

"I can't afford the time, and I don't suffer fools gladly."

"I know." She gave him a brilliant smile, eyes filled with love. "I guess just this once, Jim, we're hoist on your petard. The tour will have to be done, which means you'll have to hang on to your temper and suffer the fools gladly."

"They're going to make capital out of our marriage."

"Yes, I inferred that." She blinked, her breath caught. "Oh, Jim! Best feet forward, all that garbage. We'll survive."

"We always have, no matter what the odds."

"We've had some narrow escapes."

"And some victories."

"Why did you listen to that snake of a woman?" she asked.

"Davina?" He looked blank for a moment, then, apparently drawn by something on a wall bare of its books, turned his gaze there. "Like I told you already, I respect her opinions. She has the guts to say what other people only think, and she's worldly. You and I are babes in the woods, she says. Heads buried in our work, no experience of living."

"That's an over-simplification, Jim. Why are you so afraid of the world's judgements all of a sudden? I would have said you and I are veterans of what the world can do," Millie said stiffly. "I can't stop you regarding Davina as an oracle, but don't let her move into *my* space. I won't stomach Davina Tunbull in *my* space."

He looked stunned. "Are you jealous?"

"No. Just on my guard. Strange things are happening, and don't tell me you're not on your guard."

His desire to change the subject was transparent; he laughed, then said, "What are we going to do for furniture? Is the new place already furnished?"

"No, it's too up-market for that," said Millie, obliging him. "Mom and Dad have donated a few pieces, so have the Ceruttis, the Silvestris, and the half of East Holloman that's related to me." Her eyes and voice grew suddenly sharp. "And don't poker up, Jim! It is *not* charity. Later on we'll be buying our own furniture, when we'll return what was loaned. That's all it is—a loan. *A loan!* Okay?"

That was a tone he understood: don't mess with Millie! So he nodded. "Okay by me, sweetheart. When do we move?"

"Tomorrow." The blue of her eyes, so pure and seemingly unmarred by life, spat sudden fire. "This is my last night on State Street, and never again. Hear me, Jim? Never again!"

Edith Tinkerman was packing too, though not with such triumphant finality. Probate took time—she would ask Dean Wainfleet if he knew anyone who could speed it up a little—so the house could not be sold. However, the Dean had put her in touch with a law firm that had freed up some of Tom's staggering savings, so she wasn't worried where the next meal was coming from.

In her opinion the police had been very kind—really, really considerate. They had been obliged to search the house, especially Tom's study, but they had put everything back where it belonged. Anne and Catherine, who watched TV a lot, had thought they would create a terrible mess because the TV cops did. Well, that was the difference between reality and what Tom had called the "boob tube." Would a Delia Carstairs permit her colleagues to make a mess? The Holloman police were *civilized*.

Too civilized, as it turned out. Edith had forgotten to tell them about Tom's secret drawer, and the cops hadn't inspected that section of wall because it was covered by an ugly old Russian madonna and child Tom seemed to think far better than an Andrew Wyeth, and he was the best American painter living. In Edith's view, a thousand years of age couldn't turn bad art into good.

Now she stood, dismayed, in her husband's study and debated what she ought to do. Look first, she decided, went to the really ugly painting, and lifted it down. The wall behind was just wall save for a thin crack that outlined a shallow drawer whose handle was the picture hook. Understanding that the icon was worth more than the whole house, Carmine and Abe hadn't touched it, reasoning that nor would Thomas Tinkerman.

The drawer was where Tom always kept work in progress. It wasn't necessary to hide his efforts, he knew that well, but something in his constricted being took pleasure in pretending that his efforts were important enough to require hiding, if only from fellow scholars. Hence the drawer.

Edith pulled it out to find it stuffed quite full of loose sheets of paper, on top of which was a letter Tom himself had written using his gold Parker fountain pen. It was signed, therefore ready to be sent— why hadn't he sent it? she wondered, gazing at its addressee. Probably something to do with the papers.

Police forgotten, she moved to the phone on Tom's desk, and for the first time in her life sat in Tom's beautiful leather chair. Best call the addressee and find out what to do next.

She picked up the receiver and dialed—no push-buttons for Thomas Tarleton Tinkerman!

One of Uda's tiny hands reached for one of the baby's tiny hands and their fingers clung while he gurgled gleefully.

"Alexis is the most beautiful baby I have ever seen," Uda said huskily.

Black mop of unkinked hair glistening in the light, the baby's head came forward; up went the green eyes to his mother's face. Her heart caved in, it was all she could do not to squeeze him to death. So much love! Whoever could have guessed the ecstasy of motherhood without experiencing it? I have killed to save myself and Uda, Davina thought, but only when nothing else would answer. Whereas I would kill for Alexis if anyone looked sideways at him.

"I have decided not to go ahead with my plans for Chez at this time," she said to Uda, but not in English.

Uda blinked, lizardlike. "Is that wise? We can cope with him, we're two against one," she said, but not in English.

"Our unknown friend has let us down, and what should have been simple has turned into a mess. We must find another way."

"He will make allegations, Vina."

"That I, a very successful model, engaged in fraud and confidence tricks that I will try to blame on him—yes, we both know that," Davina said. "It is ludicrous."

Uda let Alexis's hand fall. "Chez is stupid, Vina, and life has gone too well for him. If you feel the time is not right, we should get in first. I know the Holloman police have taken his fingerprints, but have they thought to check them with the NYPD? This country is very much organized as states, his printing was routine. Let us anonymously inform the Holloman police that this Chester Malcuzinski was once Chester Derzinsky and had a record in New York City years ago. It can't hurt us, but it can switch Lieutenant Goldberg's attention to him."

"An excellent idea!" Davina stretched. "Yes, Uda, do it by telephone, with one of your American accents."

Uda went back to the baby, blowing bubbles to attract an admiring audience.

"You have disposed of the paraphernalia?" Davina asked, still not in English.

The black currant eyes flashed scorn. "It is safe."

"You did not destroy it."

"No one will find my bits and pieces, sister." Uda took the baby from Davina and held him against her meager chest. "It is time for his bottle, and my turn to give it."

Tonight there were no private moments with Desdemona; Carmine sat with his younger son on his lap, the cat wedged into the chair alongside him, while his elder son was marching up and down the little sitting room in imitation of a wooden soldier. Their house had been one of the first in East Holloman to get cable television; Desdemona wanted to search the channels for those she felt would not put ideas in Julian's head about guns and shoot-'em-deads.

But the British children's programs she had located had failed her; wooden soldiers in bearskin helmets marching up and down, wooden rifles over their shoulders.

"Julian, pipe down and read a book," Carmine said when the performance grew irritating.

He could read. Emilia Delmonico had been a famous kindergarten teacher with a genuine skill for teaching children to read, and on Julian's second birthday Desdemona had crumbled, asked her mother-in-law to teach Julian. Who was too bright, too busy, too much of a handful.

What annoyed Desdemona was Julian's tendency to obey his father as if he always obeyed every instruction or request given him: far from the truth. Though she had regained her ascendancy over him somewhat, Julian hadn't forgotten how easy it had been to bully Mommy during his defense attorney phase. So now the kid smiled angelically and went to his bean bag with his book, curled up there and did as he was told.

"He never does that for *me!*" she snapped, and could have bitten off her tongue. Carmine's amber eyes flew to her face, startled; he frowned.

"Desdemona, are you well?"

A question that made her even crosser. "Yes, yes, yes, of course I'm well!" she said angrily, sipping at her gin and tonic. "It's just that Julian has the knack of getting under Mummy's skin. He's too clever for his own good, and I find it difficult to manage him." Her hand flew out, the drink almost spilled. "It's not *right!*" she exclaimed. "I should be managing better—I ran a whole research facility, for heaven's sake! Now I can't even run a house where someone else does the cleaning. I could spit chips!"

The cat went flying, Alex was lifted effortlessly as Carmine rose to his feet. "You, my son, are going to bed." And off he went to the nursery, Alex looking a little stunned. At nine months he was crawling and jabbering; Desdemona was looking at life with another Julian to join the original model.

"Little pitchers have ears," he said when he returned, and pointing at Julian. The cat had taken all of his chair, fat body sprawled belly-up with paws sticking up. "Winston, go annoy Julian for a change," he said, dispossessing the cat with one scoop of his hand. "Go on, shoo! Where's Frankie?"

"In disgrace. Rolled in dead raccoon—I walloped him with a hollow tube and cleaned him off in cold water. Sooner or later he'll get the message that the ecstasy is not worth the icy torment afterward."

"My poor girl!" Carmine sat, his chair all to himself.

"It's early days for this case, so cheer up," she said, her own mood inexplicably lightened.

In answer, Carmine looked at his watch. "Bed, Julian."

This never provoked the storms it used to. Julian was one of those unfortunate human beings cursed with a night owl's nature—he found it difficult to get to sleep and even harder to wake up. Prunella Balducci had explained that it was simply the way Julian was made, not an impulse to disobedience. So a TV set appeared in the nursery tuned permanently to a cartoon channel, and Julian lay in bed and watched; for some reason, this lulled him to sleep far earlier than a dark and silent room did. Carmine called it a part of his defense attorney persona, though his accompanying laugh was a little wry.

Julian did have defense attorney characteristics, there was no denying it.

He came out of the bean bag lithely, as befitted such a tall and robust child. His beauty was still beauty, though it would transform into something more masculine long before he hit the playground of St. Bernard's Boys' School—dense black curls, black brows and lashes, topaz colored eyes with a dark ring around the iris that gave them a piercing look.

A kiss for Mommy, a kiss for Daddy, and he was gone, the book put tidily away on "his" shelf. Carmine's son: order and method, a place for everything.

"What's for dinner?" Carmine asked.

"Lasagna and salad, crisp bread rolls on the side."

"Fantastic!" He got himself a second drink. "What happened today to upset you, Desdemona?"

"The Monday Julians, is all. After having you to help me with him over the weekend, Monday is always hard. I love him to death, God knows I do, but we weren't fortunate with the personality of our first-born, Carmine. He's a permanent handful, not because he's nasty or malign, he isn't. But he's domineering and intensely driven. I just don't have the strength I did before this wretched depression." She flopped into her chair and stared at her drink, frowning. "No, love, don't freshen it up. I have a strange feeling that I ought to limit myself to one drink at night and one glass of wine with the meal. I'm a huge person, so I can tolerate alcohol better than a basketball cheerleader, yet . . . I don't have addictive qualities, but I know I can't let myself get fuzzy in the head. It's a feeling, that's all."

"Go with it. Gut instincts are valid, and you do seem to attract trouble from time to time," Carmine said, voice tender. "Let's talk about my case. You think it's only early days?"

"Yes. This is one of your difficult cases, dear heart, and I've come to some conclusions about them."

"Expound," he said, watching her narrowly.

"There's no concrete evidence, is that right?"

"On the knocker."

"You have your suspicions?"

"More than suspicions. Convictions."

"Oh, I see! That makes it far worse, of course. What I've noticed about the difficult cases is that the break, if and when it comes, is almost by accident."

"A fall down a leafy bank," he said musingly.

"Yes. But if no freak occurrence happens, the only way to solve the case is by confession. Which makes sense," she said, warming to her theme. "Ordinary crimes are committed by ordinary people. They don't think things through, they don't plan for every move and every eventuality. Clever criminals do, and none is more subtle than the poisoner. This tetrodotoxin nearly put you back in Thomas Tinkerman's middle ages, not so? When someone could slip aconite or cyanide into another's food or drink, and who could tell? I would judge this killer so extremely clever that he—or she!—has successfully planned for every eventuality. It's like the footprints of a complex dance pattern on a floor—left foot there, right foot here, a turn, a swirl, and who knows where the dance picks up again? This is a confession case, my love, I can see that, which means you have to force a confession not by trickery but by patience and stealth. This killer makes no mistakes."

"A confession crime," he said flatly.

"Yes. Consider! A very rare and unobtainable poison gets into the hands of people who were, if not instructed how to use it, were at least pushed sufficiently in the right direction to use it. Look at poor Mrs. Tinkerman. All she did was something she'd done a hundred times before. She had no idea that her syringe contained the rare poison. However," Desdemona said in a dreamy tone, "he didn't kill Emily Tunbull. That one doesn't fit, though I think he supplied the poison. John Hall and Thomas Tinkerman. Though Emily's murder suits him. It muddies the waters, since she died by tetrodotoxin. Oh, he's clever!"

"It's the hydra-headed monster, isn't it?"

"Yes. You have to aim for the heart, not cut off the heads." She got up, extended her hands to pull him up. "But I haven't told you a single thing you don't already know," she said, going kitchenward.

He went to wash his hands, laid the table and slid into his side of the booth as she loaded their plates.

"We don't know enough about John Hall's life before he turned up in Holloman, and the death of Wendover Hall was a bad blow," he said, watching her. "Today I sent Liam Connor to the West Coast to find out what he can. There was some kind of psychiatric illness in John's late teens involving a halfway house, and it's always possible Liam will track down someone who was at Caltech at the same time as John and the Hunters. Wendover Hall didn't employ a domestic staff except for a cleaning woman, but that's not to say there aren't people in Oregon who know all kinds of things about John Hall."

"Concentrate on his links to Jim Hunter," Desdemona said, putting his plate in front of him. "Hunter's a secretive man."

TUESDAY, JANUARY 14, 1969

Edith Tinkerman had left a message for Sergeant Delia Carstairs with the police switchboard to the effect that she had something further she wished to discuss: she would be at home on Tuesday.

The second bombshell! thought Delia exultantly, rather glad that she had worn this fabulous new coat of shaggy synthetic monkey fur with a glittering gold thread woven through it to match the thread in her mustard-and-orange suit. She drove out to Busquash to arrive around ten a.m. The correct hour in Mrs. Tinkerman's mind for morning tea.

Surprised to find the front door a little ajar, Delia knocked on the jamb and called out. "Hello? Edie? It's Delia!"

When no one answered after several successively louder calls, she pushed the door open and entered. No lights on; the hallway was dim, gloomy even, and the air was cold. As if the heat had not been turned up in the evening, when the outside temperature plummeted. A Tinkerman economy?

Edie wasn't in the kitchen, the living room or her bedroom; best check the study, a room she didn't associate with Edie in any kind of mood.

She was sitting in Tinkerman's chair behind Tinkerman's desk, her head down and resting with its brow on her hands, folded on the slab of blotting paper sheathed in a chased Morocco holder.

Death was in the room too. Delia felt its hairless leathery wings brush past her, flap away bearing its prize.

Even the sockets of her teeth crawled with horror; she stepped around the desk and looked down. Because Edie hadn't tried to stem the floodtide of grey, the blood showed up clearly in the matted home-permed hair. Someone had shot her KGB style, a bullet through the base of the brain—over and done with in a split second. The blood had ceased welling but was still very fluid: no more than half an hour ago. Broad daylight on a Busquash street that would have been full of cars taking people to their places of work.

Her tears couldn't be let fall. Delia leaped away quickly and groped in her bag, past her 9mm Parabellum pistol and her tiny .22 Saturday night special revolver to find her lace-edged handkerchief, sop up the grief. Oh, this wasn't fair! Twice she had wept for women cut short. Oh, how dared he! To cheat this poor little woman of her hard-earned Arizona retirement—it didn't bear thinking of.

"But at least he was merciful," she said to Carmine minutes later as Gus and Paul went to work. "With any luck, she never even saw it coming. Her light would have just—gone out, poof! Though the way she's lying suggests to me that perhaps he went one step farther toward mercy by drugging her heavily."

"What brought you here, Deels?"

"She said she had something to discuss."

"Something to discuss with someone else as well. If she'd confined herself to you, she wouldn't be dead."

"Whoever it was, she trusted, saw no danger involved."

"Whatever she had to say can't have appeared significant to her beyond a niggle," Carmine said. "Oh, Jesus, four deaths! He did this one himself, couldn't cope with the thought that she might suffer. However he tricked her, I'm convinced she didn't know it was coming. I wonder whose is the gun?"

"A .22 by the look of the entry wound," Delia stated, still very upset. "Dainty little thing. No one would have heard the report." she gazed around. "Why was she in Tinkerman's chair? Carmine, Abe has to inspect this room. We missed something."

"It has to be behind the icon—it's so valuable I thought Tinkerman would never fiddle with it, so I put it off limits for the search. Stupid! He had no respect for art, even worth mega-bucks." Carmine's eyes rested on Delia's coat. "You look really delectable today too. Promise me you won't take against the coat—it's fantastic."

She cheered a little. "I promise."

"Let's get out of here and leave the experts to it."

She lurched. "Good idea. My blood sugar's down."

Abe found the secret drawer behind the priceless icon, that was a given, but whatever it had contained was gone.

"No fingerprints or other hard evidence either," Carmine said to Delia, sliding back into his Malvolio's booth after a session on Luigi's phone. "I asked Abe to inform the Tinkerman daughters' lawyers that there is an immensely valuable icon must be incorporated in his estate. There's no sticker says it's on loan from the Parsons, so why shouldn't those two poor girls enjoy the fruits of its sale? Possession is nine-tenths of the law." He huffed in satisfaction.

Delia was looking better. "What do you think was in the secret drawer?" she asked.

"Hard evidence, that's for sure. But it also suggests that Tinkerman was murdered for more than his appointment as the Head Scholar of C.U.P. He knew something about the killer that survived his death, that made the murder of his wife an urgent and immediate necessity."

"I'm all out of ideas," said Delia.

"Me too. It must be dynamite," Carmine said.

"At least in scholastic circles, which were the only circles Tinkerman knew—or cared about. I am flummoxed."

"Is that an English or an American word?" Carmine asked.

"What?"

"Flummoxed."

"I really don't know, except that my potty papa would probably say it derived from an English dialect."

"North, not south."

"Carmine, honestly!" Delia squawked. "What does it matter?"

"It doesn't except it's all in how you look at a thing."

Delia groped for the right reply, found it. "I'm flummoxed."

"Exactly."

Gus Fennell was more forthcoming.

"A hollow-nosed bullet. Made soup of her brain stem."

"Had she been drugged first?"

"A very large but non-lethal dose of Seconal. I'd say she had been asleep at the desk for hours when the bullet was fired."

"Head on the desk, as we found her?"

"Yes. I think he stayed with her until he was satisfied she was virtually comatose."

"Any evidence as to how it was administered?"

"Orally, but nothing containing Seconal was found. He must have removed the glass—a drink of some woman's tipple is my guess. He would have drunk whiskey. But no glasses."

"Painless, instantaneous, right?"

"Right," Gus agreed.

"A killer with scruples," said Carmine thoughtfully. "Thanks, Gus. Her daughters will apply for burial, probably in conjunction with their father. It isn't often kids bury both parents at once."

Abe, who had hovered on the periphery of Edith Tinkerman's murder, had more to say. "Whatever was in the drawer filled it," he said to Carmine at a general meeting later on.

"How could you tell that?" Carmine asked curiously.

"There was no high-water mark, if you get my meaning. When papers fill a space, they leave fibers and fragments behind clear to the top of the space. Like in this drawer, not a deep one at two inches. I had Paul run a 3-D microscope over its insides, and they displayed the same distribution of fibers, shreds, mites. The drawer wasn't packed, but it was full. In terms of sheets of paper, the number would depend on the weight of the paper. Twenty-pound rag, about a hundred sheets to every fifteen millimetres brand new, unused. Eight- or ten-pound crap, about twice that. If the sheets were crumpled or creased or even used, fewer. I couldn't even hazard a guess without knowing what was in the drawer," Abe said in his usual calm tones. "However, the paper wasn't high grade. Ordinary crap, judging from the fibers. If you pushed me to a guess, Carmine, I'd say about a hundred-fifty sheets of ordinary paper in non-mint condition."

"Any other observations? Those are brilliant."

"From Paul, one. The blotting paper bore impressions of a letter, several pages long, written in good grade blue-black ink with a fountain pen—or a nibbed pen, at any rate. Paul is working on the blotter, but doesn't hold out much hope. The pages were blotted on top of each other and in no particular sequence. Dr. Tinkerman may have prided himself on his penmanship, but he didn't care where he blotted what he'd written, and he was a frequent blotter. So Paul has the phrase 'may not have meant' free and clear, as well as 'I cannot believe that he intended this to remain as is' followed by many sentences that cover each other up completely." Abe shrugged. "Don't hope to solve the case on a piece of blotting paper, Carmine."

"Deeply appreciated, Abe, and convey my thanks to Paul."

Tony Cerutti spoke up. "I have information on Emily Tunbull's brother, Chester Malcuzinski," he said, trying to keep the excitement out of his voice.

"Ah! The Florida businessman! Shoot, Tony," said Carmine.

"I had an anonymous call from a guy with a Texas accent you could cut with a knife," Tony said. "According to Tex, Emily Tunbull's brother has a criminal history in New York state. He went by the name Chez Derzinsky—skee with a 'y'—and was known in certain circles as the Pollack. He frequented New York City midtown between 1957 and 1964, and ran a scam using a really beautiful foreign woman as bait. Not prostitution, Tex says. Extortion. The girl, who was simply his pawn kept obedient by threats to harm her family, would batten on some rich old guy visiting town—conventioneers mostly—and tell him she was going to be kidnapped by a gang of Germans and forced into whoring. Chez pretended to be a German thug, and the old guy would cough up anything between five and ten big ones to buy her freedom. None of the victims would ever press charges, but Tex gave me the name of an NYPD Vice detective who would confirm the story."

Everyone was sitting up straight, astonished at any kind of break in this damnable case.

"What did the Vice detective have to say?" Carmine asked.

"Tex's story was true. Our Chester Malcuzinski's prints match their Chester Derzinsky, who served a year in Sing Sing for fraud when he was twenty. His only conviction. Just when New York started to heat up, Derzinsky and the girl disappeared. Derzinsky reappeared a few months later in Florida as the realtor Chester Malcuzinski—his birth name. He *is* Emily Tunbull's brother. The girl totally vanished, but she sounds a lot like Davina Tunbull," Tony said triumphantly.

"Good work, Tony," Carmine said. "Finally the pieces are beginning to fall into place."

Still suffering the backlash of his stupidity in questioning Mr. Q. V. Preston, Tony glowed.

"If the girl's Davina, how much does Max know?" Donny asked.

"He doesn't suspect Davina," Abe said positively. "It would kill him, I think."

"Maybe not, if your wife has enough power over you to con you into printing twenty thousand books without authorization," Donny said quickly.

"I don't think it affects C.U.P.," Buzz said. "Tinkerman and what was in the drawer are more important by far. The longer the case goes on, the more the Tunbull deaths look like a detour on a highway, and that goes for John Hall as much as for Emily."

"I agree that Tinkerman holds the answers," Carmine said, looking suddenly brisk. "Certainly Emily posed no threat to the killer because her death is utterly divorced from Tinkerman's. She threatened Davina, and it was Davina poisoned her. She got the tetrodotoxin from our man, but she wouldn't kill to protect him. Just herself."

"You're right," Abe said, nodding, "though John Hall is a mainstream murder our man committed."

"Emily's just dust in our eyes?" Buzz asked incredulously.

"No! Emily represented a different threat to a different person—Davina," said Carmine. "I have no idea what the threat was, but Davina knew it as dangerous to her welfare."

"We need search warrants for the Tunbull premises, Carmine," Abe said. "Printery, Imaginexa and home."

"I'll see His Honor today."

Carmine met Judge Douglas Wilbur Thwaites upstairs in Commissioner John Silvestri's eyrie at five o'clock. Jean Tasco had laid out plates of olives, cheese-and-pickle nibbles and pâté thickly spread atop savory wafers. The drinks cabinet was full, the ice bucket was full and the assortment of glasses were all of the thin, plain type the Judge was known to favor. Auspicious.

He was sitting with Silvestri and the Captain of Uniforms, Fernando Vasquez; the latter, Carmine had been thrilled to sense, was earmarked as Silvestri's choice to replace him when he retired as Police Commissioner. As Carmine had feared he himself would be John's choice, Fernando's advent had come as an unexpected gift from heaven. No way Carmine wanted the pains, politics, predicaments and pussyfooting around that the Commissioner's post involved. Fernando was a shoo-in.

Of course he was holding the floor, and speaking with fervor about his passion—paper.

"It's not the same world, Judge," he was saying earnestly. "With the hotshot defense attorneys taking more and more of the limelight and bigger legal staffs researching old cases, you as a judge have no idea what you might be hit with. Including flaws in police procedure or disruption of the evidence chain. I tell you, police procedure and method has to be more than just perfect—it has to be documented in quadruplicate."

"Paper pusher," said Carmine, going to the bar to pour himself a weak bourbon-and-soda, no ice.

His appearance had put a scowl on His Honor's face. "Oh, it's you, is it? I'm only here to be talked into dubious warrants." Then he undid the impression of enmity this implied by patting a chair near him and smiling. "Sit here, Carmine. Dotty wants to know how Desdemona's doing."

"She's well, Judge. Her cooking's paradise. Before Prunella Balducci goes to L.A., I'll give the kids to her for a few days and all of you can come to dinner. I know of no other way to prove my contention."

"She needs days to prepare a meal?" His Honor asked.

"Sure. She makes one sauce that takes three days."

"Let's get the warrants out of the way, then we can all enjoy the drinks," said Silvestri.

"What do you need, Carmine?" asked Judge Thwaites

"A warrant for a full search of Max Tunbull's house and business premises. That should include any part of the house given, deeded or otherwise to any other person, including Uda Savovich."

The Judge writhed. "Carmine, you know I abominate searches of a man's private kingdom his home. Fingers poking through his wife's underwear—reading his private papers— and yes, I know all the arguments you intend to give me, how your searches are always legitimate and almost always yield evidence. So I'll save time and grant the warrant. But strictly for evidence of your tetrodotoxin case. If you discover evidence that Tunbull is planning to blow up County Services or go on a shooting spree the next time the Holloman Huskies play at home, you may not act on it. Is that understood?"

As they went through this every time, Carmine nodded. "Yes, sir, it's fully understood. I think County Services and the Holloman Huskies are safe."

WEDNESDAY, JANUARY 15, 1969

For once Carmine caught Davina Tunbull off balance; when he and Abe Goldberg arrived with Donny and Tony to serve the warrant, Max was at the printery and Davina not long dressed.

"I suggest that you and Miss Savovich take the baby and join your husband at his place of work," Carmine said. "From this moment on I can't let you be inside this house without a member of the police force to watch you. It's more sensible to leave, ma'am."

Davina was pallid, distressed; Uda simply stood, listened.

"You called Uda by my maiden name," Davina said.

"She is your sister, we know that," said Abe.

"I get baby," Uda said, accent at its worst. "Vina, put on coat and boots."

"You will plant evidence!" Davina cried. "No one is here to watch you, you will plant evidence!"

"No, ma'am, we won't do that," Abe said, and to Donny, "Go with Miss Savovich, please."

It took half an hour to get the women out of the house, but finally it was done. All four of them had seen the baby, and made their own conclusions. A calm child, as happy with Uda as he was with Davina; both women doted on him. Far handsomer than Jim Hunter had been as a baby, they were sure, therefore not very like him except for the eyes.

"We search Uda's premises first," Carmine said. "If we find anything there, we'll decide what else to do."

The house had owned a roomy attic that had been converted to a proper apartment for Uda. Its windows were dormered and contained cushioned seats, the carpet throughout was finest wool, and the furniture expensive. Uda liked less adventurous color schemes than her showy sister: green seemed to be her favorite hue, and was present everywhere, including a green-tiled bathroom that held a large shower stall as well as a full-sized tub. She had a living room that looked across the roof of Dr. Markoff's residence toward the basaltic bluff of North Rock—a real picture in the fall, thought Abe, as it was a forest view. A kitchenette was clearly never used save to make coffee in the Turkish manner—half an inch of sludge in the bottom of a tiny cup.

The most interesting room was Uda's work place. One wall held books in German, French and Italian as well as in English. Uda was highly literate. The titles varied enormously, but among them were volumes on poison, British murder trials, psychology, brainwashing, genetics, twins. Uda had a sewing table with a professional sewing machine let into it; the surface was carefully arranged with piles of fabrics and partially finished dresses, a number of stunning hats, even silk underwear upon which Uda was embroidering tiny rosebuds. Instead of a work basket Uda preferred a tradesman's tool box that opened out in a series of stepped shelves, some divided up, some intact. On another table were inks, drawing pens, various art papers, gouache paints, brushes, sketching pads and an IBM golfball typewriter.

"A woman of many talents," Tony said.

"No, I think Davina works here as well," said Abe.

"Where do you want me, Abe? Writing down the titles of her books?" Tony asked.

"Good idea. Title, author and language," said Abe. "I might do the sewing table, I think. That leaves the art to you, Donny. We're looking for one of those home-made injection devices, syringes, hypodermics and glass ampoules. All in disguise of some sort, okay?"

They had worked together for over a year now, and knew Uda

had no secret compartments: Abe's alarm bells weren't ringing, so Carmine had gone down a floor to search.

Neat and orderly to the point of obsession, Abe was thinking as he lifted each item on a stack, shook it out, examined it, then folded it again. Sloppy searching wasn't tolerated; if the subject of the search could see at a glance what had been messed with, police advantages were lost. If things looked undisturbed, the subject had to guess.

She had a compartment in her tool box for the more esoteric of sewing's paraphernalia: devices for unpicking stitches, threading elastic through a fabric tube, other devices. But no home-made injection gizmo or anything else of interest.

"For once it looks as if we'll have egg on our faces," Abe said as he stared at the art table. "She's a tidy worker, which makes our job easier. Tubes of paint all lined up in rows and graduated according to color—she must get through a lot, each color has at least six tubes. Yeah, obsessive."

"What's phthalocyanine green?" Donny asked.

"A peacocky green," Abe said. "Rich."

"Weird name. Could be a poison."

Abe picked up the first tube in the row of six tubes of phthalocyanine green; it had been squeezed from its bottom and the end folded over. "How many artists ever bother to do that?" he asked in wonder. "Usually they just grab the tube and squeeze, so what's at the bottom never comes out—too squashed." He picked up the next tube and went down the row, a frown gathering, then he went back to the first full tube and weighed it in his hand experimentally. Each full tube was weighed like so, after which Abe put the fourth, fifth and sixth tubes aside. "I don't think these contain paint," he said.

Tony went to the sewing table and came back with two pairs of scissors, one stout if small, the other very small and fine, with pointed tips.

"The tubes are lead," Abe said, opening and closing the blades of the stouter pair. "These will cut the crimped bottom off, whereas I think Uda uncrimped the bottom so as not to shorten the tube—painstaking!" Working carefully, Abe cut off the crimped end of the tube over a drawing block to catch any leftover paint that might emerge along with whatever else was inside. But none came out. "Uda will just have pushed whatever's up there in through the open bottom, but for us to get it out the same way would take ages." He picked up the fine scissors. "I'll just slice up the side of the tube all the way to its top and then lay its interior bare like a butcher a carcass." He inserted the thin, sharp under blade of his tiny scissors into the severed base and cut the lead up one side all the way to its threaded neck, snipping through the enveloping paper label as well. That done, he took one leaf of the cut in his left hand, the other leaf in his right hand, and peeled the cladding back to reveal a glass ampoule; a clear, colorless fluid slopped inside it.

"Bingo!" from Donny. He had recorded every step of the process with his camera.

"Do we open the other two?" Tony asked, picking up scissors.

"Go to it, Tony," said Abe, smiling in quiet vindication.

"Why is it liquid?" Donny asked, continuing to photograph. "I thought the stuff was a powder."

"So did I," said Abe. "If this is tetrodotoxin, then someone put it into solution before it went into this ampoule. The answer might be in the other paint tubes, which is why we open them. Each weighs differently."

The fifth tube contained another glass ampoule, but broken into two halves, and empty; the sixth contained a tube of thick cardboard, inside which was a rolled-up piece of paper.

The piece of paper was a letter on cheap stationery typed on an old manual machine with a faded fabric ribbon.

It said:

"A little gift from a well-wisher. Break the neck of the glass and pour the liquid into a drink. No taste, water will do. Certain death for two people."

"No date," said Donny, rolling the letter up again, his hands gloved. "I wonder when Uda got it?"

"Before John Hall's death, I'm guessing," said Abe. "It's been hidden at leisure, not in a panicked hurry."

"Who has an old manual typewriter?" Tony asked.

"No one we know of, and we'll never find it," Abe answered positively. "It's sitting somewhere belonging to someone entirely unconnected to the case." He squared his shoulders. "I'm going to find Carmine."

Carmine returned with Abe to inspect the find. "Well, it's hard evidence," he said, "and you could make a case involving the death of Emily Tunbull. Do you want to try?"

"If the full ampoule contains tetrodotoxin and the empty one used to contain it, I think the D.A. will want to try Uda for Emily's murder. You know Horrie better than I do, Carmine, but that's how it strikes me."

"You're right, Horrie will prosecute for Emily Tunbull, not John Hall. If the ampoule contains an oral dose, and I'm betting it does, then Emily's the right charge." Carmine grimaced. "The only trouble is that the defendant should be Davina, not Uda."

"Right on!" Abe gave a wry laugh. "That means we cops will be working to undermine Horrie's chances of success. We can't see the wrong woman convicted."

"What I don't get," said Donny, "is why Uda ever kept the evidence. That's why I don't think it was Davina—she's too smart to hide evidence in her own home, even if she were fool enough to have kept it. The Imaginexa premises would have been safer. I mean, why this elaborate business with paint tubes? A clear, colorless solution could have been hidden in plain view."

"That implies it could have been safely removed from the ampoule," said Carmine, "and I don't think either woman had the confidence to do that. It's not their poison. Some vegetable alkaloid would have seen them comfortable. This stuff? No."

"Solution does indicate that this stuff doesn't go off after it's dissolved," Abe said. "Even so, our mastermind didn't trust the women to do it, he sent them solution. I don't think he had a time frame in mind, he was just hedging his bets against the moment when pressure on the Savovich sisters built up to murder as a desirable end result."

"I agree," Carmine said.

Abe sighed. "I'm arresting Uda for the murder of Emily. Do we oppose bail?"

"What do you think, Abe?"

"The opposite. Ask for bail, and hint that we're not worried about other murders in the Tunbull household. Bail should be set at an affordable sum."

"Then we arrest and arraign her tomorrow morning."

THURSDAY, JANUARY 16, 1969

The Tunbulls were still at breakfast when Abe Goldberg arrived, followed by a squad car with a woman cop in its back. Protesting her innocence in shrill broken English that worsened the more agitated she became, Uda Savovich was put into the squad car and driven off, handcuffed and alone.

"I suggest you find a lawyer capable of arguing for bail when Miss Savovich is arraigned later today. As you can testify, she was cautioned in the proper manner."

"You're very helpful, Lieutenant," Max said, skin ashen.

"Not at all, sir. I simply understand that news like this is a shock and you may not think of what has to be done." Abe gave Max a businesslike nod and went to his car, drove off.

"Savovich?" Max asked the stunned and stricken Davina. "He called her Savovich."

"She is my twin sister," Davina said, regained the use of her legs and marched to the nursery. What would she do without Uda? Was there more formula mixed and refrigerated?

She was greeted by a hungry, cranky Alexis, his routines disrupted, and already missing Uda. Her witch's eyes blazed at Max, who instinctively backed away. For long moments she forgot him, even managed to shut out the noises coming from her baby, all her being concentrated on this disaster. Oh, Uda, Uda, fool that you are! I told you to get rid of all of it, but obviously you didn't. Those clever cops have found it among your things . . . What do I do, what do I do?

The years rolled back, they were a pair of starving kids again, fleeing to some kinder place where the rule of men was less bestial if still a reality . . . Always looking out for Uda, always thinking of what she would do, how she would go about attaining her objective, which was to be safe, warm, lapped in luxury yet permitted to carve a career. Without Uda she was infinitely diminished, without Uda she was half a person. Now here was Uda threatened with prison, and that could not be let come to pass. Chez Derzinsky, as much devil as twisted angel: torturing Uda to make her obey his commands, yet lending her the money to found Imaginexa. Putting her under the control of Emily—had Chez told Emily his secrets about her and Uda for the sake of ongoing control, or a simple malice? Not that it mattered. Emily knew too much, yet luckily was the type who had to drop broad hints, not concrete events. Well, Em had been afraid for Chez as well as intent upon making mischief for her, Davina. Always mysterious, until after that last veiled threat when she came in her blue dress and her blue shoes implying knowledge of—what? It was only when she, Davina, visited her in her studio shed that Em dribbled her poison about Chez and the New York City years. Bolstered by her pussycats and her horses' heads, the new Michelangelo . . .

Max was staring at her, frightened and confused; the baby was beginning to howl. And there she was, her veneer in patchy streaks with the old Davina thrusting through its weaknesses. Her temper snapped.

"Don't just stand there!" she snarled at Max. "Go look in the refrigerator for Alexis's formula. If there's any there, put a bottle in a jug of hot water and bring it here. *Move, Max!*"

He stumbled away to do as commanded, came back in five minutes with the jug. Snatching at it, Davina found a towel, took the bottle out, dried it, tested it—still too cold.

"Uda was born wrong," she said, Alexis whinging on her knee. "In a family as old as ours, it happens. It's why we bred some Chinese and a lot of negro blood into our veins—a different breeding stock. I take care of Uda, who repays me with hard work. I ask nothing else of her. Many years ago, when we first came to the United States, we agreed that in front of other people I would treat Uda like—well, dirt. It saved the kind of long explanations I am forced to give you now, yet they change nothing."

"Vina, I'm your *husband!* Couldn't you have confided in me?"

"To what purpose?" The bottle was warm enough; Davina shoved its teat into Alexis's mouth and watched him suck in greedy pleasure. "Why do I have no milk?" she asked the air. "It hurts that he must get his food from a tub, and full of chemicals."

"You should treat your sister better than a slave, Davina," Max persisted. "Don't you understand how cold-hearted you seem?"

"The whole business is a crock of shit, Max. Leave Uda to me, she's perfectly happy with our arrangement. Uda and I are twins, we have a kind of love beyond ordinary sisters. Think of us as one person facing opposite ways. Vina light, Uda dark." She laughed in genuine amusement. "Sometimes it's Vina dark, and Uda light. You never can tell with twins."

An awful realization had been growing steadily in Max's mind; he stared at his wife in sudden horror. "*You* killed Em!"

"Damned right I did!" said Davina savagely.

"Where did you get the poison?" he asked, shivering.

"It came in the post with a letter. Two glass tubes with narrow necks, each with about a half teaspoon of liquid inside. In a small box, packed with cotton wool. It sat on the painting desk for days— there was no need to hide anything until after Em died. Then Uda put it in paint tubes, the silly bitch. I had told her to get rid of everything." Davina smiled sweetly. "Em and Chez threatened our well-being, so she had to go." Her lip lifted in contempt. "Pussycats and horses' heads! Pathetic!"

Max had sunk into a chair—if he stayed on his feet, he would faint. "What had Emily done to you?"

"Tormented me the way she did Martita. Then she went to black-mail. Once, you see, I was the captive of her brother, who used me as bait. A monster, Chez Derzinsky. Not prostitution, oh, no! He locked my Uda up in a cell and tortured her to force me to work for him. I cheated poor old men out of their money. It was an infamy. But that was only half of Emily's blackmail. She told me that she'd spread it far and wide that Jim Hunter is Alexis's father. A lie! A lie! But people are like starving dogs, they will lap vomit off the sidewalk."

"You'd let Uda be charged with your crime?"

"Uda will come to no harm if you do as you're told." The bottle was empty; Davina rubbed Alexis's back. "There! Done."

Downstairs again, she sat at the breakfast table and lit a blue Sobranie Cocktail, then pushed a steaming mug at Max.

"Fresh coffee, Max," she said. "If Uda comes to trial for this murder, I want Anthony Bera for her defense, is that clear? Phone Bill Wilson right this moment and arrange it."

The old Davina showed briefly as she smiled at him warmly. "My dear, this is a nightmare. Look at it as that. When it is over, you and I and Alexis and Uda will return to our lovely life. I will be the woman of your dreams again, and we will pray that you never again have to see the Davina Savovich who fought her way to haven in America. She is there, but buried, and Alexis will inherit that from her as well as all his other qualities. I am self educated. You are self educated. Alexis will be properly educated at the finest schools. You and I run a printery and design business, but our son will do something far more important. Uda has seen it in his stars."

"Did she see her own arrest for murder?" Max asked.

Davina stared; then she laughed. "I have no idea! Very possibly she did see it, but she would never put that trouble on my shoulders."

"Chez deserves to die as much as Emily did."

"Well, first we had to get him here, that meant Emily. He would have died, Max, my love. Now?" She shrugged. "I will have to reconsider my options."

Chez arrived while Max was still on the phone to his lawyers, and found Davina in the throes of cleaning the kitchen.

"What's this?" he asked, sitting down. "Val told me some crap about Uda's being arrested."

"That is correct," said Davina, turning on the dishwasher. "For Emily's murder. Nonsense, of course, but I suppose the police think her incapable of fighting back. Officials always pick on the defenseless."

She was looking magnificent, like a snake in the glory of a brand-new skin. As if she'd thrown off a layer she felt she would never need to wear again . . . For such a feral, acquisitive man as Chez, this flight of fancy was extraordinary, but her image this morning was so strong, so reptilian, so enigmatic. Just how much did she know about what was going on, about the ramifications of these murders?

Casting his mind back, he'd known the right moment to stop with the extortion, yet he hadn't wanted to let go of Davina and Uda either. Envisioning no place for them in his Florida schemes, he had decided to bank them like any other valuable assets, and that meant introducing them into Emily's sphere. Em would keep an eye on them, he could trust her for that. It had been Em's idea to introduce her to Max Tunbull, Chez's to set her up in a graphic design business; he had good reason to know that she had talent in that line of work, and would leap at the chance to go legitimate. What neither he nor Em had counted on was a marriage—Em had been beside herself—but Chez had seen its advantages at once, and Em had been pulled into line. He'd be repaid his loan, and Davina inserted like a time bomb into this rich and eminent man's intimate life. So that, if blackmail ever became an option, he still had Davina in play.

Only he should have visited to see for himself what this marriage to Max had done to Davina, what kind of person she had turned into. Having her in his mind still as that frightened, bullied young immigrant easily disciplined by a threat to her twin sister. Instead, she was powerful, dominant, brilliant and ruthless. That first meeting at Major Minor's coffee shop had shown him looming difficulties—and made him wonder about Em's murder, the one that didn't fit.

Looking at her now, his inchoate doubts suddenly crystallized into a rock-hard conviction: one of the Savoviches had killed Em!

"Uda killed Emily?" he asked. "*Uda?*"

"The police think so."

"Where's Max?"

"On the phone, arranging Uda's defense."

"He should be arranging your defense. You killed my Em."

"As bait to get you here, yes," Davina said coolly. "You're the real target, Chez. Payback for using Uda and me, torturing us like animals, which is all women are to you. But I have lost Uda temporarily, so for the moment you're safe," she said, fearless and vicious. "Don't sleep too soundly. You *will* die."

"It might be you who dies," he said, snarling, putting on his most menacing face.

She laughed. "Rubbish! Your nasty glances don't work on me anymore, Chez. I'm kill-proof. All men have to sleep. Hurt me or mine, and you'll wake up singing soprano—if you wake up at all. Emily is dead and I killed her to get at you. Don't hang around, climb into that hired Cadillac and drive to La Guardia or Kennedy, then climb on a plane for Florida."

"Cops don't frighten me," he said, trying to swagger.

"This isn't Florida. These are very smart cops, if you like that word. I prefer police."

Max appeared, shuffling, quenched: Chez stared, astonished.

Davina helped her husband solicitously to a chair, gave him coffee. "Is it arranged?" she asked.

"Yes. I waited until Bill Wilson called me back. Anthony Bera will be at Uda's arraignment."

"Excellent!" She didn't sit. "Chez is just going, darling. He came to say goodbye. Some urgent business in Florida has come up, and he must leave immediately."

"I'll be watching," Chez said, following her.

She held the door open, saw him into the tiny foyer where coats resided and the cold outside air stopped.

"I'll get you for killing Em," he said.

"It's snowing" was her answer. "Zip your jacket, you sad, aging thug. You couldn't operate in a cold climate."

His last memory of her as he trudged away was of a figure radiating power, triumph, invulnerability. Like a victory goddess he'd seen in a movie. He'd be driving I-95 out of Connecticut as soon as he packed his bags. Only the arrival of the cops had saved his neck; Vina and Uda had killed Em to lure him here so they could kill him. All his schemes of exacting revenge didn't matter a scrap; Vina had called him a has-been, and she was right. He couldn't hold a candle to this new and snaky Davina Savovich. Kill her for killing Emily? It would be far easier to go to the Moon.

Back inside her beloved home, the unmasked Davina went about mending poor Max. It wouldn't be done in a day, but it would be done. Max was a mere sixty years old; he would last long enough to see Alexis grow to manhood, the competent and crafty head of Tunbull Printing. The breaks in him were of her making and could be camouflaged. Right at this moment he didn't believe it, but when this business was over, he'd go back to being a creature full of confidence and self-esteem. A suitable father for Alexis.

The hearing before Judge Thwaites was brief. Ably argued by Anthony Bera, bail was eventually set at $50,000. This pathetic and obviously damaged little woman was no poisoning mastermind, that was clearly written on His Honor's face. Released into the custody of her sister, Uda went home to wait for her trial, not yet scheduled.

"You can never tell with Doubting Doug how he'll go at arraignment," said Carmine to Abe, "but how His Honor goes at arraignment is often how the jury goes at trial."

"I wonder who's responsible for Bera?" Abe asked.

"My guess is, Davina. She's been expecting something to happen for some time, I wish I knew why."

"She's not the brains, though, is she?"

"No. She's too enamored of the life she's living, and she wants it to continue. That predisposes people away from murder unless murder is the only way to achieve it. Which makes her only target Emily. I have a creepy feeling that the Savovich sisters have cooked this whole thing up to have Uda tried for the murder Davina committed. Because if one sister is exonerated, no D.A. in his right mind would try the other. So set the sad little one up as the culprit," Carmine said.

"I wish I didn't believe you, but I do. However, it's out of our hands. As detectives, we've found a suspect with motive in possession of the poison. Horrie wants to try her."

"Wrong sister."

"Wrong sister."

"I hear the Hunters have moved to East Holloman," Abe said.

"Yeah, yesterday. Patsy says Millie is like a kid with a new toy. The families all contributed some furniture, which she is shoving around when she's not painting the woodwork. Her lab is shut until she's satisfied the new house is fit for Jim."

"Who wouldn't notice if he ate off an orange crate."

"Yeah, well . . ."

"You have to talk to Millie again, Carmine."

"That's why I'm picking her up and taking her to lunch."

His choice was the Lobster Pot, on the shore of Busquash Inlet in close proximity to Carew. Knowing that Jim had their car, he called by the new house shortly before noon to pick Millie up. She came bouncing down the short path from the front porch looking wonderful, Carmine thought, on the sidewalk and holding the passenger's door open. If she was as thin as ever, she had somehow managed to look a trifle fatter: the new dress, he divined. Flattering, miniskirted to display her shapely legs, a blend of soft sage green and a dark lavender blue, it did wonders for her skin and streaky blonde hair, long enough to reach the bottom of her shoulder blades. Thirty-three? She looked twenty-three.

She was still chattering about the house when they slid into a booth overlooking the water.

"A king-sized bed!" she was marveling. "I can't thank Jake Balducci enough for donating it. Jim and I had never even slept in a queen-sized bed before. Jim says it's like being a horse in a huge, grassy field."

"So he approves of the fleshpots, Millie?"

Patrick's blue eyes widened in Millie's inimitable way. "I think everyone gets Jim wrong," she said. "He's not by nature one of those awful people who wear shirts made of scratchy hair and lash their own backs. That would indicate masochism, and he is *not* a masochist! It's just that he's indifferent to external things because he never notices them—his mind's too busy elsewhere. But when I put a silk shirt on his back this morning, he was thrilled. He'd never worn anything silk before, and had no idea how good silk would feel. That's Jim. From now on, he will probably demand to wear nothing but silk shirts." A smile grew. "A tiny scrap of vanity appeared, would you believe it? When he looked in the mirror, he was intrigued at the way the fabric showed off his physique."

"It's a magnificent physique," Carmine said.

"Yes, but normally he's inside his body as if it were a mere peanut shell. This morning he liked what he saw."

"What else does he like?"

"The size of his study. He's actually taking time off to make bookshelves for its walls—imagine Jim taking time off! I've always known he lusted for a study completely lined in books and journals, but I didn't expect the carpentry."

"Is he skilled with his hands, Millie?"

"Tremendously. We've lived in some awful dumps over the years—broken everythings. He taught himself carpentry, concrete work, plumbing, plastering. Electrical wiring was always left to me, I'm as skilled as any electrician. The thing is, he's such a perfectionist that the bookshelves will look hand-carved—he found some beautiful molding he can glue on the edge of each shelf, so it really will look like a high class library. And Mario Cerutti gave him a wonderful old desk—you know, huge, lots of drawers, a great work surface, room for In and Out trays—Jim's so orderly."

Millie looked at the waitress. "I'll have lobster bisque, a lobster roll, and thousand island dressing on my salad," she said, smiling, idyllically happy.

"Double that," Carmine said as the waitress poured coffee. He looked at her sternly. "Have *you* got a study, Millie?"

Scarlet flooded into her skin, she looked adorably confused. "Oh, Carmine, I hope not to need one," she said. "I want a nursery and bedrooms for kids, a basement play den."

"Sounds as if you're buying."

"Yes. Jim agreed the moment he walked through the door. A good price for a reasonably large house, Dad says. C.U.P. is going to give us our royalties as they're earned instead of sitting on them for the customary twice-yearly payments. If they adhered to that, it would be more than another year before we saw any money at all."

"Didn't they give you an advance?" Carmine asked.

She looked hunted. "If they did, I wasn't told, and Jim ploughed it into his work as usual."

"That's got to stop, Millie."

"Yes, it must."

Carmine let her eat; she was hungry enough to devour a parfait for dessert, and perpetually thirsty for coffee.

Finally he could delay the serious talk no longer.

"Millie, I need more about the tetrodotoxin," he said.

Her light went out. "Oh. That."

"Yes, that. I'm sorry to resurrect the misery, believe me I am, but enough time's gone by for both of us to see it in a far different way than when you reported its loss. Why did you?"

"Why did I what?" she asked, looking bewildered.

"It won't wash, Millie. You know as well as I do. What made you report the loss of this incredibly esoteric poison?"

"I wanted to do the right thing."

"Maybe, but that wasn't why you reported it. And reported it so cleverly. Not to me, but to your father, who you knew would pass the information on to me, thus sparing you yourself from a series of questions you might have had difficulty answering. It was imperative to make the cops aware that the stuff was out there in the community, yet you didn't know enough yourself to feel confident you could survive an interview with me."

Her laugh was forced. "My goodness, you make it sound as if I were party to a conspiracy," she said, voice trembling.

"No, I don't believe that," Carmine countered. "I think your reasoning went more like this: Thomas Tinkerman, plus a surefire best seller suppressed to feed Tinkerman's ethics and egotism, plus a livid husband who could unstitch the mysteries of tetrodotoxin as easily as he can any other complex molecule." Carmine paused, watching her intently.

She was absolutely white, but her chin was up and the eyes guarded. "Go on," she said.

"Since your fifteenth birthdays, you and Jim have been as glued together as two layers in a laminate. By this time, you hardly need to talk in order to transmit information. And you had isolated a very rare substance from its natural source, the blowfish. It was a small triumph, maybe, but one of sufficient caliber to make your husband sit up and take notice. You'd done what few had managed, and the pair of you would have discussed your feat—pillow talk, Millie, that's where conjugal confidences happen. Undoubtedly Jim was already aware what you were trying to do, and why. For you, it was a tool rather than an end in itself, but one that saved you grant money buying the stuff and represented a challenge to make. I'm sure the fish cost you a packet, but not as much as tetrodotoxin would have. And by making more than you needed, you could sell the remainder, make a profit. You can't tell me Jim wasn't interested."

Millie looked wry. "There is a lot of pillow talk in our bed, Captain, but it's entirely one-sided. Me! Jim's head hits the pillow, and he's asleep. The four hours after he goes to bed are his best sleep, as a matter of fact."

"I don't think you intended to make a lot," Carmine went on as if she hadn't spoken. "However, I'm going to speculate that you got your tank of blowfish cheaply, from a supplier to Japanese restaurants going out of business. Well, it's not actually speculation, it's the truth. Cops don't twiddle their thumbs, they investigate everything. We prowl down all kinds of avenues, including what look like dead ends. So there you were, with a whole tank of blowfish that cost you next to nothing. Why waste them? Jim asked. Make some money, sell the leftovers! That's why you reduced it to a powder—easier to cut, ask any cocaine dealer. A speck is easier to corral than a drop—smaller too."

"Fascinating," said Millie, still white-faced.

"Did you make the ampoules, or did Jim? No matter, they were made. And when your series of experiments was finished, you put the six remaining ampoules in the back of your refrigerator. When you found them missing, you knew Jim had taken them, and with what end in view. The murder of Thomas Tinkerman. You know Jim Hunter as only a devoted wife of many years can know a man, and you knew he'd kill Tinkerman. That's why you reported the loss. To let Jim know that the cops knew all about this weird, untraceable poison—that they had been furnished with the lab techniques able to detect it. You thought that would stop him. But Tinkerman died of tetrodotoxin poisoning. After John Hall did. Now you understood what you had started, and desperately rued your action. If you'd kept silent, none of the tetrodotoxin deaths would have been discovered for what they are, and Jim wouldn't be our main suspect. You do know he is?"

"Yes," she said, mouth stiff. "But he didn't steal my tetrodotoxin, and he didn't kill any of these dead people." Her eyes were dry, tearless. "Jim is innocent."

"Then give me a name, Millie."

"I can't, Captain. I don't know one. Except that *someone* stole the poison, and it wasn't Jim, it wasn't!"

"Would the word tetrodotoxin mean anything to an eavesdropper?"

"I very much doubt it, unless they were interested in animal poisons—snake and spider venom, that kind of thing."

"Is there such a person in Chubb Biology?"

"Bound to be, but I don't know a name, and no one has ever visited me to enquire about tetrodotoxin."

"Does Jim have any personnel working for a doctorate?"

Millie looked appalled. "Jim? Jim can't teach, and he's the world's worst thesis supervisor. People go to him *after* they've done their doctorates. His doctoral fellows belong to his deputies and have about as much to do with Jim as the President does with his kitchen staff."

"Interesting, that he can't teach or supervise, yet he can write this great book for the layman. Isn't that a contradiction?"

"Paper, Carmine, paper," said Millie, smiling at some private memory. "What Jim can do on paper cannot be translated to the flesh. Besides, the book is his own output, it's a part of his persona. Doctoral theses are lead weights tied around his neck."

"You mean, I think, that his entire world from government grants to dean to wife conspire to spoil and indulge Jim Hunter. If he doesn't like to do it, he doesn't have to do it."

A statement that made Millie laugh aloud. "You may have some basis in fact, Carmine, but you've exaggerated. Right at this moment I have a very rebellious husband indeed. He thought book publicity would entail a couple of days in New York, but now he's discovered it means taking a month off work for a nationwide tour. He is *not* pleased."

"I can see why that wouldn't please him, but here's a question really bugs me—how does everyone know that *A Helical God* is going to be a best seller?"

"As I understand it from his editor, Fulvia Friedkin, it's possible to predict the fate of non-fiction. The publisher can estimate how many copies a work of non-fiction will sell down to a very few. Whereas the fate of fiction is on the lap of the gods—no one can predict the sale of fiction. Weird, yet apparently true," said Millie. "Jim is certain to sell in the hundreds of thousands, which is how come our living standard has suddenly risen." She leaned forward, face earnest. "Carmine, I'm not getting any younger, and I want to start our own family. For the parents of so many girls, Mom and Dad are kinda short on grandchildren. As the eldest outside the walls of a nunnery, I want to remedy that."

"I never did understand Lizzie's vocation," Carmine said, not averse to changing the subject.

"Considering how wild she was, nor did we," Millie said with a laugh. "Nineteen, the world her oyster, and she enters the convent—the Carmelites, yet! Vows of silence, the works."

"Well do I remember the fuss. How long has she been in now?"

"Seventeen years. But conventual living, even Carmelite, is pretty enlightened these days. Lizzie seems really happy."

"I never saw a more beautiful girl. Silvestri in a totally feminine mold. She threw pure Cerutti." Carmine sighed.

"I think Liz likes the peace and quiet."

And so they left it.

Carmine dropped her back at her new house agog to continue with her renovations, and returned to County Services not much the wiser for a good lunch. It was true, however, that the O'Donnells had had a checkered career with their girls, none of whom fit any conventional ideal. Millie came closest in one respect, her science, but Annie, a pre-med student at Paracelsus College in the same year as her cousin Sophia, Carmine's daughter, was a marked contrast to Millie. Annie was militant, aggressive and fanatically left-wing politically. Her fees were a big contributing factor to Patrick's chronic shortage of funds, but she showed not one scrap of gratitude for her parents' sacrifices. Not unnaturally, she and Sophia loathed each other, not helped by Sophia's beauty, popularity—or wealth.

"What Annie needs is a million dollars," Sophia would say between her teeth. "All that left-wing crap would be forgotten in ten milliseconds."

The case was drawing toward the end of its second week, and the arrest of Uda Savovich was all Carmine had to show for the days of dogged investigation. Because her defense attorney was the great

Anthony Bera, she would probably be acquitted; the evidence was purely circumstantial in that no one had seen her commit murder. What an incompetent lawyer would have bungled, Bera would use brilliantly: her unprepossessing appearance, her servant's status in her sister's home, her sheer foreignness. The jury would go into their debate convinced that someone else had put those two damning tubes of paint there—how could a poor little soul with tiny, twisted fingers do it?

It always came back to Jim Hunter. Now Carmine and his team would have to interview every member of Hunter's extensive laboratory world, probing for mentions of tetrodotoxin without ever actually using the name. A futile business.

Delia came in, a telex in her hand. "From Liam," she said, handing it to Carmine, "and no, I haven't read it."

"On the red-eye out of L.A. tonight," Liam said, "and here's hoping no hijackers on board to disturb my sleep.

"Not much to report, but I guess you expect that. First item is that John Hall was a simple depressive, no oscillations into mania. Gold Beach enquiries showed a withdrawn kid from early childhood, a science nerd in high school, and a real loner in college, all local. Good grades. Seems to have really loved Wendover, spent his spare time with the old man. A lot of stuff about trees and forestry, also paper manufacture.

"Caltech was his first time out of Oregon and his sphere. He started there a year earlier than the Hunters, September of 1957, but dropped out a month later. The halfway house in San Francisco dates to this time, not his teens. No one admits to having kept any records, but talking to a couple of long term helpers suggests a homosexual element in his depression. Not, as far as I could ascertain, that Hall was ever involved with a man. He just had the reputation.

"He went back to Caltech in September of 1958 and met the Hunters the first week. After that he never left their vicinity. According to a classmate, he was nuts on both the Hunters, but the general feeling in the classroom was that he was more taken with Jim than with Millie. Some of the implied homosexuality may be due to his physique and his face, neither a thousand per cent masculine, seems to be the consensus.

"After the Hunters went to Chicago he broke down again and spent some months in San Francisco being treated and staying in the halfway house. Then Wendover Hall brought him back to Oregon and put him into private full-time hospitalization, which seemed to do more for him. Since 1963, he's been more or less okay, though living with Wendover.

"Talk to you some more when I get home. Liam."

"The poor young man!" said Delia, finished reading.

"It's not the Hunter story, though, is it?" Carmine asked.

"I don't agree. What Liam has garnered is hearsay, from observers on the outside. It's a great trouble to young men of John Hall's physical type— they tend to be labeled as homosexual whether they are or not," Delia said, sounding passionate. "Don't say it doesn't happen in our own police force—it does! You and I both can name half a dozen men mistakenly labeled queer. As well as one or two super-masculine types who were anything but. We have a background for John Hall, and it's a sad one, but it doesn't say anything about his relationship with Jim and Millie Hunter."

FRIDAY, JANUARY 17, 1969

At eight that morning, Carmine assembled his troops.

"By now you will have concluded that we've exhausted all our avenues of enquiry," he said, standing. They were not neatly seated in rows, but rather scattered over the fairly large room with chairs turned at different angles; each body, however, was twisted so that its eyes could rest on Carmine in comfort.

"Here's what we have: the murders of four people, three by an esoteric poison, tetrodotoxin, and one by a gunshot wound to the base of the brain. The first death, John Tunbull Hall, was by tetrodotoxin subcutaneously administered to the back of his neck before the men went into Max Tunbull's study. It could have been by any hand. The second death, Thomas Tinkerman, was by an intramuscular injection of tetrodotoxin to the back of his neck. It was administered by his wife in the belief that she was giving him his customary dose of vitamin B-12."

Carmine straightened. "We were led on a merry dance that only became obvious after we learned of the B-12. There were home-made gizmos to confuse us, valuable time wasted chasing down leads that went nowhere, a web woven to deceive. Our first break consisted of two ampoules and one letter found inside tubes that had contained phthalocyanine green gouache paint, which is absolutely water-soluble and therefore easy to get rid of. Anyone care to comment at this stage?" Carmine asked.

Buzz lifted a hand. "Is the murder of Emily Tunbull part of our guy's plans, or unconnected to him?" he asked.

"Possibly some of each, Buzz," Carmine said. "I know this is all old ground, but don't forget our guy likes to play. Not only with the cops, but with other people who may be victims, suspects, or both. Emily Tunbull definitely wasn't a part of his master plan, but she confused things. The Savovich sisters now tell a story of being sent the ampoules and letter by mail, and at first not setting much store by it. So they just left the package on their artwork desk, a space they share. Just before Emily's body was found, Davina discovered that one ampoule had been broken and emptied. It was lying on the desk in the open. Both sisters swear they didn't use what had been in it. Abe has questioned each of them, I've questioned each of them, and Delia made it three of us. Delia, what do you think?"

"That they'll never budge from that story," said Delia with a sigh. "They claim their involvement is after the fact."

"Abe?" Carmine asked.

"Davina says that she told Uda to get rid of everything, but Uda says she wanted to hang onto everything as proof of their story, so decided each of the three items would fit inside a gouache paint tube. As a graphic artist, Davina has literally many dozens of gouache colors, a minimum of six tubes per color. The tubes are lead crimped at the bottom, it's possible to open them there without cutting them down. That's what Uda did. She squeezed the paint out, rinsed them, and hid each item in a tube."

"But they wouldn't be the same shape as real ones," Liam objected, marooned on the West Coast during the search.

"Every single tube is a little different," Abe said patiently. "Lumpy, bumpy—lead paint tubes aren't sleek. It was weight gave them away, not appearance."

"And that's it," said Delia. "One sister, Davina, wanted to get rid of the evidence, while the other sister, Uda, thought it better to secrete the evidence in case it might be needed."

"Davina was right," Tony said. "If they'd gotten rid of the stuff, we'd be up that creek."

"And they would be suspect forever after," Carmine said. "Uda's way means it's out in the open and in a court of law."

"I wish I knew better why John Hall had to die," Liam said, looking worn from his flight, but wide awake.

"Complex, Liam. Old times, old sins, old jealousies."

"So who *did* kill Emily?" Donny demanded.

"Davina," Carmine said. "She's a formidable woman, as only some refugee women can be. What the Savoviches endured in their own country, what they had to do to get out of it, probably beggars imagination. And Davina looks after her own. Uda, baby Alexis, and Max. Emily was a danger to her in some way, maybe unconnected to recent events. Davina is quite capable of using the turmoil provoked by John Hall's murder to eliminate a perpetual burr under her saddle in Emily. Therefore we set that crime aside. The evidence as to its perpetrators deflects us from our real purpose."

Carmine lifted his rump from the table and began to pace. "That takes care of the three known tetrodotoxin murders, leaving us with the shooting of Mrs. Edith Tinkerman. The perpetrator knew he couldn't let her live, but he didn't want to kill her either. So, we can assume at her request, he visited her in the evening of last Monday, January thirteen, and had a drink with her—after he learned what she wanted to see him about. Obviously, the papers in Tinkerman's secret drawer. Seconal is bitter, so it must have been a highly flavored drink. Or he may have given her a capsule to swallow with some tall tale as to why she should. Whatever. Then he left her to go to sleep, which she did still sitting at Tinkerman's desk. Our killer didn't return until around nine on Tuesday morning, bold as brass, entered her home, and shot her KGB style. All of which says that he hated having to kill her, but wasn't a bit afraid of being caught in the act."

"If it's Hunter, how the hell did he escape attention?" Tony asked. "I'm still racking my brains about that, Carmine."

"It's winter. People are wrapped up. The wind had a chill factor that morning, and how much do you notice between your house and your car?" Abe asked. "The ambient temperature was 27°F in Busquash, and the chill factor brought it down into the teens. I can understand why no one noticed Hunter, Carmine, but what I can't understand is how his ancient Chevy clunker wasn't noticed—in *Busquash?* People in Busquash don't drive clunkers, even high school kids."

"He wasn't driving a clunker," Carmine said. "That's why he couldn't sneak back earlier to kill her. He had to borrow a car from someone who owned a good looking vehicle, and he couldn't do that until the person came into work. Say, eight a.m., eager to start this new project Dr. Hunter was giving him."

"Then when we find out who loaned Hunter the car, we've got him!" Liam said triumphantly.

"I don't think Hunter asked permission. He must know where his staff keep their car keys. He just borrowed the ones he wanted, and returned them later, If he was caught, he had a story ready— but he wasn't," Carmine said.

"And we won't find any fingerprints or his favorite sweet wrappers in the car," said Delia. She looked at Carmine very directly and severely. "You're sure it's Jim Hunter, Chief?"

"Yes. I've never gotten away from him. No one else fits the bill, folks. The Savovich women? Not enough know-how. I believe Hunter persuaded John Hall to show him the back of his neck *before* they went onto the study. Oh, Jeez, there's something nasty crawling up your neck, John! John's head goes right down, which means he can't see anything Hunter is doing. Out comes the syringe, Hunter lifts the skin with the tip of the needle, and slides the tip sideways, not down. Just a couple of drops under the skin. The poison takes longer to reach the vertebral artery—twenty-five minutes, say, rather than ten."

"You're right, Carmine," Abe said. "Once you take the study out of the equation, it becomes anyone's poison. Hunter could have drawn John aside for a private talk, taken him into another room, or just let it happen right there in the open. He seems to have the luck of the devil, or however you want to put it, because no one ever *sees* him! People remember Hunter having an animated conversation with Davina that occupied that space of time, but people's memories are notorious. It's equally possible that he had more than enough time and privacy for an injection."

"What it boils down to is Hunter's word. Millie was with the women in the drawing room—and so, Davina insists, was she." Carmine huffed in exasperation. "The animated conversation with Jim must have happened, but when? We don't even have a reliable time line for tetrodotoxin, largely represented in the literature by one paper from a couple of guys at Duke who isolated it in 1964. Tetrodotoxin is more of a novelty than a significant substance that's going to break down biochemical barriers."

"And we haven't a damned thing to connect Hunter to the B-12 ampoules," Buzz said gloomily.

"So what do you intend to do, Carmine?" Delia asked.

"For the moment, nothing. We close the case down and wait. I've already asked the slow-grinding wheels of justice if they could see their way clear to trying Uda Savovich fairly quickly—it would be good to get that out of the way."

"I made a terrible mistake, charging her," Abe said.

"I fail to see how or where, Abe," Carmine said gently.

"I should have charged both the Savovich Sisters with conspiracy to murder."

"Horrie Pinnerton's not the D.A. for that alternative."

"I guess so."

"Do you intend to let Hunter think he's gotten away with it, or are you going to tell him what we suspect?" Abe asked.

"I'm going to inform Hunter that we know the truth, for one very good reason—I want no more murders."

"May we listen?" Tony asked.

"On the other side of the glass, yes."

"When?" Tony asked.

"Two p.m. today."

The group dispersed; no one had wanted to discuss Millie.

Jim Hunter appeared at County Services promptly. Divested of his winter gear, he was revealed in chinos, a white silk shirt open at the neck, and a new grey buttoned sweater. He was looking as he always did—supremely confident, extremely competent, and the eyes held no fear whatsoever. Arresting in any face, Delia thought as she and Abe assumed their positions one to either side of the tape recorder. By now Hunter knew all of them, could greet them by name; he took his interviewee's chair, a comfortable one, as if attending a professional seminar at which he would chair the panels.

"This is going on the record, Dr. Hunter," Carmine said after the formalities were announced for the tape's sake, "but I want you to know that my chief reason for arranging this meeting is to prevent more murders. You may speak at any time, of course, but you are not required to speak, and I must warn you that if the interview yields criminal fruit, it may be used against you in a court of law. Therefore you are entitled to have a lawyer present. Do you want a lawyer?"

"No," Jim Hunter said steadily, after a pause. "I will make no incriminating statements, I can assure you."

"Very well, let us proceed."

Carmine led him through the murders of John Hall, Thomas Tinkerman and Edith Tinkerman with every deduction and enlightenment their work had unearthed; police skill should have surprised him, but if it did, he gave no indication of it. He simply listened as if hearing a diverting, entertaining story about someone he didn't know.

At the end of it amber eyes locked with green, an exchange of glances between two equals. Jim Hunter was a genius and Carmine Delmonico was not, but on this battlefield the advantages of Jim's superior intellect were cancelled out by Carmine's experience and doggedness.

"I know you committed these murders, Dr. Hunter," Carmine

said steadily, "but I don't have physical evidence to back that knowledge. Therefore on the surface it looks like you've gotten away with three counts of murder—John Hall, Thomas Tinkerman and his wife, Edith. All three were committed to safeguard the success of a book you have written, entitled *A Helical God*. Your wife, Dr. Millicent Hunter, made your poison as a legitimate part of her research, and you stole the considerable amount left over. Investigations indicate that Dr. Millicent Hunter is not involved in your plots and schemes. Like Mrs. Tinkerman, her role is that of a vector."

"Your prejudice is remarkable," Jim Hunter said.

"Elucidate, Doctor," said Carmine, maintaining his calm.

"If I am considered the author of these crimes, how do I figure any larger in your suspicions than my wife? As publication of my book benefits my wife as much as it does me, the motive you impute to me is just as valid for my wife. Millie and I are an identical number, you can't separate us by a plus here and a minus there." The eyes mocked. "Is this Jim Hunter being clever, or Jim Hunter pointing out that if he's guilty, so is his wife? Or maybe this is Jim Hunter showing you the error of your ways, pointing out to you that if his wife is innocent, so too might he be innocent."

The three detectives listened impassively; beneath their united front, they writhed. Jim Hunter was giving them a preview of his defense were he to be arrested and charged: Millie, he would allege, was an accessory, and just as guilty.

"I fail to see how Dr. Millicent Hunter can be implicated in the murder of Edith Tinkerman," Delia said. "She was teaching a class from eight on the morning of Mrs. Tinkerman's death, with ten witnesses to confirm it. No tetrodotoxin was employed, and thus far we have failed to locate the weapon."

"Listen to yourself, Sergeant!" Hunter exclaimed. "To my listening ears, the word that stands out is 'failed'—and yes, you have failed. You searched our apartment, my laboratory and my wife's laboratory, but could find no evidence *either* of us is implicated." He made a sweeping gesture with one huge hand. "I am tired of this inquisition, and I resent it! Either charge me with some crime, or allow me to leave."

Abe switched the tape recorder off. "Thank you, Doctor. You're quite free to leave."

"That was interesting," said Carmine after Jim Hunter had departed radiating an air of victory.

"I didn't think he'd counter with Millie," Abe said.

"It's superficially brilliant," Delia said, "but actually anything but clever. He's thrown down the gauntlet—charge him with the murders, and he'll implicate Millie. If nothing else, it indicates that you, Abe and the Commissioner have been right about her all along—she's as innocent as a babe."

"We didn't throw the fear of Hell into him," Abe said.

"That's impossible, but he does know he's skating on thin ice. Hunter has the God complex, like a lot of guys whose job or brain or talents put them way up in the stratosphere," Carmine said. "He adores to be adored. Millie is his high priestess, a role the years have cemented, but even she can be sacrificed if it becomes necessary. If it's done nothing else, this interview has demonstrated that Millie isn't privy to all of Hunter's heart, and far from privy to the greater part of his mind. Jim Hunter owns himself whole and entire."

Abe looked bewildered. "You know, they call me the master of secret compartments," he said, "but that man is composed of secret compartments—and in layers, yet. He's as cold as an Alaskan winter."

"I'm upstairs to Silvestri," said Carmine.

Carmine's report didn't improve Silvestri's mood.

"We're beaten," he said.

"Short of a confession, yes, and I can assure you that Dr. Jim Hunter will never confess. He won't even trip himself up on a verbal indiscretion."

"Millie's living with a killer."

"That she is, but she's safe, John. Hunter needs her to sustain his credibility. He's fully aware that her death would be one too many."

"How can you be sure?"

"Think of Millie in relation to Jim Hunter in the same way as Uda Savovich is to Davina Tunbull. Jim Hunter's colossal ego needs a selfless slave to minister to it, and Jim Hunter's crimes need an element of doubt only Millie can provide."

"Yes, I see your argument about Jim Hunter's reasons for wanting to keep Millie alive," the Commissioner said, looking mulish, "but what isn't so obvious is the answer to the question East Holloman's been asking itself for the last eighteen years—what if Millie falls out of love with Jim?"

Carmine's breath caught. "Don't even say it! No," he said, confidence growing as he spoke, "that won't happen now they're out of the rat-infested dumps and into a nice house in a nice neighborhood. I gather Millie's anxious to start her family, and judging from what that did to Desdemona at much the same age, she won't have time to fall out of love. She'll be too busy discovering that kids are much harder to manage than quiet, obedient laboratories. I'm delighted for her."

"I would be, if I didn't know Jim is a killer."

"Be rational, John! Hunter's not a pathological killer—killing doesn't assuage a craving in his psyche. Had the Parsons not trodden on M.M.'s toes and M.M. not trodden back, Tinkerman would never have become Head Scholar of C.U.P., and Hunter would have continued to be nothing more and nothing less than a genius biochemist. He killed to achieve his ends, not for sexual jollies."

"I wish I believed you," the Commissioner said.

"Why don't you?" Carmine yelled, exasperated. "I'm not trying to justify Hunter or minimize his deeds, I'm just trying to make you see that Millie at least isn't a target. That's the most we can hope for, given her blindness to Hunter's real nature combined with the fact that we can't arrest him."

"I fear for Millie," Silvestri maintained, unimpressed.

"We *all* fear for Millie, John, but there's not a thing we can do, so drop it," said Carmine harshly.

Desdemona sided with Silvestri.

"Millie is definitely in danger," she said, searing her frying pan with a good OP brandy and watching it hiss and bubble to a brown nothing. She stirred in some homemade tomato sauce, a little horse-radish cream, and when they were sizzling, a half-cup of full cream. A quick stir to a bubble, and the sauce was drizzled over two steaks sitting on two plates. The larger was slid in front of Carmine, who added little potato balls simmered in beef stock, and loaded his salad bowl.

"I adore you," he said, mouth full.

"Never more so than when I feed you, love," she said with enormous complacence.

"What makes you think that Millie is in danger, especially in light of what Hunter had to say about her equal putative guilt? To me, that indicated he has to keep her alive," he said when his plate and bowl were empty save for the steak fat, and a cup of tea sat steaming.

"I agree that Jim murders from necessity, not psychopathia. I also agree that Millie alive is a great protection for him. But if Millie offends him deeply enough, he'll kill her without missing a step. His ego is even bigger than his brain, but the brain will ensure that if his ego says she must be killed, you won't be able to prove he did it—and there will be another Millie waiting to step into her vacant slot."

"A new Millie can't replace the old," Carmine countered, "not from the way he talked this morning. Millie's his equal suspect."

"Even dead, she can fill that role. And since her substitute will be another slave to Jim, he can create another suspect."

Carmine gave a Bronx cheer. "That's stretching it too fine, Desdemona. You make it sound like Hunter has a whole stable of potential slaves and believes he can brainwash them the way he has Millie. Well, he can't. They were kids together when it all started. I maintain that Millie is unique."

"A replacement Millie won't be manipulated in the same way," Desdemona said stubbornly, "but Jim will make the relationship work for him exactly as he wants it to. Did you ever find the gun used on Mrs. Tinkerman?"

"No. The apartment on State Street and both the Hunter labs were searched, and produced nothing. He could have a locker somewhere, anywhere—a bus or train station—or a safety deposit box in a bank."

"Then let us hope and pray that the book does everything it's supposed to. If Millie is strong enough to divert a good proportion of the royalties into her home, they may be all right. Just may be. If you look at the situation dispassionately, Carmine, Jim has been stealing from Millie ever since she obtained a grant income—that would have been at Caltech in California. Her salary would always have been university modest, but ample for her to buy a few dresses and shoes as well as steak and fish for her table. But no, she's handed her money over to Jim, who ploughs it into *his* work, *his* facilities. How much of his equipment does Chubb or a grant committee own, versus how much is in his name? There's no law against it, it's just that most researchers like to live reasonably and so don't do it. Jim does, always has. I mean, I know what research is like. No one comes around, even once a year, to check the serial numbers on the equipment. If it's being sold off for nefarious purposes it will be found out, but if it's just taken to be used in some other lab of the same institution—who knows? The person who lost it—in Jim's case, Millie. But is she going to report Jim? No, never! She simply goes to his lab to use what's actually hers."

"Keep going," Carmine said, fascinated.

"Millie is a variation on a very common theme." Desdemona sounded stern, unforgiving. "I mean the abused wife. Think a bit about it! She's not beaten or terrorized, yet she exists at the grace and favor of a man who regards her as his property, as convenience, as an asset to advance himself, never her. He steals her income, perhaps the fruits of her research, her time, her energy and even her youth. Everything she does is to gratify him because she has no sense of self-worth. He stole that too. His world believes that he loves her madly, but does he, Carmine? Millie believes he does. Well, I don't. I think that Millie is his property, and he's proprietorial. He abuses her."

"It's a valid argument," Carmine said, his dinner suddenly not sitting well.

Desdemona wasn't finished. "They've been Chubb faculty for over two years. Millie should have been prosperous enough to dress, and the pair prosperous enough to live in a decent place. Now all of a sudden they've moved to a good house in a really good neighborhood. Why? Because, I believe, someone told Jim in no uncertain terms that he had to loosen the purse strings. It's not a subject anyone at C.U.P. would have raised because university presses don't think in personal terms. Chauce Millstone telling Jim the journalists would think it odd to find him living in a semi-slum with a beautiful wife who doesn't own a good frock? No! I think Davina Tunbull told Jim, and that makes me wonder how well they know each other."

"What would I ever do without you?" Carmine asked, awed. "Do you really think that once the dollars pile up, Hunter might see Millie as expendable?"

"I think it's a possibility," said Desdemona. "Why not take the dog for a walk? The exercise will settle your tummy."

The interview kept intruding; after two fruitless hours in his laboratory, Jim Hunter gave up and went home. He was almost to their old apartment on State Street before he realized that they were living in East Holloman now; chuckling quietly at the images of an absent-minded professor that had invaded his thoughts, he drove to Barker Street. When he noticed that a very ordinary beige car also seemed to recollect that it was going to East Holloman rather than Caterby Street, he gave an involuntary shiver. The cops had someone on his tail. His every destination would be noted down, examined. Then, after the shock wore off, he whiled away the rest of his journey in dreaming up things he could do to confuse and upset Operation Hunter. The fools!

An ideal house, he thought, walking up the path to the front porch, and groping in his pocket for the key Millie had given him. Its advent was perfect, and the royalties would buy it, just as they would better clothes for him and Millie, good food on the table—he would miss their pizza meals, the Big Macs. Food to Jim Hunter was just fuel to keep going.

Yes, the timing was perfect. Finally he had the right number of technicians and post-doctoral fellows, all the equipment he could possibly need, and sufficient space. He could afford to let Millie turn from helpmate to housewife, since clearly this was what she wanted; his next grant, a huge one, was in the bag according to a letter in this morning's post. Knowing it, he had faced Carmine Delmonico more sanguinely. Chief suspect? No, the big cop was *sure* he was the culprit, purely on lack of evidence! Well, he'd turned that one on its head! The fools! Couldn't they see that what went for him also went for Millie?

Delmonico must be desperate. First, he'd denied them the hope of demanding a lawyer: to demand a lawyer was an admission of guilt, everybody knew that. Then, he'd tossed them Millie as an equal suspect. End of game, stalemate for Delmonico.

The house's interior reeked of fresh paint—why did people bother with absurdities like a coat of paint? The underlying structure was as sound as a bell, he was engineer enough to appreciate that, and the paint hadn't even been necessary. No, Millie didn't like the *color*, therefore she would change the color. This new Millie took some getting used to.

She came flying to land in his arms, kiss his lips, hug him feverishly—poor little love, she was worried.

"It's okay, sweetheart," he said, meeting her gaze, his own eyes filled with love. "Captain Delmonico has no one to pin these murders on, so he's picked me because of the tetrodotoxin. It doesn't matter, honey, honestly! All he can do is speculate. He even had to admit that the killer could as easily be you as me, except that you're family. Seems to me like a weird way to run a murder investigation, automatically excluding suspects for no better reason than that they're family, but . . ."

The tears fell. "Oh, Jim, I'm so sorry! If I hadn't gone to Daddy and reported the stuff missing, none of this would have happened. It's all my fault!"

"Sssh, sssh! You were right to report the theft, Millie. The tetrodotoxin *was* used to commit murder, so not to have reported it would have been far worse." He gave a wry laugh. "I'd bet Delmonico is wishing I was an ordinary black man—I'd be in a cell by now, and the bruises don't show in black skin."

Her face grew horrified in a split second. "Jim, no! You can't say that of Carmine or the Holloman PD! You can't!"

"Okay, I won't." He followed her into the kitchen, where she was obviously making a start on dinner. "This is one of those rare occasions when I feel like a stiff drink," he said.

"Then isn't it lucky I started a bar in case we had house-warming visitors?" she asked, smiling. "Bourbon? Club soda? Or Coke? The new freezer makes its own ice cubes and tips them into a tray, isn't that neat?"

"Hit me," he said, sitting down on a good looking chair at a good looking table.

In answer she brought him the bottle, a bowl of ice cubes and a can of club soda. "I went to Marciano's butchery and got us some real lamb chops for dinner—New Zealand, can you imagine? He told me it's better than ours because ours is raised on grain and theirs on grass—makes ours taste muttonish. I can't make my own French fries, so they're frozen, and the vinaigrette is out of a bottle, but I'll improve. There's a lot of you to keep up, James Keith Hunter."

"I'm putting thirty thousand in an account in your name, Millie," he said, drinking gratefully. "It's payback time. Chauce says C.U.P. is happy to advance against royalties at this stage, and Vina says you should be wearing better clothes. Good quality make-up. French perfume. My fame will rub off on you, and you're still the most beautiful woman I've ever seen." He poured another drink, this time diluted with club soda. "I have to find a tailor and have some clothes made for my own back—no more hired tuxes."

"Call Abe Goldberg, he'll tell you where to go."

"Millie, are you sure you want to stop your research?"

"Absolutely."

"Do you know why I love you so much?" he asked as the warm glow of liquor coursed through him.

"Tell me again," she said, fussing at the counter.

"Because you've never believed for one millisecond that I stole your tetrodotoxin," he said, and smiled. "The latest in an endless line of selfless loyalties."

The wonderful trill of laughter she could give when utterly overjoyed erupted; her eyes went shyly to his, face beaming, cheeks flushed. "Have I really got so much money?" she asked.

"You will tomorrow, about noon. First National on the Green, and ask for the manager. He'll do the paperwork."

"I'll make you proud," she promised. "For eighteen years the world has stared at us for nothing more than our color, but in future color will be the least of why it stares."

PART THREE

From
TUESDAY, MARCH 4, 1969
until
THURSDAY, APRIL 3, 1969

TUESDAY, MARCH 4, until FRIDAY, MARCH 7, 1969

For once the judicial system had hustled. The trial of Miss Uda Savovich for the first degree murder of Mrs. Emily Ada Tunbull came on in near record time. Anthony Bera handled his share of jury selection shrewdly; when it was empaneled the jury consisted of six men and six women—four African-American and eight Caucasian-American. Their occupations ran from unemployed to a house cleaner to an accountant. Like all jurors, they were pleased at having drawn an interesting case, and as jury pay was atrocious, they were also pleased that it bade fair to be a short business.

Uda made no effort to improve her appearance. She wore the same grey uniform dress, no make-up, scant reddish hair pulled back. Unprepossessing, yes, but also quite harmless looking. Benignly damaged. To Carmine, she seemed subtly more crippled than she used to be, but if it were an act, it was so well done that he couldn't put his finger on exactly what and where the changes were. Maybe, he was forced to think, the strain of this whole business had worsened her naturally?

The office of the District Attorney ran a simple case that made no reference to any other murder than Emily Tunbull's. The woman had died of a rare and almost undetectable poison, she was vaguely related through marriage to and in fairly close geographical proximity to the Defendant, who had both a full and an empty vial of the poison concealed on her premises. There was a long history of dissent between the Victim, the Defendant, and the Defendant's twin sister, Mrs. Davina Tunbull. Only one ultimate source of the poison existed, a person known to all the Tunbulls, and therefore also to the Defendant.

Evidence was given by the Medical Examiner's witnesses that Emily Tunbull had died of tetrodotoxin orally administered in a carafe of water that stood in clear view on a shelf in her sculpting studio, a shed in the backyard of her home. The padlock securing its door was one of seven similar padlocks having the same key. Therefore to enter the studio and add the poison to the water was not beyond the Defendant's capabilities.

Millie was called to testify that she had manufactured the poison in her laboratory, and had reported the theft of a significant amount to her father, Holloman County's Medical Examiner. Born teacher that she was, she explained tetrodotoxin to the jury on a simple, understandable level. Incredibly lethal!

Horrie Pinnerton didn't try to implicate Uda or any Tunbull in the theft, preferring to concentrate on a mythical parcel of which the Defendant had no proof beyond a letter she said had been enclosed—but where was the parcel, its wrapping, the box lined in cotton wool? And if it had ever existed, why were the ampoules secreted inside paint tubes? He called Davina to testify to all this, and succeeded very well in making the story look manufactured by the intelligent sister to save the handicapped one—who was quite capable of efficiently running a busy household on behalf of her sister, a businesswoman with other interests.

Though no one had seen Uda Savovich put the poison in the water, it was an open-and-shut case, Horrie argued: Uda Savovich had the poison in her possession, and Emily Tunbull, a thorn in her and Davina's side, had perished of that poison.

Anthony Bera proceeded to tear the D.A.'s case down. First he called Millie back to the stand and pressed her as to why, if tetrodotoxin was so lethal, she hadn't locked her refrigerator? Her whole little laboratory, Millie said, composure and patience unrattled, was in effect one large safe, and kept rigidly locked. Even if she left it to go to the bathroom, she locked her door, which had a special key not available to cleaning or maintenance staff, who visited while she was in attendance. No, she had no technician, nor did her husband have a copy of her key. What kind of things did her laboratory contain besides tetrodotoxin that made this locking necessary? Concentrated acids and alkalis. Sodium thiopentone. Morphine. Several other neurotoxins: her work concerned the mechanisms capable of shutting the nervous system down. And no, nothing had ever disappeared until the theft of the tetrodotoxin. Shown the two ampoules in Uda's possession, she flatly denied having made them, and was able to point out why she was so sure of that.

Bera didn't call Uda. He called Davina, the intact twin. Who wore a plain black suit, a white blouse, and elegant, high-heeled black shoes. Her hair was piled on top of her head and she bore no resemblance to Medusa.

First Bera demolished what might have been Horrie's comeback by ruthlessly examining Davina as to why she treated her sister like a servant, and had kept their blood relationship a secret. She didn't look good at the end of it, but somehow it made a kinky kind of sense; the Savovich girls had lived through perilous times, and had concocted a dual persona that suited both of them.

Davina insisted that the parcel had been real, and that it had frightened them, given the deaths of two men from some rare poison that the accompanying letter said had also been sent to them —sufficient for two deaths. The open box had sat on Uda's work table for several days, chiefly because Davina, to whom Uda looked for guidance, genuinely didn't know what to do about it. Why hadn't she notified the police the moment she had supervised Uda's opening the box? Because they would look like murderers, Davina explained. The police had not considered them likely suspects, but if they produced this box and it did have poison in the ampoules, they would look guilty. But when Uda found one ampoule open and used, they panicked.

Why didn't they go to the police when they found one vial empty? Bera asked. And Davina, looking magnificent, snapped back that if the police doubted the existence of the parcel, what might they have thought of a used ampoule when, a day later, Emily Tunbull was dead? So they had decided not to throw the things away, but not to declare them either. They were guilty of concealing this malign attempt to involve them in a chain of murders, yes! But if in truth Uda had poisoned Emily, they would never have kept a thing.

Then Anthony Bera called Chester Malcuzinski, who didn't answer. This man, said the hotshot lawyer, was Emily Tunbull's blood brother, and, he skilfully implied, a bad lot, wanted for questioning in New York for fraud and extortion. A subpoena had gone to him in Florida, but he had vanished, despite the fact that Uda Savovich would go on trial for the murder of his sister. His testimony would help her case, but why wasn't he to be found? What had he to do with those ampoules that Dr. Millicent Hunter had *not* made? He could have sent the parcel.

Even two thousand years ago in the time of the first of the hotshot lawyers, Cicero, it was keenly felt as a great advantage that, in summing up, the Defense spoke after the Prosecution; in Holloman, Connecticut, in March of 1969, it was no different.

Horrie Pinnerton argued competently and reasonably for a guilty verdict, based on bad feeling between the Savovich twins and the deceased, opportunity to put the poison in the water carafe, and the presence of two ampoules, one full, one empty, concealed in paint tubes in Uda Savovich's work room.

Anthony Bera admitted freely that the circumstances could be interpreted as guilt on Uda Savovich's part, but that the Prosecution had not satisfactorily proved it, even remotely. It all hung on two ampoules of tetrodotoxin that at some stage had been manufactured by hands other than Dr. Millicent Hunter's—were they Uda Savovich's hands? He led the tiny woman past the jury enclosure so that they could inspect her hands at close quarters: tiny, crabbed fingers that shook with a fine tremor. This was also an ideal ploy to have the twelve good people see into her little black currant eyes, discover how small her size, and how pathetic her condition. Uda didn't make the mistake of trying to appear mentally retarded; she seemed bewildered, not sure what was happening, and very, very afraid.

He painted the story of their lives, the trek across the alps that started when they were twelve and ended in Trieste at fourteen, and the Davina who used her sister as a servant was also seen as a sister who had never, never forgotten her duty to her handicapped twin. He was frank about the role of Chez Derzinsky/Malcuzinski in forcing the model Davina to work as his bait by imprisoning and torturing Uda when she didn't obey, and he asked the jury why, having achieved respectability and a haven, either sister would dream of upsetting their status quo by indulging in murder? The motives Horrie Pinnerton had tried to make urgent and compelling were seen as no more and no less than the usual frictions that appeared between women in any extended family situation. The alternative was to see Emily as her brother's cat's-paw threatening to expose their activities in New York City, but why would Emily imperil a shady, shifty brother?

The Savovich sisters were seen as refugees from communism, a strong point in Uda's favor, and Uda herself as a poor little woman without malignity or power.

The jury believed the Defense. It returned with a verdict of "Not Guilty" in less than an hour.

Carmine and his detectives were mightily relieved at the verdict. The wrong sister had been tried; the right sister never would be now. Every last one of them had come to the same conclusion, that between them Davina and Uda had forced the police hand and the D.A. had fallen for the ploy, even though he had been warned. The consolation was that the sisters would commit no more murders.

Abe for one didn't believe the motive lay in events in New York City years ago. "Emily had some evidence of some other deed," he said to Carmine, "and we haven't a hope in hell of learning what it was, especially now Chez Malcuzinski is in the wind. I find that a mystery in itself, by the way."

"I'm betting he'll turn up in San Diego or Phoenix in a year or so doing the same kind of thing he did in Orlando," Carmine said. "He doesn't matter, he's out of our loop because you're right, Abe, Emily was murdered for reasons having nothing to do with Chez. Ask any detective involved in the case, and the answer will be that she knew something about the baby, Alexis."

"That Jim Hunter is his father? Yeah."

"Is he? I'm not so sure. It's all in the eyes, nothing else. Before his plastic surgery, Jim Hunter's looks were far different—he genuinely did resemble a gorilla. People of African origins vary in physical type even more than Caucasians do, and Alexis's African blood seems—I don't know, thinner, very dissimilar. I'm not ruling Hunter paternity out as a motive, but I have a feeling the motive is something more personal between Davina and Emily. Emily's obsession was her son, Ivan. With her history, I doubt she had enough influence over Max to estrange him from Davina, even by alleging that he isn't Alexis's father. Frankly, I don't think Max cares who Alexis's father is. He's a very happy man in his domestic arrangements—a son and heir he adores, a wife he knows is strong and smart enough to carry on the business if anything should happen to him, a brother and nephew who are loyal to him and the business as well as on good terms with Davina—he's never been a suspect, but I don't think he's ever been a patsy either. He looked and acted a bit rocky for a few days around the time that Chez left for parts unknown, but recovered quickly. No, Emily never got at him, I'm sure. Davina and Uda were her targets."

Abe sighed. "Water under the bridge, huh? So if it was aimed at Davina and Uda through the person of the baby, no one is ever going to enlighten us."

"Exactly."

"Well, Bera managed to make the situation between the sisters look as logical as necessary, which shot a part of Horrie's case down in flames. Poor old Horrie! He's not used to a Bera."

"He'd better get used to a Bera," Carmine said grimly.

Delia came in, shaking snow off her monkey-fur coat and setting the gold threads aglitter. Underneath, her tubby body was sheathed in scarlet wool appliquéd with weirdly shaped patches of shiny plastic in black-and-white checks. Even Abe blinked; it was definitely one of Delia's loonier outfits. Thank God she had not been called during Uda's trial! It had brought out the most manic side of her dress sense ever.

"So Sirhan Sirhan admitted he shot Robert Kennedy," she said, sitting down amid numerous squeaks from the plastic patches.

"That was last Monday, Deels," Abe said.

"I know, but I haven't exchanged more than a hello with you since Uda's trial started."

"Sirhan couldn't very well claim he was innocent. He stood right next to Kennedy and shot him in the head."

"That doesn't stop them pleading not guilty."

Carmine flung his hands in the air and went home.

Desdemona's mood was improving. Winter was almost over, the crocuses had come and gone, the forsythia was a mass of yellow, and Master Alexander James Delmonico was walking and talking. Desdemona had had an inspiration stemming out of her own childhood and the inevitable fate of the eldest child: she was going to get rid of her Julian blues by making him mind Alex.

"And I don't care how much he grizzles," she said to her husband triumphantly. "He can grizzle up hill and down dale, but he is still going to get rid of his excessive energies by minding his baby brother. I am in the process of brainwashing him."

"You awful woman," Carmine said, staring.

"Yes, I am, aren't I? Nessie O'Donnell rang me to say that the trial of Uda was a complete fizzle."

"Grizzle, fizzle—where do you get these words?"

"Ask Delia. Her potty papa was a don in English etymology or some such thing. A fizzle, yes?"

"Yes, but justice of a kind was done. She's innocent."

"Good. Nessie also told me that the reviews on Jim's book are appearing. *Publisher's Weekly* and—um—the *Kirkus Review*, I think she called it."

"And?" Carmine asked eagerly.

"Raves. The twenty thousand copies have all gone already, Max is printing twenty-four hours a day," Desdemona said, sitting to enjoy her one drink. "Oh, Carmine!" she burst out, "in three months we'll be sitting on the deck to have our drinks, sniff the air and watch the ships in the harbor!"

"Yeah, winter is a bummer, but it does get itself over. What else were you going to say about Max and Davina?"

"Dreadful man, dragging me back to the straight and narrow. Max and Davina have it sewn up, I'd say. Netty Marciano told me that Max has a network of smaller book printing firms lined up to help produce Jim's book if Tunbull Printing can't keep up with the orders."

"Millie looks blooming," Carmine said, deflecting her from grasshopper mode. "She was a great witness—cool, logical, right down on the jury's level—they liked her. She's put on enough weight to be curvy, and she wore a different dress every day. Things that suited her. Nice shoes, nice bags."

"Was Jim there too?"

"Of course, though he wasn't called."

"Millie's coming to have coffee with me next Wednesday."

Carmine's head lifted. "Why?"

"Cooking tips." Desdemona's lovely smile transformed her plain face. "When it comes to cooking, I am the East Holloman sybil. Millie will turn up with a fat notebook and several pens, and take notes on everything I say. Scientists make excellent cooks, at least the female ones."

"Where are our kids?"

"Outside in the snow. Cat and dog on guard duty."

"I did an imprudent thing back in January," Carmine said.

"Who and how many are coming to dinner when?"

"You are a sybil! Date not set, nor urgent. M.M. and Angela, Doug and Dotty Thwaites, John and Gloria Silvestri. Eight, including us. I know you like that number."

"Why not the Hunters?" she asked. "I don't mind ten."

"Best not," he said easily.

"I hope she's writing her tetrodotoxin paper. Millie may not be Jim Hunter, but her research is illuminating, speaking as the ex-administrator of a neurological research institute. I'm looking forward to seeing her next week."

WEDNESDAY, MARCH 12, 1969

Millie did indeed arrive at the house on East Circle bearing a fat notebook and several pens. She was driving her own car, a new Monte Carlo, and wearing a casual pant-suit in deep blue; her beauty left Desdemona feeling, as she told Carmine later, like a six-foot-three lump. The brainwashing of Julian was proceeding apace, and he was under strict instructions to keep Alex occupied elsewhere. It hadn't proved as difficult as Desdemona had imagined; perhaps Julian was the kind of child who needed a job he felt important? His feelings toward his little brother were genuinely loving, and his ego enjoyed the assumption of power. As Carmine explained to Desdemona, it would last until the day Alex grew physically bigger than Julian: then they'd have a battle royal and readjust the parameters of childhood.

"We're not cooking anything," Desdemona said to Millie, inserting her guest into the breakfast booth and pouring coffee. "Instead, I'm going to go through the various methods of cooking with you—steaming, braising, stewing, roasting, boiling, frying—from a scientific point of view, so that you understand why bread or pastry or cakes rise, why you have to cook this slowly and that quickly, and so forth. I'm also going to strip some of the hierophantic mysteries away by teaching you to make a perfect soufflé entirely on a Mixmaster, and quenelles—oh, heaps and heaps of things." She put down a plate of tiny pancakes lightly smeared in raspberry jam and topped with dollops of whipped cream. "These are pikelets with jam and cream—exactly right for putting on the dog at a morning tea."

It was done so deftly that Millie had no idea Desdemona was easing her into the position of friend as well as pupil; they were not far apart in age, and, as the chatter went on, it became obvious to Millie that Desdemona too was a scientist whose career until she had become a rather late housewife had been a respected one. They had much in common.

The notebook was used, but not in a formal lesson, and about noon she told Desdemona her most treasured secret: she was going to have a baby, due some time in early October, she thought.

"Oh, my dear, how wonderful!" Desdemona exclaimed warmly. "Are you sure of your dates? Who's your gynecologist?"

"I don't have one," Millie said, a little blankly.

"Pregnancy is the most natural function in the world, Millie, but you must put yourself in the care of a gynecologist. It's only since the advent of the National Health in Britain that women are ceasing to die in childbirth and the infant death rate has improved. Before National Health, the only help available to poor women was a midwife on a bicycle who pedaled to the home and dealt with the birth there. Get a gynecologist, girl!"

"It never crossed my mind," said Millie.

Which remark made Desdemona realize how strange Millie's life had been from the beginning of her sixteenth year and her commitment to Jim Hunter. At an age when other girls were forging active interconnections and friendships, Millie had cleaved to Jim and no one else. Choosing to estrange herself from her parents, this brilliant, widely read and amazingly competent scientist had never even begun to develop a feminine network. The scientist knew she was pregnant; the woman had no idea what its practicalities entailed.

"If you're due around the second week in October," Desdemona said, "then at the moment you're about eight or nine weeks gone. Any nausea, vomiting?"

"Not yet," said Millie, recovering her equilibrium. "May I ask for the name of your gynecologist? Would he take me?"

"His name's Ben Solomon, and, like all gynecologists, he loves the obstetrical side of his profession. Shall I call him?"

Her face lit up. "Oh, would you? Thank you!"

So five minutes later Millie had an appointment for the morrow, and had written Dr. Ben Solomon's name, address and phone number into her diary.

"Oh, Desdemona, can't you see our children?" she asked, transfigured. "Not as light as me, not as dark as Jim, and eyes of all colors!"

"Yes, I can see them," Desdemona said gently. "Have you told Jim yet?"

"Yes, last night. He was over the moon."

"Your parents?"

She flinched. "Not yet. In a little while."

Now what's going on there? Desdemona wondered, having seen Millie off the premises and going to check on Julian and Alex. It hadn't escaped her and Carmine that Patrick and Nessie had absented themselves from extended family doings thanks to that wretched sequestration, but why wasn't Millie seeking her doctor father out about this pregnancy? No gynecologist! A woman of thirty-three she might be, but an abysmally ignorant one for all that. Incredible in this day and age, it truly was. Which led Desdemona to think more deeply and detachedly about Millie. Was she perhaps just the tiniest bit "not all there"? Total love was an entity, yes, but in Desdemona's fairly wide experience it was always mixed with other emotions directed in other directions. I, thought Desdemona, love Carmine passionately, gratefully, with complete loyalty—he's my shield companion. And I love my two little sons with a visceral urgency that has led me in the past to put my life on the line for them, especially Julian. I love my mother-in-law, Emilia, all my sisters-in-law . . . But it's a tapestry that displays a rich picture, including the grim greys and blacks of post-partum depression. That's what people are, complex tapestries. But not Millie. I wonder has anybody ever pondered on—no, not her state of mind, but the state of her mind? There's something missing, or else something so inflated that it blots out all sight of the rest . . .

Driving home in a dreamy daze of future culinary masterpieces that would keep her mind occupied through the coming months of her pregnancy, Millie suddenly felt something inside her shift. Why the sensation filled her with a blind panic she had no idea, but she left the car in the drive with the keys still in the ignition, desperate to get inside the house, examine herself, see what had happened.

Blood! Nor had the bleeding stopped, though she wasn't hemorrhaging.

Her diary! Where was her diary? Hands hardly able to get the little book out of her purse, she finally located Dr. Solomon's phone number and called him.

"Don't move around, just sit and wait for the ambulance," he said. "I'd rather have you in the hospital, where I can do all the tests and investigate better."

"Should I phone my husband?" she asked, face wet with tears. "Dr. James Hunter, I've miscarried, haven't I?"

"Or spontaneously aborted, you're so early. However, the fetus might still be hanging in there, Millie. Let's see first, huh? Call your husband, but stay cheerful. Okay?"

Oh, it had been such a delightful morning! She was with child, she had made a good friend to whom she could relate, and she'd learned the scientific principles behind cooking. She had seemed to hover on two separate planes simultaneously, one a place of food, the other filled with visions of a beautiful, warm brown child with weirdly colored eyes.

Now she felt as if she would never want to eat again, and the beautiful, warm brown child was no more.

That same morning had seen a conference between C.U.P. Head Scholar Geoffrey Chaucer Millstone, Dr. Jim Hunter, Max and Davina Tunbull, and the hired publicist, Pamela Devane.

"I suggest a really big university function on Pub Day," said Pamela, leaning back in her chair and crossing a pair of splendid legs. "Is that possible, Chauce?" she asked the Head Scholar, whom she cowed effortlessly. Putty in her hands.

"A cocktail party, not a stuffy dinner," she was saying, "a function hosted, if possible, by the President of Chubb himself. Mawson MacIntosh is always news. About a hundred-fifty people, in a room large enough to permit TV camera crews and journalists of all descriptions to roam about without crowding the venue or the guests. Any suggestions?"

The Head Scholar thought for a moment, then nodded. "I'd recommend the rare book museum," he said. "It's an architectural wonder of the world, inside even more than outside. With the glass stack rising through all that white marble floor, it's spectacular. The floor is tiered, which should give the visual media a wonderful canvas, and we can confine it to as much or as little of the floor area as you want, Pamela. We use velvet ropes to fence portions off."

"No chance of Ivy Hall?" she asked.

Dr. Millstone shuddered. "After the death of Head Scholar Tinkerman there, President MacIntosh would never agree."

"Pity, but fair enough." Pamela lit a cigarette in a long jade holder. "The rare book museum it is, then. May I see it?"

"Chauce and I will take you after the meeting," Jim Hunter said. "It's only a short walk away."

"Good." She emitted a noise that bore some resemblance to a purr. "*Publisher's Weekly* is usually fairly kind, but the *Kirkus Review* is tougher, so rave reviews from both got *A Helical God* off to a flying start. Jim, the Smithsonian wants you to give an hour's lecture to a selected audience during our time in Washington D.C.—a rare honor. The university radio stations—there are dozens and dozens of them—are agog, so are the TV breakfast shows." She grimaced. "That means early starts in the morning, like five a.m. Before the hotels serve breakfast. You will have to eat whatever the station lays on, usually not much."

"I don't want to do this tour," Jim muttered.

"It's hell, but obligatory hell. At least you won't be alone, you'll have Millie and me," said Pamela complacently.

"I can't be sure Millie will come," he said.

Miss Devane sat up straight. "What do you mean? She has to!"

"Why?" Jim asked blankly.

"She's of interest. You know, black and white—prejudice—your experiences along the way. Yours is an extraordinary story, Jim, and Millie is amazing. She looks like a movie star."

For once Davina listened without saying a word, astonished at the gall of this relative stranger—she actually tried to push Jim Hunter around! So far he was taking it, but for how long?

"There is another matter," Pamela announced, discarding her cigarette. "The tetrodotoxin murders. You'll be asked about them as well, Jim. So will Millie."

"That's easy," he said through his teeth. "We will decline to comment about an ongoing police investigation. In fact, we can't do anything else. The questions will soon stop."

"Not bad," she said, approving.

Jim wasn't finished. "My wife's health may not let her travel with me, but if she does, are you implying that some of the journalists will want to interview Millie and me together?"

"Bound to," said Pamela. "You're different, you're glamorous, you're both scientifically brilliant. It's not a marriage between some famous black man and a beautiful blonde idiot. It's one doctor of biochemistry with another, intellectual and educational equals with a long history of social ostracism. Fascinating stuff."

"I see," said Jim. "Well, I'm sorry to upset the publicity applecart, but Millie has just learned she's pregnant, and I can assure you that neither of us will consent to anything that might harm our child. Millie mightn't be coming."

FRIDAY, MARCH 14, 1969

B y mid-afternoon Millie was thoroughly tired of the hospital, and feeling absolutely well. The worst of it had been the dissemination of the news that she had lost her baby; all of East Holloman seemed to know, from her grieving parents to Maria, Emilia, Desdemona, Carmine, the entire Cerutti connection as well as the O'Donnell. For Patrick and Nessie, a double shock, to be deprived of their grandchild before they had been told they would have one. Oh, the guilt! Why hadn't she been able to confide in her own mother and father about *anything?* Tetrodotoxin, from fear . . .

This was her first time ever in a hospital, but Millie was too clever not to understand that her recovery was shadowed by more than half a lifetime shutting everyone from her childhood out; now these childhood people were duty-bound to visit with flowers or fruit or chocolates, then stand without a thing to say. And she couldn't help them find words because she knew nothing about them.

Her disappointment was cruel, as her night-time pillows could have testified. To cap it, now she had no excuse for refusing to travel with Jim on this insane tour stapled together by that execrable woman, Pamela Devane. Nor had Dr. Benjamin Solomon yet told her when she could safely resume her efforts to conceive. The books and magazines palled, she dreaded the appearance of another face around the door of her private room—why *was* Dr. Solomon dodging her, what wasn't he telling her? The fears rose up, chewing, gnawing, eating away at her. *Something* was wrong!

Her gynecologist came in, firmly closing the door in a way that told her the "No Visitors" sign was on its outside.

"Thank God you've come," she said as she flopped back against her mound of pillows. "I was beginning to think that you were going to leave me here all weekend without news."

Solomon was a tall, slender man with a bony, humorous face and warm dark eyes; today he wasn't smiling. "Sorry, Millie," he said, drawing up a chair. "I had to wait for some results to come back from Histology, and those guys won't be hurried."

"It's bad news," she said flatly.

"I'm afraid so, yes." He looked uncomfortable, shifted awkwardly on the chair, didn't seem to know how to start. Cancer leaped into Millie's mind, but that didn't seem to fit either—what didn't he want to say? But now he did; now he said it. "How many abortions did you have when you were younger, Millie?"

Her jaw dropped, she gaped. "Abortions?" she faltered.

"Yes, abortions. The wrong kind. Couldn't Jim have used a condom?" The words burst out of him, but her face remained blank, uncomprehending. "You know, a French letter? A rubber?"

"Oh!" she exclaimed, her face clearing. "Yes, but they tore—we were all thumbs, and Jim was in a hurry. He *hated* rubbers! I tried foams and jellies, but they let us down too. We would think ourselves safe, then I'd get pregnant again. It wasn't anyone's fault, Doctor, honest!" The protest erupted as if she were a ten-year-old kid found out at last.

He took her hands, held them strongly. "Millie, listen to me! That you ever conceived this child you've just lost was a miracle. You're Gettysburg after the battle up there, the amount of scar tissue is horrendous. How many abortions did you have?"

She had stilled absolutely, sitting forward in the bed, and now turned her head away. "I never kept count," she said dully. "Seven, nine—I don't know. A lot, over a lot of years. We couldn't *have* them!"

"Knitting needles, whisks, alkaline douches?" he asked very gently, rubbing her back as if to help her bring it forth. From what Desdemona had told him, they'd had no one to ask, no one to whom they felt they could turn. Huge brains, utter inexperience.

"Until I learned to make ergotamine and managed my own abortions. Once the Pill appeared we were safe, we didn't have to worry anymore. I was so fertile—Jim too, I guess." She lifted her head, turned it to look at him through eyes that did understand but hadn't yet grasped the full enormity of his news. "We can afford a family now," she said. "I can't possibly be as bad as you say, Doctor."

"Believe me, Millie, you are. *You are!* Your endometrium is virtually solid scar tissue. Think about it—think! When you dislodge a fetus, you interfere with a natural process. If the pregnancy is early enough, there are no sequelae. But I'm guessing that the first two or three of your pregnancies were well along before you acted, because the indications are that you suffered post-abortion hemorrhages, infections—you're lucky to have lived." He paused, then spoke in a sterner voice. "You're a sitting duck for a uterine cancer, Millie. I must recommend hysterectomy."

"I can conceive, and I will conceive," she said.

"And if you do, it will go the same way as this one. You can't carry a child to full term or anywhere near that, Millie."

"I refuse to have a hysterectomy," she said.

"It's your choice, my dear. I've given you my opinion, and I suggest you get a second opinion, even a third. Don't make up your mind to anything until then," Dr. Solomon said.

He sat back on his chair, upset, impotent, unable to sway or to help her. "I know how big a blow this is, my dear, but it isn't the end of the world. No one is entitled to apportion blame, least of all me. Try to see this as having some purpose you just can't glimpse yet. And talk it over with your husband. Be open about it, then send him to see me."

But Millie wouldn't answer, wouldn't respond. Half an hour later Dr. Solomon gave up, wondering how he could have handled it better. Even for a physician of his experience, the Hunter situation was unusual enough to be uncertain how to proceed. A ghetto doctor would have had more insight.

After he had gone Millie lay back, the "No Visitors" sign still on her door, grateful for the privacy that gave her. She didn't cry, having wept all her tears, it seemed, during those nights worrying and wondering what had happened to kill her baby.

Like Gettysburg after the battle up there ... What was wrong with parents, that they closed their eyes to the most enormous drives of adolescence? That the only advice they could give was to "be a good girl"? What if you met a Jim, and you couldn't be a good girl? Did they tell you how to look after yourself on, say, your thirteenth birthday, as a rite of passage? No. Why? Because virginity rules. Guys can play around, girls have to go to the marriage bed with hymen intact. So either you were a good girl, or a disgraced one.

Her mind wandered, but with purpose: to retrace her history with Jim. We heavy petted through the Holloman years, then we consummated those four terrible years of anguish in such a cataclysm of passion I can still feel it now. But Jim could never get the rubbers on without tearing them, so I kept conceiving. At first I didn't know what was happening to me, so I left things far too late. We had no idea what to do. A mixed-blood baby then would have brought our careers crashing, that was how we saw it, and I couldn't be spared to have it and then put it up for adoption. Jim *needed* me. What was the year? 1955. How resourceful Jim was, even then. He consulted the professional whores, asked them where they went, how much it cost. We paid twenty dollars to an old Jamaican woman on the West Side—home of the Catholic Hispanics, plenty of business there. I was four months gone, it was a nightmare ... Next time we went elsewhere. No better.

Suddenly Millie felt weary almost to death; the anxiety was taking its toll. She dozed, woke minutes later with John Hall's face in front of her confused eyes. John! How kind he was, how sympathetic, how much on my side. Able to listen to Jim on the subject of long-chain molecules, but also happy to listen to me on the subject of birth control, how impossible it was, how much I dreaded falling pregnant. I was so exactly right for John! His problem wasn't homosexuality, it was asexuality. A vicarious participant in life, that was John. He adored Jim and me as only a man without sexual urges could. What made Jim his enemy was Jim's sudden realization that John thought my troubles as fascinating as Jim's. The famous incident of the pearls . . . Just Jim's jealousy and possessiveness. I wonder whose version Carmine believes, mine, or Jim's? The real one saw us leave for Chicago immediately afterward, exactly as Jim said. I put it back six months to make it appear less significant. Everything for Jim has been the story of my life since I turned fifteen.

Like Gettysburg after the battle up there . . . Why didn't it occur to me that there would be scar tissue? That I was ruining the riches of a substrate designed to nurture the fetus?

She dozed again, and when she woke the image of Gettysburg had gone. The book loomed in her mind. When she had the idea, she was convinced it was the answer. If Jim Hunter wrote about his discoveries for the layman, it would be a fascinating trek into the unknown for people who had no concept how exciting that unknown was, how exhilarating, how filled with the mysteries at the very roots of life. Naturally he would never have thought of it for himself, but once she proposed the idea to him, he saw its potential at once. Yes, yes! A popular book! Thank you, Millie, thank you for seeing a way out of our hell.

The frantic act of writing it, hammering away at the old IBM while she kept feeding his ego, chapter after chapter, until the six-hundred-page manuscript was done to fifth draft. Oh, the hilarious sessions as they tossed titles around until he had found the one he liked: *A Helical God*. His own choice.

Was it the book precipitated her downfall, or the horrific consequences of making tetrodotoxin? Four murders! Captain Carmine Delmonico, her own close cousin, was certain that Jim was responsible for them—Jim!

Came a light knock on the door; Jim appeared. "Does the sign extend to me?" he asked, smiling, his hands full of white roses almost into full bloom.

Her arms went out in welcome. "Never in a million years."

"Has Dr. Solomon been yet?"

How much do I tell him? "Yes."

"What's the story?"

"Apparently my womb needs a thorough rest, sweetheart. No sex for quite a while, I'm afraid. Can you bear it?"

His eyes were full of love. "What a question to ask! Sure I can bear it, for however long it takes. Are you okay?"

"I'm very well, but womb tissue takes some time to heal—Dr. Solomon explained it simply for the ignoramus I am. Sooner or later you'll have to see him, but there's no urgency," she said lightly. "Be warned! Biochemists know as much about these things as accountants do."

"I'll see him whenever he wants." He looked anxious. "The publicity tour, Millie. Will you be able to go?"

"Definitely," said Millie comfortably. "I refuse to abandon you to the wiles of Pamela Devane. Dreadful, isn't she?"

"Like a very sour lemon dipped in chocolate."

MONDAY, MARCH 31, 1969

D avina gazed around her contemporary
living room in satisfaction. It looked its
best, certain chairs banished, other chairs
fetched from different rooms, or newly purchased. The moment that
supercilious bitch Pamela Devane set eyes on this room, she would
have to admit that Connecticut too was capable of producing some
innovative interiors and design.

Uda came in, dragging her feet. Davina's eyes narrowed.

"You've been looking in the water bowl and it wasn't good," Davina said, not in English. "Tell me!"

"I have seen disaster," said Uda, not in English.

"*Disaster?* What? Where? When?"

The flat face seemed flatter, as if a veil of Saran wrap had been drawn tightly across it. "I cannot see, Vina."

"Then look again!"

"It is not our disaster, that is the problem. It touches us, but not malignly. Looking again will not help."

Davina had relaxed. "As long as it isn't our disaster, I can rest. It is not the success of the book?"

"No. The success of the book benefits."

"Alexis?"

"Is a brilliant light in the sky above a field of utter desolation. Untouched, perfect. It is not Max either. I told you, Vina, it is not our disaster."

"Then I can go ahead with my party tomorrow?"

"Oh, yes. It will be a triumph, even though you have acted stupidly in asking that woman policeman to come," Uda said.

Davina looked shocked. "*Stupid?* It is you who is stupid! Sergeant Carstairs is a socialite as well as a policeman. No one in Holloman ever has a party without inviting the aristocratic niece of the Silvestris! It was I who was mistaken, Uda, when I first met her and told her how to dress. Delia Carstairs is a famous eccentric."

"You can't say that about Captain Delmonico's giant wife," said Uda sulkily.

"She is a famous heroine," said Davina patiently, "and this is not a party for 'Mayflower' descendants, though there will be two of them as well." She looked brisk. "Mine is a delightful preview of the book's launch on Wednesday, but with better food, better drink, and far more comfortable surroundings. Chubb will hire the same old firm of caterers, whereas I have Uda, the chef supreme. The food?"

"Includes tiny curry buns, choux pastry with a four-cheese custard filling, miniature crepes rolled on caviar and sour cream, crab cakes with a sweet dipping sauce, lobster vol-au-vents, big shrimps deep-fried in batter—"

"Excellent!" cried Davina, cutting her off. "How many have accepted, especially the important ones?"

"All the important ones are coming. Nineteen."

"What about Lily?"

"Lily will be here to help me and the barman."

"Excellent! Tell her to leave her diamonds at home."

TUESDAY, APRIL 1, 1969

T hat it was April Fool's Day was of no moment to the Savoviches, whose supersti-
tions ran more to evil eyes and curses, and
the nineteen guests forebore to mention the fact, correctly deducing
that Davina's party was no prank.

Angela M.M. arrived with Betty Howard and Gloria Silvestri;
when all twenty women were assembled, everyone agreed that the
palm for best-dressed had, as always, to go to Gloria, wearing a plain
purple wool dress, the exact color of Chubb's purple. A seething Pamela Devane, also in purple, had to admit that hers was the wrong
shade, the wrong cut, the wrong everything. What did that woman
do, to create her magic? It all hinged, Pamela decided resentfully, on
a huge brooch of haphazard amethyst crystals artfully positioned on
her left hip just to one side of an enviably flat tummy. To rub it in,
Gloria had clipped a matching amethyst earring just to one side of
the middle of each purple kid shoe.

"The Duchess of Windsor would eat her heart out," Delia said to
Millie, chuckling.

"Who?" asked Millie, no follower of fashion.

"Reputedly the world's best-dressed woman. My vote goes to
Aunt Gloria, who doesn't even spend a fortune on her clothes. She
makes them herself. Just sees something in a fashion paper or magazine, and copies it perfectly."

"Isn't that stealing?"

"Not after it's in the public arena, dear. You steal designs before they're shown," said Delia. "Speaking of clothes, you look wonderful yourself."

"I went to Fifth Avenue," Millie confessed, "and spent what I would have deemed a fortune a month ago." She gazed around, frowning. "Why are we here, exactly?"

"Davina's way of checking the temperature of the water after the revelations that came out at Uda's trial. Invite a goodly representation of Holloman and Chubb's important women to a girls-only shindig, and see how many accept. If they all do—and I see they have—then her social position is not only safe, but subtly exalted. The town's women have decided that Davina and Uda are unsung heroines."

"Even if one of them committed murder?"

"There's not an atom of proof of that, dear. Not according to twelve good souls and true. They're safe and they're *in*."

"I thought Desdemona was coming."

"Two boys under the age of three can ruin any mother's plans. She's having sitter troubles."

Lily Tunbull appeared bearing a tray; Millie and Delia helped themselves on to little china plates—no cardboard crap for Davina! Thin, delicate china too. *Matching.*

"You should be a guest," Delia said to Lily.

Who blushed. "No, no, I couldn't stand that! I like to keep busy, I don't know anyone here, and I'm learning all Uda's best recipes. Take the tiny crepes, they're divine. And the four-cheese puffs. The lobster vol-au-vents are heaven, the pastry is made from scratch—on *butter!*"

Plates loaded, they found two chairs and sat. Hester Grey and Fulvia Friedkin from C.U.P. joined them.

"Davina is a wonder," Hester said.

Delia was biting into a crepe. "Caviar!" she exclaimed. "Delicious! Millie, eat up. Then we can be unashamed piggies and stack our plates again. And yes," she said to Hester, "Davina is a wonder. I'm memorizing the food to tell Desdemona."

"Desdemona?"

"Delmonico. A friend, and a formidable cook."

"What prompted Davina to give this party?" Fulvia asked.

Hester tittered. "One in the eye for Jim's publicist, Pamela Devane. That's her, in the wrong purple dress. Very snooty to us provincials—as if New York City wasn't a mere commute away! I'm not fond of Davina, but compared to Pamela, she's heaven. She also has Uda."

"I guess no one expects to be poisoned today," said Millie.

"Absolutely not," mumbled Delia, eating deliriously. She looked at Hester. "Why aren't you fond of Davina?"

"Too pushy." Hester sighed. "I did my training in textbook design under Head Scholar Walter Bingham—the one before Don Carter. His ideas were extremely conservative, and we didn't publish scientific work then. I've kept to his tenets, whereas Davina's ideas are *modern*. I admit she's right about things like explanatory illustrations and clearer layout, but I can't do it."

"Utter nonsense, my dear!" said Delia bracingly. "You're by no means an old woman—bite the bullet and go with the times! Just sweep out your mind. Davina has a child, she'll have less and less to do with her firm in years to come. Prepare to be her replacement, rather than be squashed by another import."

"Good advice I echo," said Fulvia. "You're a mouse, Hester—learn to be part rat! University presses are looking at bigger markets because more people are doing degrees, and the need for texts is mushrooming. Delia's right, change your mind-set."

Millie sat listening and enjoying the food, even let Delia put more on her plate when Uda came around. Yes, today was an acid test: Davina had deliberately tossed her guests into a food pool made by an accused poisoner. And no one was worried! There might be a few in need of a digestive later on, but no one howling for an ambulance and a stomach pump. Davina had definitely won.

She was sitting nearby with Angela M.M., and they were talking about the waywardness of genetic inheritance.

"I have two great-grandparents and a paternal grandfather who were negroes," Davina was saying. "Grandfather, whom I remember, had red hair and green eyes, but medium-brown skin and negroid features. Yet none of our negro blood showed in multiple offspring, whereas Uda's handicap, also inherited, but very rare, did. I find it extremely interesting."

"On one of our zanier trips," said Angela, "M.M. and I were in the Solomon Islands—he was on some veterans' committee, and the Solomons saw terrible fighting against the Japanese. Anyway, we were told that on one of the more remote islands there is a pure Melanesian tribe with black skin, Melanesian features, red or blond hair, and pale green eyes. They were never infiltrated by whites for any purpose, they're a natural phenomenon."

"Well, the negro shows in my son, Alexis," Davina said airily. "Would you like to see him?"

"I'd love to," said Angela sincerely.

"Oh, please!" cried Betty Howard.

"Uda, fetch Alexis."

Delia sat with skin crawling, though all the while her common sense kept asserting that this moment had to come, and that all the child shared with Jim Hunter was a pair of green eyes.

Millie had shrunk a little—a natural response in one who had recently miscarried. Of course Davina didn't know this, but if she had, would it have stopped her? Delia had to think, no.

"If I were a Muslim wife, I would have been killed," Davina was saying chattily to a growing group of listening women. "The ordinary Islamic understanding of genetics is rudimentary, I would be deemed unfaithful for producing an impossible baby. In my country, especially in its southern parts, there are many Muslims. However, I am fortunate. I am here in America, and blessed with an educated husband who understands the vagaries of genetics, of throwbacks. In actual fact, our son's features are Max's, though I flatter myself he has my nose."

At which moment Uda returned bearing a bigger version of the beautiful child Delia remembered. He sat up straight in his aunt's arms and gazed about as if fascinated by the unfolding vistas of this tiny journey.

Delia's head swung to Millie, who was staring at the baby in an apparent wonder. Her expression was gentle, her demeanor quite relaxed. Despite which, sight of a baby that echoed what her own would have been like must have moved her deeply. A private person, Millie, no heart on her sleeve.

Sensibly, Davina didn't allow others to take him, cuddle him. Watching hawklike, Delia concluded that most of the women filed Jim Hunter as a possible father, yet had taken due note of Davina's explanation and the fact that, apart from his eyes, Alexis did in fact bear no resemblance to Jim. As for Millie . . .

"Are you all right to go home, dear?" Delia asked her.

The blue eyes were tranquil; Millie smiled. "I'm fine."

Delia didn't go home immediately. She detoured to East Circle to have a drink with Carmine and Desdemona.

"If ever there was an April Fool's party, that one was it," she said with feeling. "I just haven't worked out who was the intended April Fool, though on the surface it was Pamela Devane. A frightful woman! However, the bash itself was a triumph. The invited social lionesses came, ate Uda's food as if they'd never heard of tetrodotoxin, and had a jolly time."

Desdemona was perturbed by the tale of Alexis's display to the guests. "Millie?" she asked anxiously.

"He was produced after an audible discussion about inheritance and the black antecedents Davina claims to have. Real green eyes, she said. Angela came up trumps with a story of some Solomon Island natives—at that stage she couldn't possibly have known about Alexis, so I swear M.M.'s wife is a witch. To be absolutely fair to Davina, I add, the child doesn't resemble the present Jim Hunter or the gorilla Jim Hunter. It's just the eyes. He's about twice as old as he was when I first saw him, and his facial structure has grown more European. There *is* a resemblance to Max."

"Oh, I wish this publicity tour wasn't happening!" cried Desdemona. "Jim doesn't want to do it, especially now that Millie has to stay behind for some minor surgery."

"When did this happen? She didn't mention it to me at the party," Delia said, frowning.

"She told me when she phoned yesterday. *Minor* surgery, she said. I gathered it was to do with her woman's works."

"So Jim Hunter hits the road alone," said Carmine.

"A multiple murderer," said Desdemona. "Are all publicity tours so interminable and their chaperones so—well, tactless?"

"The rub of this one," said Carmine, "lies in the Intelligence Quotient of the author. According to my sources, the publicist probably treats Jim like any other first-time author, whereas you can't. How many people deal successfully with genius? Miss Devane can't. Put her with any other first-time author, and she's probably superb. Millie's defection doesn't bode well."

"And launch party tomorrow," said Delia.

WEDNESDAY, APRIL 2, 1969

The rare book museum, Pamela Devane thought complacently, made an ideal venue for the reception launching *A Helical God* upon the reading public. The great square space in the middle of the broadly tiered white marble floor permitted a square column of clear glass to soar toward the ceiling far above; the column was filled with volumes in shelving that patently said the books could be accessed. The full impact of the cellular walls didn't manifest itself after dark, but the artificial lighting was clever and effective.

A hundred and fifty people had congregated, clad in black tie or evening gown, a glittering assemblage. If the acoustics were on the poor side thanks to the lack of small or soft objects to absorb the sound waves, that couldn't be helped; it just made the noise far noisier. M.M. and Chauce Millstone were the joint hosts, both in academic robes, and consequently much photographed. Angela, doing her best wafty impression, was circulating merrily in a beaded dress reminiscent of a 1920s flapper. Yes, thought Pamela Devane, an Ivy League institution like Chubb had a way of doing things that left political or business parties, doomed to hotel ballrooms, looking tawdry. What a setting!

Millie Hunter was magnificent. Her hair was loosely swept up on top of her head, she wore a small pair of diamond studs in the lobes of her little flat ears, and her face was made up so well that the cameras feasted on her. Her dress was long and graceful, of tawny satin that displayed her figure to perfection. She wore her large, beaded bag on a long, beaded cord over her left shoulder.

"Isn't this grand?" Patrick asked his first cousin as they stood with their wives to one side of the main gathering. "Millie is gorgeous! For the first time, Carmine, I really feel as if the nightmare of uncertainty at least is over."

When Nessie and Desdemona moved away in the direction of Gloria Silvestri and Delia Carstairs, Patrick's expression changed.

"Is it true, what Millie tells me? That you suspect *Jim* of all these murders? It's been hell existing outside the parameters of your investigations, but surely it can't be Jim," Patrick said.

Carmine sighed. This man had stood as a father to him through the stormy years of adolescence, despite his own growing family and his medical commitments. Of all the men on this earth, Carmine loved Patrick O'Donnell the most. And, as thanks, he was the harbinger of terrible news. Well, it had to come, but he had hoped not here, not tonight. "Patsy, let's leave it until we can sit over some of your coffee, drown it with bourbon if we want?"

"By all means," Patrick said stiffly, "but I need an answer tonight. Let it be short. We can have the talk tomorrow."

"Okay. First of all, I have no proof. None at all. Yet I *know* that Jim Hunter killed three people to protect the moment that's happening tonight. Not all personally. He vectored one, and brilliantly, and is implicated in a fourth killing. If Millie knows, it's because Jim told her, but I don't think he has told her. To try to check his homicidal career, I told him that I know he is a killer. That, I think, *will* stop him."

"I see." Patrick whisked away tears. "Thanks, cuz."

"Tomorrow, your office, five o'clock."

People moved in the patterns of a large party minus seating, forming small circles around certain guests like Gloria Silvestri, soignée in a limp, heavy, subtly glittering grey dress slit to mid-thigh, revealing a black-sheathed, perfect leg—how did she do it at her age?

"Complete control of her emotions," said Delia to Angela. "Aunt Gloria has no self-doubts, no money worries, and two sons who never gave their parents any real trouble. She could stand amid the ruins of Troy already planning how to have a comfortable, carefree enslavement. In short, she's a goddess of a kind."

Curiosity gratified at last, Angela eyed Delia affectionately. Tonight she was a vision in what looked like Sanderson roses, save that these blooms were hurtfully vivid blue admixed with bilious yellow foliage and magenta buds, and that the fabric of her dress had been gathered into huge puffs; search for a simile though she did, Angela could find none. The Silvestri clan was unique.

The Commissioner himself was deep in conversation with the Mayor, who paled to insignificance alongside him; his Medal of Honor was on a pale blue ribbon around his neck, and when Gloria joined him, the New York reporters deemed them the handsomest couple in the room.

Eddies and swirls, swirls and eddies, thought Carmine, doing his best to enjoy the kind of affair he privately detested. His wife, wearing three-inch heels, had the advantage of gazing over the top of almost every head, and looked superb in ice-blue lace. To Carmine, even Gloria couldn't hold a candle to Desdemona.

She forged through the crowd like a ship of the line, one of his favorite metaphors for her, and fetched up beside him.

"Have you noticed Jim Hunter's evening wear?" she asked.

"Uh—no."

"He's not wearing a cummerbund, he's wearing a brocade waistcoat with a matching bow tie," she said excitedly. "I know how you hate your cummerbund because it rolls up on you, so have a look at Jim. Please!"

Jim was moving their way: Carmine stared. Yes, he was in a waistcoat of black brocade with tiny gold fleur-de-lys, and he looked enviably comfortable.

"It's great," Carmine said to Desdemona. "Not even faggy—uh—I mean, effeminate."

"In future I'm making you waistcoats and bow ties."

Jim reached them, black skin beaded with sweat, green eyes glowing like beryls. "Isn't this fantastic?" he asked.

"Fabulous!" cried Desdemona, beaming.

"Did you ever see anyone as beautiful as Millie?"

"No," said Carmine sincerely. "That color suits her."

"That's what I said when she had second thoughts." He sucked in a huge breath. "I can't believe this is really happening!"

"Believe, Jim, believe," said Desdemona.

M.M. appeared at their elbows. "Desdemona, Carmine, Jim," he said, genial and proud. "If you think this is an event, wait until you see the party we give Jim when he wins the Nobel Prize for Chemistry."

"I can imagine," said Carmine gravely.

"If you'll excuse me, I'm going to steal Jim." Jim Hunter in tow, M.M. wandered off.

"Darling heart, I would give a lot for a chair," Desdemona said wistfully. "Heels look spiffy, but my back is growling."

"Come with me," Carmine said, leading her to a hidden flight of open marble steps.

The two chairs were on a higher tier, and had a splendid view of the area where the launch itself was going to take place, judging from the number of microphones set up there.

"How do you know where to find these places, Carmine? This chair might have been tailored for me."

"I scout the terrain before the action commences. Then I found a couple of decent chairs, flashed my gold badge at the guy in charge, and had them put here. We may as well stay here, I think they're getting ready for the speeches."

"How strange," said Desdemona as soon as her back pain had subsided, "that we can barter small talk with a multiple murderer just as if he isn't one."

"Until he's proven guilty in a court of law, lovely lady, we are obliged to. Don't forget that forewarned is forearmed. Knowledge tells you never to get on the wrong side of him. But seriously, Jim Hunter is as safe to mix with as your average Joe. He's a self-interest killer, not a psychopath."

"There has to be an element of psychopathia in anyone who kills cold-bloodedly, Carmine. And he'll kill again," she said. "Someone will endanger his survival—he's such a prominent sort of bloke, the sort some people lust to tear down."

"Sssh! Action stations," said Carmine.

Head Scholar Millstone and President MacIntosh moved together to the microphones, accompanied by the Mayor and Dean Hugo Werther of Chemistry. People began to mill, finding good spots from which to watch; Channel 6, another network channel and one New York independent jockeyed for position, and a ripple of excitement ran through the gathering. Millie and Jim were thrust through the crowd, people smiling and touching Jim as if physical contact with his person would rub some of his luck off on them. They too were stationed near the microphones, but off to M.M.'s right; the other dignitaries were clustered on his left side.

"Ladies and gentlemen," said M.M. in his democratic form of address, "in the Bible some rare events were celebrated by killing the fatted calf. What exactly did that mean? The fatted calf was the outstanding one among the year's crop of calves, destined not for the table but for the breeding of future cattle, therefore carefully fed and looked after with that end in view. However, on rare occasions a great and joyous event happened, and to honor it, the pampered fatted calf was killed for the table, a signal distinction. The famous example was the return of the prodigal son."

He stopped, smiling, then resumed too quickly for the TV people to get bored. "Tonight Chubb University and the Chubb University Press are killing the fatted calf not in honor of a prodigal son, but of a different kind of prodigy, Dr. James Keith Hunter. His extraordinary book, *A Helical God*, examines the very core of our human genetic master plan, ponders the reasons for our being, our membership in that vast family, the *gens humana*—"

The single loud bark of a gun silenced him, transfixed him.

Millie had moved farther away from her husband, as if loath to have a share in his supreme moment by being in its vicinity, and

Carmine's eyes, for one, had been turned to M.M. as he made his preparatory introduction; Chauce Millstone was to make the main address.

Amazed, stupefied, Carmine's gaze switched to Millie and Jim, saw her beyond him and completely alone, a revolver in her hands, steadying it like a professional.

Jim Hunter stood, slack-mouthed, his left arm hanging as if lifeless, blood dripping swiftly from its fingertips to the white marble floor to form a pool. A wet, faintly smoking patch in the upper arm of his coat showed where the bullet had gone in. His eyes, huge, pupils dilated, were riveted on Millie.

"That was for my baby!" Millie cried into a deathly silence. "The rest, Jim, are for the years, the life, and the betrayal!"

Carmine had gone from his chair knowing he had no hope of reaching Millie before she finished what she had begun. Scorning the steps, he dropped seven feet to the next tier.

The repeated roar of the gun was ear-splitting, bouncing in multiple echoes off smoothly planed, polished surfaces; five shots in quick succession, each projectile straight into Jim Hunter's chest. The pool suddenly immense, he stood for a second before his knees buckled and he fell, face downward, into his own blood.

Carmine walked forward, his right hand wrapped in his handkerchief, and took the revolver from Millie's nerveless fingers, then slipped it in his pocket; out of the corner of his eye he could see Patrick at a wall phone.

"Millicent Hunter, I arrest you for the murder of James Hunter," he said. "You have the right to an attorney at law and may request one. In the meantime, if you say anything, it may be taken down and used against you in a court of law."

"I'm finished, it's all over," Millie said in an ordinary voice. "He was a traitor, now he's dead. What happens to me doesn't matter."

The crowd hadn't panicked. In a way, Carmine supposed, taking place one tier up as it had, it possessed all the trappings of a stage drama that shattered its audience far beyond fleeing in all directions. To establish order wasn't difficult; people were cooperative, even Channel 6.

"Why is it," Delia demanded wrathfully, "that every time we have a public murder, it's recorded on television?"

Carmine didn't bother to answer; instead he went off to join M.M., sitting on a chair and looking ghastly.

"This is an accursed year," he said to Carmine.

"How, Mr. President?"

"Two major functions, at each of which the academic star was murdered."

"That's a pretty narrow definition of accursed. Unfortunate is a better word. After all, the two murders are related."

"I want Angela, and I want to go home."

"Angela's waiting, but before you go, did you have any kind of warning sign from Millie? You were near her just before."

"Not the flicker of an eyelash," said M.M. gloomily. "In fact, I was hardly aware of her presence. You know me, Carmine. I concentrate all of myself where I need to. In fact, I wasn't even conscious of my star, Jim. The first shot came like an overhead clap of thunder. I froze, didn't know what it was until I saw the blood running off Jim's hand onto the floor." He shuddered. "It looked black. I remember wondering if such a very black man did actually have black blood."

"Go home, sir," said Carmine, beckoning Angela. "Try to get some sleep. We'll resume tomorrow."

"And tomorrow, and tomorrow . . ."

The guests were filing out, Channel 6 busy. In the aftermath of such a public murder it wasn't necessary to do more than take down names and addresses.

Back at County Services he held a short meeting with his team. Just Delia, Buzz and Donny. He hadn't called out Abe and his men because uniforms were adequate help in this situation.

"Is Millie in the women's cell?" he asked.

"Yes," said Delia, whose puffy billows had deflated.

"Suicide watch, absolutely intensive."

"Already instituted, Captain. A woman cop is in the room with her. She didn't need an all-over shower—no bloodstains—and there is a toilet and a wash basin in the cell."

"The cop is not to leave for one second unless a replacement is already in the cell," Carmine said, iron in his voice. "I want no stupid mistakes, is that understood? Do the uniformed personnel understand?"

"Yes," said Delia.

"Did she have any tetrodotoxin on her or in her bag?"

"No."

"Did you do a cavity search?"

"Yes, thoroughly. She had nothing concealed."

Carmine sighed, rubbed his hand around his face. "Then we leave questioning her until tomorrow at nine. Does she need a doctor, by any chance? Did anyone think to offer one?"

"She declined a doctor, even after the body search."

"Goodnight, guys, and thank you."

Never having seen Carmine in this mood, Buzz and Donny left quickly. Delia lingered, wishing she knew of some magic formula could banish his—what? No use speculating, and he was not of a mind to say.

Desdemona had gotten home an hour earlier, and changed into an athlete's sweat suit because she vowed it was the most comfortable clothing she knew.

"Thank God you're home," she said to Carmine when he came in. "The sitter's complaining at the lateness, but I wasn't about to leave the kids here to run her home."

"Hang in there, I won't be long."

In actual fact it wasn't very late; when Carmine returned at ten o'clock he found that Desdemona had made sandwiches and a pot of tea; most of the launch nibbles had gone back to the caterers uneaten.

"I have never been so shocked in all my life," Desdemona said, pushing another curried egg salad sandwich at Carmine.

"Nor I," said Carmine. "Not four years of a world war and all the horrors soldiers can perpetrate could prepare me for that. Millie's my blood. What exactly did Jim do to make her snap? Because that's what this evening was—Millie so taut on the end of her tether that she snapped it."

"You know, Carmine, as well as I do. It was Davina's baby combined with the loss of her own. Go to bed, you're whacked."

"But *did* Jim father Alexis?" Carmine asked, ignoring her instructions. "Davina doesn't behave as if he did, and I gather she's been telling all and sundry about the black blood in her family for years—certainly well before the advent of Jim Hunter. It sounds to me as if she was preparing for the chance of a black baby in advance, which argues that her story of black blood is true. On the other hand, the black antecedents may be there, and she had an affair with Jim as well. This is a woman who plans."

"And we will never know the truth," said Desdemona, "since the Savovich family history is behind the Iron Curtain."

Carmine tidied the kitchen. "One day," he said, drying his hands on a towel, "there will be a foolproof test for a child's paternity. Something irrefutable. It's just a pity that we don't have it now."

"No, a mercy," Desdemona countered. "If Alexis isn't Jim's, think how Millie would feel. Best she doesn't know. The milk, in the form of Jim's blood, is already spilled, and the luck of it is that he's a multiple murderer."

"Implying that it's a lesser form of murder to kill a man or woman who is by nature a killer."

"Well, isn't it? Millie snapped, Carmine! She killed while of unsound mind."

THURSDAY, APRIL 3, 1969

The atmosphere in Detectives was peculiar: awkward and strained as well as satisfied. A multiple murderer of remarkable kind had been cut short, would never kill again, but his killer was family of some degree to at least half of the Holloman PD, and universally loved.

Nessie O'Donnell had been asked to bring her daughter fresh apparel, indicating to the experienced Nessie that the police would oppose bail, and that Doug Thwaites would probably go along. Patrick was laid flat with a rare migraine and those of Millie's sisters still at home were, in Nessie's words, "basket cases." In the end, Patrick's mother, Maria, and Carmine's mother, Emilia, helped her cull Millie's wardrobe for items containing no laces, sashes, belts, scarves, ribbons or sharp-edged ornamentation. This told her that the police feared suicide, as indeed she did herself. The worst of it was that she wasn't allowed to see her daughter, just informed that she was fine.

Millie was brought across the courtyard and upstairs to the most salubrious of the interview rooms at nine, showered, clad in jeans, slip-on shoes and a sweat shirt, her face bare of make-up and her hair pulled back into a bun. A look that suited her, in no need of artifice.

Carmine chose Delia to go into the room with him, leaving it up to the other detectives whether they wanted to observe or not. Everyone did, from Abe to Buzz and Tony.

"I'm in the soup," Millie said when she entered, smiling.

297

Looking very subdued in navy-blue, Delia set the recorder going and identified the session, its participants.

"Bearing in mind that a hundred-fifty people witnessed you empty a Smith & Wesson .38 six-shot revolver into Dr. James Hunter yesterday, April second, at eighteen-oh-one hours, and that your actions were recorded on three competing television cameras, Dr. Hunter, you are indeed in the soup," Carmine said easily. "Do you want an attorney here for this interview, or will you waive your right to an attorney?"

"I waive my right," she said, equally easily.

"Where did you obtain the revolver?"

"I've had it ever since Jim and I went to Chicago."

"Have you a license?"

"No. It never leaves me, I keep it in my handbag."

"Do you also have a .22 caliber hand gun?"

"No. The .22 is Jim's."

"It was never located on any search."

"He didn't keep it at home or in the lab, but I don't know where he did keep it."

"Why did you shoot your husband?"

"It's a long story, except that every camel's back has a last straw, Captain."

"Now's the time to tell the story, Millie."

But she went off at a tangent. "Must I have a cop in my cell all the time? I can't even use the toilet in privacy."

"It's called a suicide watch."

She laughed. "Do you honestly believe that I'd kill myself over a worm like Jim Hunter?"

"For eighteen years you've given the world the impression that you love Dr. James Hunter deeply. Now you call him a worm, now you murder him? Why? What did he do? What changed?"

"He fathered a child on that Yugoslavian Medusa."

"Mrs. Davina Tunbull speaks of negroid blood in her family, and insists her husband is the child's father. Apart from green eyes—

which are not uncommon in persons of mixed race—the baby does not resemble Dr. James Hunter," Delia said, taking over.

Millie laughed again; it held an element of hysteria, but she was working very hard to appear logical and composed. "Jim fathered that baby, not Max Tunbull," she maintained. "He betrayed me with a woman who has snakes for hair. I've always seen the snakes," she said in iron tones. "Davina is Lilith the serpent."

"Let's set the baby aside for the moment," said Carmine. "You said your reason for murder was a long story. Tell it."

"I don't know where to start."

"How about with John Hall? What happened in California when you and Jim palled up with him?" Carmine asked, his voice and manner interested but not even slightly aggressive.

"John!" Millie exclaimed, smiling. "He was such a doll, so nice to me. To Jim too, more than me. Jim let his guard down, especially after John bullied him into having his operation. I had never realized how much Jim hated the gorilla look until he lost it after the surgery. He'd spend an hour just looking in the mirror, touching his face, stroking his nose, using a second mirror to look at his profile." She shrugged, took on a happy mien. "John's generosity liberated the real Jim—is that what I want to say? The thing is, neither John nor I loved Jim for his face, old or new—we loved the person inside."

"Surely Jim knew that?" Delia asked.

"Yes, of course he did. He and I had already been together for nine years, I shared his secrets before the operation as much as I did after it, and John started sharing his secrets too."

"What secrets, Millie?" Carmine asked.

"Oh, lots of things," she said vaguely.

"You have to be more specific, dear," said Delia.

Her face twisted, she hunched her shoulders and seemed to shrink inches. "I don't really know," she said.

"I think you do, Millie. Start with one secret, even if it's only a suspicion," Carmine said, trying not to push.

"There was a student supervisor at Columbia who made Jim's life a misery, I remember," Millie said uneasily. "He died from a terrible mugging the day after he marked a paper of Jim's right down—Jim was furious, and rightly so."

"Jim mugged him?" Carmine asked.

"I thought so because he came in that evening covered in blood that wasn't his, showered, then took his clothes somewhere—I never saw them again. He wasn't a suspect, there weren't any."

"Any other muggings?"

"A couple while we were at Columbia, but I never saw Jim covered in blood, or missed any more clothes. I just—wondered."

"Did the muggings benefit him? Were they fatal too?"

"Yes, and yes."

"How did John Hall change things? Did Jim confide in him?" Carmine asked.

"No, I did," said Millie, eyes wide. "While John and I sat waiting for the surgery to be over, then sat by his bed—Jim took two days to come out of it. As soon as Jim was feeling well enough, John told him that he knew about the muggings."

"That was imprudent," Delia said.

"John didn't think so, and Jim's reaction bore him out. Jim felt like the head of a little club, I guess—he always loved anything to do with secret societies and—not the underworld, but netherworlds. Once John knew, he treated Jim like a god, a superman, you know what I mean."

"Were there any suspicious deaths at Caltech?" Delia asked.

"Two. A shooting and a road accident. I only suspected because John was more transparent, he gave things away."

"He was lucky to survive," said Carmine.

"No, he was never in danger from Jim back then, but Jim did think it was time to sever the connection."

"Did they keep in touch?"

"Occasionally, but they never saw each other until John came to visit the Tunbulls. Whatever conversation they had while Jim walked John to his car that night he came to see us on State Street I don't know, but suddenly Jim couldn't be sure his secrets were safe. I saw it coming, but the only thing I could do was report the missing tetrodotoxin. I would never have betrayed Jim, though subconsciously I must have known that reporting the loss would turn the police spotlight on Jim. Then his betrayal broke all the ties, from body to mind to soul."

"Were there murders in Chicago?" Delia asked.

"I imagine so, but I wasn't privy to them in any way."

"Can you throw any light on John Hall's breakdown after you and Jim left L.A.?" Delia asked.

"He was depressed, but some Frankenstein of a psychiatrist gave him ECT—electroshock therapy. Barbaric! It destroyed a lot of neurones," said Millie the neuroscientist. "Years went by before he recovered enough to do more than cling to Wendover Hall. Though, as I've said, he and Jim corresponded sporadically."

"So you knew your husband had stolen your poison to murder people," Carmine said.

Again Millie twisted, shrank. "No, I didn't think that at first! I thought he stole it to use in his own work—he was forever doing that to me." Her eyes blazed blue fire. "That's really why I decided to teach him a lesson by reporting the loss. Jim would be forced to admit he'd stolen from his own wife." Her shoulders slumped. "Then John died, and the next day Tinkerman died. I understood that Jim had taken the tetrodotoxin to commit murder, and I was caught."

"You're contradicting yourself a little, Millie," Delia said. "Did you report the loss of the poison to deter your husband from stealing your work or doing murder?"

"I'm not sure!" she cried. "How can I be sure? I haven't been in my right mind since I saw that baby, I'm just a mass of conflicting feelings and--and--I don't know, *rage!* He cheated on me! From my fifteenth birthday I gave him everything, and he couldn't even keep it in his pants!"

"Let's have a coffee break," said Carmine.

*　　*　　*

He spent it pacing the courtyard, tormented by almost as many conflicting emotions as Millie Hunter said she suffered. Something was wrong, and he could at least put his finger on what it was: Millie as of unsound mind wasn't ringing true. Or was that his own cynicism trying to cancel out family connections? Murder when of unsound mind did happen, even in a small city like Holloman, but its perpetrators in his experience were right out of it, no one could doubt disturbed sanity. With Millie, that wasn't so. Most of what she said contained logic rather than disordered thought patterns, so what it boiled down to was ungovernable rage. And was ungovernable rage evidence of an unsound mind?

He returned to the interview room to take a different tack.

"Tell me everything you know or guess about the reasons why Dr. Tinkerman had to die," he said to Millie.

She embarked on a logical explanation. "Tinkerman had made a fetish out of studying *A Helical God*, and extended his study to Jim's two earlier books, as well as all his published papers. He concluded that Jim hadn't written *A Helical God* at all, and wrote an essay for splashy publication that discussed the book, comparing its style to every other thing Jim had written. He proved the book wasn't Jim's, and he would have been believed."

"Is that where Edith Tinkerman comes in?" Delia asked.

"Yes. She found her husband's essay and a covering letter addressed to Jim. With them were pages and pages of his notes. Tinkerman was the kind of man who liked to rub salt into people's wounds, so he was sending Jim a copy of the essay. When Mrs. Tinkerman saw the letter addressed to Jim, she called him. He killed her and took the essay, which hadn't been submitted for publication yet. The .22 went into Long Island Sound."

"So the threat of exposure wasn't a contributing factor to Tinkerman's murder?" Carmine asked.

"No. Jim knew enough to understand that Tinkerman wouldn't rest until he'd destroyed Jim's career, he died for that alone rather than specifics," Millie said.

"You speak as if he confided in you," Delia said.

"He didn't need to. I was Jim's other half—his wife, his friend, his lover for nearly nineteen years. I loved him, and every person who died had tried to ruin him. Killing for Jim was an act of desperation. I was his for better or for worse, as our marriage vows said, and I would have protected him to my grave." Her voice changed, became high and shrill. "Then I saw his child, the child he never gave me permission to have. And suddenly my love turned to hate. He took my youth as if it counted for nothing. He adamantly refused to have children during the years when we should have been having them. Then after denying me, he informed me that Davina—*Davina!*—thought I should have a child. He spoke to me like a king to a subject. To me, his wife!"

"Millie, it is very possible that Jim didn't father Alexis Tunbull," Carmine said.

"Yes, he did," she said scornfully. "The moment I saw that baby, I knew everything."

A futile line of questioning: Millie wouldn't back down.

"Who wrote *A Helical God*?" he asked.

"I did," said Millie. "When the idea occurred to me, I knew that Jim had no gift for expressing his thoughts on paper. Well, biochemists don't really need to be able to write, it's jargon combined with basic English. Whereas I can write, and I have a more metaphysical mind than Jim. So I sat down at our typewriter and pounded it out in six weeks. Four more drafts, and it was finished. It had to be published as Jim's book—who would take it seriously if it were known to have been written by a kewpie doll? If it hadn't been for carrying the additional work load, I would have enjoyed the experience."

"You realize you can't profit from it now?" Delia asked.

Millie looked stunned. "Why?"

"No murderer can profit from murder. Jim's royalties will go to his family, I imagine."

"Those bastards?" Millie asked incredulously. "They dropped Jim like a hot potato when he took up with me!"

"It's the law, Millie," said Delia. "You're guilty."

"Jim was guilty," said Millie, tight-lipped. "He killed three times to profit from his royalties. I killed out of my mind."

"That's for a court to establish," Delia persisted.

"I must be found guilty," Millie said, "and I am not guilty. Killing is not in me. I'm one of Jim's victims." She began to weep, her hands threshing. "Stop, please stop! No more!"

Carmine terminated the interview at once.

"Was that real, or feigned?" he asked Delia once Millie was gone, still weeping.

"I wish I knew, Chief, but I don't. She's not a killer."

"I agree. Desdemona called her an abused wife, and a small number of them do reach a breaking point that sees them do murder. No, what I wish I knew was how long this alternative has been in her mind. The single day between setting eyes on Alexis Tunbull and the book launch, or extending back at least to the beginning of last year, when Jim and Davina were cementing a friendship?" Carmine grimaced. "Did she snap, or did she plan?"

"Unsound mind or premeditation? I don't know," Delia said.

"It's going to be up to a jury to decide."

That morning saw two other developments. Millie was denied bail pending psychiatric evaluation, and a slavering Anthony Bera appeared to offer Millie his services.

"I can't afford you, Mr. Bera," said Millie flatly.

"For now, let it be pro bono. If things go well, Dr. Hunter, and you are found of unsound mind when you shot your husband, you will enjoy a very large income from royalties. I would then send in a bill for my customary fee," Bera said crisply.

"You look a little like Captain Carmine Delmonico."

"A compliment. He's a handsome man. Will you accept my offer, Dr. Hunter?"

"Yes. I don't see why Jim's ungrateful family should reap the rewards of a book I happened to write." She looked satisfied. "I can prove I wrote *A Helical God*, and I have Dr. Tinkerman's essay proving that Jim didn't. Jim took the papers when he shot Mrs. Tinkerman, but he didn't destroy them."

"Am I able to lay my hands on these documents?"

"Yes." She pushed a card across the table. "Give this to Pedro Gomez, who has a convenience store on the corner of State and Caterby. He'll give you a manuscript box."

"Excellent," said Bera on a purr. He extracted a note pad from his briefcase. "Now, Millie, I am going to put you through a worse interrogation than the Holloman PD."

"You should know," Millie said, ears tearing, "that a few days before I shot Jim, I received the worst news any woman of child-bearing age can receive. From my gynecologist, Dr. Benjamin Solomon. The details are horrible." She wiped her eyes.

Bera stiffened, his dark eyes gleaming. "Ah! Naturally I need a detailed explanation, my dear, but there's no hurry. Just take your time . . ."